TEMPORARY TO TEMPTED

JESSICA LEMMON

HIS FOR ONE NIGHT

SARAH M. ANDERSON

MILLS & BOON

First Published in Great Britain 2019
by Mills & Boon, an imprint of HarperCollinsPublishers,
1 London Bridge Street, London, SE1 9GF

Temporary to Tempted © 2019 Jessica Lemmon
His For One Night © 2019 Sarah M. Anderson

ISBN: 978-0-263-27177-5

0419

MIX
Paper from
responsible sources
FSC™ C007454

This book is produced from independently certified FSC™ paper to ensure responsible forest management.

For more information visit: www.harpercollins.co.uk/green

Printed and bound in Spain
by CPI, Barcelona

TEMPORARY TO TEMPTED

JESSICA LEMMON

One

Prospect number seven was not going well.

Andrea Payne's eyelids drooped as Dr. Christopher Miller yammered on. At this rate hell would freeze solid and Satan would win a gold medal in figure skating before she found an appropriate plus-one for her sister's wedding.

Her sister Gwen was the second to last of the Payne women to marry, which left Andy dead last. Not that Andy had ever been anywhere near walking down a runner in a wedding gown, but this marriage would widen the gap already setting her apart from her married—and one soon-to-be married—sisters.

Years ago, when she'd moved to Seattle, Andy had set out to prove that she didn't need a boyfriend; didn't need anyone. She'd set out to prove that in business, *in life*, she could stand on her achievements and skills.

In her family, charm and poise were worth more than achievements, and for that she could blame her mother, former Miss Ohio Estelle Payne. Andy would settle for relationships with high-paying clients, thank you very much.

There was a contract between them, after all. That was sort of like marriage.

She returned her attention to her date, boredom having set in a while ago. It was a shame he wasn't going to work out. On paper, Christopher was everything she was looking for in a date for her sister's wedding. He was a doctor, well-dressed, nice-looking and comfortable talking about himself.

Really comfortable.

"Anyway, I was able to help out a patient in his time of need, which is what this job is all about." He arched his eyebrows and pressed his lips together, trying to appear humble. "He was lucky I was there."

Womp.

She'd tried her ex-boyfriends first—a whopping total of three of them—over the last month and a half before resorting to a dating app that had resulted in three other duds and "lucky number seven," Christopher here.

She gulped down the last of her chardonnay and flagged the waitress for a refill. Her date never broke stride.

"It wasn't the first time I've been tasked with removing a mole, but it's never an easy fight, and far more dangerous than anyone would imagine."

She sucked in air through her nose and plastered on what she hoped was a genial smile while surreptitiously checking out her surroundings. She'd noticed a trio at the bar earlier, and her attention returned there again. A guy and a girl who hadn't taken their eyes off each other and another guy who was there as a third wheel but didn't seem particularly bothered by it. She'd assumed he was waiting for his date while he had drinks with the couple, but then Andy noticed him flirting with the bartender. Maybe she was his girlfriend, though nothing between them hinted that they knew each other on an intimate level.

People-watching was one of Andy's favorite pastimes.

She enjoyed making up stories about strangers, testing her observation skills. She only wished there was a way she could find out if she was right about her instincts.

The single guy—a gut call—at the bar was handsome in an earthy way, his light brown hair winding into curls here and there like it was in need of a trim, his shadowed beard a far cry from Christopher's sharply shaven jawline. Where Christopher resembled a firm pillar in a Brooks Brothers suit, the guy at the bar was in an approachable button-down pale-blue-and-white checked shirt, his tie—if there'd ever been one—long since tossed, and the sleeves cuffed and pushed to his elbows. He was drinking a bottle of beer, an expensive IPA if she wasn't mistaken, and that made her like him more.

"Andy?"

She jerked her attention to Christopher, who was a dark-haired, poor man's version of Chris Hemsworth. Not bad for a girl who was desperately seeking a date, but something about the good doctor was bothering her. Particularly that he was full of crap. Brimming with it, in fact.

How would she tolerate the entirety of a four-day wedding with him?

"Lost you there." He smirked and then continued the story of his latest medical triumph, talking down to her as if she still held her first job working part-time at a perfume counter. Not that he'd know what she did for a living. He never asked. If this bozo knew who he was trying to impress, he'd shut his mouth like a sprung bear trap.

She wondered what ole Christopher would say if he knew she was *the* Andy Payne, master of marketers. Sultan of sales. The oft-sought-after, rarely duplicated expert who was essentially a puff of smoke.

Everyone thought she was a man…on paper. She'd kept her identity a secret from everyone—including the many publications who'd interviewed her.

The New York Times.

Forbes.

Fortune.

That random mention in *Entertainment Weekly.*

Andy Payne was known for whipping companies into shape, and throughout her illustrious five-year career she'd managed to garner the attention of others with a clean black-and-white website and zero personal or identifying information about herself. When she showed up at the company, they knew on sight that she was a woman, but by then they were under her spell…and they'd signed a nondisclosure agreement.

Mostly she worked with men and, as she'd experienced in her first attempt at beginning a business as Andrea Anderson (last name chosen for alliteration), complete with a mauve and silver website filled with flowery words and cursive fonts, male clients didn't want to pay her what she was worth.

Enter her new identity. Andrea was easily changed to Andy, and she used her real last name. She let her clients' assumptions that she was male work in her favor.

"…not that I need *another* house in Tahiti." Christopher offered a smug smile and leaned back in his chair. Apparently, that was her cue to swoon or something.

She'd wasted enough time. First on her exes and now on the Find Love app. The wedding was in two weeks and she didn't have time for another round of failed interviews disguised as dates.

Andy hated to admit it, but in a deep dark corner of her heart she longed to be more like her sisters. She desired praise and approval from her mother. She wanted not necessarily to "fit in" but she would love not to *stand out*. In this case that meant appearing happily coupled off and avoiding needling observations from family members like that cousin at her sister Carroll's wedding.

I wish I was brave enough to show up at a wedding alone. If I didn't have a date, I would've just stayed home.

It wasn't enough to have a cardboard stand-in by her side, no, no. Andy needed to impress. Ideally her date could thwart those sorts of comments before they started.

Sadly, as impressive as Christopher believed he was, he wouldn't cut it as a proper wedding date.

Still. He was all she had. Time to get real.

"Christopher. I selected your profile because I need a date for my sister's wedding. The gig is three nights, four days in amazing and luxurious Crown, Ohio. Your airfare will be covered and your hotel room will be separate, but also covered. You will be tasked with being my date, pretending to find everything I say amusing, and impressing my mother and father. You're skilled at bragging about how great you are but I will also need you to recognize that I'm in the room if we have any hope of pulling this off. Are you up for the mission I've presented you, or do you want to call it a night?"

He watched her carefully, an uncertain look on his face. "Are you— You're serious."

"As a heart attack. Which I hear you know a lot about."

"You want me to pretend to be your boyfriend."

"Yes."

"At a wedding."

"Yes."

He leaned forward and squinted one eye, his lips pursing as if deciding if the trip to Ohio would be worth his time, energy and effort.

Andy's palms were sweating. Not because she was excited by the doctor, but because her search might finally be over.

Then the idiot blurted, "Do we at least get to fuck?"

Yeah. They were *so* done.

"Good night, Christopher. I'll take care of the check."

"Wait, Andy—"

She tossed twenty bucks on the table to cover their drinks and marched to the ladies' room. The money would cover the single drink they'd each had and then she could go home and—

And what?

She was flat out of solutions. She had no close guy friends she could ask. Hell, she had no close girlfriends who might help her make a plan. What she had was money and prestige.

Just the thought of showing up at Gwen's wedding alone pissed her off. She refused to fail. It wasn't in her nature. Plus there was one other itty-bitty reason why showing up with a date was preferable.

One of her ex-boyfriends had been invited. She'd stooped low enough to call, which was bad enough, but then she learned that he was dating Gwen's best friend who was in the wedding. So that was gross.

Matthew Higgins had greeted her like no time had passed since they parted. *Well, well, well. If it isn't her royal highness.*

The Ice Queen. That was her.

Thank God she hadn't asked him to be her date. She'd played it off like she'd simply thought of him out of the blue and wanted to "catch up" and then ended the call before she died of humiliation.

At the double sink, she dug through her purse for her lip gloss, which evidently she'd neglected to pack in her clutch. She sighed in defeat. It'd been a long month.

A long *life*.

Around the time she'd dated Matt, she'd been sure she'd wind up marrying eventually. Until he repeatedly teased her about her lack of warmth. She wasn't enough for him, and as much as she wished she could refute that, she'd also seen evidence in her family of what she was lacking. She wasn't as bubbly as Gwen. She wasn't as bold as Kelli. She wasn't as stylish as Ness. She wasn't as athletic as Carroll. As one of five girls in the Payne family, Andy was the unofficial black sheep. She'd just as soon not draw even more attention to their differences by becoming the last single one. Yet here she was.

For all the confidence and kick-ass-ness she possessed at work, she didn't want to be singled out or excluded from couples' activities.

Plus, nothing chapped her ass more than giving up.

She peeked out of a crack in the swinging door of the ladies' restroom to watch Christopher exit the bar. *Thank God.* Also, her twenty was still on the table, which was a plus. The last guy had taken her money and left, and she'd had to pay the waitress again.

There were no good men left in this city.

In the *world*.

"I can't catch another bouquet without a date," she whispered to herself. As humiliating as it was to catch the blasted thing—that her sisters always aimed her way— nothing was more humiliating than returning to the table with the flowers in hand and no date in sight. Guests always looked on in pity, as if she was going to die alone.

Her gaze snagged on the attractive guy at the bar and her back straightened with determination. If she was right about her observations, he was single. He was also sort of flirting with the bartender which hopefully meant he was looking.

Approaching him would be a random shot, but so had approaching every other guy she'd been out with. Maybe instead of taking home the cute bartender, he'd agree to bail out the too-serious, frosty, desperate-for-a-wedding-date single woman hiding in the ladies' room.

Probably not.

But Andy wasn't a failure.

She wouldn't *allow* failure.

She stepped from the restroom and spotted him—alone. The guy with the attractive facial hair and almost boyish curls. Except everything about the sculpted jaw and rounded shoulders screamed *man*. He was alone. Which meant the couple he'd been with had gone elsewhere.

Now was her chance.

Maybe her last chance.

"Money," she muttered.

She didn't have time for a get-to-know-you chat followed by the prospect of a date followed by her warming up to mention, "Hey, so my sister is getting married in two weeks…" She had to cut through the small talk and arrow straight to the point. Cash would make that a hell of a lot easier. She opened her clutch to count her credit cards. Five. That should be enough.

She rounded the corner to the ATM at the back of the bar, a plan in mind and a glass of good chardonnay in her belly.

She would take the simple approach and ask him if she could pay him to come with her to Ohio. Enough with faux dating and weighing the odds. She needed a date, and hopefully this guy needed a couple grand.

On a mission, she slid the first of five credit cards into the machine and punched the withdrawal button.

She would find a date to Gwen's wedding.

And she would find him tonight.

Two

Gage Fleming finished off his IPA and tipped the bottle's neck at the bartender. "I'll take the check when you have a second."

Seattle had come out of a long winter and cool spring, and was now firmly entrenched in summer. The energy was different during the hot months. The skirts were shorter and the nights were longer, and for him, the workdays were longer, too. He hadn't left his desk until well after seven thirty—hadn't gotten here until well after eight thirty. Given the hellacious week he'd had at the office, it didn't surprise him that he wasn't as upbeat as usual.

"Sure thing." Shelly was petite, wearing a ball cap with her ponytail sticking out of the back. Her lashes were thick, and her lips were shiny with gloss. Cute as she was, he didn't plan on asking her out. Even though she was his type, from her shapely calves to her low-cut V-necked T-shirt with the bar's gold-and-red emblem on it. Even though she'd been offering her smiles freely and borderline flirting back with him, Gage wasn't feeling it.

His best buddy Flynn and Sabrina, his other best buddy

turned Flynn's girlfriend, had taken off a few minutes ago. Gage hung around at From Afar, finishing his beer after a long week and what felt like a longer workday.

He'd been friends with Flynn, Sabrina and Reid—who wasn't in the country at the moment—since college. Sabrina being in the mix was nothing new. Her being in love with Flynn and vice versa: totally new.

Gage had said yes to the after-work beer, not thinking it'd be any different than any other hangout they'd had before. It had been different, though, since the couple couldn't keep their hands or eyes on anything in the room but each other. But he couldn't begrudge his friends. A few months back, Flynn and Sabrina had slipped from the friend zone to the in-zone. Flynn was the happiest he'd been in a long while.

"Here you go, sweetheart." The cute blonde winked at him and moved away to greet another patron.

If he wasn't mistaken, that lifting feeling in his chest was relief at his decision not to dance the dance with her. Flirting was easy—hell, second nature—to him. Asking her out wouldn't be an issue. He had it down. He'd heard yes more times than no, and often heard "Yes!" shouted with exuberance later the same night in his bed.

Over the past few weeks, however, he'd noticed he was tired of the game. Going out on a few dates, a round or three of spectacular sex (or *okay* sex—but even okay sex was pretty damn good), and then finding his way out before things progressed to anything serious… If they got that far. Lately, he'd grown tired of the awkward parting in the middle of the night or the next morning. Tired of the walk of shame.

Thirty years old was too young to be this jaded.

You're just tired after a long week. Don't analyze it to death.

He leaned forward to pull his wallet from his back

pocket, ready to pay and take his gloomy self home, when he noticed a stunning vision striding toward him. He froze, the scene unfolding in slow motion.

Strawberry blond hair washed over slim shoulders in a waterfall of color, bright against the narrow black sheath dress draped over her slender form. Electric blue eyes flashed with determination. She was long-limbed, her walk confident, and her full pink mouth was set in a firm, unsmiling line. One eyebrow was arched and she homed in on him like he was the target and she was a missile.

With his next breath, his libido returned. Lust slammed into his solar plexus and dried out his mouth.

Which made no sense.

In those heels, in that dress and with no smile to speak of, it was obvious he was in the presence of a way-too-serious woman. He'd had a close call with a woman like this one in his past, and he'd since decided that cute, bubbly bartenders were more his style.

Even so. Intrigued and more than a bit curious, he shoved his wallet back into his pocket when it became clear that this striking woman was coming right for him.

This one, he'd dance with. If only to shake things up a bit.

He'd buy her a drink, turn on the Fleming charm and see what happened. It'd been a while since a woman had snagged this much of his attention. Whether it was the strawberry blonde's determination or the set of her small shoulders, he couldn't be sure, but he couldn't tear his eyes off her. How could anyone look that damned delicate and at the same time like she ate nails for breakfast?

He didn't know. But he was going to find out. Something told him that she'd be worth it, no matter the cost.

"Shelly, I'll have another IPA after all," he said to the bartender, and as the strawberry blonde placed a manicured hand on the back of the bar stool next to him, he smoothly added, "and whatever she's having."

"You got it." Shelly dipped her chin at the strawberry blonde. "What'll it be?"

Strawberry yanked her gaze from Gage, her expression almost shocked that the bartender was talking to her. "Um. Chardonnay."

Shelly fetched their drinks and Gage turned to greet his guest, pulling the stool out for her to sit.

"No. Thanks," she replied coolly, almost like the "thanks" part was an afterthought.

Instinct told him that she wasn't as cool and calm as she pretended to be. If she was actually the man-eater she portrayed, she'd look him in the eye right now. Instead, she appeared to be steeling herself for some sort of proposition. Maybe she'd had a bad breakup, needed a little rebound.

That he could do.

"Can't enjoy your chardonnay without having a seat," he replied easily, patting the stool with one hand. Her eyebrows slammed down over her pert nose and she pegged him with an expression that bordered on fury.

A *zap!* hit him low in the gut. A warning drowned out by intense curiosity.

Let's tangle, honey.

A glass of chardonnay and a bottle of beer appeared in front of him, and without breaking away from her fiery blue gaze, he handed over the wine. Strawberry's nostrils flared, but she took the glass, tipped it to her lips and had sucked down a third of it by the time he'd lifted his bottle.

Yep. She was definitely here on a mission.

She set the glass down with a loud *clink*. "I'll pay you two thousand dollars to spend a weekend with me."

Gage lowered his beer without taking a sip. His mouth was poised to say the word *what* but he didn't have a chance to say anything before she was opening her purse and showing him the contents. Stacks of twenties were packed into it, facing every which way like she'd robbed a convenience store before propositioning him.

"I'm attending a destination wedding in the Midwest in two weeks. Your flight and separate room will be paid in full. I'll give you two thousand dollars to go with me."

Just as he'd settled on the notion that this beautiful creature was certifiably insane, a flicker of doubt lit her expressive eyes.

"I need you to pretend to be my boyfriend for the duration. I know Ohio doesn't sound scenic, but Crown is a beautiful, quaint town. And there will be food," she added with a touch of desperation. "Really good food."

Her throat moved as she swallowed thickly, her outer layer of surety and confidence flaking away.

Seemed he was right about her being on a mission, but damn, he'd been wrong about her not being a man-eater. She was so similar to his ex, he wouldn't be surprised if she pulled off a mask to reveal Laura herself.

He took a long slug of his beer and then swiped his tongue over his bottom lip. This woman was either crazy or desperate or both. Figured. He should've known a woman this beautiful would be nuttier than a sack of trail mix.

"Well?" Her eyebrow arched again, her too-serious expression snapping seamlessly into place. "I don't have much time, so I'd appreciate an answer."

Was she for real?

He'd never imagined she'd march over here and demand to...to...*hire him* to be her date, let alone expect him to agree without so much as a casual introduction. For all he knew, she would lure him in with promises and then steal his identity.

Or my kidneys.

The answer was an easy no, but he wouldn't let her off the hook without making her explain first. He opened the edge of her purse with his index finger so he could examine the cash inside as he pretended to consider her offer.

"How will payment work? You just hand me all the money in your purse and then I give you my phone number?"

"No. Of course not." She snatched her bag out of his reach. "Then I'd have no guarantee you'd show up. I'd give it to you at the wedding."

"Why would I clear my weekend plans and fly with you to Ohio on a promise of two thousand dollars if I don't have any of it?"

A frown muddled her pretty face. "You can have half. But I need your phone number. And your address. And your word."

Unbelievably gorgeous and absolutely crackers. It was a shame.

"But I need your answer now."

"Right now." His gaze locked on her pink mouth and he had a moment of regret for not getting to have a taste of her lips. To feel how silky that red hair was against his fingertips. He lifted his beer bottle, delaying. The kissing and fingers in her hair were an impossibility but his curiosity to watch her reaction still burned. He was trying to decide what she would do when he said no. Would she slap him or scream at him or run from the bar?

"Yes, now," she said through her teeth.

Damn. Maybe he could convince her to stick around after he shot her down.

"I can't help you out, Strawberry. I don't particularly like the Midwest. And despite what first impression I must've given you, I don't need two thousand dollars. But if you'd like to finish your wine—"

That long swath of hair flicked as she turned on her heel and tromped toward the exit. Option C it was. She left behind a plume of softly scented perfume and a fantasy that lasted the rest of the week. One about long, silky hair and a parted pink mouth. About her beneath him naked atop those bills scattered over his bed…

Whoever she was, she left an impression. The way looking at the sun left bright light burning behind his lids for a while.

Gage turned back to his beer. Even though Strawberry was a little nutty, he honestly hoped she found a date to that wedding in Ohio.

Three

"Today's the day."

Gage rubbed his hands together and then fired up the espresso machine in the executive break room.

"What day's that?" Reid, back from his recent trip home to London, asked.

"The day that Andy Payne guy comes to save Gage's rear end," Sabrina answered as she tipped the half-and-half into her mug.

"Not *my* rear. *Our* rears," Gage corrected. "This is going to help boost sales, yes, but this will also take some of the pressure off Flynn." He grinned at Sabrina. "You're welcome."

Last year Gage had come up with the perfect solution for the senior staff at Monarch Consulting, who had been giving Flynn holy hell. When Flynn's father died, leaving Flynn in charge of the company, a lot of the men and women who were used to the way Emmons had run things hadn't taken too kindly to Flynn. Gage's suggestion—*brilliant* suggestion—was to focus on sales, create a huge boom in business, which would satisfy shaky investors and give a needed boost to everyone's bonuses. It was hard to complain when extra money rolled in.

"Oh, I'm welcome, am I?" Sabrina chuckled.

"If it's gratitude you want, mate, just ask," Reid commented.

Gage didn't want gratitude, but he did want results. The company had felt as if it was teetering on a foundation of marbles last year and he hadn't liked it at all. Monarch Consulting was the workplace Gage had called home since college. He didn't want to work anywhere else. He loved what he did, loved his friends and in no way wanted to end up working at a fish hatchery like his parents. Flynn's success as president ensured all of their successes.

Flynn stepped into the room, picking up on the conversation. "Let me guess. You have your panties in a wad of excitement over the arrival of the guy made of smoke?"

The guy who was the key to stabilizing Monarch, bringing in extra money *and* a business boom?

Hell, yes.

Andy Payne was a fixer of sorts who was known for not being known. He'd been interviewed but never filmed, and his About page was devoid of a photo or any description of him as a person. Gage wasn't sure if he bought into the hero-worship BS surrounding Andy Payne's reputation, but the man's results were rock solid. Every employee had signed nondisclosure documents before Payne's arrival.

Plus, if this Andy guy was half as good in person as he was on paper, Monarch would be set and Flynn's leadership would go unchallenged. Succeeding was the only option. Gage had never taken a backwards step since he'd set foot in Monarch and he wouldn't start now. He had goals to double the company's revenue, and making his sales department shine would tuck in nicely with that goal.

It was a big goal, but Andy Payne was a big deal. With his help there wasn't anything standing in Gage's way.

* * *

Andy strolled into the Monarch building wearing her best suit. Bone-colored, with a silky black cami under the jacket, her Jimmy Choos an easy-to-navigate height. She had to work in them, after all.

She'd never understood any woman's desire to sacrifice form for comfort. She wasn't a fan of compromise.

Andy hadn't accepted her fate from the weekend, either. Yes, she'd quit the dating app that'd been a total waste of resources. And, yes, she had felt the sting of embarrassment about propositioning a handsome stranger at a bar, but that didn't mean her search was over. There was still a chance, though slim, to find a stand-in date. Maybe she would meet a nice guy on her way out of this very building. Or maybe at the resort.

Doubt pushed itself forward but she fervently ignored it. Instead she allowed herself to feel the familiar thrum of excitement as she rode the elevator up to the executive floor. First days were her *favorite*.

She'd done extensive research on Monarch, noting that the only photo of the staff was one gathered outside the front of this very building, their faces tiny and nondescript. If businesses were to entrust Monarch with their well-being, they needed to see the trustworthy faces who worked here.

Unlike most businesses, Andy had worked hard to keep her identity under wraps. She had no qualms about pulling a bait and switch on day one. By then everyone was invested and her reputation had preceded her. She never blatantly led her clients to believe Andy Payne was male, but much like the assumption that a surgeon was always a man, so, too, was one made that the wild success of her Fortune 500 business must be attributed to someone with a penis instead of a pair of breasts.

The pay gap that existed between men and women didn't exist for her, thanks to her subterfuge. Her clients paid what was asked, and it was too late to pull the plug once the contracts were signed. She wouldn't apologize for it.

She was absolutely worth it.

She was the best at what she did and she endeavored to leave every business better than she'd found it. Monarch was going to be another link in a long chain of satisfied customers.

With a flip of her hair she exited the elevator on the executive floor. Three huge offices with glass walls stood empty, a front desk staffed with a young blonde woman in front of one of them. Andy was early, so probably the executives hadn't come out of the coffee or break room yet. Muted voices and laughter came from an unseen room in the back.

One of those voices likely belonged to Gage, the senior sales executive who'd hired her.

"May I help you?" the assistant asked.

Andy addressed her by her name, advertised on the nameplate on the front of her desk. "Hello, Yasmine. Andy Payne for Gage Fleming."

"Andy Payne?"

"That's me." She grinned.

"Oh, of course, Ms. Payne. We have you set up in the conference room as you requested."

Yasmine quickly recovered from her surprise at discovering that Andy was a woman. Good for her.

In the conference room, Yasmine pointed out the projector and offered to fetch Andy an espresso.

"Americano, if you can."

The other woman dipped her chin in affirmation and left.

Andy unloaded her bag on the table—a rigorous sales plan and a dossier on Monarch minus details on the man she was meeting, since she'd learned virtually nothing about him via the website.

Done right, they could implement her suggested changes

in the week and a half she had before she would have to fly to Ohio for Gwen's wedding.

Gag. Just the thought of that bit of unfinished business rankled her.

But Gage Fleming had hired Andy on her merits at business, not based on whether or not she was datable. She shoved aside all thoughts of the wedding and focused on what she did most—what she did *best*—fixing companies.

Flynn and Sabrina left the haven of the break room, Gage and Reid following behind. On their walk to their offices, Gage asked Reid, "How was your trip?"

His British friend, coffee mug lifted, grinned. "Grand."

"Because of..."

"Suzie Daniels. A pretty American in a foreign land who needed companionship from a local who was willing to show her a good time." Reid rested his palm over his heart. "I showed her repeatedly. Lucky lady."

Gage had to chuckle. Reid was a playboy and a half, but he was also a nice guy. No doubt Suzie Daniels had kissed him farewell and hadn't regretted a single minute of their time together. Gage hadn't been as fortunate with his past hookups. He must throw off a serious boyfriend vibe. The women he dated always wanted more, always wanted it too quickly and weren't happy when he declined. The last woman he dated had told him he'd wasted her time and said she wished she'd never met him. Ouch.

"And your weekend?" Reid asked, stopping next to Gage's office.

"Went to From Afar with Flynn and Sabrina on Friday night for a drink after work. After they left, the strangest thing..." Gage fell silent when he spotted a flash of red hair in the conference room. And when her head lifted slightly and he caught sight of her profile, he recognized her instantly.

She was the woman who'd attempted to buy him like a suit off a rack. The more he'd thought about that interaction the more it had bothered him. Not because he felt cheap or used, but because the beauty who'd invaded his dreams had truly believed the money was going to seal the deal with them. As if she didn't have enough confidence to strike up a conversation about what she needed, but instead felt the need to offer him cash.

"Holy hell." Gage grabbed Reid's arm and dragged him back into the hallway they'd just exited, Reid complaining since he'd sloshed coffee onto the carpet and narrowly missed his shoes. Gage had done a good job of spilling his own coffee on his shirt. Hot liquid burned through the pale blue button-down, and he swore.

"What just happened?" Reid shook coffee droplets off his fingers.

"She's stalking me." Gage scrubbed at his shirt with one hand.

"Who?"

Reid peered around the corner and Gage slunk farther into the hall. When he'd concluded that the redhead was "crackers," he'd thought he'd been half joking. Apparently, he hadn't.

"That's the woman I was just going to tell you about," Gage whispered, though there was no way she could hear him from the conference room. "She approached me at the bar Friday night and offered to pay me two grand to spend a weekend with her."

Reid's eyebrows lifted, wrinkling his brow. "And you said no." He stole another peek and regarded Gage dubiously. "Why?"

"Because she's insane?" That seemed the only reasonable explanation now.

"You're the insane one, my friend, if you didn't snap her

up and have your way with her right there on the bar top. Hell, I wouldn't have charged her at all."

"The offer wasn't for sex. It was for me to fly to Ohio and attend a wedding. She wanted me to pretend to be seeing her or something."

"Oh." Reid's disappointment was obvious. "That's not the same thing at all."

"No. It's not." Gage returned to the break room and set his mug aside. He grabbed a dish towel and scrubbed at the coffee stain low on his shirt.

Reid wasn't far behind. "What's she doing here?"

"I have no idea."

"Gage?" Yasmine stepped into the break room. "Andy Payne is here to see you."

"Perfect timing." Gage gestured at his soiled shirt. "Tell him I'll be right out. Who's the redhead?"

Yasmine blinked. "Andy Payne."

"Andy Payne is the fixer, love," Reid told her gently. "We want to know who the vixen in the cream-colored suit is."

"Andy Payne," Yasmine repeated with slow insistence and enough confidence that Reid and Gage exchanged glances.

"*She's* Andy Payne?" Gage asked, still trying to wrap his head around the idea that the woman who approached him at the bar was the "guy" he'd hired to whip his sales team into shape.

"Surprising, right? How sexist are we?" Yasmine shrugged. "I thought Andy was going to be a dude, too."

Reid smiled to beat all. "I believe I'll go with you to meet this Andy Payne, Gagey. Do bring up Friday for my benefit, yeah?"

"No," Gage growled, his head still spinning with the new information. "I'll go alone to meet…her."

As he exited the break room, he muttered, "Again."

Four

The projector was positioned, her laptop open and the PowerPoint presentation cued up.

Andy tidied the bound sales plans—one for her and one for Gage. She'd arranged herself at the head of the conference table and placed the report to her left elbow at the corner. She found it easier to coordinate a plan when they weren't facing each other from opposing sides.

Sometimes these meetings went smoothly, with the managers or CEOs who'd hired her easing into the adjustment as they learned that Andy Payne was the female currently introducing herself. Other times, they reacted angrily and accused her of pulling a fast one on them. Mostly it was the former.

They'd hired her for her expertise, and that was what she reminded them of when she arrived. She'd only had three men ever react poorly and had only ever lost one job because of it. The sexist bastard. No matter, her contract was ironclad and nonrefundable. She'd bought a weekend spa retreat with the money that particular time and had no qualms about enjoying her paid leave.

She sat on the edge of the padded chair and turned her head in time to see a man rapidly approaching the conference room. She recognized the scruffy jaw, the slight curl to the longish hair on top of his head…and the answering recognition in his caramel-brown eyes.

She stood slowly, feeling her jaw drop to the floor as he shut the conference room door behind him and looked down his nose at her. Although she wasn't that much shorter than him.

"*You're* Andy Payne," he said flatly.

Her mouth still agape, she managed a stunned nod. Warmth seeped from her cami, over her décolletage and up her neck. No doubt she was turning a stunning shade of pink while he watched her.

And he did watch her. Carefully. And unhappily.

As quickly as she could move, she slapped the lid closed on her laptop and yanked the cord free from the wall. "I'm—uh," she said as she hastily stacked the reports. "I have to…um…"

She yanked her bag off the chair but the strap caught, scattering the pages in her dossier on Monarch to the floor along with several pens, her cell phone charger and a tube of lipstick.

This was going well.

She crouched to the floor to sweep the contents of the bag back into it. "You must be Gage."

"In the flesh." He knelt next to her and picked up one of her pens that had fallen to the floor.

"I didn't know you were you when I approached you on Friday or I never would've done it," she said as she gathered her things. A lock of hair swept over her eye and she blew a puff of air from her lips to move it.

"You don't say." His eyebrows flinched slightly, but some of the anger simmered away, his expression almost bemused as his eyes roamed over her face.

He was stupidly attractive. Even more so in a suit. Even with a coffee stain on his shirt that looked fresh. That attraction was all the more reason why she couldn't stay another moment. She'd never be able to look him in the eye again after she'd… God…*offered to pay him* to be her date.

"I'll refund your money for the consultation contract." She snatched the pen from his hand and stood. He stood with her and the view of the rest of him was finer than it had appeared on Friday night. His muscular chest pressed the confines of his shirt, a dark blue tie in place and knotted just so. His slacks were navy as well, and a brown leather belt bisected his waist. His shoes matched—expensive and shiny.

"First you want to hire me, now you want to give me a refund. You offer to pay me an awful lot."

She blanched.

"And the hell you will." He folded his arms over his impressive chest. His unsmiling mouth pursed. "I hired you to do a job. You're not running out on me just because you—"

"Don't say it." Her eyes sank closed and she palmed one burning-hot cheek. Was it possible to die of humiliation? "I know what I did and I apologize." She reopened her eyes and turned them up to his. "Please tell me you didn't tell anyone about it?"

"I told my friend Reid. He works here. You'll meet him later."

"You told someone?" Her voice was edging along hysterical and she forced herself to calm down. "You could've kept that to yourself."

"Is that a joke? A gorgeous woman approaches me in a bar and I decide to stay one drink longer to get to know her and then she offers to pay me two grand for my companionship? It's a hell of a story, *Andy*."

He thought she was…gorgeous? And he'd wanted to get to know her?

It was far and wide two of the most flattering compliments she'd heard in a while.

"I didn't know you were *the* Andy Payne when I told him. I thought you'd tracked me down at work, and that you were going to… I don't know, try and reconvince me."

That was fair.

Why would he assume she was here for any other reason? She'd been on a mission to achieve her goal on Friday and had—incorrectly—assumed that when she ran from that bar, mentally vowing never to return, she wouldn't see Gage again.

She hadn't asked him his name, either.

"I wasn't myself that night. I was angry about my date not working out and then I noticed you—" She snapped her mouth closed before she accidentally said too much, and then rerouted the conversation. "This is no fault of yours. I'll go directly to my office from here and refund your money immediately." She added the laptop and reports to her bag and pulled it over her shoulder.

"No deal." He stepped in front of the door and blocked her path.

"Step aside, Mr. Fleming."

"Not going to happen, *Ms.* Payne." His nostrils flared as he pulled in a breath. "I hired you. You agreed to do a job. I know you're the best—I did my research. You've been cited as an asset by hundreds of companies, and I'm not letting you go because you made a mistake and now you're uncomfortable. We have a contract. I was told your fee was nonrefundable."

That was true. Normally. "I'll make an exception."

A warm, gentle palm landed on her upper arm. His voice was equally gentle when he said, "I don't want an exception. I want you to stay and double or triple our numbers like you promised. This is important."

His words were sincere. And a good reminder that she

prided herself on her work ethic. She *never* let clients down. She worked tirelessly for them because their businesses mattered. Employees had families to care for, and when she made their companies more money, the companies in turn lined the pockets of those hardworking men and women. What she did wasn't about fattening up greedy CEOs. She did this work for the people. All of them.

And right now Gage looked like someone who needed her help.

"Did you find a date for the wedding yet?" he asked.

She blinked, stunned by the change of topic.

"I'll go," he said. "You stay here for the time you promised and I'll go with you to Ohio to your sister's wedding."

"But—"

"I suspect you'll insist, so I'll let you take care of the room and flight, but you can keep the two grand." He dipped his chin in a show of sincerity. "Okay?"

As much as she hated to admit it, his offer was really, *really* tempting. She had to face reality, and the reality was that she was no closer to finding a date for Gwen's wedding than she was to sprouting wings and flying there on her own steam.

A bigger part of her was tempted simply because of Gage. He was attractive, and had found her attractive, and she wouldn't mind spending more time getting to know him. Of all the dates she'd set up in an attempt to find a companion for Gwen's wedding, Gage, from his warm brown eyes to his shiny leather shoes, was the only one who'd made her heart flutter. Dr. Christopher certainly hadn't wanted to get to know her better. He hadn't even had the decency to turn the money down.

Even so, she found herself answering, "I couldn't ask you to do that."

"Too bad. You already did, on Friday night. Now I'm accepting." He lifted her bag off her shoulder, his fingers leaving behind an imprint of heat she couldn't ignore. He set the bag on the conference room table, pulling her laptop out and extracting the reports, one of which had an ugly crease on the otherwise pristine cover.

What a metaphor for Andy herself right now. She'd come in here neat and poised and now felt more than a little bent.

He opened the laptop screen and took the wrinkled report and sat in his seat. She again considered refusing his offer. Her pride told her to bolt and never look back.

There was only one problem. She needed him.

Almost as much as he needed her.

Five

Gage had to hand it to her. Andy knew what she was doing.

A week later, he sat at a conference table with Flynn and Reid and his right-hand guy on his sales team, Bruce, reviewing the numbers. The numbers were good.

Really freaking good.

"Bonuses will look great this quarter," Bruce commented, his smile wide. A thirty-nine-year-old father of seventeen-year-old twins, he could use the extra money. Both of Bruce's daughters would be graduating and going to college soon.

"Share the good news," Gage told him. "That's all I have. Flynn? Reid? Anything?"

"Not on my end," Flynn said. "Just, good job."

Reid echoed the sentiment, shook Bruce's hand, and then Bruce left the executive floor with some really good news for the sales team.

"She's as good as she claims," Flynn commented to Gage. "Andy."

"She is."

"And bloody fast," Reid commented. "I've never seen anyone swoop in and offer suggestions that work immediately."

"She's amazing," Gage admitted. She was also all business. She strode in here Monday through Friday to train, observe and then meet with Gage on her findings. He'd done some observing of his own—of her—and he couldn't escape the idea that she'd walled part of herself off.

Last week, when he'd walked into this very conference room, she hadn't been determined and all business. She'd been flustered and embarrassed. She'd been *human*. He liked witnessing that human side of her—the flush to her cheeks as her seriousness chipped away leaving her open vulnerability visible. She was able to get shit done, took no crap from anyone, and yet he'd noticed a shier, more withdrawn part of her.

"Are the two of you still on for the wedding arrangement?" Reid asked, a troublemaking twinkle in his eye.

"I agreed to help her out so she wouldn't walk. You'd have done the same thing. It's only a weekend."

Four days, technically, but he was trying to downplay it. He'd agreed so she wouldn't walk out, yes, but he'd also agreed because learning that the woman from the bar and Andy Payne were the same person had intrigued him in a way no other woman had in years. He wanted to cash in on his fantasy vision of her beneath him, sure, but he was also curious as hell why she felt the need to pay someone— him, specifically. She'd hinted that day in the conference room that there was something about him that had drawn her in. Why him? What had she seen across that bar that made her approach him?

In the time she'd spent at Monarch he still knew next to nothing about her. She was as uncrackable as a sealed safe. He still wasn't sure what he was supposed to "do" at her side at the wedding. What role was he to play other than a date who danced with her or fetched her a glass of champagne? He needed to find out, but in order to do that he had to get her out of Monarch and into an environment where she wasn't so...distant.

"She's not light and bubbly like the women you're used to seeing. Maybe a wedding will loosen her up." Reid stood.

"She's serious about her job but that's not a bad thing," Gage said in her defense. He rose from his chair and Flynn followed suit.

"It's not," Flynn agreed. "She's a hard-core professional. Does everything she says she's going to do, and follows through like a boss." The description sounded like Flynn himself.

"I was just pointing out that she's the opposite of the type of woman you gravitate toward." Reid narrowed his eyes. "Lately."

What Reid was not-so-subtly hinting at was that Andy was, at first glance, a lot like Gage's ex-fiancée.

He didn't want to talk about Laura any more than he wanted to bring up politics at a dinner party. He'd admired her strong work ethic and serious nature. In the end, he'd believed in them more than she had.

She'd broken the engagement, coldly stating that he wasn't enough like her. He had a case of the "toos." He was *too* likable, *too* fun and *too* easygoing. She'd claimed she needed someone "serious" about the future. The corrosion of that engagement was his biggest failure.

Gage hated failure.

He'd been sure that Andy was that same kind of woman—cold, calculating—until he'd witnessed her flustered. Seeing that chink in her armor had drawn him in rather than pushed him away. He hadn't completely understood it. After the hell Laura'd put him through he'd be smart not to pursue Andy at all.

But he'd never been one to back down from a challenge,

and Gage sensed there was warmth and gentleness underneath Andy's rigid exterior that had yet to surface. The more of her flaws he exposed, the more he proved that the attraction wasn't some masochistic repeat of the past with Laura, but some new, fascinating layer to Andy herself.

He liked that she had an imperfect, human side that rarely showed, that she was a mystery waiting to be uncovered. That she didn't have it together 24/7. Plus she was downright sexy. If he found an opening to show her how sexy she was, he'd happily oblige.

Not that his agreeing to be Andy's wedding date had been totally magnanimous. He'd needed her to stay on at Monarch for both appearances and results, and a few days in Ohio seemed a small price to pay.

Flynn and Sabrina had left the office around five. Now that Flynn had a girlfriend in Sabrina, he rarely worked as late as he had before. Reid had a date as well, so he'd packed up and followed them out. That left Gage alone in the executive corner of the office, waiting at his desk for Andy's daily report, which came at around 5:30 p.m.

She strolled in wearing her office attire of black pants, low shoes and a silky white shirt. Her gold jewelry was simple and understated, except for the large-faced watch, which she glanced down at before she entered.

Mouth a flat line, determination in her eyes, she stalked toward him like a hungry lioness. Much like the first time he'd seen her, he watched her approach with an even mix of intrigue and attraction.

Could he uncover the fun, flirty girl under that armor? Was there one?

"Your team is exceptional, Gage," she said, skipping over a greeting. "Which is in no small part thanks to you being a dedicated, earnest leader."

His eyebrows lifted at the compliment he wasn't expecting. But then she spoke again and made it obvious that she'd come in here with an agenda.

"I have an itinerary, your plane ticket and a few other details to cover for this weekend's wedding if you're available for a quick rundown. I know it's last-minute, but I've been busy."

All business, he thought with a smile. He'd always enjoyed a challenge but, he was realizing, lately he'd pursued challenges professionally rather than personally. He hadn't chased women who'd challenged him since Laura left. Then again, Andy had been the only one who'd tempted him to do so since.

"What are you doing right now?" he asked her.

"Now?" Her eyes widened slightly.

"Yeah. Now. Dinner?"

She shook her head like what he was saying didn't compute.

"Are you hungry?" he pressed.

"Yes."

"Are you busy right now?"

"I'm always busy."

He waited.

She shrugged and affected an *unaffected* expression. "Fine."

"Great. I'll drive."

"Where are we going?"

"Why? Are you picky? Have allergies?"

"No." She frowned.

"Then don't worry about it." He winked, enjoying throwing her off-kilter.

He needed a little more fun in his life and Andy *definitely* needed a little more fun in her life. He liked that she seemed unused to a man strong enough or willing enough to take her on. He just liked her, dammit, though he wasn't yet sure why he liked her this much.

* * *

In the immediate seconds following Gage's invitation to dinner, Andy wanted to blurt out that she needed to change first. Thankfully she resisted that very female urge. Just because Gage was playing her date at the wedding didn't mean he was one tonight. She would pretend they were an item, enjoy the reprieve from her family's judgment, and relish showing up an old ex-boyfriend who thought she'd been carved from a block of ice. But she'd keep the boundary lines very clear in her head. Gage had agreed to be her date for one reason: because he'd needed her expertise at work.

Without something to gain, he wasn't interested in her—he'd turned her down that night in the bar, after all.

Still, being around him was a rare exception she admitted she was tempted to enjoy. She was a hard sell to any man—even without the offer to pay him. A man who was both professional *and* not intimidated by her success was a rare commodity. Like finding a unicorn.

Even though her arrangement with Gage wouldn't last any longer than her sister's reception, Andy figured it'd be good to get to know him so that her family wouldn't suspect she'd bribed him to come. The only thing more humiliating than showing up at her sister's wedding with a fake date would be everyone learning that she was faking it.

But the stray thought about changing for dinner with Gage had rocked her. Why would she care what he thought of her appearance if they weren't doing this for real? She'd long ago accepted that a forever-and-ever relationship wasn't going to happen, and yet something about Gage—about his charm and kindness—made a small part of her wish this was real.

He wasn't intimidated by her. If anything, the more prickly she was, the more laid-back he seemed to become. Laid-back and yet more than a little commanding.

It was an odd mix. She didn't have him figured out yet.

Which was why she'd spent the weekend writing up the wedding itinerary and finalizing the details of their arrangement. She needed to get them on the same page, and fast, if they had any prayer of pulling this off.

At least she'd have Gage by her side when she inevitably bumped into her ex-boyfriend Matthew. The thought of him smugly pointing out that she was as frigid as she'd always been irritated her.

She wished she didn't care. Wished she didn't want to rub her ex's nose in her business success—*and* her relationship success—in spite of the label he'd given her years ago. But she did.

She was only human, after all.

Gage chose a fairly high-end restaurant downtown for dinner. With its black tablecloths and dim lighting, candles in the center of the table and à la carte menu, it was a touch more romantic than she'd counted on. Maybe she should've insisted on going home to change rather than continue in her casual work attire—if only to fit in with the well-coiffed crowd.

The host pulled her chair out for her and she sat, lifting the menu to study the options.

"Wine, Andy?" Gage asked. "Or should I call you something else in public to protect your secret identity? Bruce Wayne, maybe."

"Ha-ha." She lowered the menu to give him a slow blink. "I'll stick with sparkling water, but thank you."

When their waiter came by, Gage ordered a bottle of Cabernet alongside her sparkling water.

"We never finished the first drink we had together," he pointed out. "Tonight would feel stuffy if we didn't indulge."

She did indulge—one glass had the rigors of her workday melting off her shoulders like butter in the hot sun.

There was something about Gage that brought out her relaxed side. Maybe it was his own casual attitude. How he could wear a suit in a fancy restaurant as well as he did and still smile as genially as if they were lounging on his sofa together...it was beyond her.

Andy had accepted that she simply wasn't the fun, carefree type. Outside of this agreement with Gage, she couldn't imagine snagging his attention. And yet being around him felt strangely comfortable—which was probably why she didn't hang around him at work. She didn't want to be unduly comfortable and slip up—she had a job to do. She couldn't pretend to be able to live up to his fun, easy-going standards. That simply wasn't who she was. Except that she needed to be *really* comfortable around him at Gwen's wedding for this charade to work.

After they'd eaten their dinners, they settled in to finish off the wine, Gage resting one masculine hand on the rim of his glass. He lifted it the same way and gestured to her with the stem.

"Let's hear the plan."

Was it any wonder he was fantastic at his job? He exuded confidence and charm, and if she were a twitchy CEO in search of a consulting firm, she'd buy an air conditioner from Gage in the wintertime. Just to urge forth that sincere, pleased smile.

To please him in general.

That thought brought forth another, one of pleasing him in a physical way. With her touch, with her kiss.

Alarming, since Andy had just tasked herself with keeping things between them strictly professional. Why did he have to be so damned attractive? Why did he have to be so damned likeable? Why did he act as if he liked her so much in return? That was the real lure. He seemed to like her just as she was—prickly and unapproachable, rigid and serious. She really wished he'd have let her pay him so the lines weren't so blurry.

"I emailed you an itinerary," she told him, firmly setting the conversation back on solid ground.

"When?"

"In the car on the drive over. Do you want to cue it up so we can review it together? It covers the schedule in detail, including what time each event starts and where we'll be staying. I left your airline ticket at my apartment but I can bring it to Monarch tomorrow."

"Those aren't the kinds of details I need from you, Andy."

"No?" She wasn't sure what else there was. Unless… "I did type up a detailed family member list, but that seemed like overpreparing. If you and I were really dating, you wouldn't necessarily remember all their names."

"Those aren't the details I need, either." He shook his head, took a sip from his wine and swallowed.

When his tongue stroked his lip to catch a wayward crimson drop, she pressed her knees together under the table. His mouth might be the most distracting part about him.

"I need to know," that mouth said, lazily pronouncing each syllable, "how much physical affection you'd like from me."

Six

"Hold your hand. Put my palm on your lower back. Those are both givens. But what about kissing? How much? How often? How *deep*?"

Gage watched Andy carefully as he doled out each option as if on a menu like the one they'd ordered from tonight. He enjoyed the surprise rounding her wide blue eyes as much as the flush creeping along her fair skin. "When we're at dinner, would you like me to feed you a bite, kiss your hand, gaze longingly into your eyes?"

"Is any of that necessary?" She sounded worried that it might be.

"Not unless we're trying to make someone jealous. In which case—very necessary. But if you have a fairly reserved family, I'll keep the touching to a minimum."

Clearly befuddled, she shakily lifted her wine and polished off the glass. He smoothly refilled it, happy to ply her with enough alcohol to have her tell him the truth. He ignored the frisson of discomfort at pursuing Andy so doggedly. She'd caught his attention. She had his admiration. Why not pursue something physical with her? It wasn't as if he'd allow himself to get in as deeply as he had with Laura. That situation had been one and done, and he'd learned not to tempt fate.

He'd recommitted to the bachelor pact with Flynn and Reid for a reason: Gage would never again consider marriage.

Flynn had backed out of the pact after he and Sabrina had obliterated the just-friends boundary, but Sabrina was the ultimate exception. She was one of their own—who better to settle down with Flynn than the one woman who would never, ever betray him?

Gage's motivation was different. He'd been thoroughly blinded by his love for Laura. He'd felt like a complete jackass for overlooking her cold-hearted demeanor, and had assumed their physical attraction and professional goals were enough to sustain a life together. He'd been young, and stupid, and all along she'd been more concerned about his financial potential than a stable marriage. After they imploded, he'd set out to make ten times as much money as she'd earn in her lifetime just to prove her wrong.

Over the years his drive became less and less about proving Laura wrong. Gage had grown to love success, and was a damn good leader. His strengths had served him well and he'd helped his best friend build a company and a sales team they could all be proud of.

Gage was a different person now than he was when he'd been engaged to Laura. Just because Andy had a similar passion for achievement was no reason to ignore the ninety-foot flames between them whenever she was near. That siren's wail he'd heard in his head was nothing more than a false alarm, concocted by the former version of himself.

"Why do you need a date for the wedding?" he asked, curious. "Why not go alone?"

"I've caught three bouquets and I don't want to catch a fourth," she answered. Strangely.

"Pardon?"

"I have four sisters. Three of them are happily married and the fourth is about to be. I don't want to catch Gwen's bouquet. If I go alone and am called to the dance floor, then Gwen will inevitably aim that bouquet right for me…" She shuddered like this was the worst fate that could befall her.

"I'm guessing not because you have an aversion to flowers?"

Andy shook her head.

"You don't want the attention?"

"I don't want the attention for being single. It's a running joke in my family."

He couldn't believe she'd admitted that much. The wine must be working. He didn't dare interrupt in case she had more to say. Turned out she did.

"I have a reputation as a hard-ass. Shocking, I know." She added a self-deprecating eye roll that he'd have found adorable if he didn't believe she was sincere. "I've never had a date to one of my sister's weddings. I'm pretty sure they think I live this lonely, pathetic existence married to my work or whatever."

"Did you date much when you lived in Ohio?"

"A few serious relationships that fizzled out. They didn't last and when we split I mostly felt relieved. One of them will be there, by the way." She chucked back the last inch of wine and waved her glass for a refill.

Gage obliged her.

"His name's Matthew," she snarled. "When we broke up he told me I'd die alone. I don't want him to know he was right."

"You're far from death's door, Andy."

"I'm not interested in permanence," she stated, a flicker of challenge in her eyes. He wouldn't argue.

"On that we agree." He clinked his glass with hers. Unbeknownst to her, she'd given him an angle to work with.

"Aside from my being your arm candy—" her impish smile emerged and brought forth an answering one of his own "—you'd like to show up this Matthew guy."

"I don't need to show him up." Bright eyes pegged him, truth in their cobalt depths. "I just don't want him to know he's won."

Gage didn't like that the bastard had coldly stated that Andy would spend her life alone any more than he liked the idea of her believing that her ex was right.

"We'll play it by ear." He reached across the table and offered a hand—handshake-style since he wasn't sure how she'd react to a more intimate touch. But when she placed her palm against his, he held onto her hand gently and made a promise he knew he'd keep. "You asked the right guy to be your wedding date, Andy. I won't let you down."

Gage had admitted during the flight that he didn't know much about Ohio. He'd told her that he knew there was a lot of corn, and that it was in the Midwest. Ohio wasn't *all* corn but there was a lot of it there.

The flight was uneventful and a straight shot to Cincinnati, but they did have to drive another hour to reach Crown from the airport. It gave them a chance to learn about music preferences—the rental car had a top-of-the-line satellite radio option—and talk about the wedding as conversationally as possible.

She didn't expect him to memorize her great-aunt's name or which grandmother, maternal or paternal, had the cane, but it made sense if they'd been dating for a while that he'd at least know her parents' and sisters' names.

"Kelli is the oldest by six years—"

"Seven," she corrected as Gage turned left onto Pinegrove Road.

"Seven. And then comes Vanessa, Carroll, you, and Gwen is the baby."

"Very good," she praised.

Gage flashed her a smile that made her tummy tighten. He really was ridiculously good-looking. She was looking forward to showing him off.

"Mom Estelle, dad Abe, but he had to work so he's coming in the day before."

"And here I sit without my gold star stickers."

"A joke. Andrea Payne, we'll loosen you up yet."

She turned to watch out the window, her lips pressed together. Gage's hand landed lightly on her leg.

"Hey. I was kidding."

"Oh, I know." She gave him what felt like an uncomfortable smile. So much for hiding her true feelings. It seemed like he could read her mind.

"Good." He turned left and drove past the wooden fence surrounding the entrance to Crown Vineyard Resort. The resort had both a man-made lake about four miles wide as well as a vineyard on-site. It made for a beautiful backdrop in the hot summer sun, the vines draped over the hills like garlands and the water sparkling under an azure sky.

Andy had secured two suites at the resort, one next to the other. She figured she could tell everyone it was a mistake made by the front desk in case it drew attention. She couldn't very well ask Gage to stay in the same room as her. He'd already been so great about not accepting payment for being here and genuinely helping her out by remembering the main branches of her family tree.

At least that'd been her reasoning until they stood at the check-in desk at the resort and she learned that there'd been an *actual* mistake at the front desk. The suite she'd reserved for Gage, paid in full, had been given to someone else.

"Unacceptable," she said, ready to fight for what was rightfully hers.

"I'm sorry, Ms. Payne. The system must've kicked that reservation out since he wasn't on the guest list. Your reservation is still in here though," the woman said brightly. "On the ground floor, king-sized bed, and a pullout sofa if separate sleeping quarters were your main concern." The woman at the counter flashed a look from Andy to Gage, probably deciding it was terribly old-fashioned to insist on separate rooms.

Gage palmed her lower back, his hand warm, and touched his mouth to her temple. "Ground floor sounds nice," he murmured, sending droves of goose bumps down her arms. "We can have coffee on the patio in the morning, and I can always sleep on the sofa if you're uncomfortable with me in your bed."

She swallowed thickly, the visual of Gage Fleming in her bed an inviting one indeed. She shifted away from him slightly. Not because he made her uncomfortable to have him near, but because whenever he was this close she was tempted to nuzzle him like a needy cat. Physical attraction to him would be helpful to convince her family and friends at this event, but she hadn't expected it in the "off" time they had together. No one was watching them, save the inept woman who couldn't provide the additional room Andy had paid for, and yet Andy had responded to him as if she had the option to have him in her bed.

She wouldn't entertain that thought. No matter how tempting it was...

He ran his hand up her back and rested it on the back of her neck, tickling her nape with his fingers and sending chills down both of her arms.

"Honey?" He smiled down at her and she forced herself to relax. He was her boyfriend for the weekend. Might as well act like it.

"Yes. That's fine."

"Great." The woman behind the counter tapped the keys on her keyboard.

How Gage's affable mood hadn't waivered today was

beyond Andy's comprehension. They'd started the morning way too early at the airport and then had gone through the discomforts of traveling—checking the bags and wedging into their tiny airplane seats. She'd fought him a little when he offered to put her bag in the overhead bin, but then realized she was standing her ground on something that shouldn't matter. If they were dating, he would of course stow her bag for her.

At the rental car kiosk, he'd insisted on driving and she'd given in on that, too. And now, the room debacle was another compromise she was making. She wasn't used to being half of a whole, or considering anyone's needs or wishes other than her own, but Gage made it easier than she'd have suspected to give up her control. It still surprised her that she'd not only let him take care of her, but that it'd also been...nice.

The woman at the front desk handed over their keycards and pointed out where their room was located, but Andy was listening with half an ear. Reason being, her mother and second eldest sister were approaching, whispering to each other as they came.

"Andrea," said Vanessa, her voice lifting in surprise.

"Hey, Ness." Andy stepped away from Gage a few inches and his hand fell away. Nervously, she smoothed her skirt with sweaty palms. "Mom."

Her mother studied Gage as well, but more dubiously than Vanessa did.

"Hi, sweetheart," her mother said, her eyes still on Gage. "Who's this?"

"Gage Fleming, this is my sister Vanessa, and my mother, Estelle."

"I've heard so much about you." Gage eased into a grin and shook their hands, and Andy felt her spine stiffen. No way would they believe this laid-back, ridiculously handsome, socially comfortable man was dating the Ice Queen.

"When Andrea RSVP'd with a plus-one, we didn't know what to think." Her mom—a beautiful woman—managed a snide smile that was somehow still pretty.

"You're the first of your kind," Vanessa added unhelpfully. "Andrea usually shows up to her sisters' weddings by herself."

"Well, unless one of you opts to remarry," Gage said as he wrapped an arm around Andy and pulled her closer, "this will be the last one."

Oh, he was good.

"We should go find our room," Andy announced, dying to run away before she inadvertently blew their cover. She was having the hardest time being comfortable in Gage's hold, especially with her eagle-eyed family staring them down.

"You're staying together?" Estelle's voice rose along with her slim, plucked eyebrows. Not because Andy's mother was old-fashioned and believed they should be staying separately but because—

"Andrea's not known for her affection." Estelle narrowed her eyes at her daughter. Andy wanted to sink into the floor. "It's…interesting to see her as part of a…couple."

Nope, her mother did not buy that Gage was with Andy for one second. Andy felt sweat prickle under her arms and opened her mouth to share the story of how they'd met at the bar—minus the part where she offered to hire him, and adjusting the timeline some—when Gage leaned in, his lips to the shell of her ear.

"Relax, beautiful girl," he whispered. "Touch my chest and smile like I just said something deliciously dirty to you."

He hadn't said anything dirty to her but her cheeks warmed like he had. She followed his instructions, tickling her fingers over his T-shirt-covered chest and closing her eyes as she pulled her mouth into a smile. It wasn't hard to do with him so close, his low, sexy voice in her ear.

He finished by kissing her temple, and when Andy faced her mother and sister, they both looked away like the intimate public display had made them uncomfortable.

She liked that. *A lot.*

Vanessa mentioned "drinks in the bar" in an hour and then she and their mother wandered off in that direction.

Andy grinned at Gage, barely able to keep her excitement in check when she blurted, "That was amazing!"

But he wasn't smiling with her.

"Are they always that rude?"

"Who cares! You should've let me pay you. You're worth every penny."

His mouth flinched like he wanted to smile, which seemed to be his default expression. She pulled her hand off his chest, having forgotten she'd left it there this whole time. "Sorry about that."

He cupped her cheek and tipped her face up to his. She was lost, admiring his handsome face for one stunned moment. "Stop acting like we're acting. You have to immerse yourself in this role, Andy. We're always being watched."

She stole a look around the room, and sure enough, another group of family members was heading their way. "Oh. Right."

"Right. Do we need to say hi to them, too?"

"I don't feel like it."

"Okay, then, let's not." Gage lifted their bags as she shouldered her purse.

Her cousins approached, wearing matching shocked expressions, one of them going as far as to say, "Andrea. You have a date."

"One who's been itching to get her alone since this morning," Gage said. "Come on, beautiful. Let's test out that bed."

Leaving them gaping in her wake, Andy followed, wanting to punch the air in triumph. Damn, it felt good not to be alone for once. To have someone have her back—hired or no.

Maybe her fears and worries about pretending with Gage were truly unfounded. What was the harm in immersing herself in this role the same way he had?

He wasn't expecting more from her, and he'd already overdelivered on her expectations. She didn't see a reason not to return the affection Gage so easily offered. Especially when they both knew this attraction was pretend.

He walked down the long corridor toward their room and she bit her lip as she watched him carry her bags. He looked strong and sure hefting her luggage. Plus he had a great ass.

She watched his butt, satisfied that she could without worrying what anyone might say if they noticed.

Mostly pretend attraction, she thought to herself.

Seven

"My sister's husbands are nice guys for the most part," Andy was saying as she walked back and forth in the hotel room.

Ever since Gage had placed their bags on the floor in their suite, she'd been a flurry of activity from changing her clothes to touching up her makeup to fixing her hair.

"Kelli and Boyd are the snobby country-club type, but Alec, Kenny and Garrett are okay. I mean, I guess. I don't really know Garrett." She huffed as she tried again to latch a necklace around her neck and Gage stepped in to help.

"Which one's Garrett? Lift your hair." She did and he easily clasped the delicate chain at the back of her neck, smiling at a cute smattering of freckles at her nape.

"Garrett's the groom." She turned, her eyes on his, her high heels bringing them almost nose to nose. "Gwen's fiancé."

She looked away quickly, like maintaining eye contact was hard for her. When she backed away, he crooked a finger, beckoning her to him. She visibly squirmed but came as requested. Sort of.

"Closer, Andy."

One more tentative step brought her to the spot where she'd been standing a second ago.

He smoothed her hair off her neck. "You and I have been dating for eight months, right?" he asked, reminding her of their agreed-upon pretend history.

"Right."

"You're going to have to learn how to be near me without flinching. Am I that unattractive?"

"No. Not at all." She looked genuinely stricken. "I'm sorry if I made you feel that way."

He had to smile. This take-charge, in-charge woman who blew into a room like a frosty chill and froze everyone around her into submission wasn't as cold as she pretended to be.

"Andy."

"What?" Now she looked just plain hurt. "This isn't going to work, is it?"

"Yes. It's going to work." He trailed his fingers down her arm and grasped her hand, brushing her knuckles with his thumb and placing his other hand on her hip. She touched his chest like she had in the lobby, and he heard her breath hitch. "How can I make you more comfortable around me?"

"I'm not comfortable?" she seemed to ask herself. "I thought I was doing better."

So she'd been trying. Interesting.

"We should kiss," she said with a curt nod. "Get it over with."

Now he did chuckle. "Get it over with? It's not going to be like a dental appointment, Andy. I promise." He gestured to his mouth. "I know what I'm doing with this."

Her tongue darted out to wet her bottom lip as she stared at him almost in wonder. He felt the charge in the air—the sexual tension radiating between their bodies. He couldn't get past the idea that she was a live wire, even if she was contented to play the role of the "Ice Queen."

He knew this was pretend—they both did—but he couldn't help wanting to pull warm, responsive Andy from her recesses. He'd started out thinking she was a challenge, but he had the distinct impression that succeeding would be an even bigger win for her.

"I'm all for kissing you. I'll let you come to me, though. I want you to be ready. Once you touch your lips to mine, I'm going to give as good as you do," he promised. "I'll match you stroke for stroke."

"Okay." She rolled her shoulders, readying herself. "I can do this."

He banked his smile as she seemed to steel herself. She closed her eyes, pulled in a deep breath and blew it out. If he hadn't already worked with her for almost two weeks and knew what a goal-oriented achiever she was, he might've been insulted. Andy did whatever it took to win, and evidently winning included kissing him.

Her eyes popped open, determination brewing in their depths. She palmed the back of his neck and slanted her face. He leaned in, mirroring her movements. A fraction away from his lips, she whispered, "Are you sure you're okay with this?"

"God, yes."

As soon as he said the words, she pressed her mouth to his. It was more of a lengthy pucker than making out, but he gripped her waist to encourage her to stay close. He wanted her to take what she needed from him.

When her lips softened, he teased them open with his tongue. She slid her tongue into his mouth and that was when that live wire jolted him. She tasted like mint and smelled faintly of cinnamon. From her hair stuff or her perfume, he wasn't sure. He hadn't noticed it in the lobby, but now it infused every inch of his immediate vicinity.

He'd expected kissing Andy to affect her, and he'd expected to enjoy it. What he hadn't expected was to be towed in by her so thoroughly. The connection—the spark—that had resulted from their fusing didn't stop at their mouths.

She held onto him—her palm gripping the back of his neck, her smallish breasts against his chest—like she never wanted to let go. He tightened his hands on her hips and aligned them with his own. She was an absolutely *perfect* fit. He allowed instinct to drive him as he took the kiss deeper. What had lit between them was a hell of a lot more than he'd bargained for, but he had zero interest in stopping. Unfortunately, she did.

Andy tugged her lips from his, her delicate throat moving as she swallowed.

Gage was still leaning forward, his lips parted, completely dazed by that kiss. Here he thought he'd be the one walking her through the lesson. He'd expected to be the one guiding her. Instead, she'd taken him hostage with her mouth and her skill. He hadn't minded at all.

Take me, honey.

"So." She cleared her throat. "I guess that's not going to be a problem."

"No," he agreed with a grin. "I guess not."

"Ready to go meet the family?" She smoothed his T-shirt that she'd wrinkled in one fist while they'd kissed.

"Sure. Let's do it," he answered automatically, and then on his way down the corridor realized that the last time he'd agreed to such an invitation it'd been when Laura asked him to meet her parents.

Gage had met Andy's sisters at the bar last night—they'd been there with their husbands, who huddled together and talked like they were comfortable with each other. Rather than mingle with them, Gage had chosen to stay by Andy's side.

He was still trying to figure out the dynamic between her and her four sisters. The mother, Estelle, was stern and unfriendly, yet as gorgeous as the rest of the women. They were all tall or tallish, long-limbed and attractive, with varying shades of red or blond hair. Estelle has passed down her high cheekbones and bright blue eyes to most of her daughters.

Andy was reserved and distant, where the other sisters were mostly cozy with each other. Gage wondered if it was because she'd moved away and they'd remained in Ohio. He'd asked her as much when they returned to the room last night, but she'd only shrugged and said, "They've always been like that."

He wasn't sure if it was her sisters who'd ousted Andy or Andy who'd ousted herself. It appeared to Gage that Andy was the one keeping her distance. Although after that run-in with her mother and Ness at the front desk, who could blame her?

But Andy had come alive when Kelli asked her about work, citing her recent successes without an ounce of gravitas. Andy didn't have to overstate her accomplishments. He knew from the experience with her at Monarch—Andy was just that good.

He'd slept like crap last night since the sofa bed was about as comfortable as a pile of cotton balls and wire hangers, but he'd lied and told his pretend girlfriend that he was fine sleeping on it. She'd tried to offer him the bed and said she'd take the sofa, and then he'd had to wonder what kind of dopes she'd been dating.

Whatever ease had come as a result of the explosive kiss last night was gone by this morning. Part of him was relieved, since he'd been thrown so off-kilter by their abundant physical attraction. Andy didn't seem the type to embark on a temporary physical affair. But most of him still wanted to kiss her again and damn the consequences, if not to slake the thirst he'd developed for the confusing redhead over the last couple of weeks.

This morning's activity, according to his itinerary, was brunch with Andy's immediate family. She stalked ahead of him across the green grass, her straight spine evidence that she was back to her no-nonsense self.

The small, catered affair was for the wedding party and close family. Andy fell into both categories since she was a sister and a bridesmaid.

After a quick greeting to a few people he'd yet to meet, they lined up at the buffet packed to the edges with mini quiches, fried potatoes, fruit and every imaginable breakfast meat there was, including prosciutto-wrapped figs.

He picked up two plates and handed Andy hers.

"Thank you," she said. "I'm not accustomed to anyone fetching my plate for me."

"What cavemen have you been dating, Andy? This is boyfriend 101." Gage didn't realize anyone was paying attention to them until a bulky guy on the opposite side of the buffet table spoke.

"I was one of 'em, wasn't I, Snowflake?"

Andy bristled, her back going even straighter—Gage hadn't thought it possible. She introduced him, her voice cool and robotic. "Matthew Higgins, this is my date, Gage Fleming." Her tone softened some when she turned to Gage and said, "Matthew and I dated about seven or eight years ago."

"Oh, right. You mentioned him. The one with the protruding brow and big head." Gage kept his smile easy.

"Very funny." Matthew really did have a caveman vibe about him. He snapped his attention back to Andy. "Nice to know we regard each other with similar admiration, *Snowflake.*"

"Don't call me that."

"Do you prefer Elsa?" To Gage he said, "*Frozen* wasn't

out when we dated, so I had to make up my own ice-queen nickname for her."

That was what Snowflake was about?

"Freeze you out, did she?" Gage set their plates aside and pulled Andy close. His lips to her ear, he whispered, "You want a repeat of that kiss from last night, now would be a good time."

Her mouth curled into a smile of uncertainty—like maybe she thought she'd heard him wrong.

"I'm game if you are," he announced, happy to have shut out her asshole ex-boyfriend and thrilled that Andy's attention was on Gage instead. Thrilled further when Andy draped one arm over his shoulder and leaned in for a demure kiss. Not a tangle like last night, but the kiss didn't last as long as Gage would've liked.

She lowered to her heels and accepted her plate from Gage, who sent Matthew a smug smile. "She's nothing but gooey with me, big guy." He enjoyed Matthew's deep frown almost as much as him leaving pissed off.

"Thanks for that," Andy muttered as she piled her plate full of fruit. She picked through the croissants while Gage put another spoonful of scrambled eggs on his plate.

"When in doubt, make out."

Her laugh was genuine and he liked it a hell of a lot. He might have first agreed to come here in exchange for her help at Monarch, but he found he also liked protecting her from the vultures circling.

"You're not intimidated by difficult people," she pointed out. "Did you learn that at work, or is your family also challenging?"

"Sorry, can't claim dysfunction. The Flemings are scarily normal. My sister, Drew, and I are close and our parents are supportive. Although they still do weird parent stuff that embarrasses the hell out of us."

"Your sister's named Drew." Andy smiled. "What's she like?"

"She has bad taste in men, a big heart and a lot of spunk."

"Sounds like me except for the big heart. It's always been assumed that mine is missing." She sent a derisive glance in Matthew's direction.

"Sounds to me," Gage said as he placed bacon strips on his plate, "like your ex is in your head."

Eight

Andy followed beside Gage as he made his way to a table with their breakfast. He set down their plates and pulled out one of the folding chairs for her.

The theme was navy and red—Gwen's favorite colors. The tables were decorated with white tablecloths and blue vases filled with dark red roses, the silverware wrapped in navy blue cloth napkins tied with red ribbon.

Like Gwen, the décor was bold and beautiful.

Portable air conditioners stood at each corner of the tent to thwart the summer heat. Andy was glad for them since it was warm already and it was only noon.

"Care to explain your last comment at the buffet?" Gage asked as he sat across from her.

She unwrapped her silverware rather than look at him. "What?"

"Don't 'what' me. You stated you're heartless as casually as you might tell me what time it is. You can't believe that." He jerked his chin over to where Matthew sat with his girlfriend, Amber, one of Gwen's friends and bridesmaids. "You don't believe you're an ice princess."

"Ice *Queen*," she corrected, spearing a chunk of pineapple with her fork. "That was a long time ago."

"That isn't an answer."

"I know my limitations. It's part of being a good leader. I'm not warm. I can't help that."

"You were plenty warm when you kissed me a minute ago," he murmured in a low, sexy tone.

He had her there. She'd kissed him to show up Matthew, but the truth was that the second her lips touched Gage's, she'd forgotten her stupid ex was standing there. She'd been lost in Gage's mouth, in his scent. Matthew gaping unhappily was a nice bonus, though.

"That was pretending." She ate the pineapple.

"That was *not* pretending."

"Oh? Are you secretly an escort on the side?" she whispered.

"Maybe." His caramel eyes twinkled before he sent her a roguish wink. "I have been kissed enough to know the difference between a woman who's frigid and one who's—"

"Don't say out of practice." She didn't want to talk about how lame her sex life had been over the last two years. About how she'd tried to be those attributes that didn't come naturally: Bubbly, fun, laid-back. In the end the real her came forward. While she knew she wasn't heartless, she definitely kept a wall around her heart. She felt she had to after the way she'd been let down in the past. No one really understood her. No one had tried.

"I was going to say nervous." Gage's eyebrows lifted. "How long's it been?"

"Long enough that there are tumbleweeds blowing around." She didn't know what made her tell the truth. Although, maybe she did. If anyone could understand the real Andy Payne, it might be Gage. He didn't look at her like a problem to be solved. He saw her success, her timidity, her vulnerability. It'd been a while since a man had bothered to see past her cool exterior.

"Cute *and* funny." He laughed as he dug into his food and Andy was struck with the oddest sense of pride. Gage was cute and funny but she couldn't recall a single time she'd ever been accused of as much.

Throughout her childhood she'd been told she was stiff. Her mother had instructed her to "loosen up" more times than Andy could count. When she and Matthew dated, he'd asked her if she could at least "appear to be having fun" when they were out. She'd always hated that comment. Like she should smile to set everyone else at ease.

Now that she thought about it, all she did around Gage was smile. Not because he goaded her into it. He made her smile just by being himself. He made her feel comfortable even in stressful situations. He helped her crawl out of her head and be in the moment. And she'd really enjoyed kissing him in front of Matthew.

You enjoy kissing him just to kiss him...

"How long did you date that bozo, anyway?" Gage shoveled a bite of scrambled eggs into his mouth.

"A little over a year."

"A little over a year. You're going to let a guy you dated for *a little over a year*, seven or eight years ago, dictate what you think about yourself?"

"This sounds like a lecture," she pointed out blandly.

Andy was accustomed to being misunderstood and/or made to feel less-than. She could hold her own. Until she was with her family, and then those old hurts crept in and made her defensive. The difference here was that Gage was new. He was part of her work, not her personal life. She could compartmentalize that.

"Are you telling me you have no damage? That no one in your past has ever inflicted a wound that carried through into your adult years? That you didn't change some aspect of your behavior because of it?"

Gage was resolutely silent.

That was what she thought.

"Everyone has skeletons in their closets," she told him.

Before she popped a strawberry slice into her mouth, she noticed two of her sisters barreling toward her.

"Hey, you two," Gwen, the blushing bride-to-be, flicked a gaze at Gage and then back at Andy.

"Good morning, Gwen. Ready for the big day?" Gage asked. It was predictable banter but somehow it sounded fresh coming from his mouth. He really was skilled with people. Andy was better with plans. Numbers. Websites.

After Gwen answered that she was "so ready!" Andy's other sister Kelli spoke up.

"Ready for the couples' cruise today?" Kelli gave Andy a saucy wink. "It'll be Andy's first, so we're pretty excited about it."

"*Kelli*." Andy let her tone be her warning, but her eldest sister was not intimidated.

"Couples' cruise?" Gage flashed a smile at Andy and she felt her cheeks heat. She hadn't exactly called it a couples' cruise. She'd told him that they were going on a boat ride, which they were. It was a sizable pontoon boat, which was basically like a floating patio, and Andy was absolutely dreading it. Unfortunately—

"I'm making her come," Gwen chirped. "Andy is totes uncomfortable about it because she's Andy, but I want all of my sisters there."

And that was why Andy was allowing this ridiculous charade to go on. She loved Gwen, and this was her big weekend.

"It's just a boat ride," Andy told Gage, though he didn't look like he needed soothing.

"With champagne and kissing!" Gwen clapped.

"It's tradition in our family," Kelli explained, pressing her fingertips to her collarbone. "I started it with my pre-wedding festivities, and everyone has carried it forward."

"Because it's fun. All eyes will be on you two. You know what you have to do when it's your first CC."

Yep. Andy's face was flame red. She could feel it. Gage's inquisitive look paired with his indelible smile of his and then, to her sisters, he said as smooth as you please, "I look forward to finding out what that is."

What was it, exactly, that had Andy wanting to hide beneath the tablecloth right now?

Gage wasn't sure, but it intrigued the hell out of him. He bade Kelli, who had a conniving glimmer in her eye not unlike Estelle's, and Gwen adieu and turned back to his wedding date.

"Are they going to make you walk the plank or something?"

"Something like that" was the only answer he got.

After brunch Gage and Andy returned to the room to change into "boat clothes." Other than a ferry, Gage wasn't really a boat guy. Not that he was intimidated by a pontoon, or by her family. He wasn't intimidated by much, especially not the couples' cruise initiation that had made Andy twitchy since brunch.

"I packed a few towels from the room into this bag, along with…" He trailed off when Andy came out of the bedroom and into the suite, hair pulled back into a slick ponytail. She wore a gauzy white cover-up over her blue bathing suit. The sight of her legs glued his tongue to the roof of his mouth and stalled his brain. Long, pale, smooth legs. Andy was tall, and at first glance appeared almost too slim. But her curved calves and delicate ankles thwarted that notion immediately. They were subtle, but oh, yes, Andrea Payne had curves.

Her eyes rounded, and her eyebrows rose. "Along with…"

It took him a few seconds to realize he'd been in the middle of speaking.

"Sunscreen." He gestured to the bag. "You're fair-skinned, so I didn't want you to burn."

Very fair-skinned. Her freckles stood out in subtle contrast like her peachy-pink lips. Lips he'd tasted and was already itching to taste again.

"Okay, thanks." She bounced past him and he shook his head. He didn't know how, but was it possible Andy had no idea how gorgeous she was? "Ready to go?"

"Yep." Board shorts and T-shirt on, he pulled the tote over one shoulder and followed Andy to the car. Twenty minutes later they were standing on a dock in the hot summer sun while her sisters and their husbands—or fiancé in Garrett's case—settled onto the wide vinyl seats.

"Whose boat is this?" Gage asked Garrett as he settled in next to him.

"Rental. Biggest, newest one they had." Garrett was Gage's height, a few years younger, but not by much. Gage had talked to him at the bar that first night. The guy seemed cool. Kelli's husband, Boyd, waited by her side while she talked animatedly to her other sisters. Gage sensed a distinct taming-of-the-shrew feel from those two.

Vanessa's husband, Alec, took the captain's chair, wearing a captain's hat to go with it. Gage had pegged Ness as a mean girl the moment she and Estelle pecked at Andy, but he didn't think she did it on purpose. She seemed to like being in charge, though, and he could tell she approved of Alec manning the boat.

Carroll, Gage decided, was the quiet sister. She was amiable and polite, with no real dog in the fight over whether or not Andy would arrive single to the wedding. Her husband, Kenny, was as laid-back as she was, more so actually.

His scraggly goatee and hippie wear gave him a definite I-smoke-weed vibe. Gage had decided Carroll and Kenny were also cool.

"Let's do this!" Gwen called, earning applause. She was the shameless youngest child, happy with the attention, not because she craved it like Ness, but more because she expected it. Cute and plucky, she beamed with an infectious smile that was hard not to return.

Andy sat primly beside him, a pair of sunglasses on her nose and a tentative, nervous smile on her face. Gage lifted her hand in his and kept his gaze on her while he pressed his lips to her knuckles. Her smile shone as bright as the sun overhead…until Ness spoke.

"Aww! Look at those two!"

Everyone focused on them and Andy promptly stiffened and snatched her hand away.

"So shy! Honestly, Andy, who would believe you two have been dating for eight months?" Ness added and sat on Andy's immediate right on the L-shaped cushion.

"Not everyone is as comfortable making out in public as you are," Andy told her sister.

"That's true. And I happen to be really good at it," said Alec from the captain's chair.

Ness smiled, but her expression was as stiff as Andy's spine.

In moments like this, when Gage bore witness to Andy's chillier side, he felt like his past had walked over his grave. As sure as he was that Andy wasn't heartless, he had doubts that pursuing a physical relationship with her—even temporarily—was wise.

During those chillier moments, he was reminded of the idiot he'd been when he promised forever to Laura. She'd made him look like a bigger idiot when he was left holding the engagement ring she returned and the remnants of his broken heart.

Since then, Gage kept things on the surface with the women he dated. He liked women and loved sex, but getting in any deeper wasn't an option. What had started out with a simple agreement to keep Andy on board at Monarch had turned into meeting her complex family, and her ham-handed ex-boyfriend.

And yet he couldn't help coming to Andy's rescue and changing the subject.

"I notice Estelle didn't make the trip," he said to Ness.

"This is a sibling-only affair." Ness swept her hair off her neck and piled it on top of her head in a sloppy bun.

"Hang on to something," Alec announced as they puttered from the no-wake zone into the larger portion of the lake. Cheered on by his passengers, he pushed the speedometer to the middle, sending Andy's ponytail whipping behind her.

Gage settled back, his arm on the bench and Andy sent him what appeared to be a gracious smile. She leaned back into the curve of his arm and he rested his palm on her shoulder. Whatever cooler moments he'd witnessed from her, she was warm where it counted. Andy was completely responsive to him and he enjoyed the hell out of getting her to respond.

Enough lingering in the past. He'd rather sit here, his arm around Andy, and enjoy the cool breeze, hot sun and random splashes of water kicked up by the buoys on the sides of the boat.

Nine

Alec dropped anchor in a private cove surrounded by trees and a few villas. Kelli and Ness opened coolers and divvied out drinks into plastic flutes. Sparkling rosé for the ladies, and ales brewed and canned by a local brewery for the guys.

Andy gladly accepted her drink, letting the bubbles tickle her throat and relying on the summer sun as well as the alcohol to take her down a notch.

Or ten.

No one made her as prickly as her sisters. She wasn't like them—any of them. Sure she might have a dose of Kelli's self-assuredness, but Andy didn't have her eldest sister's confident, sexy vibe. And while Ness was a go-getter, she wasn't plagued by Andy's shyness. Carroll was genuine and sweet, whereas Andy had never been referred to as "sweet," and the bride-to-be, Gwen, was adorable and fun. Andy hadn't been accused of being either of those.

She was the black sheep among her reddish-flaxen-haired sisters, sharing their coloring but not their personalities. Every time she was around them she felt as if there was an invisible yardstick measuring her to see if she'd blossomed into a *Payne lady* yet, and if her mother's assessment was anything to go by—Andy hadn't.

She'd settled for being the best at her job, and excelling in her field rather than competing socially. They all knew what she did for a living—that she was the mysterious Andy Payne who was often imitated, never duplicated—but praise was more often given for personality and looks—especially by her former-beauty-queen mother.

As a teen Andy had been lanky, thinner than any of her sisters. Fairer, too. By age sixteen her nose was a touch long and her feet a *not*-dainty size ten, and she'd felt firmly entrenched into the black-sheep role she'd assigned herself.

She'd moved away from Crown, Ohio, to become someone else, someone new. Someone who wouldn't be contrasted and compared to her sisters. Her nose was still a touch too long, she was as curve-free as she ever was, and her feet were still a size ten, but she'd used her frosty personality to help build an empire. And she wasn't as socially awkward as she used to be. She was open and polite, even if she didn't exude warmth.

"That went fast," Gage said, taking her empty plastic flute. "Can I refill it for you?"

"Yes."

He pushed his sunglasses on top of his head and studied her, his eyes a lighter shade of brown in the sunlight. The stubble on his chin and jaw was short and rakish, his hair windblown and curling on the ends.

"You have nice hair."

The moment the words were out of her mouth she wanted to die. What a boring compliment. Not to mention it was more the kind of thing you'd say to someone when you'd just met them, not after you'd been in a relationship for eight months. Thankfully no one was paying attention to them or she would've just given away that they'd known each other only a few weeks. Her brothers-in-law were behind them stripping off their shirts to dive in and her sisters were huddled over the ice-filled coolers at the front of the boat, chatting.

"So do you." He wrapped her long ponytail around his fist and gave it a subtle yank, smiling as easy as you please. She swallowed thickly, unsure what to do with the attention.

"H-has it always been curly?" she stammered. Gage looked at her with a combination of heat and admiration, curiosity and a bit of bemusement. Like she was a puzzle he wanted to solve. Another new feeling for her. "Sorry. Stupid question. Of course it's always been curly."

"The bane of my existence." His smile didn't budge. "I try to keep it short, but it still curls." He pushed his hand through his hair again and the wave snapped right back into place. She had to grin. And before she thought of what she was doing, her hand was in his hair, sweeping the strands. It was soft and thick, adding a boyish charm to a man who was *all* man.

"You two are positively adorable," Gwen said, sneaking up on them. Although, you couldn't really "sneak" on a twenty-four-foot boat. Andy had been completely absorbed in her pretend boyfriend. "Did you pick your movie yet?"

"Movie?" Gage asked as Andy returned her hands to her lap.

Gwen aimed her wide grin at Andy. "You didn't tell him." Back to Gage, she said, "If it's your first couples' cruise as a couple, you have to reenact a movie kiss for everyone. Extra points for authenticity."

"Boyd and I did *Gone with the Wind*," Kelli announced proudly. "Ness, *Dirty Dancing*—"

"Complete with dance moves," Vanessa called over.

"And Carroll," Gwen said, "chose *The Princess Bride*, while I went with *Twilight*." The youngest of the Payne sisters swooned. "How I love my sparkly vampires."

"Sorry I missed that one," Andy said, genuinely meaning it. She hadn't made it home for the engagement party here at the resort, which is when the *Twilight* magic must've occurred.

"It's your turn now," Carroll told Andy. "Don't screw it up."

"But first, swimming! It's too hot not to jump in." Gwen tore off her cover-up and revealed a perfect-ten body complete with a belly-button piercing she'd insisted was still "in." A tattoo graced her shoulder blade, a smattering of butterflies and flowers in full color. When her groom called down for her to jump, she did.

Kelli wrinkled her nose. "I'm not getting in that water."

Vanessa agreed and they moved to the other end of the boat farthest from Andy and Gage, while Carroll argued they were "spoilsports" and leaped in behind Gwen.

"Movie kiss, huh?" Gage asked.

"The good ones are already taken," Andy argued.

"Not true. There are lots of great movie kisses available. What about *Dumb and Dumber*, where he tries to eat her face?" At Andy's aghast expression, he chuckled. "I'm kidding."

"I was thinking more like *Lady and the Tramp*. What could we use as spaghetti?" She looked around at a few ropes and wrinkled her nose. Definitely not. But something similar—something tame and not embarrassing.

"What about *The Notebook*?" he asked. "The kiss in the rain is iconic."

It was also…intimate. Plus, Gage would have to lift her and that would be weird. It wasn't as if Andy was dainty.

"No," she told him. "It's not raining."

He narrowed his eyelids as if he knew why she'd bowed out of that suggestion. Then his face lit up. "I've got it."

"What?"

"Nah, I'm not letting you shoot this one down or reason us out of it. I'll tell you right before it happens."

"What if I haven't seen the movie?"

"Trust me. You have."

"What if I haven't?" She liked being prepared—especially for a kiss in front of her relatives.

"You have. But if you haven't, I'll walk you through it."

But that didn't make her feel any better. Her stomach jumped in anticipation, nervousness and excitement switching places in a do-si-do.

"Why me?"

She blinked at the question. "Sorry?"

"Why did you approach me in the bar that night and offer to pay me two grand?" he asked, his voice low so as to not be overheard. "Were you out of options, or was there something else?"

She studied his rakish curls, warm caramel irises and affable smile. She could lie, but she decided not to. "You looked nice."

She winced, worrying that the comment was almost a repeat of the "nice hair" one earlier, but Gage grinned.

"And? Am I?"

"Very."

There was a distinct pause where they watched each other and the pretending seemed to fall away. A moment where Andy caught a glimpse of the possibility of more if she would only open herself up to it... if only he would.

She blinked to break the intense eye contact and Gage's smile snapped seamlessly into place.

"Take this off and swim with me." He plucked the edge of her cover-up.

"That's okay."

"No. It's not. It's a hundred-and-fifty degrees out here. Let's get wet."

Something about the way his voice dropped suggestively made her consider doing more than kissing him. If her tingling innards were anything to go by, she was starting to consider a host of other possibilities.

Naughty possibilities.

"Your face is red already. See? You're hot." He tugged at her cover-up and she let him take it off, holding her arms overhead. She was hot, all right. When the white gauzy material was done obstructing her vision, she came face-to-face with an expression on Gage she'd never seen before. Playful was his typical MO, but this look was…fiery.

Heated and scintillating.

Suggestive, and not in the "pretend" way.

"Hot," he repeated, his smirk twitching his lips. "Damn, Andy." He took her hand and helped her to her feet. Then he grabbed the personalized tote that read Gwen ♥ Garrett where he'd stuffed their towels and sunscreen and produced a bottle.

Wide, warm hands on her hips, he turned her. "I'll do your back."

Gage momentarily lost the thread of whatever he was talking about when he removed Andy's cover-up.

Beneath the shapeless square material was hiding a lithe body. Her shoulders were delicate and round, freckles dotting them like they'd been misted on with a spray bottle. Her back was muscular and strong, and he noticed more freckles as he smoothed sunscreen over her shoulders. There was something intimate about slipping his fingers under the straps of her suit, especially where her bikini top tied into a bow at the middle of her back. His fingers flinched as he imagined tugging that string loose and releasing her breasts, maybe smoothing his hands around to cup them. He'd thought she was a B-cup, but now that she was mostly undressed, he guessed she bordered on a C.

Leaning close to her ear, he said, "Is this okay?"

"Hmm?" She sounded distracted, like maybe she'd been enjoying his hands on her skin as much as he was.

"Are you comfortable with my touch?" He applied the cream to her lower back and braced her sides with his hands. "This is how our kiss will happen," he murmured into her right ear. "I want to make sure I'm not weirding you out."

In a perfect reenactment of what was to come, she turned over her shoulder to look at him, blue eyes wide and curious. A high-pitched voice rang out—Gwen's.

"They're doing it! I know the movie!" she called up from the water.

Gage jerked his attention to the guys and girls in the water, and then to Kelli and Ness on the boat. Everyone was watching.

"No practicing! Do it now!" Gwen shouted with a happy laugh.

"Gage?" Andy's voice was a soft, curious pant. "What are we doing?"

He slid his hands up her waist, lifting her arms and holding them straight out to her sides. He walked her forward to the edge of the boat as their audience cheered.

"*Titanic*!" Carroll shouted.

Over her shoulder, Andy sent him a smile.

"You've seen it?" he asked.

"Of course."

"Then you know what comes next." He tugged her hair from her ponytail, releasing the silken strawberry blond strands, gripped her waist and lingered over her shoulder. As if God was helping out, a breeze kicked her hair at same moment she turned her face to his and he lowered his lips.

The kiss was soft and expected, but what was unexpected was the way her curved bottom nestled perfectly against his crotch as he used every faculty in his brain to keep from hardening against her. She raised a hand to the back of his neck in perfect movie form and held him against her, her fingernails tickling into his hair as he moved his lips over hers.

More cheering erupted from the water and on the boat and Andy eased away from him. Perfectly comfortable and confident.

He loved seeing her that way around her family. Since they'd arrived, she'd been walking on eggshells...or thumb-tacks, depending on which of her family members was around. Now, though, the feisty glimmer in her eyes was one he'd seen time and time again in a business setting, where she was cocksure and definitive.

Nothing turned him on more. Especially when she reacted that way to him.

"I'm calling it, guys," Gwen shouted. "Best couples' cruise kiss. Now you two have to stay together forever. You just won first place."

Ten

Andy showered after Gage, insisting he go first so she could take her time. He agreed since his showers took all of two minutes. Now he sat on their suite's sofa, where he was watching TV. The true crime documentary wasn't keeping him from picturing her in there, water sluicing down her trim form and droplets hanging off nipples he'd seen the outline of in her bikini top but had yet to taste.

"Dammit." He adjusted a budding erection and addressed his lap. "We're faking. Understand?"

That wasn't sinking in for any part of his anatomy, including his brain. After the *Titanic* kiss, they'd swum in the lake, the water warm on the surface and bone-chillingly cold at their feet. Since it was sand-bottomed, they'd found water about four feet deep to stand in while everyone enjoyed beer or rosé and the coolness of the water in contrast to the baking-hot sun.

During that time, Gage allowed himself to touch Andy freely and she'd glided against him, her skin slippery from the combo of smooth water and creamy sunscreen, turning him on in a way he hadn't known possible.

She was his colleague, and this was an act. She'd made that clear when she'd invited him, and by footing the bill for his stay. But he couldn't escape the niggling feeling that she was enjoying herself as much as he was. That their chemistry was hot enough that her sisters kept pointing it out.

She'd thwarted her sisters' teasing by batting her lashes at Carroll and rolling her eyes at Ness, but Andy liked him. He could tell. She responded to him. If they were to go to bed together, he would blow her mind.

The only problem was that he wasn't confident he could disentangle from her as easily as he had from, say, Heather, the last woman he'd dated. What he'd experienced with Andy so far—whether working closely with her at Monarch, or hanging out with her family—was deeper than mere surface attraction. Sex wouldn't dampen the simmering attraction between them. It would *ignite* it.

That would make walking away harder and Gage would eventually have to walk away.

The bathroom door swung aside, steam billowing from the small space. Andy emerged, her cheeks rosy, her hair wet and combed straight, a white towel wrapped around her body.

Speaking of igniting...

"I'm sunburned." She pouted.

"What? How?" He moved to her, flicking the TV off as he went and tossing the remote onto the couch.

"I don't know. Maybe the sunscreen washed off."

She turned around and peeked over her shoulder, reminding him of the boat kiss and the press of her ass against his front. He swallowed a groan.

"Here." She pressed two fingers into her red shoulder and the color changed to creamy pale before quickly fading to red again.

"Does it hurt?" He repeated the move on her back where

her reddened skin resembled her shoulders. "Did the hot water of the shower hurt?"

She paused in thought. "No. Not really."

"Then you're fine." He smoothed his fingers along her back and over her shoulder, the feel of her soft skin having a drugging effect on him. Touching her sent his fears of future entanglements up in smoke. The devil on his shoulder assured him she'd be worth it, and damned if the angel on his other shoulder didn't agree.

She came closer and gazed up at him with an earnest gaze almost as naked as she was. Such vulnerability.

Those warning bells made one more attempt to stop him but he justified that Laura had never had this much vulnerability in her eyes.

Or was that longing?

Only one way to find out.

"Do you have any idea how sexy you are?" he murmured.

Her reaction wasn't a gasp of surprise or a sigh of capitulation but instead a challenging smile followed by "Ha! You must have me confused with Gwen. Or Kelli. Or... any of my sisters."

She threw a hand of dismissal that he caught in midair. He tugged her to him, and she gripped her towel with one hand to keep it from slipping.

More's the pity.

"No. I mean you." He didn't smile, making sure she knew he wasn't playing around. "You're sexier than all your sisters put together."

"Gage." She released her hand and patted his chest as if leveling with him. "Save this stuff for an audience."

He gripped her waist and pulled her against him, her towel gaping when she let it go to steady herself by grabbing his biceps.

She didn't believe him.

She had no idea how sexy she was. And that invited a fun challenge that far outweighed his concerns of getting in too deep.

"Want me to show you?" He had to ask. She was too skittish to ask him for what she needed. Plus, he respected her. If she had no desire to find out what he had in mind for her tonight, he'd go back to that horrible pullout sofa bed. He'd go there rock-hard and in need of an ice bath, but he'd survive.

"Show me what?"

He stroked his fingers over her collarbone to her shoulder. "Well. I could point out that you're delicate and strong at the same time." He gripped the towel hanging precariously on her body, holding it closed but allowing his fingers to graze her cleavage. "Then I could mention how much I'm dying to see your breasts after they teased me by bobbing in the lake in that sexy string bikini top you wore."

Her smile slid away, lust blowing out her pupils.

"My breasts...?" Her brow crimped like that phrase didn't compute.

"And those legs." He closed his eyes, flared his nostrils and grunted for effect. "They've been killing me since you started working at Monarch."

"Gage..."

"Am I making you uncomfortable?" His eyes moved to her pink mouth.

"No. I—I was going to ask you if you were serious about showing me."

Hard-on. *Achieved.* His shorts tented and he shifted to bump into her hip.

"Hell, yes, I'll show you. Over and over if you like." He grinned. Excited. Wanting that.

"No making fun of me." She pointed, her voice stern, her finger an inch away from his face. He bit it and soothed the bite by suckling and then letting go in a long, smooth motion.

She licked her lips in anticipation.

"Definitely, you're in need of a lesson, Andy. That is... if this is a yes." He had to be crystal clear she wanted this.

"Yes," she breathed.

Oh, it was *on*.

He yanked her towel aside and dropped it in a damp pile at her feet.

Cool, air-conditioned air hit her body as goose bumps rose on her arms. Gage kept his hands on her sides, but the look in his eyes was feral in the best way. He wanted *her*. He thought she was sexier than all her sisters combined.

She dismissed the possibility that he'd lied about how attractive he found her simply to get into her pants—or *towel* as it were. Andy was no dummy. She'd worked with Gage in close proximity and had been around him enough to see his guard dropped. Gage might very well be the last salesman on the planet who wasn't full of crap.

Which meant he'd been sincere about every nice thing he'd said to her.

"I want to look so bad," he said with an impish smile, and then she realized he meant down at her nude body. He'd kept those melted-caramel eyes on hers ever since he pulled her towel off. The fact that she still held his gaze was a powerful feeling indeed.

Confidence surged through her at earning his attention, at holding the cards. Her *yes* determined how far they went tonight. He'd made that abundantly clear.

Hands on his T-shirt, she gripped twin fists of the material and tugged upward. "I'll show you mine if you show me yours."

"Deal." He had the shirt off in record time and she thanked the good Lord for her sight. Gage's chest was beautiful. The strong, firm pectoral muscles and ridges of his abs. He wasn't so much thick as lean, his waist tapering to a tantalizing V that disappeared into his shorts. Shorts that were straining against a part of him that was definitely, if outer appearances were to be believed, *thick*.

She lifted her eyes to apologize for ogling, only to find his gaze on the ceiling.

"Gage," she whispered, leaning in and brushing her lips over his. There was a benefit to being almost as tall as he was, though now that she was sans heels, she had to climb to her toes a little. "You can look now."

He cocked an eyebrow and lowered his eyes, his smile fading into an expression of awe as he perused her body. He took a full step back, holding her hands out at her sides.

"Damn."

Were a headshake and a *damn* signs of disappointment? She wasn't sure…

"Not what you expected?" She tittered a nervous laugh.

"No." He didn't let her squirm away, cupping a breast and thumbing her nipple. "Better."

His other hand held her jaw and he didn't wait for her to answer before he kissed her, sliding his tongue into her mouth to tangle with hers.

They made out long and slow, his hand moving from one breast to the other as her tender buds peaked at the attention. Her wet hair dripped down her back, leaving trails of water over her backside and doing a good job of mimicking the wetness between her legs.

By the time Gage moved to her neck and was tonguing the very sensitive patch of skin behind her ear, she was wrestling with his shorts and shoving them down his thighs.

"There she is." He sent her a grin that could only be described as wicked. "I've been waiting for you to let go with me, Andy. Since you stalked over to me in that bar, I knew this was in there. All that cool control didn't fool me for a second. You take what you want, don't you, sweetheart?"

Her heart thudded like it'd punched the air in triumph.

She *did* take what she wanted.

At work. In her business life.

But in her personal life, she'd never been so bold.

It was Gage.

He provided a very big safety net for her high-wire routine. Maybe it was their arrangement, or maybe it was simply him. He was easy to be around, comfortable in his own skin, and she'd begun replicating his smooth confidence.

"Are you asking me to take you?" she asked, her smile incurable.

"No. I'm *telling* you to take me. Have at it." He held his arms to his sides as his shorts slid past his knees. Somehow, with his shorts around his ankles and his boxers distorted by the ridge of his erection, he didn't look silly. He looked *scrumptious*.

"We're doing this." She freed him and shoved his boxers down, stomping on them with her bare feet.

He stepped from the inconvenient clothing and kissed her again, moving them to the couch. "Wait, not there. I've slept on floors that are more comfortable."

He routed them through the living room to the tiny kitchenette instead, which wasn't all that far away given the diminutive size of the suite.

"Why didn't you tell me?" Concern wrinkled her forehead. "I would've let you have the bed."

"I know." He gripped her waist and plopped her onto the tiny square of countertop. He had to move the mini coffeepot aside and bodily brace her against the counter to keep her from toppling off.

"What are you doing?" she asked through a laugh.

A laugh! While she was naked, damp parts of her freshly showered body sticking to his sexy, tanned form... She'd never had sex and laughed at the same time. What was it about this guy?

"Countertop sex. I hope. We have a serious real estate problem." He looked behind them at the tiny table and chairs that might collapse under the weight of a stern glance. "Not many options around here."

"What about the bed?"

"*Definitely* the bed. I was saving that for tonight." He kissed her softly. "Assuming I impress you enough to earn a repeat."

"Hate to break it to you…" Looping her arms around his neck, she rested her forearms on his trapezoids and tilted her head. "But considering how long it's been for me, and how forgettable sex has been in my recent and not-so-recent past, that bar is pretty low."

Eleven

And she's funny.

Funny in a clever way. He found nothing funny about her admitting she'd had forgettable or bad sex in the past. He found it…exhilarating. Not to brag—what the hell, it wasn't bragging if it was true, right?—but Gage didn't leave women unsatisfied. And he was never forgettable. Which was part of the problem, since the women he slept with began nudging him toward boyfriend status pretty soon after they did the deed.

He wanted to have a release with Andy—to experience every amazing part of her lithe body—but he also wanted to show this woman how beautiful she was. It seemed like no one had taken the time or effort to show her, and that was a crime.

She didn't curl away from him or appear the least bit bashful now. If she'd been honest about the mediocre sex in her past, he'd raise the bar so fucking high no one would ever compete with him. Gage aimed for 100 percent success in all attempts and right now, with a wet and willing

Andy Payne holding onto him and smiling at him like he was her shiny new present, he'd happily blow her mind.

"Ever done it on a hotel countertop?"

"Can't say that I have." She wobbled and he steadied her by pressing against her. The move had the added effect of his hard-on rubbing against her slick folds and, *God have mercy*, did she feel warm and welcome and good.

So good.

"I have a condom in my purse," she told him, then offered a chagrined twist of her mouth. "It's really old, though."

"Mine aren't." He didn't miss the subtle flinch. He cradled her face with one palm. "I don't mean because I had sex recently. I meant because I *bought* them recently."

"When is the last time you had sex?"

"Long enough."

"I'll tell you how long it's been for me."

"Andrea."

"Yes?"

"Do you want to talk or do you want to fuck?"

He tested her with the harsh word to learn what she liked. To his delight a smile burst forth on her face. "The second one."

Then she bit her lip and his erection gave a happy jerk.

"Okay, then. Don't fall off this countertop while I grab a condom from my bag."

"Okay." She kicked her legs back and forth, knocking the cabinets with her heels and sending her breasts bouncing in a rhythm he could watch all day. He raced back to her, fumbling with the packet, and she took it from his hand.

"Gage Fleming, I think you must be excited." Package ripped open, she reached for him. "Do you mind?"

"From now on, you don't have to ask that." He held the back of her neck as she rolled the condom on. He watched her long, graceful fingers as she sheathed him, and let out a groan.

"Did you like that?" she asked.

"I like everything you do to me. Haven't you figured that out yet?" At her entrance, he nudged, his gaze drilling into hers. He notched the head, blew out a breath and closed his eyes. Nerves tingled and his arms shook. He hadn't been this excited to slide home in...*a while*. More than that, he hadn't been this intrigued by the prospect of sex since he was a hell of a lot younger.

"Gage, yes." She sighed, a breathy exhale that tore him open. He obeyed her tugging hands and slipped inside of her, slowly thrusting as her eyelids sank to half-mast and her mouth dropped open in ecstasy.

This. This was *fantastic.*

"You feel so good," she breathed, wrapping her ankles around his butt to pull him forward on the next long slide.

She raked her nails into his hair and he slammed his mouth over hers.

"So thick," she gasped when their mouths parted. "Big. No. *Huge.*"

He gave her a pleading look. "Andy. Keep that up and this will end a lot sooner than you want it to. Got it?"

She bit her lip and nodded and that sweet, chaste expression did absolutely nothing to help him pull himself together.

He'd started this physical interaction to show her how sexy she was and yet she'd turned the tables, flattering him so much he could hardly keep his head in the game.

Scooping her to him, he tilted her hips and sank into her again. She let out a squeak of delight, her nails scraping his back.

"Yesss," she hissed in his ear. She only got louder as he continued working them into a sweaty lather, especially when he found her G-spot and pulled her down on him hard. It was awkward and clumsy at first but now she clung to him, her limbs wrapped around his while she finished him off. When she shouted her release, he buried his face in her neck and let go.

Seconds, minutes or, hell, hours, he didn't know, later, he surfaced from her cinnamon-scented skin to give her a lazy smile. It was one Andy returned, her cheeks rosy, her body sated and lazily draped over his as he held them against the countertop with what little strength he had left.

"How was that?" he asked, shameless.

The sex had been incredible and he was fishing for as many compliments as she'd dole out.

Fingers finding the curls of his hair, her mouth widened in an equally shameless grin. "You've proven you know your way around a countertop. I guess we'll see what you can do tonight in bed."

The wine tasting that evening doubled as a bachelorette/bachelor party for the bride and groom. Since this was a private event, the wedding party plus guests had the run of the patio, which had been decorated with strings of twinkle lights.

Andy was impressed by how low-key Gwen had kept the weekend's festivities. Her itinerary was nothing like Kelli's or Ness's had been—which were almost military standard by their punctual schedules—though Andy was sure if she was a bride in the future, she'd be much less laid-back than Gwen or Carroll. Gwen's wedding was happening at breakneck speed, somehow fitting in brunch, boating and a wine tasting along with a bachelor/bachelorette party into a single Friday.

"This is such a beautiful venue. Were all of you married here?" Amber, Gwen's good friend and Matthew's date, asked. Andy's ex-boyfriend wasn't sitting with the girls but with the guys, who'd poured cognac instead of wine and held unlit cigars on the other side of the winery's huge patio.

"I started it," Kelli announced, her I'm-the-firstborn-and-pioneer-of-all attitude shining through. "I found the venue and Boyd agreed it'd be perfect. Vanessa followed suit."

"Only because they had the option to be married in the vineyard," Ness defended.

"It's so funny that you all married in order, too!" Amber exclaimed with a sweep of her hand. When that hand reached Andy, Amber caught her mistake. "Oh, well. Almost in order."

Andy gave the other woman a brittle smile. *Rub it in.*

"I'm sure Andy will choose a venue that is on the West Coast when she weds," Ness said. "She's always been one to do her own thing and snub tradition."

Kelli sent a smirk to Andy that wasn't hard to decode. *If she gets married.*

"I'd love to see what kind of beautiful West Coast wedding you come up with, Andy. I bet it'd be gorgeous." Carroll smiled in support and Andy appreciated her sister speaking up for her.

"How long have you and Gage been seeing each other?" This from Amber.

"Eight months," Andy answered automatically.

"So, it's serious," Amber said.

"Looked pretty serious on the boat this afternoon." Kelli trilled.

"Yeah, I thought maybe he'd come as a friend until I saw that kiss," Ness said. "Not to mention you are absolutely glowing-happy right now."

Andy blinked around. The girls were sitting in a circle on metal chairs around a firepit dotted with citronella candles. They were all nodding their agreement.

"What happened after the boat and before this wine tasting, anyway?" Carroll asked with a teasing wink as she raised her wineglass to her lips.

A rush of confidence pushed a smile to Andy's lips. "Oh, you know. We went back to the room and showered. Then...watched some TV," she said coyly.

A round of *woots* and giggles lifted on the air and she looked up in time to see Gage smiling his approval.

She wasn't used to taking her sisters' teasing in stride, but their playful pokes didn't so much as ruffle a single one of Andy's feathers. She supposed she had Gage to thank for that, too. He'd praised her for being sexy, had turned her on like a light switch and then made love to her standing up, giving her the discretion to invite him to her bed tonight.

Andy had practically floated here on a balloon filled with her own confidence. Confidence at work, she was used to. Confidence around her family was a whole other experience.

One she embraced.

"You two are seriously compatible," Gwen said, noticing Andy and Gage's eye-lock from across the patio. "I love you together. Reminds me of me and Garrett when we first met."

"Which was what, about seven minutes ago?" Ness teased, and everyone laughed.

Gwen and Garrett had been seeing each other less than two months when Gwen announced her engagement. As crazy as it'd been to receive that email from her sister, Andy had passed it off as kismet. True love had the reputation of finding people when they weren't looking for it.

Andy bit her lip in thought. True love wasn't what was between her and Gage, but there seemed to be *something* there. She wasn't willing to deny herself the experience of sex with him, but now that it'd happened she wondered what life would be like when they returned to Seattle. When she followed up with him to ask how the team was doing in the office. She'd only asked for his help for the weekend...but what if it blossomed into more?

Did she want it to?

"Gage is yummy. Am I allowed to say that?" Carroll refilled her wine and gave Andy a cute but slightly sloppy wink.

"Yes. I think we can all drink to that. If it's not too weird for Andy that we objectify her date," Ness said.

"Gage can handle it." Andy sneaked a glance to find him laughing with the guys, though when he ducked his head to take a drink from his glass, she noted him glaring at Matthew. That made her like him more.

"Those curls are to die for. He has this sort of school-boy charm," Kelli said. "But one look at his ass and it's clear he's all man."

Andy blushed, but couldn't help adding, "You should see the rest of him."

Howls of laughter erupted in their circle and Gwen gripped Andy's forearm in support. "I love you like this! So open and happy. It's awesome."

It *was* awesome. Andy shook her head, but not in disagreement—in surprise. "I guess I always felt like the black sheep. The odd one out."

Gwen abruptly sobered, her eyebrows twin slashes of concern. "We don't see you that way."

"At all," Kelli chimed in.

"If anything you're the pioneer of all of us," Carroll agreed. "Over there in the big city making a name for yourself."

"Living life on your own terms," Ness added, and Andy blinked at her in shock.

Whatever brought forth that moment of rallying, whether the wine or the weather, Andy welcomed it.

"Thanks, guys." She raised her wineglass. "Cheers to Gwen and Garrett!"

Everyone joined in on the toast and Andy, as relieved as she was to have the attention off her, also allowed a little part of her to bask in the newfound feeling of fitting in.

Twelve

Gage caught Andy peering over her wineglass at him and had to smile. Damn, but his sexy strawberry-haired vixen would be the death of him. And if that was the way he'd go, he was sure he'd die a happy man.

Nothing had turned him on more than turning her on. Watching as she surprised herself by liking him so much, by liking sex on the countertop so much. He'd enjoyed the delighted, satisfied smile on her face as much as he'd enjoyed the sex itself. Pleasing her pleased him, and the prospect of doing it with her in a bed tonight was a welcome one. Especially after she'd had a few glasses of wine and was loose and sleepy.

Whatever flashbacks of his ex-fiancée had haunted him before, he was glad to have pushed them aside in favor of indulging with Andy.

"You and Andy, huh?" Matthew Higgins, known to the rest of the guys as "Higgs," asked.

It was rhetorical, though, a way to bring up Andy and goad Gage into a fight. Gage knew Matthew's type. Mean. Stupid. The kind of guy who had to prove he was the biggest, strongest man in any gathering. Gage couldn't care less about bravado. He knew exactly what Matthew's insistence on drawing attention to himself meant. It meant that Matthew had a small dick.

"She's always been a puzzle," said Kenny, who stroked his beard in thought. "But then I saw you two together and it was like the puzzle was a whole picture."

"Uh, thanks." But Gage's smile, though slightly perplexed, was also grateful. Ness's husband, Alec, spoke next.

"Andy surprised us, is what Kenny means, I think." Kenny gave him a thumbs-up, and Alec's eyebrows jumped. "Anyway. She's been a loner for as long as I've known her. Except, well…when she dated him." He gestured to Matthew, who puffed out his chest.

Moron.

"Eh, Andy and I weren't long for this world. She doesn't mesh with me. She's brisk and curt. Professional and cold. Smart as a whip, though. I'll give her that."

Gage's blood was set to simmer. Between clenched teeth, he managed, "Must've been you."

Matthew's lips oozed into a smile. "That so? Did you thaw our little Ice Queen, Gage?"

"She's not *our* anything, prick." Gage's anger spiked and he took a step toward the larger, dumber man. Andy might not belong to Gage, either, but he'd be damned if he'd let her ex stake some sort of claim over her.

"Okay, Higgs." Alec put a hand on Gage's chest and patted a few times. "Last thing Gwen and Garrett need is a fistfight on their wedding weekend."

"If you do anything to make Gwen cry, I'll beat your ass myself," Garrett promised, his eyes on Matthew. "Including upsetting her best friend, your date."

Garrett capped off that statement with a smile, but it was a humorless one.

"Far be it from me to ruin anyone's weekend," Matthew

grunted. To Gage, he said, "If Andy's happy with you, I guess congratulations."

"Gee, thanks, Higgs," Gage grumbled.

"I like Andy," Garrett told him, trimming the end of his cigar and passing the trimmer to Gage. "She's probably like the rest of our girls in that there's another layer to her when you two are alone. Another side of her that she doesn't share with the world."

"Gwen has a side other than bubbly and cute?" Alec asked, disbelieving. "And here I thought she was a fairy princess."

The rest of the guys chatted about their wives, but Gage found his mind wandering to his own Payne royalty. Gwen was a fairy princess, and Andy believed she was the Ice Queen—no thanks to the Neanderthal "Higgs" across from him who puffed on his cigar. Matthew had set himself away from the guys as if by choice, but they'd shunned him by subtly turning their backs.

Gage peeked over at Andy, who was sitting, legs crossed, in a pair of white capri pants and a radiant red blouse. She was smiling, her wineglass aloft, her eyes light and happy. It was so good to see her comfortable around the women she'd compared herself to for years and never thought she'd measure up to.

Gage had told Andy she was sexier than all of her sisters combined and he'd meant it. He perused the Payne women, including her mother, who was just joining them, and noticed a tall, older man—Andy's father, Gage would bet—angling for the guys.

Andy stood out in stark contrast from the women surrounding her because he knew that secret side of her the guys had hinted their wives had, too. Gage knew a part of Andy few others did, and that made him want to uncover more.

"Well, well. If it isn't the man who's stealing away my

baby girl." The tall man with white hair boomed as he held out a hand to Garrett.

"Abe. Good to see you." Garrett straightened some, taking the man's hand in a solid pump.

Greetings happened all around, with newcomer Garrett visibly less comfortable around Abe Payne than the rest of the guys. Admittedly Gage also felt a pinch of discomfort when Abe settled his navy eyes on him.

"You must be Andrea's date."

"Gage Fleming." He shook Abe's wide palm, noting the way Andy's father hulked over him, and Gage wasn't a short guy.

"Hmm. Surprised she brought someone."

Gage prepared for a comment like Estelle's or Vanessa's had about Andy not being able to scrounge up a date, but Abe surprised him by saying, "She's usually too independent and discerning to bring a date. Except for this bozo." He shot a thumb over his shoulder at Matthew, who for once looked nervous.

"How are you, sir?" Matthew extended a hand. A hand Abe ignored before sending a barely tolerant headshake to Gage.

Gage grabbed a cigar from the table behind him. "Cigar?" he offered Abe, suddenly a big fan of Andy's father.

"Thank you, Gage." Abe clapped his shoulder. "I think we're going to get along just fine."

"One more, c'mon!" Gwen goaded as she tipped the bottle of chardonnay precariously over Andy's glass. It was the end of the last bottle, however many that'd been. The waitress had efficiently removed the empties, which made counting hard.

"*Fine*. But that's it," Andy acquiesced as Gwen drained the last few ounces of wine from the bottle to the glass.

The Payne women, with their Irish blood, were no strangers to *the drink*. Andy's mother, Estelle, sat rosy-cheeked and laughing, her air of superiority drowned after the first glass. Kelli and Vanessa had relaxed, too, and Carroll and Gwen were punchy and giggly...even more so than usual.

Andy was somewhere in between, as she'd always been with her sisters. She wasn't as ruthlessly serious as her older sisters, but not as laid-back as the other two. She'd often landed in the middle, and where they'd been comfortably paired off with each other, she supposed it made sense why she'd labeled herself the odd woman out.

"Oh, great, cigars. When did they light those?" Vanessa grumbled, her good mood ebbing.

"Eh, boys." Kelli threw a hand. "Boyd knows he's not getting any tonight, anyway."

"Uh-oh, what'd he do?" Carroll asked playfully. "Forget to iron your socks again?"

Andy and Gwen sat forward in their chairs and laughed heartily at the insult. Even Kelli and Vanessa couldn't keep from joining in.

It was a true rarity for Andy to have this kind of evening with her sisters. Where every one of them was loose and relaxed and no one was passing judgment. Gwen's best friend had since collected Matthew and left, so it was only the Paynes and their significant others on the patio. Andy decided to hell with sizing them up. For the remainder of the weekend, she'd just *be*.

They might've been the dominant excuse for her bringing a date in the first place, but Gage had become more than a stand-in so that she could avoid judgment from her family. She now saw that each of them had their own issues, less concerned with Andy than she'd originally imagined. Gage accepted her, liked her, for who she was. It was past time she accepted *herself*.

"Looks like Gage is abstaining," Estelle pointed out, tipping her chin toward the group of guys. Sure enough, Gage stood, arms folded, unlit cigar cradled between two fingers. He was participating in the conversation with everyone, but not smoking. Interesting.

"That must mean he and Andy have some sexy plans tonight." Gwen elbowed Andy in the arm. "Do tell, sister. How is he?"

"How *big* is he?" Carroll chimed in.

"Girls!" Estelle covered her ears. "I'm not listening to this." Vanessa pulled their mother's hands from her ears and then Estelle said, "Unless you'd like to hear details of your father's—"

"No!" all five sisters called out in unison.

Estelle grinned, pleased that her bluff had worked.

"You don't have to be graphic," Carroll stated.

"But be a *little* graphic." Vanessa leaned forward in her chair. Even Kelli looked curious.

"I'm excusing myself to the ladies' room." Estelle threw her hands into the air and hustled off to the restaurant. When she was gone, Andy's sisters raised expectant eyebrows.

"Gage is…attentive."

"Oh, I love attentive," Carroll said, nodding in support.

"Is he a slow kisser? A deep kisser?" Gwen asked, chin in her hands and elbows on her knees.

"Yes to both," Andy answered, and sighs of delight echoed around her. "I don't know what's going to come next. He goes from kissing my mouth, to my neck, to that part behind my ear."

"I *love* that part." Kelli sat up now, too, her attention on Andy.

"What about the first time you ever had sex?" Vanessa asked on a whisper. "Where was it? How long did you wait?"

"Well…it was…more recently than you might think," Andy said, her tongue loosened from the wine, and yeah, she was caught up in the attention.

"How recent? And where? How did it happen?" Carroll asked rapid-machine-gun-style.

Andy opened her mouth, unsure what would come out of it when a low male voice interjected, "Whoa, whoa, whoa… What did I walk in on?"

Every one of her sisters sat up, backs straight in their chairs as Gage rounded behind them and aimed accusatory looks at each one.

"Leave you alone for a few minutes, and you're telling all." Hands on Andy's shoulders, Gage kneaded her tight muscles. He'd done a good job of loosening her up earlier, but now that easy-breezy feeling ebbed away.

She shut her eyes, mortified that he'd overheard her. This was why she never allowed herself more than two glasses of wine! She became caught up, the wine an elixir urging the truth from her. She'd forgotten that she had a story to keep up with: a *pretend* boyfriend she was *for real* sleeping with.

How had the lines gotten so blurry?

"Gage. We were just—" she started, lamely.

"You women are worse than those guys over there," he said, but she could hear the smile in his voice, the teasing tone that was good-natured and so *Gage*. "Ready to head back, sweetheart?"

"We noticed you didn't smoke a cigar," Kelli said, crossing her legs. She'd recovered from being busted quicker than any of them. Even Ness looked a bit chagrined.

"Not tonight."

"Oh? Why's that? Plans with Andrea?" Kelli asked.

Gage took Andy's hand and helped her stand. When she faced him, he said, "Yes. I have *many* plans for Andrea tonight."

Thirteen

"That was a close one." Andy had been on the spot in front of her sisters. The jig would've well and truly been up if she'd even hinted at the fact that hers and Gage's first time had been *today*.

"I thought I'd whisk you out of there before you had to make up a story about the first time we had sex. You liked me coming to your rescue." He tossed their suite's key card on the counter where they'd had sex hours earlier, and then he gripped her hips, pulling her in front of him. "Admit it."

He'd been dying to kiss her again all evening, and while he hadn't minded leaving her sisters with something to chew on, out-and-out PDA seemed over-the-top for Andy.

"I did love it." She swept her fingers into his hair and toyed with the curled ends. "You claimed me."

His eyes sought hers, lost in the depths of those earnest blues. Andrea Payne was a woman who was smooth and detached on the outside. A woman who knew what she wanted and how to get it. A woman who, to achieve a goal, would approach a man in a bar and offer him two grand to come with her to a wedding. What she didn't know about herself, and what Gage was trying to show her, was that she was also soft and caring, giving and loving. She was sensitive and demure, and the slightest bit shy, and every one of those attributes did it for him. Especially when they came wrapped in a package of freckles and strawberry hair and blue eyes so bright he could sink into them for days.

He blinked, jerking his chin back in shock. Normally when it came to women he wasn't this...poetic. Could be the cognac. Could be the setting—love was in the air.

Or it could be that he'd been taking this pretend role of boyfriend to real extremes.

He hadn't been a boyfriend in a long, *long* time. The last time he'd escalated to fiancé and that wasn't something he was interested in repeating. When Laura left, he'd felt filleted. Like someone had stripped out his bones and left him a heap of flesh on the floor.

Yeah, no repeats on that, thanks.

"No one would've believed we waited eight months before making love on a countertop at my sister's wedding retreat." She played with his hair some more. "We didn't wait more than a few weeks before we caved."

"Two weeks too long," he admitted, his earlier reminiscing forgotten.

Right now was about *right now*.

He'd didn't typically worry about the future and he'd be damned if he ruined the weekend with it now. He moved her hair over her shoulder. "When you came at me like a lioness in that bar, I'd decided to take you home and damn the consequences."

"Is that so?" She tilted one eyebrow. "What about that cute bartender you'd been flirting with all evening? Did you swap her for me so easily?"

"You were watching me." He narrowed his eyes in accusation.

"I—" Her mouth gaped for a second. "Only between bouts of my date talking incessantly about himself."

"What did you see when you looked across the room at me, Andy?"

"You mean other than an opportunity?"

He smirked at her deflection. "How'd you know the bartender wasn't my girlfriend?"

"I didn't. I…assumed."

"And you also assumed I was a sorry sap in dire need of two thousand dollars."

She squeezed her eyes closed, her cheeks going the sweetest tinge of pink. "I didn't think you needed two thousand dollars." When her eyes reopened, she looked up at him with such raw vulnerability, his heart clutched. "I thought it'd take two thousand dollars to convince you to say yes…to me."

He gripped her chin and lifted her face just enough to keep her eyes on him while he made sure what he said next sank in.

"Honey, I was going to take you home based on one look. Based on you stalking toward me like you wanted to make a meal out of me. And trust me when I say, I have a very good reason for not liking that look on a woman."

"Sounds like a story."

"For another day," he said. "I liked your determination. You saw what you wanted and you were coming to get it. Certainty, *honesty*, is a huge turn-on for me."

"But you said no." Her eyebrows pinched.

"You offered to pay me!" He let out a chortle, his fingers threading in her hair. "Tell me if I'd have offered you the same you would've gladly accepted."

"Oh. No. Of course I wouldn't have… I'd never…" Her fingers came up to cover her lips as she pushed his arms aside. Between her hands she said, "Gage, I'm so sorry I made you feel…cheap."

"You made me feel confused, Andy. Not cheap. In no way should you have ever felt like you couldn't earn a yes from me instead of buying it." He tugged her hands from her mouth and kissed her fingers. "You're worth it."

In the distance of Gage's mind he was aware that this was how he gave women the wrong impression: by being likable. By being honest about what he liked about them. But he couldn't help being likable any more than he could help liking Andy a bit too much. A bit more than common sense suggested he should...

Her hand came to rest on his chest and she gave him a push. "You like me determined, Fleming?" she asked, her voice hard and unyielding.

His lips twitched, but he didn't dare smile. "Yes, ma'am."

At her playful shove, he walked a few steps backward toward the bedroom.

"Good. There are things I want from you," she stated.

"Oh?" He was intrigued as hell. "What things?"

"I want to taste you." Her fingers trickled down his button-down shirt. "I want to feel you hard and heavy in my mouth."

His eyes zoomed in on her plush lips as she—God help him—swiped her bottom lip with her tongue. *Slowly.* His cock gave an insistent twitch from behind his fly.

"Take off your pants," she commanded.

Gage wouldn't allow her to do all the commanding. He had things he wanted to do to her as well. Instead of obeying, he cupped her jaw with both hands and kissed her sweetly. The sweet turned to hard, the hard to long, the long to soft. When he pulled away, she whimpered her protestation at losing his mouth. He took advantage of her being dazed and unbuttoned her pants, sliding his hand into her panties to find her damp and inviting.

Against her parted lips, he whispered, "You first."

* * *

Waves of pleasure streaked up her spine as Andy came at Gage's command. He hadn't even taken her pants off yet. Instead, he'd rooted them to the spot on the floor and moved from stroking her to sliding a finger deep inside of her. When a second finger joined the first, her talented wedding date thumbed her clitoris once, twice…and the third time was a charm.

She opened her eyes, her breathing erratic, her palms resting on his shoulders. She might topple over if she didn't hold on to him. But she didn't find a pleased smile on Gage's face, no. He was all heat and seriousness when he lowered his lips to hers. His whisper was hot, his breath coasting over her lips when he said, "That was beautiful to watch."

She'd never been with anyone like him. Someone so confident and easygoing, and…well, who *liked her*, quite frankly. She'd never liked someone as much as he liked her back, so the mutual attraction was brand-new.

"Thank you," she breathed.

That brought forth his brilliant smile. "Show, don't tell, Ms. Payne."

She bit the inside of her cheek, knowing what he was referring to. She'd made him a promise. Reaching for his hard-on, she massaged him and earned a deep kiss for her efforts. In a blur of movement, Gage maneuvered them backward into the bedroom while keeping their lips sealed. She unfastened his pants as he tore at her shirt, leaving them in a pile on the floor.

When he reached the bed, she undid his shirt one button at a time, revealing his chest and smoothing her fingers over the scant hair whorling around flat male nipples, dusting his clenching abs, and finally to that trail of hair that disappeared into his black boxers.

"I've never been so excited to have someone naked before," she said, half surprised she'd said it aloud.

"Honey, have at it." He thumbed her cheek as a deep breath lifted his shoulders and broadened his bare chest. Anticipation hung heavy in the air between them. She let it linger for a few agonizing seconds and then dropped to her knees and tugged on his boxers.

"Look at me when you do it." He wound her long hair around his fist and held it away from her face.

She licked her lips and his hips surged forward. He was suddenly intense, not the same playful guy from earlier. She couldn't wait to experience his flavor, and was trying to decide if she would linger at the head or pepper the shaft with kisses.

She started with a sweet kiss to the tip. His answering groan spurred her on, bolstering her confidence and making her sit a little taller. When she opened her mouth to accommodate him, she did as he asked and turned her eyes up to his…

Gage typically held off coming by reciting the last quarter's sales numbers in silence, but with Andy's eyes zeroed in on him, he couldn't concoct a single thought that didn't involve her. On her knees, her fingers lightly tickling his balls, and those blue, blue eyes fastened to him and holding him hostage.

He locked his thigh muscles as she took him deeply into her mouth again and again. He didn't think of sales numbers or baseball stats, or any other helpful distraction that might keep his release at bay. He didn't want to miss a single second of Andy making love to him with her mouth.

She was a glorious sight. Her pink-tipped breasts bare as she knelt there in nothing but a pair of black panties. The way she gripped his shaft with nails painted the same color red as her shirt had been.

Mercy.

She'd be his undoing. He was sure of it. He wasn't sure what that meant yet, and he wasn't sure he would've changed a damn thing if he'd known before now, but she was not unlike a female praying mantis. He was willingly, gladly allowing himself to be devoured.

Thoughts of cannibal insects and his imminent doom faded away when she swirled her tongue and took him deep. His hand that had been holding her hair out of the way tightened into a fist and he let out a grunt, followed by a plea.

"Can't…believe I'm…saying this…"

She let him go before slowly taking him deep again and his brain blanked. Seriously, he had nothing in his head during the next slick slide, but his memory returned when the telltale tingle of his pending orgasm shimmied up his spine.

"Stop, sweetheart. I need to be inside you. *Now.*"

He watched as she let him go, his length slipping from her wet, parted mouth.

God.

Damn.

He blinked. Hard. Resetting his brain and hopefully gaining a modicum of restraint. He lifted her by the elbows, helping himself to exploring her plush mouth when it reached his.

"You are so hot it's ridiculous," he panted. "You could lead me around with that move, you know that?"

She offered a pleased grin as he worked her panties down her legs. "Does that mean you're my sex slave now?"

"Yes," he said without hesitation. Though he didn't like the idea of any woman leading him around by the pecker, for Andy—for this weekend—he could make an exception and forgive himself for it later.

"On your back, beautiful. Let's do this properly."

She lay down and pushed herself up the bed, gloriously naked—all that smooth skin exposed for his eyes and his twitching fingers. He slid his hand from her hip to her ribs and back up to her breasts.

"So much better." He kissed her lightly. "No complicated countertops or vertical maneuvering."

"Yeah." Her smile the slightest bit shaky. Before he could work out what that meant, she said, "Condom."

"Right." Right! Wow. Where was his head? He'd been consumed with being inside her and totally forgotten about protection. *Rookie move, Fleming.*

Again that distant alarm rang, a little louder than before. It hinted that he was in deeper than he'd intended, but that was stupid. This was a temporary arrangement between them—they were completely compatible physically. No reason not to enjoy themselves.

Repeatedly.

He retrieved a condom from his wallet and rolled it on, returning to Andy. Then he lifted her leg and lined up with her center, enjoying teasing her. Enjoying watching her hands clench the sheets into a wad, her lips parting in anticipation.

"You want me, Strawberry?" he asked.

She didn't take him to task for the nickname, only hastily nodded.

He didn't tease either of them any longer, thrusting inside of her in one mind-melting slide. She cried out, her pleasure infusing the air with a scent not unlike the cinnamon of her perfume.

He repeated the action again, again, until she locked her legs around him and cried out with wild abandon. He lost track of his voice as well, especially when he came on what would qualify in most countries as a roar and collapsed on top of her. His entire body was buzzing, his head detached, a slight layer of sweat sticky between them.

He returned to earth when Andy's fingers found his hair. A move that was already becoming familiar to him, and was unique to her.

That caused another alarm to break through the haze of his orgasm.

But he ignored that one as well.

Fourteen

Gage woke to the telltale clicking of computer keys, his head swimming through a seascape of dreams. He opened his eyelids a crack to notice two things: one, it was still dark outside, and two, Andy was sitting up in bed next to him, laptop on her lap, naked breasts highlighted in the bluish light emanating from the screen.

He stretched his hand across the bed—king-size, so he had a way to go—and brushed her thigh with an open palm. She started, jerking her head over to him before flashing him a grin. And flashing him, period, considering the movement also shifted her long hair from where it covered her breasts and out peeked a nipple.

"What are you doing?" he asked, his voice sleepy and craggy.

"Working," she whispered. "Did I wake you?"

"Yes." He sat up in bed next to her, propping a pillow behind his back. He pressed a kiss to her shoulder. *Mmm.* She smelled good. He lingered on the second kiss and she sighed, a soft sound from her throat, before giving in and turning her head for a kiss. A kiss he almost gave her.

"Hang on." He wandered out of the suite and into the bathroom, using the facilities before washing his hands, face, and finally scrubbing his teeth. He wasn't going to kiss her long and slow if he had dragon breath, that was for damn sure.

When he emerged, she was standing in the living room, bare-ass-naked. "If you're going to brush your teeth, then I have to, too." She seemed inconvenienced by this, but he was glad to see that the laptop on the bed was closed.

He climbed back into bed and glanced at the clock, doing a double take. When Andy meandered back into their shared room, teeth brushed, he pointed at the digital readout. "It's barely five a.m."

"I know."

"Does the word *vacation* mean nothing to you?" He rarely saw the other side of six o'clock in the morning. Whenever he'd tried to start his day earlier than that, he'd met it grouchy and groggy. He was still groggy, but his grouchiness had been replaced by another feeling entirely, considering Andy was crawling toward him in bed, her breasts shifting temptingly with every move she made, her hair tickling up his body.

She rested on him, chest to chest, and Gage cupped her bottom, his grogginess dissipating when she leaned in to kiss him slowly.

"I'm an early riser."

He pushed his pelvis into hers, his arousal making itself known despite what time it was. "Me, too, but never this early."

Not that he usually had a reason to wake hard and ready. Rare was the occasion a woman stayed over. And on the off chance she had, he pretended to be fast asleep until she left so they didn't have to do this dance. Many, *many* lines were being crossed with Andy, and while he knew

that wasn't cause for a panic attack, he reminded himself
not to get used to it.

"What time's the rehearsal?" he asked around a yawn.
"Early, right?"

"Ten o'clock."

In the morning, he knew. Evidently Gwen and Garrett
had opted to rehearse for the wedding the morning of the
wedding, which wasn't typical. He remembered that from
the quick scan of the itinerary.

"That gives us several hours," Andy purred before pressing a kiss to his shoulder. Then his neck. When she opened
her mouth at the base of his throat, he slid his arms to her
back and squeezed.

"I need my beauty sleep," he joked.

"Sex first, then you can sleep, princess." She nipped his
bottom lip and soothed the twinge with a kiss.

"There is some serious role reversal going on here," he
pointed out. "I don't like it."

"You don't like not being in charge?"

"Correct." He was all-the-way hard now, the languid,
teasing kisses and verbal sparring turning him on regardless of what ungodly time of morning it was. "I have a
better idea."

He reversed their positions, rolling Andy to her back and
sliding down her body as he laid kisses here and there. Her
eyes widened with excitement.

"What are you doing?" The question burst from her like
a bottle rocket, capping with her stopping him when he
began kissing a line down the center of her breasts.

"Making sure you go back to sleep when I'm through
with you," he mumbled against her skin, shaking off her
hands to kiss her flat belly.

"Gage." She clamped her legs together, her hands returning to his hair. He gave her his attention and that was when
she shook her head. "You don't want to do that."

"Oh, but I do." He removed one of her hands from his head and kissed her palm. "You touch my hair a lot."

The panicky expression gave way to a shaky grin.

"I don't remember any woman I've been with who played with my hair the way you do."

"Sorry."

"Not a complaint. And right now a big turn-on." He put her hand back on his head. "Pull when I do something you like and I'll keep doing it until you explode." He gave her a wink, licking a line just under her belly button before moving to her thigh and kissing there, too.

Her clean scent hit him, musky and inviting. He absolutely could not wait to taste her. To make her scream his name.

"But…"

With a sigh, he raised his face from the cradle of her thighs.

"You're sure?"

"Andy, haven't you ever done this before?" A rhetorical question, because surely…

But she slowly shook her head, and in the sparse light from the digital clock he could see her cheeks darken with color. He had no idea how that was possible, or what dickweeds she'd dated who didn't take the time, energy and effort to satisfy her—but…

He knew of one, didn't he?

He kept his eyes on hers as he lowered his lips to just above her center. "Step one—" he licked her seam, thrilling when desire bloomed in her eyes and her mouth dropped open "—let me do all the work."

Shifting her so that her knees were resting on his shoulders, he opened her to him. "Step two—" he placed another reverent lick to the heart of her "—instructions are encouraged. Faster, slower, left, right, that kind of thing."

She bit her lip—to keep away a smile, he was guessing.

Her shoulders had come down from her ears, and he wondered if that was because he'd just made it clear she had no need for performance anxiety.

"Step three—" instead of one lick, he delivered several in rapid succession, loving the way she thrust upward toward his seeking tongue "—enjoy yourself. This is all for you."

Her fingers were in his hair, seeking, pulling and pushing or a combination of all three when he went to work. When she was close, she rewarded him with a high cry and he doubled down on his efforts, concentrating on that one spot in particular designed to make her lose her mind. She never gave him instructions but she never had to. Soon she was coming, clenching around his fingers, which he'd added to help her get there, and crying his name on a weak, sated shout.

Hell.

Yes.

He kissed her hip bone and then her ribs, placed a loving peck on each of her nipples and then suckled her earlobe when he reached it. Her heartbeat was erratic, her breathing labored and her eyes closed.

"Wow" was the first word she said. And Gage, who'd meant that exploration as a precursor to some really great morning sex, decided he'd let her ride this wave into oblivion.

"Sleep well, Strawberry." He gave her one last kiss and she grunted what might've been a word if he hadn't rendered her every muscle useless. Proud of himself, he rolled over, his erection protesting. He ignored it. She needed that—worse than he'd originally known, apparently—and he'd been the first to give it to her. That special sort of release when you're the center of the attention—the very attention she'd given him without hesitation last night.

In the dark, she began to lightly snore and he smiled in

wonderment at the creature who'd brought him here, bedded him and confused him constantly.

Who was this woman?

And how, in all of his years of folly and dating, had he never met another like her?

Andy showed up for the casual brunch rehearsal wearing a light floral dress rather than the navy blue bridesmaid's dress she'd purchased for Gwen's navy-and-red-themed wedding. Gwen had eschewed the traditional rehearsal *dinner* for a casual brunch rehearsal, which was being held in a tented-off area in view of the lake.

The sky was heavy with clouds, but the weather was warm. The app on Andy's phone showed the skies clearing by noon, and nothing but sun after, which was good news for Gwen and Garrett's 4:00 p.m. ceremony.

Gage accompanied Andy to the rehearsal even though she'd assured him he didn't have to come. He didn't need to rehearse for anything. He'd insisted, though, saying he'd better regain his strength and *"have something other than you for breakfast,"* which made her remember how completely he'd spoiled her this morning.

After he'd successfully tranquilized her by going down on her, she'd slipped off into the most pleasant sleep of her life before waking him an hour later in much the same fashion. The sex had been electrifying and gratifying, and yet lazy and languid, the way morning sex should be.

She'd ridden him, her hair tickling her back, and he'd held onto her hips, lifting to meet her with each languid thrust. It was the kind of sex a girl could get used to, but that thought made her melancholy, so she'd ignored it all morning. If there was one clear boundary line between her and Gage it was that they shouldn't get too used to being together.

"I'm grabbing a bite to eat that's guaranteed to be less satisfying than you," Gage whispered in her ear.

She ducked her head, suddenly shy at the copious attention. He placed a kiss on her temple before leaving her to her sister Gwen, who appeared uncharacteristically nervous.

Uh-oh.

"Hey. Everything okay?" Andy asked.

"No." Gwen's gaze flitted left, then right. "Carroll is my maid of honor, and Garrett's best friend is Kenny, so that worked out perfectly. But you're my bridesmaid and so is Amber, and Amber is dating Matthew, who is your ex."

"Right," Andy said, waiting for the other shoe to drop.

"Garrett doesn't really like Matthew."

Andy didn't really like Matthew, either.

"But he's in the wedding party. Because I love Amber and she's in love with Matthew and wanted him to be her partner. So I talked Garrett into it, which makes me feel awful…but worse than that—" Gwen winced "—I didn't warn you about Matthew being here. I'm a giant coward."

Andy tracked her eyes past Gwen over to where the wedding party was gathered near the wedding arch. Granted, she didn't like Matthew any more than Garrett did, but she wasn't going to ruin her sister's day. "I'm sure it'll be fine, Gwen. We've survived this weekend so far without incident."

Except him referring to her as Ice Queen. But Gage had been there to stand up for her.

"He said you called him and he told you he'd be here."

Andy stiffened. She'd called Matthew to ask him to be her stand-in date, in a fit of insanity, apparently, but luckily never had to ask. Matthew had interrupted and bragged about attending with another date—Gwen's best friend, Amber.

"I did… I did call him. I was curious about how he was doing. It was a random whim," Andy lied.

"I should have been the one to tell you—to warn you. It'd been so long since you two dated… I guess I didn't give it much thought." Gwen pressed her lips together before adding, "Are you sure you're not mad at me for not warning you?"

Andy palmed her youngest sister's shoulder, relieved Gwen wasn't instead suspicious over the reason that Andy had called Matthew in the first place. "No, Gwen. I'm not the least bit mad."

"Good." Gwen's shoulders sagged in relief. "You're walking with Garrett's good friend Jon, who arrived this morning. He's in the blue shirt."

Andy spotted the slender, smiling man in khakis and a golf shirt. "Okay."

"Don't be mad about this, either, but I sort of told him you were single."

"Gwen!"

"I didn't expect you to bring a date! If he hits on you, break it to him gently."

Andy sighed. Just what she needed. First, she'd barely scrounged a date for this wedding, then she'd learned Matthew would darken the wedding's doorstep, and now she was sleeping with her pretend boyfriend *and* had another suitor asking if she was available? She'd never had so many man problems in her entire life.

One more look at Gwen showed that she wasn't her normal happy-go-lucky self. This must be what the pre-wedding bridal jitters looked like on her. Kelli had had an outburst about her bouquet containing the wrong kind of roses, Ness had dissolved into tears when her flower girl refused to wear the tiara that matched her own and Carroll had done a shot of peppermint schnapps to ease her last-second nerves before she walked down the aisle.

"I'll let him down gently," Andy assured her.

"Thank you." Gwen beamed. "I'm getting married."

"You are!" Andy couldn't help smiling back at her youngest sister. She was enjoying herself so much now that she was here. Andy had Gage to thank for that. He seemed to be the common denominator in every moment she'd been at ease. "I'm so, *so* happy for you and Garrett."

Gwen embraced her in a tight squeeze that made Andy's eyes watery. "I'm so happy for you and Gage. I know Ness and Mom can be complete pains in the rear about pairing you off, but they want what's best for you deep down on the inside."

Andy hoisted a brow. "It must be buried deeper than the mines of Moria."

Gwen giggled, loving the *Lord of the Rings* reference, as Andy knew she would. "Thanks, Andy. I appreciate you being understanding."

"Sure thing." She followed Gwen to the wedding arch, toward Matthew and the stranger she'd be paired with in the wedding, and drew back her shoulders in determination.

She could do this.

And maybe it was better if she did. She'd used Gage as her security blanket for long enough. Andy could handle this part on her own.

Better get used to it, a tiny voice warned.

Soon she'd be back in Seattle and their bout of pretending would be over. But their physical connection wasn't pretend for her at all. She wondered if it was for Gage, or if, like her, he was steeling himself for the end.

Fifteen

Around noon the clouds swept aside like curtains, parting to reveal the sunshine. By the time Gage made his way to the wedding area, the grass was dry and the day warm but not too hot.

He was invited to sit with the remaining Payne sisters who weren't included in the wedding. He overheard Ness say she'd begged off, not wanting "to deal with another useless bridesmaid's dress."

Not that he'd ever accuse any woman of being an "Ice Queen" but he wasn't entirely sure how Andy had earned that moniker over Vanessa.

Gage took the seat next to Boyd on one of the white plastic folding chairs arranged in rows. He turned to smile at the tiny flower girl walking down the aisle beside Carroll, who was helping the little girl throw petals. The tot probably had no idea why she was dressed in a white confection and all eyes were on her.

Next came the bridesmaids, and Gage turned expectantly to see Andy. She'd left him in the room, her dress in a bag tossed over her arm, and promised to see him at the wedding. There'd been an awkward moment when she'd debated whether she should kiss him goodbye or not, and then she had. Just a quick peck on the side of his mouth. He'd wished her good luck.

The sight of her now stole the moisture from his mouth. She was...ethereal.

The navy blue dress was knee-length, the sleeves designed to reveal her creamy shoulders. Her hair was pulled back on one side, the strawberry blonde color a stunning accent to the blue. The photographer leaned out of an aisle to snap a photo and Andy smiled, her plush lips shining with sparkly pink gloss. When she caught sight of Gage, her smile stayed but turned demure, the joy in her blue eyes zapping him where he sat.

Then she walked past him to take her place up front, and Amber followed. By the time the music changed to introduce the bride, Gage didn't want to take his eyes from his date. And when a white-dressed Gwen strode down the aisle to take her place next to Garrett, Gage felt his forehead break into a sweat.

Could've been you.

He'd been to weddings since his engagement with Laura had imploded. He'd always had a date, so that part wasn't new. He'd never pictured himself in the role of the groom, with a bride in white coming toward him down a long aisle.

Until right now.

Gripping his hands in front of him, he forced himself to take a few long breaths. When Boyd eyed him curiously, Gage gave him a pained I'm-fine smile. Eyebrows bowed in sympathy, Boyd patted Gage's back gruffly and then turned to watch the ceremony.

What was that about? What was the back-pat and that knowing smile supposed to reinforce? Gage swiped his brow again. When it came time for the prayer he ducked his head, but his eyes and thoughts stayed on Andy.

Andrea Payne was a puzzle, like Kenny had said.

But Kenny had also said that when Gage and Andrea were together, Kenny could see the full picture. That picture spread out before Gage now, even though he didn't quite know what to make of it.

He saw Andy in his future.

That wasn't something he'd been able to say of any woman besides Laura. But he was enamored with Andy in a way he'd never been with any woman—and that *included* Laura.

In the midst of pretending to be Andy's boyfriend, Gage was feeling particularly boyfriend-like. He was going against several rules he'd set up to protect himself, including endangering the bachelor pact he and Reid were still upholding.

Gage wouldn't muster up a version of a wedding of his own—lest he throw up on his and Boyd's shoes—but he could safely state that when he and Andy returned to Seattle, he'd like to keep seeing her.

Thing was, he wasn't 100 percent sure she wanted to keep seeing him.

So.

That was new.

Typically, it was the woman he was dating who was leaning on him a little too hard. Crowding into his space and wanting the "more" he couldn't give her. Meanwhile here he was, literally a few days into this…fantasy romance, and starting to feel a whole host of things he shouldn't.

Particularly when Andy rested her hand on the arm of the groomsman she'd been paired with and they both smiled at the camera.

If Gage were to let this affair end, he imagined Andy would eventually find a man worthy of her time. They couldn't all be duds. Maybe even after she and Gage split, the nice-guy-looking groomsman would call her up.

"Hey, Andrea. You remember me? Pencil Neck from Gwen's wedding? I thought we could get together sometime for a bland dinner before I try to impress you with a few of my lame bedroom moves."

Gage felt his lip curl at the idea of another guy trying to spend time with Andy. Possessive was another trait he'd never had to contend with. But here it was, as gritty and basal as he'd ever imagined.

Whenever he looked at Andrea Payne, a bolt of certainty shocked his gut with a single word.

Mine.

He wanted her, and he'd had her.

But he hadn't had *enough* of her.

Even though previously he'd decided beyond a shadow of a doubt that he would never get married or engaged.

Was there an in-between? Was Andy the kind of woman who would settle for some but not all?

He was beginning to think he wasn't that kind of guy. That he was instead the kind of guy who'd like to get married someday. That he was the kind of guy who'd like to have a family and a wife and buy a house with a yard he had to mow.

But only if that future included Andy.

So.

Yeah.

What the hell was he supposed to do with *that*?

Thankfully the tradition of a formal wedding party dance wasn't one Gwen and Garrett kept. The happy couple finished their dance as husband and wife and then the DJ played a song about single women that would inevitably herald the bouquet toss. Andy settled in at the round table decorated with red roses in navy vases, her hand in Gage's, content not to move. Until…

"Get up there, girl," Kelli goaded.

"Me?" Andy shook her head. "I'm not single. I'm here with Gage."

"Yes, but you're not married to Gage. Or engaged to Gage." A small frown marred her sister's forehead. "Are you?"

"No." Andy shook her head and met Gage's eyes. He looked slightly green and she could imagine why. Pretending to be her boyfriend was one thing. Pretending to be her fiancé was a whole other level of OMG. "But I'm not single."

"That's not how it works." Kelli grabbed Andy's hand and dragged her to the dance floor, where Amber was already boogying to the music.

Andy stood behind Amber and the other four girls who were on the stage, arms in the air. Gwen searched the crew of available bachelorettes and Andy quickly shook her head. Gwen smirked, slapped her hand over her eyes and threw the bouquet high.

It arced toward Amber, but the toss was high and Amber was about six inches shorter than Andy. Either the gorgeous bouquet of blue roses with red ribbon hit the dance floor and exploded into a shower of petals, thereby ruining her youngest sister's day, or...

Andy held out her hands in a show of an attempt. The bouquet landed prettily in her palms like Gwen had aimed directly for her.

Cheers rang out and Andy held her prize overhead, her headshake a combination of chagrin and *that-figures*.

But when she caught sight of Gage applauding, she felt happy she'd gone along with this farce anyway. Just to have him here with her—just to be in his company. Even if it was only for the weekend.

The DJ called for the single guys as Andy stepped from the dance floor, and this time it was not Kelli but Garrett

calling to the men who'd rather not stand up and catch
Gwen's garter.

Garrett shoved Jon onto the dance floor as a random
smattering of single guys shuffled into their spots, beers
in hand. Andy tried to hold Garrett off when he angled for
Gage, but Garrett only winked at her.

"Sorry, Andrea. He has to make an attempt. Especially
since you have the bouquet." When Garrett slapped Gage
on the back, she also heard him say, "You don't want Jon
slipping a garter onto your girl's thigh, now do you?"

Gage sent a heated glance over his shoulder at Andy and
flames licked along her body like he'd touched her instead.

Saucy, silly burlesque music piped from the speakers
as Garrett shimmied a garter belt from high on his bride's
thigh. He slid it down the remainder of Gwen's leg with
his teeth, which made everyone cheer and clap except Abe
Payne, who covered his eyes when he received a few elbows to the ribs.

"Okay, gentlemen!" Garrett called out. "Who's next?
Hey! Hands out of your pockets." After calling out a few
of his buddies, Garrett flipped the garter into the crowd
like a slingshot, and Jon made a hearty reach for it. He had
a few inches on Gage, but Gage made a play for it, launching himself higher by using Jon's shoulder as leverage and
snatching the garter out of midair.

Andy applauded when Gage sauntered over, spinning
the garter around his finger as several of the guys patted
his back.

"All he needed was the right motivation," Garrett shouted
as he grabbed a chair and dragged it onto the dance floor.

"Come on, beautiful." Gage offered his hand to Andy.
"Let's do this."

She tucked her palm into his. His easygoing attitude had
shifted slightly. He was still fun-loving Gage, but a ribbon
of seriousness threaded through him as he sat her on the

chair and she lifted her leg. His smile was there, his silliness as he verbally urged the crowd on while he slid the garter up her leg, but she couldn't escape the idea that something had changed within him without her knowing. Especially when he tugged her skirt down, helped her stand and asked her to dance as the fast beat slowed into the next ballad.

Couples joined them on the floor and Andy rested her arms on Gage's shoulders as they began to sway.

"Sorry about that." She forced an eye roll even though she wasn't very sorry at all. "I appreciate you defending my honor, though."

"No way was I going to allow Jon—or Matthew—to win that prize and touch even an inch of your leg with their grubby paws."

She giggled. "All my life I've never known a man to be possessive over me, Gage. I think maybe I was lowballing you with my offer of two grand. You're worth much more."

His smile fell, and again she felt as if he was more serious than before. He pushed her hair off her neck, tracing the line from her collarbone to her shoulder. "Have I told you how good you look in this dress?"

"Thank you."

He had. At the start of the reception, when they had parted ways, her bridesmaid chores complete.

"I'm glad you asked me to be your date," Gage said, sneaking a look around to make sure no one was near them. "And for allowing me to share your bed. I have a proposition for you in return."

"Oh?" She bit the inside of her lip, a parade of naughty possibilities lining up to conga through her brain. Would he suggest sex somewhere public, but hidden in shadows? Maybe he wanted to make love by moonlight on the boat. Or maybe, when they went back to the room, he would get a bucket of ice and tease a cube along her inner thighs...

"When we return to Seattle, what if we don't stop?"

She swayed in his arms, not understanding his meaning. "Don't stop what?"

"Any of it. You coming to my place. Me to yours." He turned them in a smooth circle. "I can't promise opportunities for garters or dancing, but the rest of it—the meals, the dates, the waking you up by going down on you—" he whispered, leaning in "—why stop now?"

Sixteen

Andy had been putting off thinking about life back in Seattle until after the wedding was over. But the weekend was winding down quickly, wasn't it? It was nearing the end of the time she and Gage would spend together and now that she allowed herself to think about what that meant for them…well, *not* seeing him didn't sound even a little appealing.

"You want to keep seeing me?" She was still trying to wrap her brain around that. It wasn't a typical discussion she'd had with her mediocre dates and underwhelming boyfriend prospects.

"We're good together, Andy. I didn't come here expecting…this." He raised their linked hands to gesture around them. "To be this comfortable with you. Especially in this scenario."

"Hmm. You're going to need to explain that." He'd hinted that there was a story from his past before, but he hadn't shared it. By her estimations she had him right where she wanted him.

"Wondered if I could escape explanation." He sighed heavily.

"You can," she told him, quickly changing her tune. "You don't owe me anything. But since we're planning on *not stopping*, it would be nice to know you a bit better. Beyond the biblical sense, I mean." She winked and he chuckled, settling into their dancing rhythm with ease.

"Since you've just agreed to my terms, I suppose I could indulge you with a few details of my sordid past."

"Oh, sordid. That's a good beginning to any story."

He took a deep breath before he spoke, like there was still a part of him that was resisting. "I was engaged when I was a junior in college."

"Young."

"Quite." He lifted a sardonic eyebrow. "Laura and I… ended our engagement."

"Code for she dumped you."

"Precisely. After that engagement ended, I decided this—" he jerked his chin to indicate the wedding guests, tent and the bride and groom themselves "—wasn't for me. By then there was a pact issued by my buddies that we'd agree never to marry."

"Which buddies?" But she had a guess.

"Reid and Flynn."

"Ha! But aren't Flynn and Sabrina…?"

"Yeah, they are. He broke the contract, but after seeing them together it made sense. You've seen them. It's undeniable how they feel about each other."

"It's pretty obvious," she agreed.

"Anyway, he's been married before, and once the divorce was underway, he was the one to reinstate the pact. He was upset, as well as he should've been since his now ex-wife cheated on him with his brother."

Andy sucked air through her teeth. "Yowch. Tell me

there was nothing that ugly behind the ending of your engagement with Laura."

"No, nothing like that," he said easily enough that she believed him. "We were young. It wouldn't have lasted."

The music faded into another slow song, and they kept on swaying.

"So what is your modus operandi with dating now? Or do you exclusively bail out women in need of wedding dates so long as they pay your room and travel?"

"Believe it or not, you are my first. Typically, I just… date. I don't have any weird rules or anything, but I don't ask for more. And if she does…" He shook his head.

"So you sleep with these women and then leave a trail of broken hearts when they start wanting more?"

"First of all, there aren't that many of them and few leave brokenhearted, so stop making me sound like a lothario." He tugged her so that they were dancing cheek to cheek and lowered his lips to her ear. "Secondly, you didn't ask for more. I did."

He pulled away and pegged her with a look that said, *There you go.*

Andy digested that information, feeling like it was substantial in a way that it wasn't before.

"You haven't wanted more with the women you've dated since college, but now, after only a weekend with me, you know you do?"

"I know I'm not ready to stop talking to you. Or kissing you. Or sharing a bed with you. So I guess my answer is yes. After this weekend, I *know* I'm not through with you."

There it was. Out loud.

Right about now he should be shaking and nervous the way he'd been when he was watching the wedding procession and eyeing Andy like she might be the cause of his pending breakdown.

But he didn't feel that way. He felt like pulling her closer and inhaling her cinnamon scent.

So he did.

He clasped her back and held her to his chest and let his lips hover just over hers. Her fingers wrapped around his neck, and when she slid them into his hair, he had to smile.

"I'm not sure what to say about any of this except the truth." Vulnerability danced in her eyes but she didn't look away. His brave girl.

"Hit me. I can handle it."

"I've never had a relationship like this with anyone."

"You mean fake for the sake of your family?" he teased.

"No." But she smiled like he'd intended. "I trust you, Gage. Maybe more than I should, but I'm acting on instinct whenever I'm with you. Which is probably why I haven't denied myself much where you're concerned."

"That makes me sound like an indulgence and I really, *really* like that."

"You are an indulgence. And I never indulge."

He'd bet. Every lean curve on her not only reflected good genes but also suggested a rigid workout regimen and being mindful of every calorie she ate.

"Especially in the bedroom," she whispered before covering his lips with a soft kiss.

"Check, please," he muttered, only half kidding.

"I'm going to visit the ladies' room." The song ended and the couples on the dance floor moved away. Perfect timing.

"I'm going to the bar, where I'll grab a water and dump it over my head." When she laughed, he added, "And down my pants."

"I'll meet you over there."

But when they parted, he didn't want to let her go, holding her hand until the last possible moment when her fingers slipped from his.

"Sap," he muttered to himself, quelling the panicky feeling in his belly before it bloomed in his chest.

So, he'd asked to keep seeing her. So what? He didn't promise her forever. He could be with Andy and not end up like Flynn and Sabrina.

Gage wasn't done with her yet, and that was enough for him. They were in a safe space to continue riding the middle until it made sense not to be together any more. There was no reason to believe what they had would doom him to forever.

And there was no way to deny that her agreement to keep doing what they were doing made him damn glad he'd brought it up.

Andy walked from the frigid air-conditioned building into the warm, welcome summer breeze of the tent.

She moved to her table to grab her purse and found her sister Vanessa cradling a half-full glass of white wine and looking unhappy, which seemed to be her normal expression. Ness had always been a serious sort. Andy had that in common with her sister, but she wasn't pessimistic, as evidenced by the conversation she'd just had with Gage.

He wanted more. She wanted more. It wasn't a bad way to strike a bargain, either—he'd held her on the dance floor while telling her he'd suffered an ill-fated engagement. And that pact. She'd have made a similar deal with her girlfriends if she'd come that close to matrimony and then had her heart broken.

Andy took a swig from her water glass, lingering next to Ness for a moment.

"Everything all right?" She probably shouldn't ask, but she loved Vanessa, grumpy or no.

"It's always like that in the beginning," her sister responded darkly. Ness gestured with her wineglass to Gwen and Garrett, who were all smiles while dancing to a swing song. "The infatuation and love…and *blindness*. Then a few years go by and what's left is disillusionment and disappointment."

Andy followed Ness's gaze to where Alec stood chatting at the bar with Kenny and Gage, the three of them looking chummy. Andy lowered into the white folding chair next to her sister and leaned in. "Are you and Alec okay?"

Ness's mouth hardened into a flat line. For a moment she looked as if she might cry, but she blinked and jerked her face around, her expression flat but still pretty.

"I don't mean this in an unkind way, Andrea," Ness said, and Andy felt her back stiffen with dread. "But what you have with Gage is fleeting. So enjoy him. Enjoy the sex. The rapt excitement whenever you two lock eyes. But don't become entrenched. Don't put yourself in the position of being in a relationship you can't escape. And whatever you do, don't involve paperwork."

"We're…not planning to" was all that Andy could muster as a response.

"Save yourself." Ness finished the remaining wine in her glass and stood. "I'm getting a refill. Want one?"

Andy shook her head, shocked by…well, pretty much everything her sister had just said.

She'd thought Ness and Alec were doing fine. Thought they were happy, even. Granted, Andy hadn't seen them together much this weekend.

A niggle of doubt crept forward. Ness wasn't wrong. Even if one does make it to the altar, the ultimate step in any relationship, everything could still fall apart. And if that was the case, what could any of them count on? She stole a glance at Garrett and Gwen. How long would they be happy?

How long will Gage and I be happy?

Another peek over at Alec proved there was more under the surface than Andy had previously noticed. His smile fell when he met his wife's glare across the tent, his shoulders lifting as if bracing for bad news. Ness approached the bartender to order and Alec curtly smiled at Gage and Kenny, excusing himself before walking off in the opposite direction.

"Oh, Vanessa." Andy sagged in her seat, sad for both her sister and brother-in-law.

They'd been married, what, five years? Six? Wasn't that the point when you could relax in a relationship? Weren't things supposed to get better and better? A closer look at Kelli and Boyd showed they were having no qualms about their own marriage, slow-dancing despite a fast song playing. Even Carroll, who was shimmying with Amber, paused to blow Kenny a kiss that he pretended to catch in his fist. And obviously, Gwen and Garrett were at the peak of happiness today.

Gage parted from Kenny with a wave and walked toward Andy, his sights set on her. He held a glass of whiskey—or some kind of brown liquid—with a single, large ice cube floating in it.

"Danced out?" he asked as he sat next to her.

"Just…resting." She didn't want to air Ness's dirty laundry. It wasn't her story to tell.

"You sure?" He swept her hair aside and kissed her bare shoulder.

She wasn't sure. Not really. But at the same time she wasn't willing to mire herself in her siblings' problems. What would come of Andy and Gage remained to be seen.

They weren't five or six years into a relationship potentially circling the drain. Hell, they hadn't even put a timeframe on what they had. Continuing to see each other back in Seattle might not last a month.

She wasn't willing to stop kissing him or sleeping with him or enjoying him just because the clock struck midnight on Gwen and Garrett's wedding. No matter what the future brought.

"I'm positive," she said instead of sharing her tumultuous thoughts.

She stole a kiss from Gage, letting her lips linger over his, palming his scruffy jaw and then slipping her fingers into the open placket of his shirt.

There was one surefire way to dissolve the worry Ness had planted in the back of Andy's mind, and that was to do what she and Gage were best at doing.

By the time she ended the kiss, he was on the literal edge of his seat, his breaths hectic and erratic.

"Want to get out of here for a few minutes, have some fun, and then sneak back in and eat some cake?" she asked in her best sex-kitten voice.

"Hell, yeah, I do." He stood and pulled her with him, thrusting her purse into her arms. "Lead the way."

Seventeen

Gage pressed a kiss to the left of Andy's spine, then to the right of it, continuing the line of kisses as he drew the zipper on her dress up, up, up until she was dressed.

She sighed, contented, and admittedly sort of lost. Not literally. They might've stolen off to the woods for a quickie disguised as a nature walk, but they weren't far from the festivities. She could see the lights twinkling from the tent and hear the faint sounds of the band playing.

"That was a first," she said when Gage kissed her shoulder.

"Outdoor sex?" He scooted closer to where she sat in the grass and wrapped his arm around her waist. "I like hearing that."

"What about you?" She shifted to face him, her legs damp from the dew. Now that night had fallen and the sun was down, the humidity sitting in the air had fallen to the ground. She recognized her error in asking when a firm line found his lips. "Oh. I guess… Never mind."

"Not what you think, Strawberry." He tucked her hair behind one ear.

She'd worn a clip holding that side up earlier but had no idea where it'd disappeared to since her and Gage's...*dalliance*. Having sex outside should've felt needy and shallow, but it had been deeper to her.

"The truth is I'm experiencing a few first times with you, too," he said. "You're different."

She opened her mouth to give him a snarky "I know," but he cut her off with a finger to her lips.

"Ah-ah. Your differences are all good ones. When I'm with you, it's not about the setting or the act." He tipped her chin. "It's about what it feels like to be with you. Like I can't get enough."

Nervous at his admission, she swallowed. "Don't go endangering your pact now." The mention of him never being serious with a woman was supposed to ease her nerves and his, too.

"The pact? You think you're in danger of being proposed to?" He canted one eyebrow and gave her an easy smile.

"God, no. What was the catalyst for Flynn reinstating it, anyway?"

"Veronica. He proposed to his first wife pretty quickly. They'd only known each other a month before tying the knot. Flynn believes if he hadn't married her, they would've imploded naturally, and way before an ugly divorce, or her cheating on him with his brother. A lot of pain could've been avoided."

"Garrett and Gwen had a quick engagement." Andy cast a worried glance in the direction of the tent. "Did Flynn and Veronica start out as happy as Garrett and Gwen?"

"No." That made her feel marginally better for her youngest sister. "Veronica and Flynn were never compatible where it counted."

"He and Sabrina seem to be on the same page."

"Those two." Gage emitted an amused sniff. "They've been best friends since college. Sabrina predated Reid and me by a few weeks. Somehow Sabrina and Flynn had circled each other for years. Too distracted by dating people other than each other, I guess."

"That's sweet." And it made sense. A relationship built over years and years had a strong foundation. "They seem solid. I can see why he didn't stick to his pact... But you did."

"Yes, the Brit and I carry that torch." A self-deprecating smile decorated Gage's handsome face. "For me it was about not being engaged again. For Reid, well, who the hell knows? He was in no matter what. He's never been one to get too attached."

"I know what that's like." When she found Gage regarding her with a curious head tilt, she explained. "It's hard to get attached and then be left behind. If you're not careful, your identity can become wrapped up in someone else."

"You're the independent sort."

"As are you."

He seesawed his head like he was turning over the thought. "Not exactly. I'm a team player. I like having someone. I like dating but I rarely turn and burn them like Reid."

"You're a serial monogamist."

"I don't know about that. But I can definitely feel when I'm getting in too deep, or when she's getting in too deep, and that's when I button things up."

"Sounds sort of awful."

"You mean I sound awful now that you know how shallow I am?"

"No. I mean it sounds like an awful way to live. Like you're too afraid to keep going when there's potential for a real connection."

He watched her in silence for so long that a breeze swelled and she became aware of the music again. It also made her aware of the party they were missing.

The truth was she was afraid to pursue more with Gage, too. She'd never pursued deep connections in the past, even with her sisters. She'd gradually accepted that those sorts of relationships were for other people—people other than the Ice Queen, though that nickname had lost some of its sting.

She was changing, little by little, and the man next to her in the damp grass was a big reason why. She didn't know what that meant for them, but she did know that she wasn't giving him up just yet.

Outside of the "wedding bubble," and when they stopped pretending, did they have a prayer of making it last?

She wasn't sure that was the right question, considering Gage had made a pact never to marry anyone. She wasn't in the market for a husband, either, but she'd be lying if she said she'd never imagined what marriage might look like for her. How could she hang any hopes on what she and Gage had together, knowing that he'd walk away with hardly a second glance?

Since those thoughts were too big for her, and much too big for the end of a wedding reception, she shut them down.

"Come on." She stood and extended a palm to Gage, who was still sitting, his back to a particularly stout linden tree. "I need one more glass of champagne."

One more glass of champagne, one more dance and at least one more evening in Gage's arms before she lost her glass slipper at midnight.

Then it'd be airport, home, work and…whatever else followed. She hoped he still fancied her as much as he did in this moment.

Only time would tell.

Gregg and Lee Fleming had been residents of Leavenworth, Washington, for every year that Gage had been alive. The town was rich in Bavarian/German ancestry and boasted a festival every year to celebrate.

Gage's parents had been coworkers at the Leavenworth fish hatchery until recently, when his mother retired to start her own online business crafting quilts and pillows. His father still worked there and loved every moment of it, even though Gage had paid their mortgage off last year so that his father could retire. Stubborn old man.

Leavenworth was a shortish two-hour jaunt from Seattle, so Gage saw his parents often enough for his tastes.

His sister, Drew, admitted she'd like to see them a little *less* often, but Gage had goaded her into hosting the family visit this time around.

Drew's apartment was in a nice, newish building in Seattle teeming with millennials and career-driven singles. She'd ended up as career-driven as Gage as it turned out, the worry of ending up at the hatchery a worst-case scenario for her as well.

"Mom is driving me crazy," Drew said in a harsh whisper as she pulled the lid off a pineapple upside-down cake their mother had brought for dessert.

Dinner had already been consumed—fish tacos, of course. Gage's father insisted on bringing his hard work to the table even though Gage had eaten enough fish to sustain him for a lifetime.

"I told her *three* times that Devin couldn't come to dinner because his schedule is too demanding and still she accuses me of 'hiding' him. I don't know why they want to meet him so badly anyway. He's a chef, not a celebrity."

Gage bit his lip. To Drew, chefs *were* celebrities. She was a public relations manager for various restaurants under the corporate umbrella of Fig & Truffle. She managed soft openings mostly and was a self-proclaimed foodie. She poked at the pineapple upside-down cake and frowned.

"I should've had Devin make crème brûlée."

"Don't be a snob."

She stuck her tongue out at him and he smiled. She left

the room with a confidence that didn't used to be there. He admired the hell out of her for it—his sister hadn't always been so sure of herself.

She'd always been petite, though, which had been her downfall when she was younger. Her curvy figure had been named a "weight problem" by their less-than-eloquent mother, and Drew had referred to herself as "chubby" which showed even less eloquence.

Gage might have noticed his sister looked different at age sixteen versus age twenty, but it wasn't as if the fifty or so pounds she'd lost had made an iota of difference in how much he loved her.

He was glad she went after what she wanted. She'd always contended that good food was her number one passion, and she wouldn't sacrifice a pat of real butter for margarine no matter what health magazines suggested. She'd balanced her fitness goals and her passion, never indulging in too much of either one. Gage couldn't be prouder of his only sister.

He turned to resume making his and Drew's drinks, not the least bit intimidated by the fancy espresso maker in her apartment—they had one like it in the executive break room at Monarch. It made him laugh that while her dining room table was a scarred hand-me-down from their parents, her espresso maker was top-of-the-line and probably cost close to what it would take to replace that entire dining set twice over. Drew had her priorities straight, Gage thought with a smile.

Their parents had retired to the living room, which was connected to the kitchen. Drew came from that direction now to grab dessert plates as he finished their espressos.

He handed Drew one of the petite cups and she sagged against the countertop. "Why aren't they giving you a hard time about meeting who you're dating?"

"Because I never tell them I'm dating."

The TV was blaring so loudly that he was confident neither Mom nor Dad could overhear the discussion in the kitchen. Fine by him. The less they knew about his love life, the better.

"You would've been smart to keep Devin to yourself. Or Ronnie, for that matter," he said of her last bad breakup. Devin didn't have much more potential than Ronnie in that arena. Gage had met Devin once and, culinary degree aside, had determined he was a self-indulgent butthead, and that was putting it kindly.

"I *like* talking about my feelings." She sipped her espresso and her eyebrows jumped. "Mmm! This is delicious. So, big bro, do tell. Are you seeing anyone?"

He debated his answer for one sip, then two, from his espresso cup. Finally, he opted to level with Drew, since they'd been nothing but honest with each other for most of their lives. "Her name is Andy. I met her at work and she asked me to attend her sister's Ohio wedding with her last weekend as a favor."

As he spoke, his sister's eyebrows climbed her forehead until they were lost in her mahogany, previously mouse-brown hair. He hadn't gotten used to the darker hue yet.

"You went to a wedding in Ohio?"

"Yes."

"And then what?" She smiled like a loon.

"And then we came back to Seattle."

"Do you like her?"

"It'd be weird to attend a wedding with someone I didn't like, wouldn't it?"

"So coy. Where is she?"

"She's working."

"Monarch isn't open on Sunday."

"She works for herself. She was freelancing at Monarch." He and Drew had a mini standoff. "It's too soon to bring her in to meet the fam." *If ever.*

"I can't remember the last time you brought a girl around to 'meet the fam.'"

She was right. It hadn't been something he'd even considered. He couldn't say that he was considering it now, but when he'd mentioned to Andy he had a family thing today, he'd briefly entertained the idea of inviting her. He didn't, of course, because that would've been insane.

"What girl?" Their mother, Lee, strode into the kitchen.

Enter: the reason he hadn't invited Andy. His very loving, oft-prying mother.

"I want to hear all about her. Can you Face-Call her so we can meet her?"

"It's called FaceTime, Mom," Drew said.

"Face-Call, FaceTime. Whatever. Pull her up on your mobile phone so we can say hello."

Gage opened his mouth to say "hell, no," but their mother interrupted with "Do you have any real coffee, Drew darling? I don't like expresso."

Drew ignored their mother's mispronunciation of *espresso* and pulled a "real" coffee maker out of a lower cabinet. As she set up the drip pot, she smiled over her shoulder. "I don't think Gage is ready to introduce us to his girlfriend."

"She's not my girlfriend," he grumbled, sounding like a less mature version of himself.

"Well, why on earth not?" their mother asked. "The same reason you won't introduce us to Devin? Are we that embarrassing?"

Gage grinned at his sister, content to have the topic swivel to her. "Yeah, Drew. Where *is* Devin tonight?"

"Working," she said between her teeth.

"Well, so is Andy."

"Oh! Her name is Andy! Isn't that darling?" Lee clapped her hands. "Tell me about her while Drew makes some real coffee."

Lee wrapped her arms around Gage's arm and dragged him out of the kitchen, peppering him with questions the whole way.

He couldn't be sure but he could swear he heard his sister's tinkling laughter follow him from the room.

Eighteen

The door to Flynn Parker's top-floor penthouse opened and Andy thought for a second she'd walked into a tomb. Gray walls, black floors and dark cabinetry greeted her from the kitchen, the room closest to the door. A few flickering jar candles on the surface further reinforced the "tomb" decor.

The feeling inside was nothing like a tomb, however, and neither were the people. Andy didn't typically hang out with a group of friends. She was a loner by nature, maybe in part due to her upbringing, and rarely spent this much time with anyone when the hours weren't being billed. Conversely, Gage had a strong network of friends, which was no surprise given his abundant charm.

She'd been working like a madwoman since they'd returned to Washington, but she'd made sure to allow time for Gage and his friends. She'd even sent a nice bottle of bourbon to him at the office. She was simply happy. And "simply" anything in a relationship had been an elusive beast until now.

"Andy!" Sabrina, dressed beautifully in a bright red knee-length dress, wore a smile that was both wide and infectious. "I'm so glad you could come. I wasn't sure if you would."

Honest as ever. Andy gave a demure smile, aware of Gage's palm warming her back. They'd been home for a little over a week now and things were surprisingly…good.

They'd been back to work, back to their own beds. Andy had seen Gage twice last week. Once for a late dinner that, thanks to a troublesome new client, had happened at 8:45 p.m., and once when she went to his apartment for what was supposed to be pizza and a movie and had ended up being pizza, half a movie and sex on the sofa.

"Well, you did corner her, love," Reid said, stepping into view to pour a glass of white wine, then turning to hand it to a blonde woman standing at his left elbow. "Kylie, this is Andrea Payne. Andy, Kylie Marker."

The blonde gave Andy a limp handshake and accepted her wine. "I like your…pants."

The compliment was forced, and so was Andy's smile. She'd worn simple black slacks and a pale blue silk shirt for work and hadn't had time to change. Kylie, on the other hand, looked like she'd been poured into her little black dress, her curvy form testing the seams. She was exactly the kind of woman Andy would expect to see Reid with, but somehow not… Reid's shrewd sense of humor and elegant wit seemed better suited for a woman who could match him blow for blow. Then again, according to Gage, Reid wasn't in the market for a challenge.

Anyway.

Andy had been near Monarch today, so she'd stopped by under the guise of "checking on the sales team" but in reality had wanted to see Gage. She'd been busy since she'd been home and was trying to fit him in when she could.

Missing someone was a new concept. She normally had her work to keep her warm at night. When Sabrina had poked her head into his office to invite him over to Flynn's penthouse for "Hump Day drinks," she'd swept her hand to include Andy in the invitation. Andy had automatically refused but Sabrina had instructed Gage to bring her with him.

Andy liked Sabrina. Liked all of them, truthfully. She hadn't expected to pull a lover out of offering to hire Gage as her fake boyfriend much less three new friends, but somehow she had.

"Red or white?" Gage asked her, helping himself to the line of wine bottles sitting on the countertop.

"White, please."

"That's what I have!" Kylie exclaimed with a grin. Reid arched one eyebrow like maybe he'd just now realized he'd settled for less than his equal.

"How about champagne?" Sabrina sent a saucy wink to Flynn, who was already moving for the fridge. She bounced over to the cabinet and began pulling out flutes to line up on the countertop.

"What's this, then?" Reid asked.

"An announcement of some sort, apparently." Gage relinquished the wineglasses and stepped back, waiting while Flynn popped the cork off not one, but two bottles of Dom Pérignon.

"We're getting married!" Sabrina said as Flynn started pouring. She reached into her pocket and pulled out a shining diamond ring.

Whoa.

Andy suddenly felt out of place for an announcement this big.

The moment Sabrina slid the ring onto her finger, Kylie was on her like white on rice.

"It's beautiful." Kylie hugged Sabrina around the neck and Reid gently removed his date, who was now dabbing her eyes. "Sorry. I'm so moved when people get engaged. Or pregnant. Are you pregnant?"

"Um. No. But thanks for asking," Sabrina said with a wince.

Kylie shot a loving look up at Reid, and he turned the color of his sage-green tie. Yes, he'd recognized his short-sightedness when it came to Kylie. She was hearts and wedding bells and Reid wasn't looking for anything more than a good time.

"Congratulations, Sabrina. You two are good together and I'm happy for you." Andy accepted a champagne flute from Flynn. "Tell us how you asked."

Always a popular conversation starter in this situation.

"She was painting," Flynn said, his low baritone not hinting at what a softie he was on the inside. Andy had seen him around Sabrina at work. He virtually melted whenever she was near.

"He brought me a little paper sack from my favorite art store and when I pulled out the new paintbrush—" Sabrina couldn't finish, her throat clogging as tears came forth as easily as her smile.

"The ring was on the paintbrush. I said some stuff. The end." Flynn wrapped an arm around his fiancée and kissed her forehead while Sabrina swiped at her eyes.

Seriously. How sweet were they?

"Congrats, man," Gage said. Reid chimed in, too, lifting his flute and toasting their friends.

"Well, that was a surprise." Gage corralled Andy to one side, his hand on her back. Whenever he touched her, the stresses of the day vanished.

"A surprise? Even I could've guessed that was coming."

"I *suspected*. I wasn't sure."

"I like your friends. You're all sort of puzzling."

"Meaning?"

"Sabrina," Andy said, lowering her voice as they stepped farther into the apartment, "is so quirky you'd expect her to wear a peasant dress and flowers in her hair, but she favors fancy dresses. Flynn is gruff but it's for show, although this penthouse does make me question if he has a soul…or if he stores it in a trick wall somewhere in the penthouse."

Gage chuckled. "Sab's working on that. He inherited this place from his father. Emmons wasn't the warmest of men."

The painting over the mantel featured a pair of chickadees sitting side by side on a Japanese maple tree. The warm golds, blues and pinks were adorable and light and completely out of place in this house.

"I'm guessing that artistry was Sabrina's doing?"

"Definitely. Wait'll she moves in here. Her apartment is the equivalent of a peasant dress. Come on. I know you've got more to say." He made a give-it-to-me gesture.

"Okay. Reid is British class and pomp, the textbook playboy, but there's something about him that makes me wonder if he's acting. Though I'm not sure *he's* aware that he's acting."

"That's what every woman says about him. They've all tried to crack the Reid Code." They both looked at Kylie. "She's going to be disappointed when she doesn't succeed."

"Terribly. I can tell already she's not the one. Reid needs a woman who challenges him."

"To duels?"

"Challenges what he knows about himself." She gave Gage a playful shove.

"And what about me puzzles you, Andy?" He paired the question with his hands on her hips as he moved behind her to study the Seattle skyline out the window. In the background, his friends' laughter and banter continued.

"You were engaged before and made an unbreakable pact never to be married," she told Gage's reflection, "and yet you volunteered to come with me to a wedding and then didn't break things off after." She shrugged. "*Puzzling.*"

"I needed your expertise."

"Is that why I'm here right now?" Was she a version

of Kylie? A temporary placeholder before he moved on to someone else?

"Andy."

"You like me more than anyone ever has, Gage." She spun in his arms and even though there was a time she would've died before doing something as casual as drape her arms on a man's shoulders within sight of a crowd, she did it anyway.

"Good." He placed a gentle kiss on her lips.

"Don't tell me you two are next," Reid said with a groan.

"Aw, but they're so cute!" Kylie chimed in.

Andy and Gage separated and she studied the floor for a beat. He had a way of making her forget where she was— who she was. Was she becoming one half of a whole? The idea of her being with anyone intrinsically was foreign, and after talking with Ness, frankly a little frightening.

"I know about the pact. He's safe," Andy said with a soft smile.

"Pact?" Kylie asked, her brow denting with a frown.

Ruh-roh.

Reid's nostrils flared. He sent Andy a withering glare and she mouthed the word *sorry.*

"Kylie, let's you and I step outside for a moment." Reid took a long look at the balcony and seemed to reconsider. "Actually, let's go out into the hallway. You'll catch a chill."

"In July?" Kylie asked as Reid hustled her out of the penthouse.

"I don't think he was comfortable telling Kylie about the pact with the prospect of a balcony and a long drop to the street," Gage said.

"Right." Andy's smile faded. "It's a strange pact for the three of you, considering your goals are so different."

"You didn't see Flynn when he was married." Gage shook his head.

"I didn't see you engaged to what's-her-face, either."

"She was a lot like you." This from Flynn, who strolled into his living room, his fiancée, and her million-watt smile, by his side. "Driven. Ambitious."

"But *not* like you," Sabrina offered, "in that she was about as warm as…"

"This penthouse?" Andy supplied.

"Exactly." Sabrina's smile was approving, her eyes narrow as she studied Gage. When her gaze snapped to Andy, it said *we'll talk later*.

Andy nodded. She was looking forward to learning more of Gage's secrets.

"Give it to me." Andy refilled Sabrina's flute in the kitchen.

Reid had returned from the hallway without Kylie. He told everyone that she'd left because she had an early morning tomorrow. No one believed him, but no one asked him to explain. Now the guys had vanished to parts unknown in the five-thousand-square-foot penthouse to shoot pool, while Sabrina and Andy lingered around the drinks and snacks.

"Give what to you?" Sabrina dragged a cucumber slice through the hummus and offered it. "This?"

"The way you were looking at Gage earlier, I could swear you came to some sort of conclusion."

Sabrina covered her smile by eating the cucumber slice, and then took a sip of her champagne before speaking.

"Gage and I have been friends for a long time. Almost as long as I've known Flynn. I've seen him date, and I remember Laura, although that was a long time ago. I know that he's charming, relaxed, a great date."

"He is all of those things," Andy said carefully.

"And yet with you—" Sabrina tilted her head "—he's serious, too. I can tell by the way he looks at you that he's not as light in his approach."

Uncomfortable and almost sorry she'd asked, Andy squirmed. "I'm fairly serious myself. I can see why he'd react accordingly."

Sabrina donned her best Mona Lisa smile before humming to herself.

"You're falling for him."

Andy coughed on her next sip of champagne. "What?" she croaked, trying to recover from inhaling her Dom.

Sabrina's knowing expression didn't change as she dragged a carrot through the hummus. "I can tell by the way you act around him. The way you look at him. Not in the same way Kylie looked at Reid, which was...*needy*."

Agreed.

"But like you're seeing a future without an end date."

"I'm in no danger of being proposed to by Gage," Andy sputtered. She was thrown by Sabrina's suggestion that she was "falling" for him. Thrown because she wasn't that well-versed in relationships. She was enjoying herself, that was all. But falling for him? Hmm...

"That dumb pact." Sabrina rolled her eyes. "They act like it's carved in stone. Then the right girl comes along and they learn it's more like chalk on a blackboard."

That made sense for Sabrina and Flynn. They'd been friends since college—best friends. For Gage and Andy it was different. They'd known each other for what, a handful of weeks?

"You never know," was all Sabrina said.

But the lingering glance to her shining engagement ring told Andy everything she needed to know about what was going on in the brunette's mind.

Sabrina had changed Flynn's mind about the pact. If Andy and Gage were serious about having a future, could she change his mind, too?

Nineteen

"**W**here's Andrea tonight?" Reid lifted his beer and pegged Gage with a meaningful look. They sat side by side at the bar they usually haunted, though it was fairly dead for a Thursday night.

"Working."

Andy worked a lot. He'd had no idea how much he wouldn't see her when they returned to Seattle. But she was never too far away, either texting or visiting in between busy nights.

"Shouldn't you two be celebrating your three-week anniversary tonight?" Reid smirked.

"Very funny." Gage frowned.

"Refill?" Shelly, the bartender, gestured to Reid, whose glass was empty. The bar's overhead lights glinted off the ring on her finger, practically throwing sparks.

"That's new, love." Reid took her hand and turned the ring this way and that. "Are you spoken for?"

"I've *been* spoken for, but I suppose this makes it official. Bryan proposed this weekend." She beamed, her eyes sparkling like her new diamond ring.

That was a giant coincidence. Flynn had asked Sabrina this week. Love was in the air, Gage thought, shifting uncomfortably in his seat. He'd been flirting with Shelly the night he met Andy and he had no idea at the time that Shelly was someone else's.

Reid ordered two more beers and Gage tipped his draft back to drain the contents of his glass. Might as well have another.

"Soon I'll be the only keeper of the pact," Reid said with a melodramatic sigh.

"What's that supposed to mean?" Gage asked as Shelly delivered their beers and cleared away their empty mugs.

"Andy sent you an expensive bottle of liquor. To the office."

"It was a bottle of bourbon. Don't sound so foreboding."

"It means she was thinking about you. And then she unexpectedly dropped by before coming along with you to Flynn's." Reid's tone was conspiracy-theory low. "She's getting comfortable, mate. *Girlfriendy.*"

"What are you talking about?" Gage laughed to dismiss the whole "girlfriendy" thing, but he had to admit she sort of was and it wasn't bothering him as much as it should.

"With anyone else you'd be letting her down gently. But you haven't yet, have you?"

"Not yet." The words settled into the pit of Gage's stomach. He wasn't sure why. He'd been the one to suggest they keep seeing each other after Andy's sister's wedding. He'd been the one to insist on her coming to Flynn's that night. *Where another engagement was announced*, he thought nervously as he caught the glint off Shelly's ring.

"Keeper of the pact," Reid announced, lifting his beer again.

Reid was being ridiculous. Gage was no closer to proposing to Andy than he was to climbing on top of this bar and stripping.

And yet…

Something had been welling up inside him. An uncomfortable…what was the word? *Rightness*.

He felt *right* with Andy and he hadn't had that feeling in a long, long time. And never this soon. Even with Laura, he'd been acting more on expectations than emotion.

Why was that?

"It's in the air," Reid said, echoing Gage's earlier thought. He sneered. "Love. You've not caught it, have you?"

"Love?" Gage laughed. "No. Definitely not."

If love was like an airborne virus, he could write off that weird pit-of-his-gut feeling to proximity. He'd been at a weekend wedding with Andy where every event dripped with romance. And now two of his closest friends were engaged to be married. Romance tended to be like glitter. It stuck to you, undetected unless the light hit it just right, and almost impossible to get rid of once you noticed it.

Was Andy like glitter?

Yes. And no.

She wasn't annoying or clingy. She wasn't staying at his place or leaving her stuff there. She was good on her own and didn't need his reassurance. But she was different than she'd been when they first met. She was independent but including him in her life.

Like he'd asked. Because he'd caught the airborne glitter virus and was infected. He swiped at his sweaty brow.

Possibly he was freaking out.

"It's not too late," his British friend warned, his tone scarily serious. "You've been down this road with plenty of women. If it's time to insert some distance, you know how to do it. Is it time?"

Gage let out a choking sound. "You make it sound like there's a lot of them. I date less than you do."

Deflection was the best tactic whenever backed into a corner.

"I date because I'm great at it. You date because you like being part of a couple."

Gage blinked at his friend. He liked having company, yes, but the "part of a couple" accusation wasn't true.

Was it?

Andy had accused him of being a serial monogamist. He wasn't like Reid, showing up with a new girl at every event, but neither was he Flynn and Sabrina, attached at the hip. Gage was somewhere in the middle. A "gray area" when it came to women in general and relationships at large.

"You're quite good at having girlfriends. Women like you so bloody much."

"They're not girlfriends." Aware he sounded like a twelve-year-old, Gage stopped slumping and sat straighter on his stool.

Reid smirked. "Well, they're different from hookups, which is what I'm best at."

"You're bragging about being forgettable, Reid."

"Not forgettable. Just...*unkeepable*." He nodded, happy with his own conclusion.

Gage had sworn to uphold the pact in part for Flynn, but also for himself. After his engagement imploded and Laura left, Gage never wanted to feel that unmoored again.

Success was important to him in all things. In school, he'd graduated with a 4.0 GPA—even though it meant working harder to lift his suffering grades. When he dated Laura and determined she was as ambitious as he was, it was a perfect match. He'd *known* she was The One.

Until he didn't.

Laura had come at him with a whopper of an announcement just one month after announcing their engagement. He wasn't good enough for her. Wasn't as successful as she wanted him to be. Worse, she said he never would be. *"You don't want to be in a partnership where your wife is earning more than you, Gage."*

It rankled him that she thought he'd care about how much money she earned, and how it compared to his salary. That he'd be that shallow. And then it rankled him all over again that she'd basically hobbled him, telling him he couldn't be as successful as her, when she knew damn well that success and Gage went hand in hand.

Nothing he'd said to that effect had changed Laura's mind. Her mind was made up when she'd invited him to that diner for lunch. She'd set the stage for a public breakup, and had pulled out an actual bullet-pointed list. She'd read from the notebook, never stopping to look at him.

On the surface they'd seemed like a good match, but Laura found him too "casual" and not serious enough for her taste. "We're too different," she'd told him. He'd learned that day that she was right about that. Gage was a human being with real feelings and a heart, while Laura was a cyborg with faulty programming.

It was the biggest failure of his life, that relationship— the engagement that never produced a wedding. He'd been certain of a future with Laura. One that stood the test of time like his parents' marriage. Being that wrong had thrown him. It wasn't any wonder he'd leaped into the pact the way he did…twice.

Failure in business happened, of course. He wasn't so delusional he thought himself impervious to stepping in it now and again. But failing with relationships was trickier to pull out of. His grades had temporarily dipped when Laura and he split. His social life exploded, and he'd chosen to go to parties instead of study. Hookups were a tack he tried and failed at. He didn't like meaningless flings. And yet he didn't want to be roped in again by a woman who promised forever and backed out before giving him a chance to be a success.

Laura thought they were too different? Fine. He'd date fun-loving women who valued him for who he was. He'd back out before it became too much for either of them. It was hard at first, learning how to let them down easy and walk away whole, but he'd been successful at that, too.

Then came Andy.

Independent, driven, successful Andy.

Vulnerable, open, *fascinating* Andy.

The idea of them splitting sent his mind reeling. Made his stomach toss. He'd suggested they not end things and she trusted him. He cared about her and didn't want her hurt. Would she carry his rejection with her like a wound? Or would she harness her driven, independent side and soar without him?

Option B was the *only* option. He couldn't even think about leaving a scar as deep as Matthew Higgins and his "Ice Queen" comments. Andy was better than that.

But she was also better than sticking around with a guy who wouldn't give her what she ultimately deserved.

Forever.

He'd seen the way she looked at her sister, Gwen, at the wedding. Andy might not be able to admit it to herself yet, but Gage could tell she was a woman who wanted to be married someday. And he couldn't—*wouldn't*—allow himself to take those vows.

A sigh came from the depths. He knew what he had to do. He couldn't let Andy settle for less than she deserved any more than he could string her along. Their relationship would end eventually. And maybe if he ended it sooner it'd save them both a lot of heartache.

His chest seized at the thought of not seeing her or holding her again. Of not kissing her ever again. He'd miss her like hell. He already felt like part of him was tangled up in part of her. He couldn't let his unreliable heart call the shots, though, arguably, he'd already let it call a few.

No part of this was going to be easy. He already cared

about Andy ten times, hell, *one hundred times*, more than he'd cared about Laura. And he'd been *in love* with Laura.

Or so he'd thought.

It was possible, even probable, that he'd been fooled into thinking what he was feeling for Andy was deep, unfathomed and long-lasting. As if he'd been glamoured by the couples-in-love around him and had acted on what he thought was instinct but was more...conditioning.

And if he didn't proceed very carefully, Andy could fall into the same trap.

At his elbow, Gage's phone buzzed with a text message from her.

I have dinner for us. It's Thai. Your place or mine?

Gage's chest tightened when he thought of Andy's bright eyes and strawberry-blond hair. When he thought of what he had to do he knew he had to do it before either or both of them said or did things that were unable to be taken back.

He realized now that he'd made a mistake not ending this after the wedding. He wasn't too big of a man to admit he was wrong, even if he had let things go on for far too long. Andy deserved that same respect.

My place, he texted back.

His home turf would be better. Then she could storm out like he guessed she would. Drive to a girlfriend's house and curse his name a thousand times over. There was no time like the present to recover from the misstep—before she expected more than he'd be able to give. Before she got in any deeper, or he gave her any *wronger* of an impression about himself.

He pulled money out of his wallet to pay and Reid's eyebrows rose. "Duty calls? Or should I say booty calls?"

Gage was so miserable he couldn't crack even the smallest of smiles. "You're not in the pact alone, Reid."

"No?"

"No." Gage shoved his untouched beer in front of Reid and nodded. "I know what I need to do."

He'd been pretending, which was fun at first, but now it'd gone too far. It was time to wrap up this farce with Andy.

Past time.

Twenty

Andy had never been so cheery. Happy, sure. Contented, absolutely. But joyful, humming a tune as she strolled into the high-rise holding Gage's posh apartment? She couldn't remember ever feeling this buoyant.

She hadn't been very good at balancing her time at work and her time with Gage. Tonight she was going to make it up to him. She was ambitious and she was driven and, frankly, didn't have a lot of experience including another person in her plans.

Andy wanted to include Gage for one simple reason: she loved him.

She was certain of it.

She'd been ordering shrimp pad thai and basil fried rice and it hit her as she paid for their dinner.

For the first time in a long time, she was half of a whole.

As unexpected as it was, and in such a short period of time, she'd fallen in love with Gage Fleming. She hadn't seen it coming but now that it was here, she welcomed it. As much as she contended that she didn't need anyone, she needed him. And what's more was that she didn't mind needing him. It didn't make her feel weaker or less independent. She felt stronger for it.

Love.

She finally was beginning to understand what all the fuss was about.

Excited about her newfound discovery, she'd grinned at the cashier and said, "My boyfriend and I are having dinner together."

The cashier smiled quizzically but wished her well, having no idea the monumental shift that had occurred in the ten minutes Andy sat in the restaurant and waited for her takeout.

Falling in love *was* monumental. And even though it was after nine o'clock, and even though the food was greasy Thai instead of a five-star meal, Andy was certain of her feelings for Gage.

She couldn't wait another second to tell him how he'd changed her. There'd even been a stray thought about how they could tell their grandkids one day about how they'd met. The bar story. It would kill!

Humming and happy, she pushed the number eighteen button in the elevator and rode to Gage's floor. She'd tell him tonight. He deserved to feel as great and whole and happy as she did.

She stepped out and admired her surroundings. The building Gage lived in was historical, with charming woodwork and brass handles on the doors. The lighting fixtures appeared original to the building, though Andy guessed they'd been rewired. Everything functioned and felt modern while at the same time throwing her back several decades. It was remarkable the way history worked. She was making some for Gage and herself tonight.

His apartment door was cracked, the soothing notes of jazz coming from inside. Andy knocked lightly before letting herself in. The entryway opened to a wide living room with a wall of windows letting in the moonlight. The couch was navy with deep red pillows, which had reminded her of Gwen's wedding colors the first time Andy had been here.

It was a sign. She never would've thought that before tonight, but being in love had given her new vision. Who knew what a superpower that could be?

Gage stood in the kitchen beyond the living room, pouring wine into two glasses. Red.

The color of love.

Andy was so excited she was about to burst.

"Your dinner, sir." She set down the paper sack and sidled over to kiss him. He delivered a kiss but his lips were firm and pursed, his brow a furrowed thundercloud.

"You okay?" she asked.

She lifted her wineglass and took a sip, wondering what it was that had turned Gage's mood sour. Work, most likely.

"You go first," she told him. "I had a not-so-great day at the office, too. I'll commiserate with you."

Her smile faded as a look of hurt crossed his features.

"Andy." The way he said her name was ominous. A premonition of something horrible.

The food that had once smelled tantalizing and tempting now caused her stomach to flop like a dying fish.

"I've never lied to you before and I have no intention of starting now."

"Oh?" Her hand shook, and her wineglass with it.

He pulled in a deep breath, paused to drink down half the contents of his glass and then faced her. He put the glass down. Then warm hands braced her biceps and a million alarms rang out in her head.

In a panic, she blurted, "I love you. I realized when I was picking up your shrimp pad thai that we belong together. What we have, this isn't impermanent. This is the real thing. I know it's fast and I know you have that pact, but Flynn ditched the pact for Sabrina. Do you know why?"

Gage's expression teetered on mortified, but for Andy her dam had broken. She couldn't stop talking now that she'd started.

"Flynn realized that being in love with Sabrina was more important than some silly pact," she continued. "Sabrina was someone worth making new decisions for. Flynn wanted to move forward with her because he'd seen a part of her he'd never seen before. *Gage.* That's you and me." She didn't dare slow down until she said the rest. "You were the one who excavated that part of me. I didn't know how to be half of a couple. I didn't know how to be in love. You were the one who opened those doors—who taught me how to love you."

Her voice broke. She swallowed thickly and waited. She'd said what she'd come here to say, and as naively as a virgin bride on her wedding night, she expected him to have come to the same realization as she had. She hadn't even considered that he didn't feel the same way. How could he not?

She saw now that she'd been dead wrong. The evidence was written all over his stricken face.

"Say something." Her voice was a broken whisper, her heart threatening to break right alongside it.

"We went to a wedding together," he said. Bizarrely.

"Yes." She let loose a shaky smile.

"And then Flynn and Sabrina announced their engagement. Shelly's engaged, too, by the way."

"Who?"

"Bartender at From Afar."

"Oh." She wasn't following.

"I was engaged, Andy. And Laura ended that engagement because she didn't believe in us. She was cold and calculated and completely dismissive of who we could've become."

"I'm not." Andy gripped his hands, trying to head off

another argument before it brewed. "I'm forever material. I'm a single Payne sister—the last of my kind. You opened my eyes to the fact that I'm valued and worth it. You opened my eyes to a life outside of my business. You opened my eyes to love."

"I can't love you, Andy. I can't let this go on any longer." His voice was hard and tight, like the words were fighting being spoken. "It's irresponsible."

"You...*can't*?"

"No."

Such a final word. She dropped his hands and he backed away from her a step.

Backed.

Away.

"You weren't supposed to fall in love with me, Andy. Hell, I'm not sure you are in love with me. You were caught up in your sister's romantic getaway, and I'm sure Sabrina said something last night that made you think you were— and that's not your fault. She's in love. Completely smitten. She thinks everyone can have what she and Flynn have."

For as gobsmacked as she felt, Gage might as well have reached out and slapped her.

"You think I don't know if I'm in love with you?" Gage was *deep* in the danger zone and hopefully her tone was conveying that fact. "You think I was swept up in wedding bells and engagement rings rather than coming to the con- clusion about my feelings on my own?"

"Yes—" his voice rose incrementally "—I do. So was I. Too caught up to recognize we were both flirting with disaster. I'm not too big a man to admit I'm sorry."

"You're *sorry*?" she snapped.

"I never should've asked for more when I knew damn well I couldn't be the guy to give you more. Staying to- gether is setting us up for a huge fall. A huge *failure*. I won't keep you from your future husband and waste any more of your time. What we had at Gwen's wedding was a perfect weekend. I should've left it at that."

Her hand twitched at her side. She'd never wanted to slap someone before. She did now. Just so he could feel the way she felt—like her stable footing had crumbled beneath her and she was in a free fall toward the cold, hard ground.

She settled for lifting her glass and throwing her remaining wine at him. Unaccustomed to being physically reactive, she sort of chickened out at the end and the splash fell short of his chest, landing on one side of his crisp white button-down shirt. Right about where the coffee stain was the day he'd talked her into letting him be her pretend boyfriend.

God. She'd never been so stupid.

"Bastard." Tears threatened but she swallowed down her rioting emotions.

"I'm sorry."

"The sorriest," she agreed. "Enjoy your meal."

She stomped out of his apartment without looking back, rode the elevator to the ground floor and marched to her car parked on the curb. She'd congratulated herself when she'd parked there, thinking how "lucky" she'd been to find the coveted space.

Lucky and in love.

"I'm *so* stupid," she reiterated aloud as she turned the key in the ignition. She'd known in her heart of hearts that forever wasn't for her. She'd let that doubt go, trusting Gage so implicitly that she'd agreed when he suggested they keep seeing each other. She'd allowed herself to believe the future was an open expanse with wildflowers blooming and horses galloping...

A fantasy.

One she wouldn't let herself wallow in no matter what her stupid heart thought. She could be in love with him all she wanted, but it didn't mean she couldn't move on. Gage might've put the final nail in the "them" coffin, but she had the power not to allow him in ever again.

Maybe someday she'd find it in her heart to be grateful to him for teaching her how to open up and trust and love someone.

Today was not that day.

She drove home without a backward glance, lecturing her tear ducts most of the way. The moment she twisted the lock on her front door and she was safely ensconced inside her own dark apartment, those tears came anyway, and showed no signs of stopping.

Gage stuffed his soiled shirt into the trash can hidden beneath the sink and washed Andy's wineglass, standing it on end in the dish drainer.

Then he moved to the kitchen counter, palmed the back of his neck and eyed the untouched bag of food with the receipt stapled to the paper bag.

He'd done the right thing.

But he still felt awful about it.

He finished his wine, surmising that Andy might never forgive him, but she could be free now. That he could continue working and upholding the pact because he believed wholeheartedly that engagement and marriage weren't for him. That his "feelings" couldn't be trusted because everyone in his vicinity was drunk on love.

It sounded like bullshit, even to him, so he couldn't imagine how badly it'd sounded when Andy was standing in his kitchen dumping her heart out.

What he'd done was the equivalent of stabbing her in the center of that heart with a dull knife.

"She'll get over it."

She'd have to. *He'd* have to. Viruses had to run their course, and the one he'd caught from her was a doozy. The "L" virus. He couldn't so much as think the four-letter word that hovered in the room like the scent of Thai food. His stomach gave an insistent rumble.

"Screw it." He tore open the bag, pulled out his shrimp pad thai and stowed the other container in the fridge for later.

Things didn't work out, that's all. And if the only carnage left behind from their breakup was a bag of Thai food, well, then they'd escaped relatively unscathed.

But as he dug his fork into his dinner and chewed forlornly, he questioned if he'd escaped unscathed after all.

The flavor should've burst—the shrimp was utter perfection, and the seasoning on point. Instead it was as if he was navigating a mouthful of foam packing peanuts.

"Virus," he said around another big bite. Viruses changed the flavor of food and altered a person's physical being. Which also explained that ache in the center of his shirtless chest.

He didn't hear any loud, blaring alarms like he had early on with Andy. There was only a low hum after the fallout. The sense that the worst wasn't coming, but had already come and gone. The sense that he'd made a giant mistake—one he could never take back.

He carried his dinner and wine to the couch where his heavy limbs dragged him down. Then he turned on the television and zoned out.

This, too, would pass.

Twenty-One

Gage looked up from his keyboard. Yasmine was typing away on her own laptop, and behind her Flynn's office was dark. Sabrina's, too. Flynn and Sabrina had left earlier. Something about meeting with a wedding planner and the only time the woman had available was three o'clock today.

When Gage glanced in the direction of Reid's office, he found his British friend wasn't in his chair, but heading Gage's way, whistling.

What the hell is he so happy about?

"Gagey, Gagey, Gagey." Reid said as he entered Gage's office.

"What?"

"Let's bugger off and grab drinks at Afar. It's dead in here. Everyone else has gone." He gestured to the empty-save-for-Yasmine floor.

"Pass." Gage returned his attention to the computer screen, where literally nothing was happening. He'd opened a blank document to type up a progress report for Flynn… that wasn't due for another month. He'd been spending a lot of hours in the office since he had nothing better to do than pass the time alone in his apartment.

The past nine and a half days had been absolute torture.

The feelings he'd convinced himself were fleeting and temporary hadn't gone anywhere. He'd given himself a week to recover from breaking things off with Andy, even though his instincts were bucking like a wild bronco. Everything about her leaving his apartment had felt wrong. Three days, five days—hell, nine and a half days later, it still felt wrong.

"You need to talk to someone and I'm offering my ear. But I'd rather do it over a beer." Reid unbuttoned his suit jacket and sat in the stuffed chair next to a plant.

"You and I talked already."

"I'm your best friend."

"You *were*."

Reid ignored the jab, pulling a hand over his face and muttering a swear word into his palm. "I tried to tell you."

Since Gage held Reid mostly responsible for leading him to think he needed to end things with Andy, that arrogant "I tried to tell you" comment sent his anger through the roof. He spun the chair to face his "friend."

"What, exactly, did you try to tell me, Reid?"

"That you had a girlfriend. That you liked being part of a couple. That I, alone, would hold true to the pact." He put a fist to his heart like a knight taking an oath.

"I seem to remember you telling me that it was past time to let her down gently."

"I never said that. I said I expected you to have let her down gently by then."

Gage's frown intensified; he could literally feel an ache forming between his eyebrows. "You planted a seed of doubt."

"You've got a whole garden of doubt in there on your own. Don't pin this on me. I don't want to see you hurt any more than you do, but I'm under no delusions when it comes to who I am and what I want. You, on the other hand..."

Reid shrugged and Gage wanted to hit his friend's perfectly square jaw. Or hit *someone*. At the moment hitting *himself* was justified.

"That night we went to From Afar," Gage started. "I broke up with Andy under your advice." When Reid opened his mouth to argue, Gage added, "Encouragement. Whatever. You weren't rooting for us, so don't pretend you were."

Reid's turn to frown. Good. Gage liked watching his friend's smug face slip into an expression that was borderline apologetic.

"I love her, Reid." Gage said it like he was announcing that he had only days to live. That was what that epiphany felt like.

He loved Andrea Payne and she hated him.

"Does she love you?"

Gage's heart suffered another fissure, but he barely felt it. He'd been in so much pain over the last week-plus he'd gotten used to it. "She loved me nine and a half days ago."

"Love." Reid's tone was as grave as Gage's. "It is soon."

"I don't need your commentary. You've helped enough already."

He stood and Reid did, too, stepping in front of Gage to block the path to the door.

Reid put his hand on Gage's chest to keep him from walking out. "You can't blame me for this. I was being myself. Doing what I've always done. Which is bust your bollocks. It was your job to tell me to shove it. To stand up for what you and Andy had if it was so bloody important."

Gage's shoulders sagged. "You're right."

His buddy was right.

Andy had been right.

"Andy mentioned that Flynn had thrown aside the pact because Sabrina was worth it. He was able to see it. We all were. But that was Sab." Someone who'd been in Flynn's life for a long time, not a brand-new relationship with a vulnerable, gorgeous, cautious redhead.

"First," Reid started. "Sab is a unicorn. When it came to him tossing aside the pact, we never would've stood for it had it been the wrong woman. Second, you're wrong about Flynn being the white knight. He had his head up his arse until you and I dragged him to the conclusion that he'd always belonged to Sabrina."

Gage blinked. Damn. He'd forgotten that day in Flynn's office, where Reid and Gage had to have a "come to Jesus" talk with their third musketeer.

"Points to you for realizing you're in love with Andy before Flynn and I had to come in here and pull it out of you as well." Reid patted Gage's chest and dropped his arm to his side.

"Doesn't matter. I'm too late."

Reid's mouth pressed into a line.

"Andy vanished. She's back to being the unreachable Andy Payne. She's a puff of smoke. I tried her assistant after Andy ignored a few of my calls." Gage shook his head. "Nothing."

"Did you text her?"

Gage nodded. He couldn't lay his love for her out in writing and watch it be ignored, so he'd settled for one We need to talk and a follow-up At least let me apologize.

Unsurprisingly, she hadn't responded.

He understood her caution. She'd come to him, her bright blue eyes shining with happiness, and told him to his face that she was in love with him. She deserved the same from him and he'd been too chickenshit to admit as much. Then he'd broken up with her, telling her he was sorry. *Sorry.* Like an apology would undo the hurt.

He'd never regret anything like he regretted letting her walk out of his apartment that night.

"Not like you don't know where she lives," Reid offered.

"I don't, actually. We always met at restaurants, or the airport, or she'd come to my place after she was done with work. She's impossible to track down."

"Nothing's impossible." Reid's eyes twinkled knowingly.

But it was too late. Andy had moved on. And really, wasn't it fair to *let her* move on? To let her go and heal when he'd wadded up her love for him and thrown it in her face?

"This came for you." Yasmine interrupted them before Gage could share his thoughts. She handed him an envelope and he blinked at it stupidly. "I'm done for the day, unless either of you need me?"

"Take care, Yasmine. We're heading out soon ourselves," Reid told her.

She grabbed her purse and left while Gage stood frozen in the doorway of his own office.

"What is it, then?" Reid asked.

Gage showed Reid the envelope. The printed return address in professional block lettering read *Andy Payne, LLC* followed by a PO Box number.

Monarch had paid the invoice for her services upon her arrival, so what was it? Gage half expected it to be a letter saying, "You're a dick," or maybe another invoice with a line item for "breaking my heart" with a dollar amount next to it. Two thousand dollars, maybe.

He tore open the envelope and pulled out the single item within. A check.

His guess wasn't far off. But instead of being billed, he was being paid.

His eyes locked onto the words *Pay to the order of* and then snapped to the dollar amount—$2,000.00.

She'd written him a check for two thousand dollars.

On the memo line it read *Payment in full for business trip.*

There was nothing else in the envelope. No note. No

"Fuck you." It was no less than he deserved—a final middle finger for what had happened in his apartment nearly ten days ago.

Reid let out a long, low whistle. "Harsh."

Then Gage arrived at a conclusion that hit him as hard and fast as a shot. "Except it's not."

"No?"

"No." If Andy was mad at him, she *never* would've sent him this check. What better retaliation was there than freezing him out and never speaking to him again? Instead she'd *reached out*. She might even be as brokenhearted as he was, which could mean she still loved him. Receiving this check meant she cared. About him. About *them*.

She wasn't an Ice Queen.

They both knew it.

Gage's smile found his face without him trying. "She loves me. Still."

"You're insane. That's a cold move."

"I know what it looks like, but trust me when I tell you that this—" he waved the check "—means she's not over us yet." He knew it in his heart. A heart that he'd have to serve up on a platter if he had a prayer of earning her back. "I have to tell her that I love her, too. Right now. And in person. Can you find her?"

Reid's mouth flinched into a grimace briefly—likely at the prognosis of his friend falling in love. Couldn't be helped. Gage loved Andy, and distance and time hadn't done anything to dampen that love. In fact, his feelings for her had only intensified.

"Please."

With a sigh, Reid announced, "I'm a computer-hacker-turned-IT-wizard. Of course I can find her." He tilted his head toward his office, where no fewer than three large computer screens decorated his desk. "Tell me everything you know about the mysterious Andy Payne."

Twenty-Two

Andy reread the email to her webmaster for the third time, a zing of excitement and nervousness comingling in her belly. It was past time she came out of hiding and let the world, or at least the world wide web, see her for who she truly was.

Mike, attached you'll find my headshot. Please update the website to include my photo and an About page. My bio is below. If you have any questions, let me know.

She'd never had the confidence before to stand on her own merits. She'd made many, many excuses about why she needed to keep her identity a secret from her clients, but since the breakup with Gage she'd taken a long, hard look at her life. She was done hiding. Done trying to live up to the tough-as-nails woman she'd created as a persona. She'd thought it would protect her, but instead she only felt like a coward for hiding behind that persona. It was time to step into her power. A power, ironically, that she wouldn't have if it wasn't for Gage.

He'd undone her completely. He'd peeled back layer after layer and had seen her in her most vulnerable state. He'd wooed her from her shell and defended her honor and made her realize that above all else, she was enough.

Exactly as she was.

She closed her eyes and willed back the torrent of emotions that had plagued her since the night they broke up. She couldn't change what had happened any more than she could keep from still loving him.

He'd texted. He'd called. She'd ignored both, knowing she couldn't face him with her tender underbelly showing. She had been desperately trying to rebuild her armor, to rebrick the wall that she'd been hidden safely behind that evening at the bar, when she'd offered Gage two grand in exchange for his accompaniment to Gwen's wedding.

Hiding had proved impossible.

Gage hadn't only lured her out from behind that wall, but he'd also demolished the way she'd seen the world prior to him.

Andy knew she was desirable and, unlike Gage, she wasn't afraid to face her future.

That didn't mean her heart didn't ache, or that she didn't soak her pillow every night with fresh tears, but it did mean that she wasn't the Ice Queen Matthew had accused her of being. She was a feeling, sensitive, vulnerable woman. Beautifully vulnerable.

Being vulnerable sucked.

She sent the email and shut her laptop, mind on the bottle of white wine chilling in the door of the fridge. It was ten thirty and her eyes were heavy, drooping from the fatigue of both work and personal matters.

Wine would help.

Before she'd taken her first sip of crisp, light pinot grigio, her cell phone rang. The jingle made her heart leap to her throat even though she'd silenced Gage's phone number days ago. She couldn't bring herself to delete his phone number yet. Soon, though, she'd have to close the door on what they had.

The screen showed Vanessa's photo, and Andy took a steeling breath. Rare was the occasion Ness called her, and the news was rarely good.

"Ness, hi."

"Is it too late to call?"

"No. Just wrapped up work, actually. I poured a glass of wine and was about to have my first sip."

"I'll join you. I have a bottle open." There was the sound of a cabinet opening and closing, liquid pouring. "Cheers, sis."

Andy joined her in a cross-country sip and waited for Ness to say why she'd called. She didn't have to wait long.

"Alec and I are separating. Separated. Past tense. He moved out this afternoon."

"Ness." Andy's heart, which was already crushed, hurt for her sister. "I'm so sorry."

"I wanted to tell you personally. A divorce is probably on the horizon, but we're trying living apart to see how things go."

Andy guessed that could go one of two ways. Either absence would make the heart grow fonder, or that other adage—out of sight, out of mind—would make them forget why they'd ever liked each other.

For Andy, it was option A. She wanted to believe that Gage reaching out meant that he felt the same way, but there was no way to be sure unless she contacted him. She hadn't been brave enough to do that—and quite possibly never would be brave enough.

"How's life?" Ness asked. Caught off guard by her sister's conversational tone, Andy surprised herself by answering honestly.

"Horrible. Gage and I…" She swallowed down a lump of sadness. "We broke up."

Ness let out a cynical laugh. "You should consider yourself lucky you didn't invest years in him before things went downhill. What I'm going through isn't for the faint of heart."

An insensitive comment was completely expected from her sister, but Andy didn't clam up like she used to. The new Andrea Payne didn't make herself smaller to avoid hurt feelings. She stood up for herself.

"You know you're not the only one with problems, Vanessa," Andy snapped. "Your pain doesn't eclipse mine or make what I'm going through any less upsetting. I'm a human being with feelings, not the Ice Queen whose heart is frozen into a solid block. I was in love with him. *Am* in love with him."

"Andy—"

"I told him," Andy continued, her voice watery. "I told him I loved him, because while I might not be the Ice Queen, I am very, very stupid. I laid everything on the line even though he told me from the beginning he didn't want to be married. Why didn't I listen?"

Her mini rant ended with tears slipping down her cheeks. She went to the couch, wineglass forgotten. It wouldn't help her to drink it.

Nothing would help her but time.

"Sweetheart." Ness sounded almost motherly, definitely sisterly. The hard edge from her voice was gone. "You are not stupid. You're the smartest of all of us. If there was a mistake made, it wasn't you falling in love, it was that Gage was too blind to see what he had. He really missed out on an incredible life with you."

The tears dried on Andy's cheeks as she held the phone gently against her ear. "Thanks."

"What a jackwagon."

Andy surprised herself by laughing at her sister's choice of name-calling. Even Ness let out a little chuckle.

"I have a way of letting my own misery overflow onto others," Ness said. "I'm bossy and rude. I want what's best for you, but somehow it comes out like I'm judgmental. No wonder Alec is leaving me."

"Stop talking about my sister that way."

Ness let out another laugh.

"Are you and Alec going to counseling?"

"He asked me if I would." A pause. "I told him I'd think about it."

"Ness, don't let your pride ruin what you and Alec have. I can't pretend to know what it's like to be married as long as you have, but I've seen you two together. You're good for each other. You were at some point, anyway. Is it un-fixable?"

"I want to believe it's fixable but I'm afraid to try." Ness's voice trembled. "I don't ever want to feel this way again. I wonder if it'd be easier to make a rule to never get this close to someone rather than to try again and fail."

A rule...or a pact.

Andy thought of Gage and wondered for the first time since he dumped her if she wasn't the braver of the two of them. She was the one who faced her fears and won—he'd faced them and retreated.

"Don't make a rule," Andy told her sister. "Don't rob yourself of something great—whether it's Alec or a man in your future you overlook because you were hurt once before. Don't let the pain you're feeling now keep away the joy you could have later."

"See?" Vanessa sniffled, but there was a smile in her voice. "I told you that you were the smartest one."

They chatted for another twenty minutes, until Andy's eyes grew heavy and Ness begged off. She promised to call Alec and schedule the counselor, and thanked Andy for her help.

They exchanged I-love-yous, another rarity between them, and Andy curled up on the couch and closed her eyes, contented at least in part that she'd helped Ness through a rough evening.

Andy woke up to the insistent buzz-buzz-buzz of her phone. She cracked open one eye and checked the screen. It was her apartment's front desk, and typically they called only when there was a visitor or a delivery.

She blinked, her bleary eyes fighting to focus on the clock on the wall. Midnight wasn't prime visiting or delivery hours.

"Hello?" Her voice was groggy and sleepy, her mind not doing a very good job of understanding what the woman who called was saying to her.

But Andy made out two pertinent bits of information.

Gage Fleming was in the lobby.

And he wanted to come up and see her.

"He said it's urgent, Ms. Payne."

She had no idea how Gage had found her address. She hadn't purposely kept it from him—it'd been easier to meet him on her way home from work or at the airport when they'd flown to Ohio—but she was grateful he didn't know where to find her when her wounds were so fresh.

That he'd found her at all meant one of two things. A) He was angry about the check she'd sent and wanted to throw it in her face; or B) He wanted to explain himself since he hadn't shown an iota of tact when he'd broken up with her a week and a half ago.

Not that there was any great way to tell someone you didn't love them.

"Send him up." She'd hear what he had to say. She was brave. Strong. And unafraid.

How much more could he hurt her after he'd tossed her heart into the dirt?

After a quick check in the mirror by the front door to make sure her mascara wasn't on her cheeks—it wasn't—Andy opened the door and waited in the doorway with her arms folded.

She unfolded her arms and straightened, unsure if she wanted him to see her in a defensive position. Then folded them again anyway.

Dammit.

She was nervous.

Even though she wanted with all her heart not to be.

But you don't have all of your heart, do you?

No. The man currently riding the elevator up to her apartment had at least 30 percent of it.

Maybe forty.

She refused to give him more. Not without him reciprocating.

From her front door she had a vantage point of the elevator, so she watched when Gage stepped from it. He was still in his office clothes, a pale blue pinstriped shirt and trousers, a navy tie knotted at his neck. In one hand was an envelope.

She froze when he spotted her. His mouth was unsmiling and his gait long and strong. As he strode toward her she had no idea if he'd chosen A or B. His first words to her didn't clear it up, either.

"You're not an Ice Queen." He stopped in front of her and held up the envelope, torn open unevenly. A good representation for how she'd felt over the last week. "This proves it."

She didn't follow his meaning, so she said something neutral. "Paynes always repay their debts."

"You're not in debt to me. I'm in debt to you. You gave me the best gift of all." His mouth curved, reminding her of the taste of his smile. "It didn't cost you a thing but it was far more valuable than anything you could've bought."

The dangerous emotions she'd packed down into a tight ball at the bottom of her heart threatened to unravel. She crossed her arms tighter to keep it there.

"You showed me *you*. The real you. The unsure, vulnerable, shy you. And when it came time for me to man up and show you that part of me—" he shook his head "—I failed you."

That tight ball unraveled like a spring.

"This—" he held up the check inside the envelope "—is proof that you still love me."

She felt her cheeks go white as the blood drained from them to her toes. She shook her head. Not because it wasn't true but because he wasn't supposed to know that part. That check was intended to be proof that she *didn't* love him. She needed to learn how to be whole without him. She needed space and giving him the money he'd never wanted was supposed to guarantee that space. To allow her to close the door on what they had for good.

"You never would've sent me this if you didn't still love me. If you hated me, you wouldn't have given me another thought," he told her. "Like I said, you're not the Ice Queen. In fact, everything about you is fire. From your red hair to your flaming honesty to the way you heat me up with your vulnerability. I thought I'd walk away and save us both further pain but the truth is… I'm scorched, Andy. *Ruined.* I will never again be whole. Not without you."

She closed her eyes and sensed Gage stepping close to her. She'd never imagined this scenario—not in all her multiple-choice options. He'd given a speech that absolutely owned her in the threshold of her apartment.

And he wasn't through yet.

"I was trying to rebuild my own walls and failing miserably. I fell in love with you, and because I'm so hopelessly out of practice at responding to that much love, I blew it. I had a chance to claim your heart and defend your honor and I didn't."

"The pact…" were the only words she could utter. She couldn't address the "fell in love" part or the fact that she'd "scorched" him and "ruined" him for all others. That was too big.

"Fuck the pact."

She took him in—those boyish curls and caramel-brown eyes. The way being near him felt so, so right.

"If I promise to love you forever, will you forgive me?"

"I…" But more words wouldn't come.

"If I promise to be brave from now on out, can you let me in?"

A shaky nod was the most she could give him before she covered her mouth to stifle the cry. Then she was in Gage's arms, being held and shushed, the words *I'm sorry* and *I love you* on a loop on his tongue.

When he let her go, he held the envelope between them. "An Ice Queen would've kept the money as the ultimate screw-you. You, Andrea Payne, are no Ice Queen."

He tore the envelope in half and then in half again and dropped the pieces at their feet. His eyes flicked to her lips and just like before their first kiss, he said, "I'll let you come to me."

She gripped the back of his neck. "But you'll give as good as you get?"

"You bet your perfect breasts I will."

They met in the middle, their mouths crashing and their bodies fusing together—as close as they could get without being naked. But they were naked in another way—their souls had been bared.

Walls had come down.

Hearts could heal.

Pacts, like the envelope at her feet, could be torn into pieces.

"I missed you," she whispered, the tear sliding down her cheek a happy one.

He thumbed it away and smiled warmly. "You'll never have to miss me again."

Epilogue

It was a gorgeous, sunshiny, perfect day to be on the water.

The pontoon swayed gently in the cove where they'd anchored, Andy's four sisters holding out their flutes while Gage filled each to the brim with sparkling rosé.

It was a beautiful summer day in Crown, Ohio.

"Carrying forth the tradition of the couples' cruise was never not an option," Andy explained as she pulled out a plastic flute for herself. Gage winked as he uncorked a second bottle and filled Andy's glass as well as his own. "This time around, we have a new couple who will reenact a movie kiss and attempt to steal first place from Gage and me."

"A tough act to follow," Gwen offered. "Good luck, Ness."

All heads swiveled to Vanessa and her date, Mitchell. Mitch was forty years old, had two daughters who were ten and eight, though they hadn't come to the Payne-Fleming wedding, and he had a nice smile and a smooth-as-butter Southern accent.

Andy liked Mitch.

Vanessa and Alec had gone to counseling, and although it didn't result in a reunion, Ness was much happier with her new beau. Andy could see it in the loose way she draped over him on the boat's seat. Sometimes things had to break to be fixed, like Andy and Gage, but other times the break was too final and new parts were needed.

"We're a hard act to follow," Gage said. "Andy and I nailed *Titanic*."

A round of teasing "ohhs" lifted on the air.

"You say that like we didn't prepare." Ness arched one eyebrow in challenge.

"I know better." Andy playfully rolled her eyes. Vanessa and Alec had rehearsed for their *Dirty Dancing* kiss for weeks.

"Get ready to be dazzled. But not yet. We have to practice. Into the water with all of you." Ness shooed them off the boat.

"Not a hard sell today." Gage polished off his bubbly and stripped his shirt over his head. The late July afternoon was a stifling ninety-eight degrees and the humidity was set to "stun."

Within minutes of Gage cannonballing off the side of the boat, everyone save Ness and Mitch was in the water.

Arm around her waist, Gage tugged Andy to him and she wrapped her legs around him.

"God, they're as bad as we were," Gwen told Garrett.

"Worse," her husband concluded.

"Do you think they're really going to beat our couples' cruise kiss?" Gage asked Andy, ignoring the ribbing of her family to nuzzle her nose.

She held onto her gorgeous fiancé, squinting against the blindingly bright sun. "Possibly. Ness hates to lose."

"Sounds like she has a lot to learn." His eyebrows jumped in self-deprecating humor. At one point he'd been the one who was so afraid to fail he hadn't given them a chance.

He'd come a long way. Especially when he proposed at Monarch Consulting. He'd lured her to the building under the guise of meeting for lunch and then was on his knees before her, proclaiming his love for her in front of his friends.

Andy pulled her hand out of the water to admire the engagement ring. A teardrop-shaped diamond with smaller stones on the band. Gage had told her he liked to think that it was shaped like a flame.

She liked that, too.

"We're ready! Although you're going to get the PG version." Ness came out from behind the beach towel Mitch had used to shield her and stood on one of the boat's seats. She was wearing a short pink skirt, an argyle-patterned neckerchief and knee socks in the same jaunty design. Her hair was pulled back at the sides but distinctly ruffled to make her look like she'd had a few too many.

Once the song started playing, Gwen gasped. "I know this one! I know it!"

Andy watched the scene unfold, from Ness leading Mitch across the boat to her falling on a seat and letting out a loud laugh. By the time she tossed aside the kerchief and they vanished from sight, Kelli and Gwen were cheering.

Carroll was grinning, too. The husbands, including Andy's husband-to-be, looked as clueless as she felt.

Vanessa popped back into view, Mitch with her. "Sorry the kiss happened out of sight. We got a little carried away. Any guesses?"

"*The Wedding Date*, and bravo," Kelli answered.

"Yes!" Vanessa shot her fists into the air as everyone clapped.

"What movie?" Andy had to ask.

Gwen looked affronted. "Debra Messing. Dermot Mulroney. The boat scene."

"The movie where she pays the guy to be her date for her sister's wedding. Total fiction, right?" Vanessa added with a wink.

Next to her Gage laughed. "That was a good one."

"The best!" Ness corrected, and then awarded herself first place.

"Close," Gage murmured as he pulled Andy into his arms. Then he whispered so that only she could hear, "But not the best."

* * * * *

HIS FOR
ONE NIGHT

SARAH M. ANDERSON

To my mom.
Here's to new beginnings and fresh starts!
Love you!

One

"It's a good crowd tonight," Kyle Morgan said as he slipped down the narrow hallway that qualified as the backstage of the Bluebird Cafe in Nashville, Tennessee. He winked at Brooke Bonner. "But I don't think any of them came for me."

Brooke gave the older man a shaky smile but didn't stop humming to herself. The Bluebird was usually full—it was a small space where songwriters and singers came to test out new material. She'd been coming here for a decade now—first as a patron, then as a performer. She hadn't been back in almost a year and a half, though.

She hadn't been anywhere since she'd had Bean.

This night marked the beginning of her official comeback. After almost seven months of what felt like house arrest, she was walking back into the spotlight.

She was done hiding.

Mostly done, anyway. No one but a few select people knew about James Frasier Bonner—who she still called Bean, even though he definitely had grown. At three months, Bean was already smiling and cooing at her.

He had his father's smile.

Kyle wasn't in the know about Bean. Which made Brooke feel bad because Kyle was almost a father figure to her. He'd been at the Bluebird for her very first show and had taught her more about songwriting than anyone else. At every step of Brooke's journey from "girl with a guitar" to "country music phenomenon," Kyle had been a cheerleader, giving her advice and gentle pushes forward.

"Missed seeing you around," Kyle said. "Been quiet without you."

If she could've picked a father, Kyle might've done the trick. Sadly, Crissy Bonner would never tell Brooke who'd sired her. And the fact that she was walking in her mother's footsteps by keeping Bean's father a secret was a huge problem for Brooke.

But what choice did she have?

She didn't *want* to repeat the mistakes her mother had made. She wanted to do better.

But first, she had to get back out into the music scene.

Kyle's smile crinkled the lines around his mouth. It was a damn shame he refused to even talk to Mom. They could've made a good couple, and Kyle was rocking a silver-fox thing. Plus, if Mom had had a boyfriend or a husband, it might've taken some of Crissy Bonner's focus off Brooke. But the few times Brooke had managed to get them in the same room, the barely concealed hatred had been enough to crush any dreams of an instant family.

Of course, if Kyle and Crissy had hooked up, that might've meant Brooke wouldn't have a Grammy and a couple of chart toppers to her name. And it also might've meant she'd never have performed at that All-Stars Rodeo where Flash Lawrence had been riding, which would've meant no Bean. And she loved her son with her whole heart.

"Does this show mean you're off hiatus?" Kyle asked as he packed up his guitar.

"Yup. I'd been touring for almost four years straight before I hit big last year. It just wiped me out."

That was the official position her record label and family had cooked up. Brooke had needed a break to work on her new material. There might have been something in there about resting her vocal cords, she couldn't remember.

It'd all been a load of crap.

No one *rested* during the last three months of pregnancy. New mothers with fussy babies didn't *rest*.

Not for the first time, Brooke wished they'd just announced she was pregnant and dealt with the issue head-on. Yeah, the press might've been brutal—but there was no such thing as bad PR, and she'd argued that her surprise pregnancy might've taken her second album, *White Trash Wonder*, from double to triple platinum. After all, an unexpected pregnancy was on brand.

She'd been overruled because of one fact and one fact alone: she wouldn't tell anyone who Bean's father was. Not that it was any of their business, because it wasn't.

Her mother hadn't forgiven her yet for sitting on that particular secret, as if Crissy hadn't done the exact same thing by refusing to acknowledge Brooke's father.

Which meant Brooke was stuck lying, which she hated.

Kyle stood and wrapped an arm awkwardly around her shoulder. "Welcome back," he said, giving her a friendly squeeze before he headed out to the front to watch. "You need anything, you just give me a call. I mean it, Brooke—anything at all."

Brooke's eyes stung with unexpected emotion at Kyle's thoughtfulness. She forced her shoulders down and started humming again, keeping her vocal cords warm.

Alex Andrews, her bodyguard and friend, squeezed her big frame into the hallway and handed Brooke a mug of hot tea. "They found some honey," she practically growled.

Brooke accepted the tea gratefully and took a sip. Ah, the perfect temperature. "Thanks, hon."

Alex was big and gruff, but underneath her tanklike exterior she was a softie with a heart of solid gold. They'd been friends since junior high, back when Brooke was a band geek just starting to perform and Alex had been the first girl to play offensive lineman on the football team. Long before *White Trash Wonder* had hit big, Alex had been right beside Brooke in every dive bar and county fair, doing her best to keep away grabby, drunk assholes.

Thirteen months ago, Alex had stayed home because her girlfriend had the flu, instead of joining Brooke in Fort Worth for the All-Around All-Stars Rodeo. If Alex had come, would Brooke and Flash have spent that white-hot night together? Or would Alex have been the voice of reason, keeping Brooke far away from cocky cowboys who were good in bed? And against the wall? And on the floor?

Brooke must have been frowning, because Alex asked, "Worried?"

Damn it—it was hard to get anything past that woman. Especially since Alex was one of the few people who knew about Bean. "It's fine. He's home with Mom," she said, stretching her facial muscles to loosen them up.

"They'll do great. Crissy only wants what's best for him," Alex replied, which was probably supposed to be reassuring. Except it wasn't and Alex knew it. Her eyes widened as she realized what she'd said. "Oh, crap—I didn't mean…"

"It's fine," Brooke repeated, taking this opportunity to test out her fake smile. Crissy Bonner's favorite saying was 'It's for the best.' Brooke starting singing lessons at the age of five was *for the best*. Guitar lessons at the age of six was *for the best*. Hours of practice every day were *for the best*. Slumber parties, birthday parties, pets or boys— they *weren't* for the best.

Knowing who her father was? That definitely wasn't for the best.

Brooke kept humming. She was the last act of the night and she was surprised to realize she was nervous. It had been almost seven months since her last public appearance. Seven months since cleverly cut dresses and long, swingy cardigans hadn't been enough to conceal her baby bump. Seven months since she'd sung in public.

After years of constantly touring—starting with bars on Nashville's Music Row and then to county fairs to state fairs, to being the opening act for some of the biggest names in country music—Brooke had paid her dues early and often. And it'd all paid off last year when *White Trash Wonder* had hit. Suddenly, sold-out rodeos like the All-Stars had led to sold-out arenas. Years of lessons and performances and navigating the business world as a teenager had suddenly paid off, and Brooke had officially been labeled an overnight success, country music's Next Big Thing.

And she'd ruined it by getting knocked up by Flash Lawrence.

She'd had to miss the Grammys, for crying out loud. She'd been in labor when she'd won Best New Artist.

She wanted to be home with her son right now, she realized. She wasn't ready to do this again—the long and lonely nights, the negotiations, the travel and, most especially, the constant media scrutiny. But she didn't have a choice. Her uncle and former manager, Brantley Gibbons, had embezzled not just most of her money but a great deal of his other clients' funds and invested them in the Preston Pyramid Scheme—which had, of course, collapsed around his ears just about the time Brooke was breaking out.

Brooke and her mother weren't penniless—she still had royalties coming in on her two albums and had managed to keep the bulk of her profits from the last few months of touring after Uncle Brantley had "relocated" to Mexico to avoid criminal charges. But she couldn't afford to stay out of the spotlight any longer. She had to strike while the iron was hot.

Getting back out there was for the best, her mother had said. Because of course she had.

"Ladies and gentlemen," the MC began. "Our final act tonight is none other than the Grammy and Country Music Association winner, Brooke Bonner!"

Brooke took a final sip of her not-quite-hot tea and locked her smile in place. She'd been fourteen when she had first performed at the Bluebird, just a scared little girl and her acoustic guitar. It seemed fitting to start over where it had all started.

Brooke stepped out of the hallway to an impressive roar of applause. She smiled and nodded and tried to turn her body so no one would make a grab at her ass as she worked her way to the center of the Bluebird, where chairs and mikes had been set up.

As she settled into her chair, the hairs on the back of her neck stood up and she had the strangest feeling that *he* was here—Flash Lawrence. Which was ridiculous. In the thirteen months since their one-night stand, she hadn't heard from him. And she hadn't contacted him, either. She'd come so close when she'd realized she was pregnant. But she'd Googled him and seen all these horrible headlines about barroom brawls and trials and...

And she'd passed.

Her life was crazy enough with her career. A baby would make it crazier still. But a violent, immature cowboy? That was a hard *no*. She wanted her son to know his father but not at the risk of his well-being. Or hers.

A shiver raced down her back. She was imagining things, that's all there was to it. There was no way that her one-night stand was in the audience. It just wasn't possible.

Just to be sure, she turned in her seat to wave at the people behind her who were still clapping.

Damn. There, at the bar—a long, lean cowboy was perched on the last seat, the brim of his black cowboy hat throwing his face into deep shadow. He wore jeans with an absolutely huge belt buckle, with a leather biker jacket over a black Western-style button-up shirt. She couldn't see his eyes, but she could feel him looking at her.

Oh, no. Oh, *hell*.

Maybe she was wrong. It wasn't like cowboys of a certain height and weight wearing black hats and big belt buckles didn't exist around Nashville because they absolutely did. But her blood pounded in her veins and her hands shook, and there was no mistaking the flight or fight reaction.

Because she wasn't wrong.

The cowboy shifted in his seat, tilting his head back. His gaze collided with Brooke's, and even though she hadn't seen him for thirteen months, even though she'd only ever spent one amazing night with him, heat pooled low in her belly and she trembled with want.

Her big mistake was sitting less than thirty feet away. The one time she'd gone off schedule and done something just for herself—not for her career or her mother or anyone—and she'd been paying the price ever since. She loved her son, but…

She wasn't ready. Not for Flash Lawrence.

Not for any of this.

The lights dimmed and an expectant hush fell over the crowd.

Well. The show had to go on, so Brooke did the only thing she could.

"It's so good to be back, y'all. I've been working on new material for my next album—should be out in a few months—and we're thinking of calling it *Your Roots Are*

Showing." The crowd laughed appreciatively as she flipped her hair back with an exaggerated toss of her head. "Aw, you guys are great."

She desperately wanted to turn in her seat for this next part. If that was Flash, what would he think when he heard the song title? But she didn't. She was giving him nothing to work with, and, besides, there was a literal audience here tonight. All it would take for the wildfire of gossip to catch and burn would be one too-long look, one touch, one wrong move, and her comeback would be forever tainted.

So she didn't turn, didn't even acknowledge that there was anyone behind her. She played to the people she could see when she said, "So the first song that'll be on the new album that I want to sing tonight is called 'One-Night Stand.'"

Two

God, she looked amazing.

Brooke Bonner wasn't wearing the skintight crop top and leather miniskirt she'd had on the last time Flash had seen her. For this small crowd, she was wearing a black hippy-style skirt that came just below her knees and showed off her turquoise cowboy boots. A long sweater vest thing without sleeves was held in place over a deep-cut white shirt with the kind of studded belt that Flash's sister Chloe sold for her Princess of the Rodeo clothing line.

Turquoise dripped off her ears and around her neck but—he had to lean to the side to see—her fingers were bare. He couldn't tell for sure, but he didn't think there was even a tan line for an engagement ring on her finger.

Thank God.

When she'd disappeared from the public eye a few months ago, Flash had been terrified to think she might have met someone, might have gotten married. If she had, he'd have had to walk out the Bluebird's door without a look back. He wasn't going to screw up a marriage. But no ring meant he settled in and ordered another ginger ale. He was here for the duration.

Had he ever seen a more beautiful woman? He'd met a lot of hot women and slept with his fair share of them, but there was something about the way Brooke was put together that drew his eye. He couldn't look away, hadn't been able to since the very first moment he'd seen her in Fort Worth. He'd kissed her hand and that had been that.

Brooke wasn't wearing a hat tonight, so he could see the glory of her dark red hair as it flowed down her back in long waves. His fingers itched to bury themselves in that hair, wrap it around his fist like he'd done the last time, holding her head so he could kiss her again and again.

Apparently, absence really did make the heart grow fonder, because Flash was so glad to see Brooke right now that he wanted to sweep her into his arms and carry her far, far away from this crowded little place and show her how damned glad he was to see her.

He'd spent a year trying not to miss this woman. A year of trying to put the most intense sexual experience of his life out of his mind. He'd tried to pick up buckle bunnies since that night, but he hadn't succeeded. Not once in thirteen months.

He was afraid Brooke Bonner had ruined him for any other woman.

And that would be a damn shame.

No way in hell he wanted to be tied down. Especially not this year, when the All-Around All-Stars Cowboy of the Year was in his sights. After a wreck of a year—mostly brought on by Flash's own hot temper and alcohol-fueled brawls—he was back and ready to prove he wasn't just a chip on his shoulder with a good right hook.

For too long, people had assumed that Flash only won the All-Stars because the Lawrence family owned the circuit, and he understood now that most of his fights had been about proving he wasn't just a Lawrence, but that when it came to the rodeo, he was one of the best.

Getting suspended from the rodeo after that last fight—along with forfeiting his winnings up to that point—had been a blessing, although it sure hadn't felt like it at the time, especially not with the busted jaw Flash had gotten brawling. But it'd forced him to come to grips with his temper and grow the hell up. Plus, it'd shown everyone the All-Stars wasn't just a family business coddling the baby of the family. The rodeo family understood now that Flash had earned his place in the rankings.

This was *his* year and, for once, he wasn't going to shoot himself in his own foot. That included this thing between him and Brooke.

He just wanted…well, he wanted another night with her, to see if there was still that same electric current between them.

Best case, they'd make an effort to meet up on the road a few times a year, whenever his rodeo was in town during her concerts. He wouldn't say no to something like that. Not with her. He could focus on winning it all and she could focus on her career, and they'd get the chance to enjoy themselves during their downtime, like they had in Texas.

Then she announced the name of her first new song. "One-Night Stand."

The tips of Flash's ears went hot. That wasn't about him, right?

Couldn't be. It was the height of egotism to think that one night with him had left Brooke with anything other than a fond memory.

"Everyone should have one good night stand, don't you think?" Brooke went on, and the crowd chuckled approvingly. Someone to his left wolf whistled. Flash didn't see who, but he'd like to bust whoever it was in the jaw.

But the moment that thought crossed his mind, Flash clamped down on it. He was not going to lose his temper here. People were allowed to be jerks. He wasn't responsible for teaching them the errors of their ways when they crossed the line. Throwing a punch to defend Brooke's honor was something the old Flash would've done. The new-and-hopefully-improved Flash settled for glaring in the direction of the whistler.

Besides, causing a scene didn't serve his goals. He wanted to get reacquainted with Brooke Bonner. He needed to find out if there was something worth chasing between them or if he just needed to man up and move on.

If he got lucky, then he'd get lucky. If not, well, he still had to win it all.

The All-Around All-Stars Rodeo was in Nashville this weekend and he'd been hoping to find a way to run into her. When she'd posted on social media she'd be at the Bluebird tonight, he'd driven like a bat out of hell to get to Tennessee five days early just to see her.

At the bare minimum, he needed to make things right between them. Starting a brawl less than two minutes into her set would pretty much guarantee he'd never get another shot. So he kept a lid on his temper and took another drink of his soda.

When the crowd settled down, Brooke leaned in close to the microphone and said, "I'm so glad to see so many people agree—it's my favorite piece of furniture, too!"

Flash let out a slow breath, grinning in spite of his nerves. He'd loved her snarky sense of humor last year, too. She hadn't fawned over him and he had done his best not to fawn over her. There'd been an…understanding between them, almost. And a woman with a sense of humor was surprisingly erotic.

Thank goodness that a year of superstardom hadn't changed that about her.

Then Brooke began to sing as she played her guitar, and something in Flash's chest let go as the sound of her voice washed over him. By God, he'd missed the hell out of her.

She might not remember him—although, given how her eyes had widened slightly when they'd made eye contact, he thought maybe she did. And she might not want to see him again. But for a little while, he could lose himself in her world.

Until he realized what she was singing.

"It's just a one-night stand,
No tomorrow, no plans."

Well, damn. Yeah, she remembered him. But it wasn't a good thing. Especially not when she got to the chorus.

"You weren't worth the fun.
My one-night stand."

And the hell of it was, it was a great song. She had the audience eating out of the palm of her hand.

"Don't want to hear your excuses,
I don't care about your plans.
Not waiting any longer.
Screw your demands.
It's time I made my one-night stand."

Chills raced down his back as she held the last note, strong and powerful. He hadn't even had the chance to say hello and she was already shutting him down.

When the song ended, she did not look at him. She didn't sneak a peek out of the corner of her eye, didn't pivot in her chair, nothing. If she'd recognized him, it was clear she was ignoring him. "Whoo, y'all like that? That's just the beginning—I have a whole album of sass coming your way!"

Anger—an old, familiar feeling—began to push through his veins, but Flash refused to let it win. It was entirely possible that Brooke Bonner had forgotten all about him after her whirlwind breakout year. There was also a distinct possibility that, if she did remember him, she didn't hold him in any particularly high esteem.

He should've anticipated the song, though. He should've anticipated her anger. Anger was his second language. It came as naturally to him as breathing. But he hadn't seen this *attack* coming.

Okay, yeah, there'd been a superhot one-night stand. They'd hooked up in her dressing room before the show, which had made her late to go on because leather miniskirts weren't easy to work around. And it'd been good.

God, he still went hard just thinking about taking her against the wall in that tiny room, staring into her eyes as they both fought not to make a single sound. So damn *good*. And she had to have agreed, right? Because he'd hung around after the show, and when she'd seen him waiting for her, her entire face had lit up and she'd crooked her finger at him. They'd spent the rest of the night wrapped around each other in her hotel suite, having hot sex and ordering room service and, in between the seductions, making each other laugh.

They'd parted friends the next morning. He'd made damn sure to leave her with a smile on her face. He knew he hadn't stopped grinning for days. Weeks, even.

So how had they gotten from *that* to *this*?

"My next song—now just wait for it," she all but purred into the mike, "is called 'How Many Licks' because that was always the question, right?" The crowd hooted. "How many licks to get to the center of the sucker?"

"Three!" some jackass yelled.

"As many licks as it takes," a different ass yelled. Brooke wagged a scolding finger at him.

Flash had to close his eyes and focus on his breathing. Behind his eyelids, the world was red. They weren't disrespecting her. She'd chosen that title to get that exact reaction. She knew what she was doing and it wasn't his job to defend her from every slight. He'd already tried that once and had the criminal record—and nemesis—to prove it. He'd busted Tex McGraw up pretty damn good because the man had dared to put Brooke's name in his mouth.

Obviously, Flash understood why Tex hated him with a white-hot fury—Flash had knocked the man out of the All-Stars with a solid right hook. But Tex hadn't let up any with his online attacks since then, and he sure as hell hadn't accepted either of Flash's apologies—not the court-mandated one and not the more sincere one Flash had made after a few months of sobriety. But it was fine. Flash had gotten to a place in his life where he could handle online swipes from Tex without being driven to fits of rage. That was how far Flash had come in a year.

Brooke launched into the song, which cut off any other outbursts. The red haze behind his eyes faded, and he was able to breathe without feeling like punching someone.

Not surprisingly, this song felt personal, too. The double entendres flew fast and furious, but the core of the song was about a guy who couldn't take his licks and bailed.

A lot of people didn't like Flash. He'd never made it particularly easy for anyone to like him, but at least he knew it. However, he'd never inspired such strong feelings that someone could write an entire album based on how much they hated him, for God's sake.

Right. Instead of being insulted and letting it get to him, he was going to focus on feeling…flattered. Yeah, flattered. Not just any rodeo rider had an entire album dedicated to him, officially or unofficially. And if she publicly acknowledged that he was the inspiration, well, Flash was sure that his sister, Chloe, would find a way to spin Brooke's new album as a positive for Flash and the All-Around All-Stars Rodeo. Probably.

Besides, Brooke had said herself the album wouldn't be out for a few more months. She was still fine-tuning some of the material, still recording. Forewarned was forearmed. It was a good thing he was here tonight. He could work with Chloe to plan for a couple of different contingencies.

His sister had already basically figured out that Flash was crushing hard on Brooke.

Although…she'd want to know why Brooke was so furious with him. And he did not have an answer for that. Brooke had kissed him goodbye. Thanked him for the amazing night. Told him to take care.

And that was *it*.

At least she hadn't forgotten him, right? If there was one word that described Flash Lawrence, it was *memorable*.

When Brooke started the next song—titled "Not Going Down (Without a Fight)"—Flash almost couldn't take it. What the hell? If it'd been any other club or dive bar in Nashville, he would've bailed. But when a songwriter or a singer started their set at the Bluebird, no one moved and no one talked—house rules. So he had no choice but to sit there and listen.

He'd spent a year trying to make sense of the fact that Brooke Bonner was an itch he hadn't finished scratching. Before her, he'd bounced around bars and rodeos for four, maybe five years, picking up buckle bunnies and beautiful women in every town from Phoenix to Peoria while riding on the All-Stars circuit. Brooke Bonner should've been just one more woman. It'd been a one-night. Meaningless. Satisfying.

Except that that night had meant something to him and he'd spent nearly thirteen months unsatisfied.

Coming here tonight hadn't been a good idea. But damn it, he needed to know if their night together had meant anything to her.

Something more than raw material.

Finally, her set ended and the crowd came back to life. Because she was the last act, she stayed in the center of the room and signed autographs and posed for pictures. Flash hung back at the bar, debating his next move. Should he wait for the crowd to thin and then approach her? Or would it be better if they didn't have an audience? In that case, he should head out to the parking lot and wait by her car. Or was that too creepy?

Brooke glanced at him, a frown wrinkling her forehead before she quickly looked away. Nothing about that said *invitation*.

But he didn't care about that little frown. He didn't care about the songs or the radio silence that had lasted over a year.

He wanted to look her in the eye, make his case and then hear whatever she needed to get off her chest in person—without losing his temper. He wanted to know how they'd gotten from that wild night to this.

And if he didn't get lucky…he'd walk.

But he wasn't playing this guessing game.

He paid his tab and headed outside. The Bluebird was in a nondescript strip mall, and it took some work for Flash to work his way around to the back of the building. There—that plain sand-colored sedan had to be hers. She'd told him that she drove a boring car because it blended in.

He took up residence against a wall a good ten feet from the door of the Bluebird, giving her plenty of room. Lying in wait for her was a terrible idea, especially after that window into her mind and most especially after that frown. Frankly, he wouldn't be surprised if she pulled a gun on him.

But that was a risk he was willing to take.

Three

"Great set," Kyle said, a note of pride in his voice. "It's going to be a massive hit. The whole album. Very girl power. I wish I'd written half of it."

"Be sure to tell the record label that, okay?" Brooke said, her cheeks beginning to hurt with all the smiling she was doing. She valued Kyle's opinion and the crowd had seemed to enjoy the songs as well, so this was all great.

Except Flash Lawrence was here. What was she supposed to do now?

"I'm so proud of you," Kyle added, giving her an awkward hug.

She hugged him back but her mind was stuck on Flash. She'd almost, *almost* gone up to him out there. There were a lot of people milling around, so it wouldn't have been a big deal if she'd walked up to the bar and asked for something else to drink, right? People wouldn't have made any connection between her getting a drink and making small talk with a random cowboy, right? Then she could've at least figured out why he was here. The only two possibilities she could think of were—this was either a stunning coincidence or...

Or he'd come to see her.

And as she had only mentioned the Bluebird appearance on her Twitter feed two days ago...

She'd bet good money Flash was outside waiting for her. Which meant she had to talk to him. Which meant she had to tell him about Bean. Her son.

His son.

Oh *God*, this was going to suck.

"Hey," Kyle said, putting a hand on her arm. "You okay?"

"Fine," she said, working hard for that smile. She'd kept Bean a secret for a lot of good reasons, but none of them came to mind now that she knew she'd *have* to tell Flash. Because the alternative was to do exactly what her mother had done—keep on hiding and lying for the rest of her life—and Brooke couldn't do it. She was done hiding.

Or would be, just as soon as Flash knew. But to Kyle, she said, "Just relieved the new stuff is solid."

Kyle gave her a worried look. "You sure? I know you, Brooke. I know how you write. That stuff...it seemed kind of personal."

"We need to get going," Alex said, all but hip checking Kyle into a wall. Bless her heart. "Sorry, Morgan."

"Jeez, woman," Kyle said, rubbing his shoulder. "You should've stuck with football."

Brooke gave him another quick hug and made a not-exactly-quick stop in the ladies' room. Damn it, she was stalling.

Not hiding anymore, she repeated to herself as she picked up her guitar case. Alex opened the back door for her and, as she walked out into the humid Tennessee air, Brooke felt it again—that tingling at the base of her spine.

"Brooke."

That was all he had to say for her worst nightmares and her fondest dreams to come true at once because this was really happening.

Flash had come for her.

Oh, God—she wasn't going to be strong enough because even just the sound of her name on his lips was making her resolve weaken.

It didn't have the same effect on Alex. "Hey—back off," she rumbled, stepping in front of Brooke. "Show's over, buddy."

"Brooke?" Flash said again. "I just want to talk. Privately."

Yeah, she knew what happened when she and Flash had any privacy. At least the first time they'd hooked up, in her dressing room, she hadn't planned to have sex with him. At least, not right then. But Flash was that rare, dangerous creature—an irresistible man.

Okay, so not total privacy. But maybe semiprivate would work.

Brooke put a hand on Alex's shoulder. "It's okay," she said quietly as she stepped around her friend. "I know him."

Alex leaned down to whisper, "I don't like him." Of course, her whispering wasn't exactly quiet and, given Flash's smirk, it was clear he'd heard.

Yeah, neither would Crissy Bonner. The record label executives would love Flash, though—a showy pro-rodeo cowboy would be great for PR.

But she didn't want Flash to be a public relations bonanza. She wanted…hell. She didn't know what she wanted. Except for some privacy. She owed him that much.

"It's fine. Can you wait in the car?"

Alex glared at Flash and growled. But then she said, "Fine—but only for a few minutes," as she took the guitar case from Brooke.

Then he did the ballsy thing and approached Alex. "Hi. Flash Lawrence. And you are?"

Alex gave him a look that made lesser men turn tail and run, but Flash held his ground. He wasn't a coward, that much was for certain.

With a quick look at Brook, Alex said, "Alex Andrews.

Don't try anything funny." She jabbed a finger in Flash's direction and pointedly did *not* shake his hand.

"Wouldn't dream of it. As Brooke can tell you, I don't have a sense of humor." She couldn't help the smile that danced over her lips at that bold-faced lie. She remembered quite well how easily she'd laughed with Flash. It would've been one thing if he'd just been amazing between the sheets. But he'd been so dang easy to be with—kind and funny and tender and hot and...

He'd made her like him.

She'd liked him a good deal. Seeing all those news headlines about his violent temper and plea deals had felt like a betrayal, almost.

Because she'd been wrong about him.

Had any of it been real?

Flash stood his ground as Alex crowded into his personal space on her way to the car. The one with the baby bucket-seat base in the back seat. True, there was a blanket thrown over it because God forbid anyone should notice that Brooke Bonner had a child restraint system in her car, but still. Hard evidence of Bean was practically within line of sight.

How was she supposed to do this, damn it?

Because Flash looked so much better in person than he did in her dreams. Maybe it was just the jacket. But maybe it was him. There was something almost...calm about him.

With a huff, Alex slammed the driver's side door. It wasn't like Brooke and Flash were alone—the door to the Bluebird's kitchen was still propped open and Kyle might come out at any second. But for this brief moment, she and Flash had something resembling privacy.

"You look great," Flash began.

Brooke barely managed to avoid rolling her eyes even as the compliment sent a thrill through her. She was still at least one size above where she'd been before she'd gotten pregnant, and her mother was pushing her hard to lose the last of the baby weight so people wouldn't get suspicious. To know she looked okay was a relief.

No, no—she was not falling for superficial compliments. Because that was just the generic sort of statement that any man trying to get laid would open up with.

"What do you want, Flash?"

Please don't say something romantic ran through her mind in the key of G at the exact same moment *say something romantic* did the same thing in harmony. She'd have to write that down later—could be a good hook.

Flash whipped off his hat and launched the smile at her that had melted her heart—and other parts—so long ago. "I wanted to see you again, but I get the feeling that you're not exactly happy with me right now."

"You picked up on that, did you?"

"It was subtle," he replied, that easy grin on his lips, "but I did notice a little anger in those songs."

"Well, your powers of deduction are in fine form." She made a move to step around him, but he mirrored her movements. "What, Flash? I'm tired."

"I want to apologize," he said, moving closer.

She inhaled sharply. This sounded like a trap. "Oh? And what, exactly, are you apologizing for?"

"Don't know. But—" went on when Brooke scoffed heartily "—clearly I hurt you and, judging by the songs I heard tonight—which were great—I hurt you badly. So let me apologize, Brooke."

Lord, did he have to sound so damned earnest about it? She almost wished he was cocky and overconfident. This would be so much easier if he was trying to talk his way into her panties again. This time, she'd be ready for him. This time, she wouldn't make a mistake.

But, no—the cocky cowboy she'd taken to bed was nowhere to be seen, and in his place stood a serious man staring at her with so much longing and tenderness that, if Brooke allowed herself to think about it at all, he might take her breath away. So she didn't think about it.

"Fine. Apology accepted. Good night, Flash."

"Brooke," he said, her name a whisper on his lips. "I've missed you so much and the hell of it is, I don't know why."

"Really?" she snapped at him. *Anger* was great. *Anger* was not being seduced by his sweet words or intense looks. *Anger* was reminding her exactly who he was—a smooth talker with a violent streak—and, more importantly, who she was. He'd gotten her pregnant and she'd had to deal with the fallout without him because she couldn't trust him. Her whole life had been upended because of this man because she'd fallen for his sweet words and right now, he wasn't even that smooth at the talking. "That's not an apology, Flash. That's an insult."

"Would you listen?" he said, a warning in his voice. But then the weirdest thing happened—he took a step back and drew in a deep breath before letting it out slowly. "What I mean to say is, you were amazing—gorgeous and funny and smart and so easy to be with, and I'd be a fool not to want more of that. With you," he added quickly.

She snorted again, crossing her arms in front of her chest as different harmonies for *don't say something romantic* played in her mind.

"We had one night. A one-night stand, as you so eloquently put it." He ran a hand through his hair and then looked at her again, and this time the need in his eyes really did take her breath away. "That was all it was supposed to be, damn it, and…and it wasn't. Not for me. I wanted more with you then and I want more with you now."

"That's all well and good, Flash, but it's not enough. Not for me."

She needed to tell him about Bean. It wasn't fair to him

to keep his son hidden away, and it wasn't fair to Bean to deprive him of his father when the man was right here.

But she couldn't.

Not until she knew what he wanted and not if all he wanted was another night. Because she couldn't make a mistake like Flash Lawrence again. She needed him to be a father to his son. She needed him to be a co-parent, at the very least.

She needed to know she could trust him. And right now? Not a lot of trust to go around.

Eyes closed, he took another one of those weirdly deep breaths and then he stepped up to her. Even though the night was warm and sticky, she felt the warmth from his body as if he'd shined the heat of the sun down upon her. And it only got worse when his hand came up to cup her face and his thumb stroked over her cheek. She knew she should push him away, but when he touched his forehead to hers she couldn't help leaning into his touch, breathing in the clean scent of him—leather and man and, Lord, it was wonderful.

"I followed your career, watched your climb up the charts. Celebrated your number-one hits and cheered your award-show wins. Saw your face every night I closed my eyes," he said, his voice soft as his breath brushed over her skin like a lover's kiss. Her body clenched in an involuntary response to his touch, his words. His *everything*. "I tried so hard to forget you, but I couldn't. And I'm so sorry."

He wasn't making any sense. He *wasn't*. But damn it all if he wasn't reminding her exactly why she'd taken him into her bed, because even when he was speaking in riddles he still made it sound so good—and feel even better. "Because you can't forget me?"

"No." He laughed a little. She looked deep into his eyes and saw unflinching honesty as he said, "I'll never be sorry for that. But I looked you up and I realized, what if you'd looked me up, too? What if you read about the arrest and trial and plea deals? So I'm sorry for how you must've felt when you read the headlines. I'm sorry you saw the worst of me, playing out in real time on the internet. I'm sorry I destroyed a perfect memory of a perfect night, because that's what you were to me. A perfect memory."

She inhaled sharply, her eyes stinging even as she squeezed them tight. That was a *very* good line, one that was already weaving its way into the chorus her brain was trying to write.

"I came here tonight not to tell you I wanted you—although I do," Flash went on. His other hand settled in the curve of her hip, gently pulling her into him and, weak as she was, she let him.

Her breasts brushed against his chest. "Then why?" she whispered, afraid of his answer even as she was desperate to hear it.

"I came here to tell you what happened after the headlines. After I got sentenced and suspended from the circuit, I did my community service and completed my anger management courses. I made a promise to myself and my family that I was going to rein in my anger and stop letting it rule me."

"You did?" Somehow, her hand was underneath his jacket on his chest—not pushing him away but resting right over his heart. She could feel it beating, strong and steady.

He turned his head ever so slightly, his lips brushing against her temple, then down her cheek. "I also quit drinking. I won't say I'm an alcoholic, but when I drank I couldn't keep a handle on my anger, and that's when I got into trouble. I've been sober for eight months and counting."

"Tonight?" Her voice came out breathy and tight, and the space between her legs felt warm and liquid with want because she hadn't had a man in her bed since him and she missed him.

No, no—she missed sex. Which was normal. She'd been cleared to resume her nonexistent sex life from the private OB/GYN—who her mother had made sign a nondisclosure form, HIPAA be damned—six weeks ago, as long as she used reliable birth control, and it had taken everything Brooke had not to laugh in the woman's face.

So she didn't necessarily miss this man. She just missed men in general.

Right.

"Ginger ale. In a beer glass." Then he brushed his lips against hers, and she was powerless to do anything but open her mouth for him. When he licked inside her, she tasted sugar and ginger, not beer.

Pop shouldn't be so seductive, but this was crazy. How did he know that was exactly what she needed to hear? How could he taste so good?

How could she still want him so damned much?

Because she did.

He broke the kiss but he didn't pull away. Somehow, they were closer now and she could feel the heat of his erection pulsing against her belly. She could feel her pulse matching his, beat for beat.

"I want to see you again," he murmured against her lips. Then his mouth was trailing over her cheek, toward her ear. "I need more than just one night, Brooke. But I won't ask you for anything else."

"Yes." The word slipped out before she could think better of it, before the logistics of another night in Flash's arms could rear their ugly head. She needed more from him, too.

"Where? Say the word and I'm there, babe. I'm anywhere you need me." As he spoke, he pressed his knee between her legs, putting pressure right where she needed it. She couldn't fight down the moan. God, it'd been so long since another person had touched her for pleasure. *Her* pleasure. "Just tell me you need me."

"My house. I need..."

But reality reared its head.

Her mother was at her house, babysitting her son. Mom didn't live with Brooke and Bean, but she did live in what the real estate agent had described as the mother-in-law house on the property, a completely separate building almost 250 yards away from the main house—close enough for baby emergencies, but not under the same roof.

However, if Brooke waltzed in with Flash on her arm, they'd never get to the bed. Mom and Flash—that was a scene Brooke wasn't ready to face tonight. Maybe not ever.

"I need half an hour before you come over." She could get Mom out of the house and give herself a chance to change her mind. Or at least make sure she had some condoms because she wasn't going to make the exact same mistake again.

A honking horn tore through the night. Flash and Brooke jerked apart just as Kyle Morgan emerged from the back of the Bluebird. Guiltily Brooke glanced at the car, where Alex glared at her, then at Flash, then back at her.

Right. They had an audience and Flash had just kissed her, and she'd probably been about twenty seconds from completely throwing herself at him.

"Hey, Brooke—everything okay?" Kyle asked, sounding meaner than she'd ever heard him. "Where's Alex?"

Flash took another step back. He looked at Brooke like he was waiting for her to lead here.

"In the car." Kyle stopped next to her, eyeing Flash with a healthy dose of warning. "This is a friend of mine."

"Great set tonight," Flash said, cutting through the awkwardness and stretching his hand toward Kyle. "Flash Lawrence. Sounds like you had some big hits waiting to happen in there. Eric Church, maybe? He could bring down stadiums with that one song about rebels."

Kyle glanced warily at Brooke before returning Flash's

handshake. "Thanks. Toby Keith was also eyeing 'My One, Her Only' for his next album."

Flash whistled appreciatively and Brooke felt Kyle relax. How did he do that? Flash Lawrence could charm his way into any situation. She'd fallen for that charm once.

She couldn't afford to fall again.

As Flash and Kyle made small talk about country singles and Flash offered his opinion on what played well at the rodeos, Brooke had to accept that somehow, Flash had known exactly what she needed to hear—that he wasn't the same man he'd been when he'd made all those awful headlines. He'd worked on being a better man.

Had he become the kind of man she'd want around her son?

Except she wasn't *just* a single mother thinking about dating again, and Bean wasn't *just* her son. He was Flash's son, too, and she couldn't keep his baby away from him, no matter what. She knew what it was like to grow up without a father. She couldn't do that to Bean. Not if Flash was willing to step up.

Was he?

"Well, it was great meeting you, Morgan," Flash said, shaking Kyle's hand again. "Looking forward to hearing your next big hit."

Kyle actually blushed at that. "Always great to hear from a fan. Will we be seeing you again soon?" He held out his hand to Flash.

Brooke didn't miss that *we*.

Flash heard it, too. He cut a glance at her as he shook Kyle's hand again. "That depends on Brooke."

Kyle leveled an intimidating look at Flash and didn't let go of his hand. Instead, he pulled Flash off balance. "You're damn right it does. Alex isn't the only one you'll have to go through if you hurt her." Then, just as quickly as it had appeared, the threat of violence dissipated into the night air.

Surprise registered on Flash's face but, after a beat, he broke out that smile Brooke saw every time Bean grinned at her. "Trust me, hurting Brooke is the last thing I'd ever want to do."

Then both men turned to her.

So this was the moment when she had to make a decision. Was letting Flash back into her life and her son's life a good idea, or was it another mistake waiting to happen?

Knowing her luck, both.

Just like Bean had been both the biggest mistake of her life and the best thing that had ever happened to her.

"Let me give you my info," she told Flash, holding out her hand for his phone. She would have preferred not to do this with Kyle standing right next to her, but this was still better than having Kyle catch them kissing.

Flash unlocked his phone and handed it to her. Her heart going a mile a minute, she put in her address and number and added the note, "half an hour" to give her enough time to get Mom out of the house and…and decide how she was going to handle Flash.

She was not bringing Flash home to have wild, crazy, *great* sex with him again. Absolutely not. This was about Bean. Her world began and ended with him now. That's all there was to it because a boy needed his father. Even if that boy was only three months old.

She handed the phone back and turned to Kyle with a studied casualness she definitely wasn't feeling. "Hey, if I need a little help on a few songs, you're interested?" Because everything on the *Roots* album was…energetic, to say the least, and Kyle was good for ballads.

Kyle's eyes lit up. "Hell, yeah, sweetheart. Just give me a call. Good meeting you, Lawrence."

But the man didn't move. He just stood there, watching her and Flash to see what was going to happen next.

"Morgan." Flash tipped his hat. "Brooke. I'll be seeing

you." He packed a hell of a lot into his gaze before he turned on his heel and strolled out of the parking lot.

She about broke out into a sweat as she watched him walk away. One thing was for sure—if anything, Flash's ass had only gotten better in the last year. A man who rode broncos and bulls for a living had the legs and backside to go with it. The first time they'd had sex—against the wall of her dressing room—he hadn't even taken his chaps off. She'd had a view of that ass in her dressing room mirror that even now threatened to make her melt.

She wasn't inviting him over for sex. She had a single-minded purpose here—informing him he was a father.

But Lord, that man made every part of her weak. Always had and, apparently, always would. She just needed to be strong enough to get through the next few hours.

Honestly, she wasn't sure she was *that* strong. Especially when he turned and tipped his hat to her, the model of the country gentleman.

"Honey," Kyle started when Flash was out of sight. "Did I just meet the inspiration for all those new songs?"

"It's not like that," she protested, and to her own ears, it sounded weak. "He's a friend."

Kyle gaped at her. Yeah, he wasn't buying it, either.

"The way he looked at you? No way. That's a man who wants a lot more than 'friendship,'" he said, throwing in air quotes for good measure. "And the way you're looking at him? Come *on*. I may be an old man, but I'm not blind."

Brooke didn't have a snappy comeback to that, but Alex saved her. "Are we going?" she all but shouted through the car window.

"Be careful!" Kyle called as Brooke climbed into the car. "And call me if you need backup!"

Yeah, like that was going to happen. She just waved as Alex sped off.

How would people like Kyle react when he found out

that she'd been sitting on the juiciest of details for months? She hoped people wouldn't be too hurt that they hadn't been important enough to be in the know, but, seriously, aside from the executives on her record label, the private OB/GYN and nurse who'd delivered Bean at Brooke's home, the equally private pediatrician and Alex—and Mom, of course—no one else knew.

But she couldn't hide her son forever. She wanted to take him to parks and the zoo and…and just out. She wanted to talk to other moms she knew about what was normal and what wasn't. Hell, she wanted to take some pictures with Bean, not just cell phone shots. She wanted to do all the normal stuff with her son.

She didn't want to hide. Not from her friends, not from her fans and not from Flash.

Worse, when she daydreamed about all those fun things, she wasn't alone. Flash was next to her.

In her perfect world, Flash was by her side during the day and in her bed at night. Her son didn't have to grow up without his father, like Brooke had. And she didn't have to feel so alone anymore.

But that fantasy was just that—fantasy. Instead of that perfect world, she'd invited him home to tell him about Bean and also to *not* have sex with him.

The tension rolling off Alex was palatable, which had to be the only reason Brooke heard herself repeating the lie, "He's just a friend."

"Uh-huh." Yeah, Alex wasn't buying any of that as she took off for the 440.

From there, they'd take 40 west to the house she'd bought with the money her uncle had managed not to embezzle. Her home was on five fenced-in acres. If she had another hit record and successful tour, she had plans to completely renovate the sprawling mid-century ranch house. She hadn't even been able to paint the rooms while she'd been pregnant because the smell of primer had made her sick.

"The show went well, don't you think?" Brooke tried again, desperate for a subject change.

"Hon," Alex said in her growly voice, "did you tell him about Bean?"

This was the problem with best friends. There was no hiding anything from them. Because of course Alex had figured out that the one show she'd missed was the rodeo in Texas.

"No," she said, because more lies would only be an insult to Alex's intelligence.

Alex thought that over as she began to weave through traffic like the devil himself was hot on their tail. Finally she asked, "Are you going to?"

Brooke had closed her eyes. Flash was the boy's father. She simply didn't have a choice.

"Yes," she admitted, wondering why it felt like such a defeat. "But…"

"Yeah, I know—don't tell your mother," Alex grumbled. "She'll find out sooner or later."

Later, Brooke prayed. Please let it be much, much later.

Her mother had sat on the secret of Brooke's paternity for twenty-some-odd years. Brooke could keep Flash a secret for just a little bit longer.

She was going to tell Flash about Bean and hope all he'd said about not letting his anger rule him was the truth. But…

God, it was selfish and wrong, but she wanted just one more time with him before she told him she was the mother of his child.

One last grasp at the woman she'd been a year ago. A lifetime ago.

Humming a melody that built itself around the words, she had to wonder—was bringing Flash to her home another huge mistake or the making of another perfect memory?

Four

At exactly eleven forty-five, Flash walked up the front walk to Brooke's house, which was a long rancher that looked a bit shabby around the edges. The whole thing was set almost half a mile back from the road, creating the appearance of privacy. Flash didn't see any other lights and the night was hushed. He did his best to tread quietly, afraid to disturb the quiet.

Clearly, Brooke didn't want anyone to see him coming or going and he respected that—after their night together, she'd become the subject of a lot of media scrutiny.

The temptation to whistle was strong, but he tamped it down. It was a nice night and Brooke had kissed him. Sure, her new music was a broadside attack on him, but she was stunningly talented and she'd kissed him. He'd said what he needed to say and then *she'd kissed him*. She needed him and, by God, being needed was freaking amazing. This had all the markings of another amazing night.

All in all, things were looking up.

But doubt was trying to crowd out his good mood. Why did she need so much time to get ready? Possibly she just needed to pick up—as if he gave a flying rat's ass if there were dishes in the sink or clothes on the floor.

Another possibility bugged him. Because what if she needed the extra time to get rid of someone?

The thought of her being married or hustling some dude out of the house made his stomach tighten, but he breathed through the pressure. He was not the boss of Brooke. He had no claim on her whatsoever, and it'd been over a year since they'd been together.

He wanted her but not enough to ask her to cheat with him. The bonds of marriage were unbreakable. Hell, his own father still deeply mourned the loss of Flash's mother and that'd been fourteen years ago. Trixie Lawrence was still Milt's wife. Not even death would change that.

Flash would do damn near anything for another night with Brooke. But he wouldn't wreck a marriage.

Everything else, though…

Kissing Brooke Bonner again had brought it all back to him. The feel of her body flush against his, the taste of her singing on his tongue. She was honey sweet and he wanted to sip her. Just thinking about her hand on his chest, how her fingers had curled into his shirt to hold him close while he'd done his damnedest to show her how good he could be for her—he was downright giddy.

A long, painful year of "self-improvement" and "introspection" was behind him. All that time without women to relieve the pressure, without beer to dull the frustration. Months of reining himself in, no matter how much some jackasses deserved a punch to the mouth. Thirteen freaking months of watching Brooke from a distance, wondering if he haunted her dreams like she haunted his—and now he was so close to having her again that it was physically painful to walk.

The need to bury himself in her body beat a steady rhythm through his veins, all because she'd kissed him.

Flash had to stop just outside the circle of light cast by the porch lights and wait for his blood to cool. He wasn't expecting anything from this...*visit*. There was no way six songs worth of percolating rage had been erased with some good groveling and a kiss.

But...best case, they'd be naked at some point before dawn broke and stay that way until at least lunch tomorrow. He had a pack of condoms in his back pocket, purchased in a fit of optimism after discovering she'd be at the Bluebird. He didn't have to report in at the Bridgestone Arena before Friday afternoon. He could happily spend a few days wrapped up in Brooke.

But that was best case. Hope for the best, plan for the worst, and the worst case was Brooke taking advantage of what seemed like acres of privacy to read him the freaking riot act. Just because she'd molded her body to his and whispered, "I need you," in his ear didn't mean Flash was about to get lucky.

Failure to plan is planning to fail. He'd learned that the hard way over the last year.

So this was the plan. If she got mad, he wasn't going to get mad back. This wasn't a screaming contest and he didn't have to win. Yeah, it would suck, but he deserved to be put in his place, as his brother Oliver and brother-in-law Pete loved to remind him. He would grit his teeth, focus on breathing, take a walk if he started to lose his cool and hopefully figure out what, exactly, he'd done to inspire such passionate songwriting. Then he'd make his apologies—again—and do what he could to make things right and...

And then he'd walk away.

If that's what she wanted, that's what he'd do.

And if he had to walk away, he wouldn't go to a bar and pick a fight. He'd go pound out a few miles on a treadmill at his hotel workout room until he couldn't move.

There. That was a plan.

With his emotions firmly under control, Flash strode up the front steps.

Before he could knock, the door swung open and there she was.

"Brooke," he said, his body tightening at the sight of her.

She'd lost the vest thing and the belt, as well as the heavy jewelry that'd been around her neck. Which gave him a hell of an unobstructed view of her cleavage. But the worst thing of all was she'd lost her boots. The sight of her bare toes slammed into his gut, and he went hard when she placed one delicate little foot on top of the other. Her toes were painted a deep, sultry red, and he wanted to suck on each one until she screamed.

The space between them sparked with electricity, just like it had the first time he'd clapped eyes on this woman. There was something about her that lit him up, and he was tired of trying to ignore that elemental reaction.

She needed him. She'd asked him here. He wanted her. Simple.

He realized he was still staring at her toes. He jerked his eyes up.

Brooke stared up at him, her mouth forming a round little O. Then she dropped her gaze, blushing furiously. "Flash. You're on time."

"I would never disappoint a lady."

She tucked her lower lip under her teeth and he fought back a groan. Was she trying to torture him?

He desperately wanted to believe her hesitation was because she didn't know how to ask for what she wanted. She hadn't had any problem telling him where and how to touch her last time, and he'd done his best to give her what she'd needed. Because he wanted to give her anything she wanted. *Everything* she wanted.

And he couldn't do that outside the house, so he stepped

inside. Into her. Her head popped up, her eyes wide and dark with what he prayed was desire.

"I missed you," he said, cupping her cheeks in his hands and lifting her face to his. He didn't kiss her, but they were right back to where they'd been earlier, before they'd been interrupted. Brooke was in his arms and he didn't know how he'd get her out of his system.

"You said that."

"Well, it's true. I've never missed anyone like I missed you."

Her hand snaked up behind his neck, holding him against her. It was the sweetest thing he'd ever felt, that touch of possession. "How much?" Her voice was whisper soft as she backed up, pulling him with her.

He slid one hand down her neck, tracing the valley between her breasts before he settled it on her hip and pulled her into him. The last time he'd held her like this, she'd looped her arms around his neck and her legs around his waist and begged him to make her come. He'd done exactly as she'd asked. Twice.

"So much, babe. I'll do anything you want—you know that, right?"

Her eyelashes fluttered, the blush spreading down her neck and across her magnificent chest. He leaned down and pressed his lips against her pink skin, the warmth of her body setting his blood on fire. The last time he'd seen her breasts, he'd sucked on her rosy nipples until she'd moaned and thrashed beneath him.

Her chest heaved at his touch as her fingers curled around his neck, pulling him closer. "Anything?"

Yes—it was right there in her voice, waiting for him to come get it. Brushing his lips against her cheek, he slid both hands down her waist, around to her backside. He filled his hands with her, lifting her and pulling her against his erection. She gasped and he thought he might come right then. "*Anything*. You want me to stop, I'll stop," he murmured, pressing kisses that trailed over her skin until he could whisper in her ear. "You want me to leave, I'll leave. Just say the word."

Then he waited, the lobe of her ear resting against his lips, her bottom firm in his hands, the warmth of her breasts heating him up. This might be the last moment he could walk away from her, and it sure as hell wouldn't be a dignified walk. Every square inch of his body—a few inches in particular—throbbed to be closer to her, to pull her into his arms and hold her for as long as he could.

He felt her inhale, then let the air out slowly, her honey-sweet breath caressing over his cheek. Each second that ticked by was an eternity of torture, but he forced himself to be patient.

"Don't leave, Flash," she whispered, her lips touching his cheek. He shuddered as she leaned forward, bringing her body completely flush with his, and kissed his neck. "Stay."

Then she bit him—not hard, but with enough pressure to take everything that was already throbbing in his body and kick it into overdrive.

She didn't have to ask twice. He kicked the door shut behind him and spun her around. Her back hit the door with a muffled thud and then Flash was kissing her, her sweetness overwhelming his senses, her body erasing everything but this moment.

He squeezed her ass and ground his aching erection against her, and, God help him, he couldn't get enough. He closed a hand around one of her breasts, letting the heavy weight fill his palm.

She sank one hand into his hair, knocking his hat off. With the other, she grabbed his hand and jerked it away from her breast at the same time she pulled his head back.

"Shh!" she hissed, real fear in her eyes. "Quiet!"

"What is it, babe? What's wrong?" He swallowed and, holding himself in check, did the right thing. "We can stop. We don't…"

Shaking her head *no*, Brooke released his hand and stroked her thumb over his cheek. "I don't want to stop but…it's complicated, that's all."

"Just so we're clear—you're not married?" She shook her head *no* again and he almost sagged in relief. "Engaged?"

She gave him the saddest of smiles, one that did some mighty funny things to his heart. "No. Just… I need you, Flash. Like before." Her voice was barely a whisper, something he felt more than he heard. "But you have to be quiet and don't touch my breasts."

He gave her a strange look—if he was remembering correctly, she'd absolutely loved it when he'd played with her breasts.

"Please," she said softly, pulling him back down to her. "Just one more time, like it used to be. And afterwards… I'll understand, no matter what happens."

He stared at her. What the hell was going on? He was missing something, and he couldn't tell if it was *bad* or *really bad*.

"Babe," he said, hoping to reassure her, and he made damn sure to do it quietly. "If another night—or another weekend is what you need—that's what I want, too." He touched his forehead to hers. "Just tell me."

Breathing hard, she didn't reply right away. Then her beautiful green eyes fluttered open, and even before she spoke, Flash knew what her answer would be.

Yes.

He covered her mouth with a hard kiss, stuck in between this exact moment right now and an almost identical one last year. This is what he wanted—Brooke pressed against him, her mouth opening for his, her teeth scraping his lip.

She dug her fingernails into his scalp, the flash of pain burning bright into pleasure.

Oh, yeah—she pushed him and tormented him like no other woman ever had and he loved it.

Then she jerked her head away from his. "Condoms," she hissed, her voice soft but serious. *"Now."*

"Bed?" he asked, reaching to get the packet from his back pocket.

"No—can't wait." While he struggled with the foil wrapper on the condom, she went to work on his belt buckle.

God, she really couldn't wait.

He groaned as her fingers closed around him, and he almost dropped the condom when she stroked up, then down.

"I missed you too, Flash," she said, her mouth at his neck again. "No one makes me feel the way you do."

Then her teeth scraped over his skin and she squeezed him, and if he had been able to think right now, he might pause to break that statement down. But he couldn't think, couldn't do anything but feel her hands on him, feel the warmth of her breasts pressing against his chest.

She needed him. It was a hell of a thing.

Somehow, he got the condom on and got her skirt lifted. Thank goodness she had on a thin pair of panties. Flash didn't even bother to pull them down. He just shoved them aside and positioned himself at her entrance. The smell of her sex hit his nose like a bomb going off, and he groaned again.

"Now," Brooke breathed in his ear, hitching one leg over his hip. "Now, Flash. Now, now *now…*"

He slid his hands under her ass to lift her and then, with one thrust, he sank into her wet heat.

"Oh," she moaned, and he swallowed that sound with another kiss.

For a moment, he couldn't do anything but stand there as sensations swamped him.

For a year he'd been trying to forget how right she felt surrounding him, how perfectly they fit together.

It hadn't worked.

He couldn't forget what they had together, this electric physical connection.

"Brooke," he said, his words coming out a strangled whisper. He touched his forehead to hers and stared down into her eyes. He desperately wanted to believe he saw his own desire reflected back at him. "Oh, *Brooke.*"

"Shh." Then she was kissing him with all the passion he remembered from last year, all the pent-up desire that had been driving him slowly mad.

He began to rock into her, each thrust threatening to destroy him anew—especially when she whispered, "More," in his ear before she bit down on his lobe.

"Yes, ma'am," he whispered back.

It'd been like this in her dressing room, hard and fast and quiet against the door because people were right out in the hallway. It'd been exciting then. It was still exciting.

He paused long enough to shift his grip on her bottom, lifting her up and bracing his feet so he could support her with one hand. With the other, he reached down between their bodies to where they were joined. Brooke's head dropped back, her chest heaving as Flash pinched the folds of skin right above where he was buried inside of her.

Beneath his touch, her body shuddered. Her head thrashed against the door and he felt the spasms of her orgasm begin to move around him, clenching him so, *so* tight. A low roaring sound filled the air around them as he came and she came, too. It was only after that he realized the roaring was him, groaning in pure bliss.

He collapsed against her body, pinning her to the door, still inside of her. Breathing hard, he couldn't think, couldn't talk.

Home.

That was the only word he had, one that repeated itself over and over again when Brooke kissed his neck, then his mouth.

This was what coming home felt like.

Which was wrong. She wasn't home. He followed the rodeo. This was just…one of those things. A good night. Maybe a great week.

He pulled free of her body but not her arms. "Babe," he murmured against her hair, but then he stopped because he wasn't sure what was going to come out of his mouth next.

"I'm so sorry," Brooke whispered, and he heard the catch in her voice.

He reared back, staring down at her. No, he wasn't imagining things—she was on the verge of tears. "Don't apologize to me, Brooke. You and I…"

But that was when a new sound reached his ears—something high-pitched, almost a whine. Something that sent a shiver of real fear racing down his back.

A single tear spilled over and ran down Brooke's cheek. "So, *so* sorry," she whispered, slipping out from under his arm and leaving him hanging—literally. "I didn't want it to be this way."

"Brooke?" He turned but she was already halfway up the stairs. Her skirt had already fallen back down and she didn't look like she'd just changed his world.

And she didn't stop.

"Brooke!" he said as the noise got louder, grating over his nerves like sandpaper. "What—"

"We woke the baby," she said, choking on the words.

"The baby? What *baby*?" Flash stared up at her, the hairs on his arms standing at full attention, like lightning was about to strike.

Someone else's baby. That was the only thing that made sense. Not hers. Not…

Oh, God.

She made it to the top of the stairs and still hadn't answered.

"Brooke," he shouted. *"Whose baby?"*

"Mine." She turned around then and looked down at him, crying hard. "And yours. Our baby, Flash. *Our son.*"

Then she turned and ran.

Five

"Oh, Bean," Brooke murmured, scooping the baby into her arms. "Momma needed just a few more minutes." Five more minutes to break it to Flash that his son was upstairs. Five more minutes to untangle her body from his.

But it wasn't meant to be.

The baby howled his displeasure, and Brooke quickly realized what the problem was. He was soaking wet and probably hungry, too. He'd already been asleep when she'd gotten home.

Everything was wrong. That wasn't how she'd wanted to tell Flash. It wasn't fair to just drop that bomb on him. Not mere seconds after he'd been inside of her. Not when her legs were still shaking with the force of the orgasm he'd unleashed.

She hadn't planned to have sex with him again. No, that was a lie because obviously, she *had*—God, he was still so good—but she'd resolved to do the right thing and tell him about Bean first. And that resolve had lasted all of thirty-seven seconds. Right until he'd touched her.

She handed Bean his rattle shaped like a frog that croaked when he shook it. He only got to play with that toy when she was changing him and Bean was endlessly fascinated with it. Thankfully, it worked and the baby quieted down as she got him cleaned up.

That was when she realized the house was silent. Too quiet.

Was Flash still here? Or had he opened that door and walked out of her house and her life? Oh, Lord. Not that she would blame him for that, because she couldn't. She'd hidden Bean from him. An entire pregnancy, a birth, *a baby*—and she hadn't breathed a word of it to him. Really, that was unforgivable.

If Flash walked, that didn't change anything. She was still responsible for Bean, just like she'd always been. But now that Flash knew, she wasn't going to hide the baby anymore. It was time to show the world she had an amazing little boy. She'd tell her mother and her record label that she was going public and that was *that*. Her next album would get some extra PR, so everyone would win.

Brooke focused on the job before her. One day at a time and, when that didn't work, one hour at a time.

The sound of heavy tread on steps ricocheted through her body like a gunshot, and she gasped. The baby began to fuss again.

Flash hadn't left. Instead, he was coming upstairs. Somehow, that was worse.

Breathe. She had to breathe. It was good Flash hadn't left. Yay, he wasn't abandoning them! That was great, right?

Then he was standing in the doorway, staring at her with his mouth open and his eyes bugging out of his head, white as a ghost. He didn't say anything. She wasn't sure he was breathing.

This felt like something out of a nightmare, the reoccurring one she'd had after she'd realized she was pregnant, had looked Flash up and seen all those news stories. A shiver of panic raced down her back as she remembered everything she'd read—the drunken bar fights, the criminal charges for assault.

But as she stared at Flash staring at her, she knew she wanted more than just a fight-or-flight reaction out of Flash, more than sex against the door.

Well. The show had to go on, didn't it? She picked up Bean and turned to Flash. "Can you hold him?"

His mouth shut, then opened. "What?" The word sounded like she'd tortured it out of him.

"Here." She held Bean out to Flash. "This is Bean." She swallowed. "James Frasier Bonner, but I call him Bean."

She wouldn't have thought it possible, but Flash got even paler as he stared at the baby in her arms.

"He's yours," she said. "Please, Flash. I have to change his sheets and wash my hands. Can you hold him? For just a minute?"

Bean seemed to notice Flash for the first time. His little body went stiff and he made a noise of concern. On instinct, Brooke tucked her son into her arms. "It's okay," she murmured, watching Flash over the top of Bean's head. "It's…" she swallowed. "That's Daddy, baby. That's your father."

"You… I…" Flash stuttered. Then, without another word, he spun on his heel and was gone.

It felt like a punch to the gut, but before Brooke could do anything but stiffen in pain, he returned, his eyes blazing. "I am coming back," he said, his voice quiet and level and, somehow, all the more unsettling for it. Then he was gone again. This time, she heard his footsteps thundering down the stairs.

She hurried to the doorway. "Flash?" she called after him. Was it a good thing that he was coming back?

He stopped when he got to the bottom of the stairs, his back to her. His hands were definitely clenching and unclenching. He looked like he'd just been bucked off a bronco a half second too early to win it all.

"I need a minute," he said. The look he shot her over his shoulder made her stumble back, it was that intense. "Just give me a damned minute, Brooke."

He straightened and walked out the front door. At least he didn't slam it. That had to count for something, right?

Brooke had a baby.
Brooke had *his* baby.
He had a baby.

Flash paced relentlessly around his truck, struggling to breathe. The old Flash would've probably already punched the side of the truck a few times, breaking his hand and denting the metal. It was a pointless, destructive way of coping with a problem, striking out like that.

He'd thought she'd been giving him the gift of forgiveness with her kiss, her touch, her body.

And the whole time, the baby had been upstairs.

Jesus, he and Brooke had a baby *together*.

How old?

Flash did the math and, oddly, counting months helped him breathe. Thirteen months. Babies took nine months, right? No, wait—Renee, his sister-in-law, had been pregnant for ten months. So thirteen minus nine and a half, just to be safe, meant that baby boy was…

Three, maybe four months old.

Flash's knees threatened to buckle, and he had to hang on to the side of the truck bed just to keep from collapsing. He had a son who was almost four months old already and he hadn't known.

Because Brooke hadn't told him.

The world went a deep, crimson red at the edges again at what he'd missed—the first heartbeat, the labor and delivery, his son's first breath, first smile, first *everything*. All those moments, gone. He'd never get them back. All because Brooke hadn't told him, goddammit.

That was unforgivable.

But the moment the thought crossed his mind, Flash pushed back at it. He had to reframe this right *now*, because he was many things but he didn't like to think *stupid* was one of them.

He was angry, yes. Flash let the anger flow but he didn't try to hold on to it. He let it pass him by and forced himself to look underneath. Before he'd started court-mandated anger management therapy, he never would have thought there was more to anger than good old-fashioned rage, but he knew better now.

For starters, he was surprised. Not that *surprised* was a strong enough word, but it'd have to do. Brooke hadn't told him and then the baby had been crying, and Flash had been *stunned*—and that was a perfectly normal reaction to discovering a one-night stand had a child that was his.

What the hell did he know about being a father?

He'd gone over to his brother Oliver's house and played with his niece, Trixie, but that didn't mean he was qualified to be a father. He rode bulls and wild broncos for a living and did stupid stuff like having one-night stands. Not exactly the kind of thing a good dad did.

He didn't know how long he paced in circles, but eventually the world went back to being plain old dark.

He paused and looked up at Brooke's house. One light was on in what might be the baby's room. No, Flash couldn't keep thinking of that child as "the baby." That boy had a name. He was James Frasier Bonner, which was a good, strong name—even if she had given the boy Flash's real, awful name. James could be a Jim or a Jimmy or even a Jamie—*never* a Frasier.

What had Brooke called him? Bean? What the hell kind of nickname was that, anyway?

He took comfort in the fact that he must have been right—she'd tried to look him up and found those headlines and seen the pictures and decided it was safer for her and her child if Flash wasn't around. That was the only thing that made sense. He understood that on a rational level. It was a good thing that she'd do anything to protect their son.

But that didn't change the fact that *she hadn't told him.* She'd kept his son away from him. She'd never even given Flash a chance to show he had what it took to be a good father.

He would not let his anger get the better of him, but, by God, he had no idea how he was supposed to forgive her for what she'd done.

Forgiveness could come later. Right now, he had to make sure that Brooke never again managed to hide his son from him. That boy was his just as much as he was hers.

Brooke was the mother of his child.

He knew what he had to do.

He pulled out his phone. Brooke probably wasn't going to like this, but that was too damn bad, wasn't it? He wasn't about to try to handle a situation of this magnitude by himself. God only knew that'd be a disaster. Something like this required finesse and PR skills, not to mention a sensitive touch. None of those things would ever describe Flash, in this life or the next.

But they did describe his sister, Chloe.

He got voice mail and, scowling, hit Redial. He knew Chloe and her husband, Pete, were already in Nashville. They always got in a few days early to get everything set up for the All-Around All-Stars Rodeo. Finally, on the third try, Chloe answered and said in a breathless voice, "This better be important, Flash."

He cringed, trying not to think about what he'd interrupted. "Sis," he began, but the words, *I have a son with Brooke* got stuck in his throat.

Not that Chloe would've listened anyway. "I swear to

God, if you're in jail, I'm going to leave you to rot this time," she snapped.

In the background, Flash heard Chloe's husband, Pete Wellington, growl, "Now what's he done?"

Well, sometimes she had finesse. "Go to hell," Flash muttered. "I am having a legitimate problem and I thought I could count on you, but if you both are going to treat me like I'm a child, I'll do this myself." He hung up and then had to walk around the damn truck a few more times.

Yeah, he'd done more than enough to screw up his own life in the past. He knew that. Hell, everyone knew that. But since he'd started therapy, he would've thought he'd demonstrated that he was serious about being a better man. But maybe Chloe would always see a failure when she looked at him and, frankly, Flash didn't have the time or space to deal with that. Especially not right now.

He hadn't gotten far when his phone rang. Chloe. If he wasn't desperate he'd ignore her, but…

"Sorry," he gritted out. Chloe had always been the one to bail him out before, and he knew she hated it. "I'm not in jail or drunk. Not in a bar."

"What's wrong?" At least now she sounded concerned. And, oddly, that was what Flash needed.

"If I send you an address—a house—can you and Pete be here in…" He mentally calculated how long it'd take them to get from the hotel next to the Bridgestone arena in downtown Nashville to Brooke's house. "In twenty minutes? Quietly, without attracting any attention?"

After all, Flash hadn't known about his son because no one did. James Frasier Bonner hadn't shown up on any social media or paparazzi site. Brooke had gone dark months ago. Probably about the time she'd been unable to hide her pregnancy anymore.

"Flash," Chloe said, and finally she sounded about

right for this situation—worried, a little scared. "What's going on?"

He looked up at that lit window, where the one woman he couldn't forget was holding a son he hadn't known he had. This was how it had to be.

"I have a baby."

Chloe gasped, a noise of pure pain. Flash could hear Pete in the background saying, "Hon? You okay?" Belatedly, Flash remembered that Chloe had been trying to get pregnant for months now with no luck.

"Sorry, sis. I just found out. And I need help."

"Yes." He could hear her pulling herself back together. "Yes, of course we'll help. Who's..." She swallowed nervously. "Who's the mother?"

He looked up at the window again. Brooke was standing there, James Frasier Bonner in her arms. She'd always been the most beautiful woman he'd ever seen, but there was something about the image she presented, his son resting his head against her breast, her arms holding the baby tight—there was something right about it.

Why hadn't she told him? Damn it all to hell.

"It's Brooke. Brooke Bonner had my son."

He exhaled slowly. He was going to make things right, starting *now*.

Six

What was he doing out there?

Flash appeared to be pacing around his truck, which was hopefully an improvement over the way he'd all but bolted out of the house like the hounds of hell were nipping at his heels.

It was a good sign, she decided as she quickly washed up. He hadn't driven off in a blind fury, and even though he'd obviously been upset—what a pitifully weak word *that* was—he hadn't done anything…scary.

God, this was a freaking mess. She was nauseous with worry. For crying out loud, she could face down an arena filled with fifty thousand screaming fans with little more than a few butterflies in her stomach, but one man was going to be her undoing.

As if he could sense her panic, Bean looked up at her from where she'd set him down on the rug and smiled like he was trying to reassure her. He had his father's charm, but Bean's drooly grin was all sweetness and innocence, whereas Flash's grins promised wonderful, dangerous things. Things like long nights in hotels and hot sex against the door.

Brooke clung to that innocent baby grin. "Oh, you're having a grand time, aren't you?" she cooed to him as she swept him into her arms. "All sorts of excitement happening here tonight, and none of it involves sleeping."

Bean gurgled appreciatively and Brooke kissed his little head. At least someone was having fun.

Bean in her arms, she peeked out the window. Flash was still out there, leaning against the side of the truck. Wait— was he on his phone? Oh, hell.

Just then Flash glanced up, and even through the dark and distance, she *felt* the moment their gazes locked.

Who was he talking to? This could be a disaster. Of course there was a contingency plan for when she announced Bean's existence and, knowing her publicist, there was one for if the information leaked. She didn't want Bean to be gossip. She wanted to be the one controlling the information. She wanted to introduce her son to the world.

She could still get in front of this. She was supposed to meet with the publicist about tonight's show and approve a series of small shows on Music Row in downtown Nashville until the album officially dropped. Then there was a tour that was already set up, even though it hadn't been announced yet. She had to go over the album the final time with the producers. And then there were the interviews— so far, all by phone.

They might have to spend all that time talking about her one big mistake instead of her album, but she was going to control this narrative, by God.

With or without Flash.

Would he acknowledge the baby publicly? Would he sign off on the inevitable PR that would go along with introducing Bean to the world?

Or was this about to be a fight?

She didn't want a fight. She didn't want to be on opposite sides of Flash, stuck in a tug-of-war with the baby as the rope. She wanted Flash on her side.

Especially since Brooke was going to have to tell her mother about him. At the rate things were going, Brooke would have to tell her soon. Like, in a day or two. God help her, Brooke didn't want to.

Flash Lawrence was the sum total of things Crissy Bonner hated and Brooke knew it. Crissy would do the exact same thing Brooke had done—she'd start by researching Flash, and the moment those headlines came up it'd be all over.

It wouldn't matter how much Flash would claim he'd changed. Crissy Bonner would see only the irresponsible, immature ass who'd knocked her daughter up and abandoned her to brawl in bars and ride bulls—all of which put the carefully crafted career Crissy had been arranging since Brooke had turned five in danger of collapsing under the weight of scandal. Brooke didn't know anything about her father, who Mom claimed had split when Brooke was still crawling. But, needless to say, Crissy Bonner was not a big fan of any man who abandoned a woman and a child.

Nope. None of that was *for the best*.

Cuddling Bean to her chest, Brooke settled into the rocker. No matter what, her son came first. She and Flash would…work something out. Shared custody, maybe. Brooke wouldn't allow her mother or her record label or anyone—not even Flash himself—to hurt her child.

But what if there could be something more? For the first time since Bean had announced himself to Flash, Brooke's thoughts turned not to what'd happened months ago or what was going to happen tomorrow, but to those last few moments before it'd all gone to hell.

Flash, pressing her back against the door. Flash, kissing her even better than she'd remembered. Flash, bringing her to orgasm like no time at all had passed between this night and the one thirteen months ago.

Flash, reminding her who she'd been before she'd become a mother.

She shuddered, her body tightening almost painfully with need. She didn't know how this would work—would they date? Be co-parents? It seemed pretty obvious that she couldn't spend any time with Flash without having hot, *great* sex. She was too aware of him, too needy for him. So could they be co-parents with benefits, maybe? She'd be okay with that. Bean could spend time with his father, and she could keep Flash in her bed.

Anything more seemed unlikely—he'd be chasing the rodeo and she was supposed to go on tour. They'd rarely be in the same town at the same time, much less in the same state.

Of course, that all depended on if he was calling his lawyer or the press or, hell, his girlfriend, didn't it?

She stared down at Bean, his eyes already half closed as he held on to her thumb with his tiny fingers, nursing happily. She'd never been away from her son for longer than a few hours, recording her album in between nursing him. She wanted her son to know his father, she really did. It pained her to think of him missing that part of his life, his history. She had no idea who her father's people were. Her mom had erased any trace of that man from the record.

She wouldn't allow that to happen for Bean. She was *not* going to turn into her mother.

But she couldn't bear the thought of a custody battle with Flash, couldn't even consider the idea that she might lose her son.

Brooke made her decision.

She wouldn't ask for anything more from Flash than he was willing to give, and she wouldn't let him reject his son. And there was no way in hell she would let him take the boy away from her.

She might have dozed, she couldn't tell. The next thing she knew, Flash was sitting on the footstool before her, staring at where Bean was still barely latched on.

Flash didn't look mad. If anything, he looked...focused. He wasn't pale and that wild look was gone from his eyes. When he glanced up at her, that ghost of a smile played over his lips, and she felt a smile of her own answer his.

"I'll put him down, then we can talk," she whispered. Flash nodded. She moved Bean to her shoulder and gently patted his back. Flash studied her every move with an intensity that sent little shivers down her back. When she pushed to her feet, he stood with her.

She put Bean on his back in the crib and stared down at her perfect little boy, clinging to what might be the last moment of peace for a while. The moment she left this room, things would change—quickly.

Then Flash stepped up next to her, shoulders touching, his hip warm against hers, his fingers brushing hers on the crib rail. She fought the urge to wrap her arm around his waist and lean into him.

This was what she wanted, this closeness. This feeling of being part of a team. Yeah, she had Alex and her mother, but it wasn't the same. Only Flash could seduce her with that smile, make her feel like he did.

But it was an illusion, one shattered when he leaned over and said against her ear, "We need talk. *Now.*"

She nodded and, after leaning over to brush her fingers over the baby's forehead, headed down to the library. At least, that's what she called the room, because it's where all the books were, as well as her piano. It was mostly where she went when she needed a little peace and quiet to write, because the library was on the complete opposite side of the house from Bean's room. If there had to be shouting, hopefully they wouldn't wake the baby back up.

Flash didn't follow her at first. She turned back to see him lean over the crib, a look of what she hoped was adoration on his face as he touched Bean's forehead almost the exact same way Brooke had.

"Sleep for Mommy, little man," he whispered, and if it were possible to fall in love with him in a moment, she might have done so because Flash was going to love Bean, and the baby would know his father and everything would work out.

A vision of a happy family assembled itself in her mind's eye, one where Flash got up with Bean when he fussed at night and kissed her awake in the morning. A lifetime of teaching Bean to walk and swim and ride horses, of singing along to her songs when they came on the radio and watching Flash ride from the bleachers at the rodeo. She wanted it all with him, everything that went into being a family—first steps and first words, first *everything*.

And when Bean went to bed, she wanted Flash waiting up for her after a show or coming home to her after a rodeo, celebrating his win and her hits with hot kisses and hotter sex. A lifetime of losing themselves in each other, where the sex only got better and Flash was a man she could count on, through good times and bad. Where she was the only woman he needed or wanted.

Then Flash turned to her and another icy shiver raced down her back. That intensity was still there, but anything sweet or adoring was long gone.

Say something romantic. She didn't miss that the other chorus line—*Don't say something romantic*—had disappeared completely. She couldn't stop the melody from running through her head, couldn't stop wishing Flash would hear the same song.

But it wasn't meant to be because even if Flash wasn't

throw-things-against-the-wall mad, it was obvious he was still freaking furious.

Right. Best get this over with.

She headed down the stairs, determined to hash this out. She could like him and she could want him, but she wasn't going to torpedo her career or risk her son's happiness to soothe over Flash's ruffled feathers. He could just be mad. She would protect her family.

By the time she reached the bottom of the stairs, Flash caught up with her. He grabbed her hand, as if he were afraid she might bolt. "How old?" he asked softly, even as his fingers were as hard as steel around hers.

He was hard and soft all at once, intense and gentle. She wanted to lean into him, but she wasn't entirely sure she could trust that he wouldn't push her away.

"He'll be four months next Wednesday. In here," she replied, leading him into the library. "I was in labor the night of the Grammys. I had him at three in the morning."

"Ah. I wondered why you weren't there." Flash guided her to the long blue couch arranged in front of the fireplace, but instead of sitting next to her he moved to the mantel. "Did everything go okay? Any..." He swallowed, looking ill. "Any problems for you or him?"

"No. Labor was long and not fun, but everyone was fine. Seven pounds, six ounces, all his fingers and toes. The doctors say he's right where he should be."

Flash slumped against the mantel in relief. "Good. That's good. I wish I'd been there for you."

"I wish you had been, too."

Flash stared down at the floor. "Was I right earlier? You looked me up and found the headlines?"

Her cheeks blazed with heat, but the hell of it was, she had no idea why she was embarrassed. "I did. I'm sorry, Flash. I—"

"Don't apologize." His voice was harder now. "I brought

that on myself, as my sister is so fond of reminding me." He closed his eyes and another few moments passed. Was this normal for him? She should know—but she didn't because every time she was around him, they wound up having sex instead of deep, meaningful conversations.

"Just for the record," he began suddenly in a low voice, "if I walk out of the room, it's because I don't want to lose my temper, not because I'm walking away from you. I'll come back when I'm in control because we are nowhere *near* done, Brooke."

Honest to God, she had no idea if that was a threat or a promise. "All right." She shifted nervously, trying to find something to do with her hands. She wished she could go sit at her baby grand piano and let her fingers work out a melody. She thought better when she let the music carry away her anxiety.

"Are you mad at me?" she asked. As if that answer wasn't obvious.

"I am extremely upset," he said, his voice oddly level. His eyes closed again, and he exhaled for a long moment before going on, "I am mad at you because you didn't tell me about my son. I am mad at myself because I know we used protection, but obviously it failed and I failed you. Repeatedly. I obviously wasn't as careful with your health as I should've been, and I wasn't the kind of person who you thought you could trust."

Wait—was he not throwing her under the bus here? Was he taking *responsibility*? At least some of it? "I don't blame you for this, Flash. We used condoms, but it takes two to tango."

He nodded curtly, which was the only way she knew he'd heard her. "I've learned that, for me, anger is a catch-all for my emotions, and it takes work to understand the other things I'm feeling. I am *damned* hurt right now. And surprised and a little scared and…*mad*. Because how could you hide him from me, Brooke? How could you not even give me a chance?"

His voice had begun to approach a shout, but he checked himself and began to pace in a tight circle in front of the mantel. She was reminded of an unbroken horse in a corral, running back and forth and trying to decide if it was going to charge the fence or not.

Would he bolt? Or would he settle?

"I was going to tell you," she explained.

"When?" he snapped. "Because that baby's well past newborn, Brooke."

She winced. She hated this guilt, but he was right. "I always meant to tell you, but it was easy to put off contacting you until tomorrow and tomorrow and tomorrow, and the longer I didn't tell you, the more I was afraid that you'd…"

"That I'd punch a wall or wrap my truck around a light pole?"

She winced at the truth of that. "No one else knows about him except Alex, my mother and a few medical professionals, all of whom signed nondisclosure agreements in addition to their legal obligations to keep my medical history private. Oh, and a few record executives, all who had a vested interest in keeping the news quiet."

Confusion flitted across his face. "Why, though? Are you ashamed of him?"

"Of course not." Brooke slumped back against the couch. Suddenly she was tired. She'd done a show tonight and hooked up with Flash, and now had to defend the choices she'd made during the most stressful moments of the last year. Of her *life*. "It's because I wouldn't tell anyone who you were. Not a single person knows you're Bean's father— or knew. Alex figured it out tonight. I never wanted to keep this a secret, but I got overruled by literally everyone else, all because I didn't want to bring you into it."

His eyes bugged out. "You didn't tell anyone about me?"

"You were my secret. Those headlines…" She shuddered. "Because I wouldn't identify you, my mother and my record label decided to keep the pregnancy quiet."

"Damn it," he growled, but at least he growled quietly. "I was following your career and you suddenly fell off the map and I had no idea. If I'd known, I…" He stopped and suddenly paced to the doorway, but he didn't walk out. Instead, he turned back around. He looked tortured and it hurt her.

She'd made the best of a bad situation, but she'd never stopped second-guessing herself. And the fact that he wasn't screaming and blaming her for getting pregnant in the first place—that was what she'd feared. And what she'd expected, to be honest, after reading all those headlines.

His response gave her hope. Maybe this could work. Somehow.

She went to him, resting her hand on his arm. His eyes softened as he cupped her cheek with his hand and stroked her skin with his thumb. "I wish it'd been different," she whispered, leaning into his touch. "I'm so sorry, Flash. I'd change the past if I could but…"

"Neither of us can."

Somehow, she and Flash were getting closer. His arm slid around her waist and her head rested on his shoulder. God, it felt so damn good. This was who she wanted—Flash at his best.

"He's such a great baby, Flash. I want him to know his whole family—your family."

"I called my sister," he told her. "Chloe—remember meeting her at the Fort Worth rodeo?" Brooke nodded and Flash went on, his arms tightening around her waist. "She and her husband Pete run the All-Stars and they're in town. They're heading over."

"That's fine. Chloe seemed nice."

Actually, Chloe had been more than a little upset with

Brooke because hooking up with Flash had made Brooke late to start her show. But Brooke couldn't hold that against the woman. The show had to go on, after all. If someone had to be the first to find out about Bean, it was probably for the best that it was family.

Flash snorted. "She's a bossy know-it-all, but she's saved my butt more times than I can count. And she loves babies."

"That's nice. I…" Swallowing nervously, she tilted her head back and stared up at Flash. It was wonderful that this conversation about the past wasn't a fight, but that didn't mean a discussion of the future would be easy. Especially as his fingers stroked over her skin again, warm and encouraging. Brooke got the words out before his touch distracted her. Again. "I want to make this right. I don't know if you realize this, but to this day my own mother won't tell me who my father is, and I refuse to let my own son grow up like I did. I want us do this parenting thing together."

He took several long breaths, but he didn't close his eyes, didn't walk out of the room and he wasn't yelling—so this was all progress, right? Instead, he pulled her closer, her chest flush against his. Languid heat began to build in her body because even though she was exhausted and relieved and so, *so* thankful that Flash was finally here and it was all going to be okay, she'd had all of one orgasm in months and she selfishly wanted more. With this man—no one else.

Say something romantic, she silently begged him as she molded her body against his. Something sweet and hot that would let her know it would all work out just fine. Something that would take this perfect melody between them and make it into a song.

He didn't. He didn't kiss her or offer to hold her for the few short hours of sleep she might get before Bean woke up hungry. Instead, something in his eyes hardened as his arms crushed her against him. When he spoke, his voice was silky smooth and it sent a chill down her spine.

"We're absolutely in this together from now on. That's why we'll get married as soon as possible."

Seven

"What?"

Flash didn't miss the way Brooke's body went stiff in his arms. "Married," he repeated, feeling his blood pressure rise. "As soon as possible. That boy is a Lawrence by blood and by right."

Brooke moved but, instead of curling into him, she twisted out of his grasp. "Flash—what are you *talking* about?"

Not that he expected Brooke to start jumping for joy or anything, but hadn't she just said they were in this together?

"We need to get hitched," he said. "Quickly. Tomorrow, even."

Brooke stared at him with a look of horror on her face. "No. Absolutely not."

No? *No?*

Obviously, they needed to make this legal, especially if she was going to announce *their* baby to the world at large.

"This is nonnegotiable, Brooke. You can't keep pretending that I don't exist because it's convenient for you. That's my son, by God, and I won't let you keep him from me. You *will* marry me!" he yelled.

"I have no intention of keeping your son from you," she shouted back.

Oh, if that didn't just take the cake. "More than you already have, you mean?"

A little of the shock bled into fury as her eyes flashed with righteousness. "We are *not* getting married, Flash. Under *any* circumstance."

She couldn't have hit him harder if she'd actually punched him. He had to grab on to the door frame to hold himself up.

"The hell we aren't," he snapped. "That's my son and we're good in bed—against the door—together. Why wouldn't we get married?"

Dimly, he was aware that probably wasn't the best way to phrase it but, damn it, he was *pissed*. This was not complicated. Brooke was the mother of his child and he liked her. Simple.

Her cheeks blazing, her mouth opened for what looked like a blistering response, but just then headlights flashed through the parlor, cutting her off. They both turned toward the windows as the sound of doors slamming filled the air.

Brooke went to push past him but he grabbed her arm. "This conversation isn't over," he said, trying to make it sound nice and gentle.

But the way her eyes flashed a warning and the way she jerked out of his touch made it plenty clear he hadn't succeeded. "I will *not* be forced into anything I don't want," she said, her tone icy.

Then the doorbell pealed through the house. "Oh, no—the baby!" she said, making a break for the door. "Come inside—quietly," she said to Chloe and Pete, but it was too late because that was when James Frasier Bonner decided he needed to be part of the festivities.

"Oh, I'm so sorry," Chloe Lawrence said in a quiet voice,

even though they were way past whispering. James began to wail. "We didn't mean to wake him!"

"My bad," Pete Wellington said, whipping his hat off his head. "I rang the bell. Didn't think."

Brooke heaved a mighty sigh even as she launched a forgiving smile at Chloe and Pete. "It's okay. Things haven't been exactly *quiet* here tonight," she added, shooting a look at Flash that was part challenge, part scold and all mad.

Was she going to blame this on him? He hadn't been the only one yelling! "With good reason," he shot back, crossing his arms over his chest and trying not to glare. Given the way Pete frowned at him, Flash was pretty sure he hadn't succeeded with that whole not-glaring thing.

But then again, neither had Brooke. "You'll excuse me," she said, her voice tight. "I need to go see to *my* son."

"*Our* son," Flash snapped.

Chloe and Pete took in the tension, shared a look and then moved like a calf-roping team with years of competitions under their belts. "I'll come with you, if that's okay? I can't wait to meet this little guy, even if he's grumpy," Chloe said gently, putting an arm around Brooke's shoulders and turning her toward the stairs. "I'm sure it's been a long night—for all of you."

"You have *no* idea," Brooke said, almost sagging into Chloe. Even through the haze of emotions he was barely keeping in check, Flash heard the sheer exhaustion in her voice.

Well, if that wasn't enough to make a man feel like crap.

But before he could open his mouth—regardless of what was going to come out of it—Pete advanced on him, crowding him back into the room where Flash and Brooke had ended up before.

"How's it going?" the man had the nerve to ask, his hands up as if he were ready to give Flash a hard shove should the need arise.

"Great. Freaking great. Thanks for asking," Flash said. Okay, *snarled*.

He turned and began to pace around the couch. The one where Brooke had sat and said things about understanding and co-parenting, and why, for the love of everything holy, was she so hell-bent on not getting married? Was it marriage in general? Or was it just *him*?

It wasn't like he wanted to get married. He rode the rodeo. He lived out of his suitcase ten months out of the year and rarely saw his own home. That wasn't a lifestyle that lent itself to raising an infant. And this was the year he would win it all. He was off his suspension for fighting, he was sober and focused, and he did not have time to settle down. He'd make time, damn it, because that's what family did. But if he wasn't extremely careful about how this played out, he could kiss his championship year goodbye.

Damn it all to hell. If Brooke had told him about the baby months ago, he could've spent the off season getting to know his son and making plans. Now he had to scramble—and rely on Pete Wellington, of all people, to help him out.

Flash hadn't punched a single person in months—not since he'd gotten into a brawl with his father, his brother Oliver and Pete over Pete's underhanded tactics to win the All-Stars and Chloe away from the Lawrence family. And even then, Flash hadn't been as mad as he was right now. The last time he'd felt this dangerous had been...

It'd been when Tex McGraw had said those things about Brooke and Flash had been booted off the All-Stars as a result of the fight.

"What happened?" Pete kept his voice calm and level, but he wasn't inspiring anything calm or levelheaded in Flash.

"She had my baby and didn't tell me! Come on, Wellington—keep up!" Flash realized his hands were fists now, swinging loosely at his sides as he stalked Pete around the room. He was primed to throw a punch. God, it'd feel so good to just let go...

But Pete had been around Flash long enough that this outburst didn't faze him. "You need to hit something?"

"You volunteering?"

"Jackass," Pete said easily, dancing just out of reach. "Here." He bent over, grabbing the cushions from the seat of the couch. When he had two of them stacked, he held them in front of his stomach and stood in front of Flash. "Go."

"Seriously?" Was the man actually giving Flash permission to punch him?

Pete smiled. Not a big thing, but it was there. "Afraid a cushion will bruise your tiny little—oof! Damn, man— you've got a hell of a kick," Pete wheezed out, stumbling back a step.

A minute passed with nothing but the muffled sounds of Flash punching light blue couch cushions and Pete grunting as he absorbed the blows.

"I told her we had to get married immediately, if not sooner, and she said no, and that's when you showed up." He finished this off with a quick three punches. "This is *supposed* to be my year to win it all. She was *supposed* to be a one-night stand. And we have to get married because I'm not going to let her keep that boy from me, even though it'll screw up all my plans. But she said *no*."

Now that he'd hit something, he felt his anger going from a roiling boil to a low simmer. He punched the cushions one more time and sagged forward, his forehead resting on the top.

He had a son. The enormity of that fact still made him see stars. A healthy little boy who Brooke obviously loved and...

And she hadn't told him.

"Better?" Pete asked, sounding winded.

Flash nodded. He was breathing hard and his hands hurt, but the throbbing pain was good, anchoring him to his body.

Pete shifted, one arm coming up and lying over top of Flash's shoulder. Not that Flash needed a hug and not that this was a hug—but there was something comforting about it, all the same. "I guess I'm not as calm as I thought I was," he mumbled into the cushions.

"Did you hit anyone?" Pete asked, patting Flash on the back.

"Do you count?"

"Not today."

Flash shook his head. "Walked away when I needed to. Called you guys for backup when I realized I couldn't handle this myself."

"Didn't punch me in the face, either. All things considered, you're doing real well."

Flash snorted. It didn't feel like he was doing anything but losing it.

"You said you told her you were getting married?"

"Yeah." The thought left him uneasy. Marriage was... forever. Lawrence men—and Pete by extension—were one and done. If Flash married Brooke, that was it. He was *done*.

He'd do it. He'd do it in a heartbeat because that's what a father did for his son and, honestly, the sex was great. People throughout time had gotten married for less.

But...*marriage*.

To a woman who had no problem keeping secrets from him.

It was a recipe for disaster. And that was if she agreed. Huge *if*.

Pete was silent long enough that Flash lifted his head. When he'd been a hotheaded kid, he'd looked up to Pete

Wellington. The older man was a hell of a good rodeo rider, one Flash had aspired to be like. But for ten years, they'd been on opposite sides of a feud about the ownership of the All-Stars Rodeo. They'd made their peace, mostly, but it was still hard to think of this man as a friend.

Even if Flash suspected that's what Pete was. Who else would take a cushioned pummeling for Flash?

And now Pete was staring at Flash with a look of incredulous amusement on his face. "Where's the charm, Lawrence? I thought—*ow*—you were this legendary ladies' man. You could talk your way into any woman's bed and—*ugh*—make her feel like she was the only woman in the world."

"I am," Flash said, throwing another punch. He was going to owe Brooke a new couch, probably. "I was," he corrected.

He hadn't been that man since, well, since Brooke.

Maybe it wouldn't be so bad, a traitorous voice whispered in the back of his head. Great sex, yeah—but Brooke had gotten under his skin well before infants had come into play. Hell, he'd never looked up a one-night stand before, much less a year later. It might even be good…

But he'd have to trust her for that to happen, and she'd have to believe he wasn't the same asshole he'd been before he cleaned up his act, and, yeah, that felt like an impossible mountain to climb.

"You told her," Pete said yet again. "You *told* that woman to marry you, you giant jackass."

"Do you have a point?" Flash punctuated this with another combo punch. "Or are you just going to repeat yourself until the end of time?"

"What did you think would happen, issuing orders like that—to Brooke Bonner, of all people?" Flash paused midswing to stare at Pete, who rolled his eyes. "Next time, try *asking* her." Then he shoved Flash with the cushions.

Stumbling back, Flash gaped at Pete, who shook his head tauntingly.

Ask her?

Ask her to marry him. Like, down on one knee, with a ring and a promise.

Not an order. A proposal.

Like he cared about her.

Oh, hell—what had Flash done?

Eight

"I'm so sorry about this," Brooke said, leading Chloe Lawrence upstairs into the nursery, where Bean was screaming.

She felt like screaming, too. The nerve of that man, demanding that she rearrange her entire life—again—to get *married*.

Married! She had a comeback to orchestrate, a record to release, a tour to get through and a baby to announce to the world. Not to mention the whole mom thing, which was a full-time job all by itself. Who the hell had time for a wedding? Maybe in a few years...

Besides—Flash wasn't exactly making his case.

Yes, the sex was as amazing as ever, but she was not going to permanently tie herself to any man, much less one with an arrest record and a penchant for issuing orders. She had enough people in her life telling her what to do and when to do it, treating her as if she couldn't possibly make her own decisions about her life and her career. And now she had to deal with his sister because, of course, Flash had called in reinforcements to try and wear her down, no doubt.

She was more than tempted to call Alex for backup, but

that would undoubtedly lead to a brawl. And calling Crissy Bonner was out of the question—that'd be a brawl *and* a police report. For a brief second, Brooke debated calling Kyle Morgan, but that wouldn't work either, because Kyle would be just as stunned to find out about Bean as Flash had been.

No, Brooke was on her own here.

Then Chloe said, "Do not apologize for anything involving my brother," in a way that made it seem like she might consider Flash to be a butthead or something. When Brooke gave her a funny look, Chloe merely shrugged. "Look, I know he's got it bad for you and I also know I don't currently have all the facts, but just because he *wants* you doesn't mean he *deserves* you."

Brooke gaped at the woman in surprise because that was the thing she'd needed to hear right then. The second part, anyway.

What did she mean, Flash had it bad for Brooke?

"Thank you."

But Chloe wasn't listening. Instead, she'd moved to stand next to the crib, staring down at Bean with absolute adoration in her eyes. "Oh my. Oh, my *goodness*," she whispered, clutching her hands to her chest. "Look at you, sweetie. Hi, honey—I'm your aunt Chloe."

Brooke stepped around Chloe and picked Bean up. Chloe gasped, "Oh, he's *perfect*," her eyes filling with tears. "What's his name?"

"James Frasier Bonner, but I call him Bean," Brooke said.

"Can I hold him?" Chloe was already reaching out for the baby, but she stopped before actually plucking Bean from Brooke's arms. "I'm sorry. I'm just—this is such a surprise and I love babies so much and it's Flash's baby. You even gave him Flash's name!" She gave Brooke a watery smile.

"Sure. Here, take the rocker and we'll see if Bean is feeling sociable."

"Do you want to tell me what's happened?" Chloe said. "I gather that Flash didn't know about that little angel before a few hours ago?"

"No, he didn't. No one knows, really." She nestled Bean in Chloe's arms.

"Oh, goodness," the other woman whispered as Bean stared up at her. Then he turned on his father's charm and smiled at his aunt, who promptly began crying. That startled Bean and made him cry. Frankly, Brooke had no hope of holding herself together. It'd been *such* a long night.

"I'm so sorry," Chloe said again as Brooke took Bean back. "We've been trying to have a baby and..."

"It's okay." Brooke snatched the tissues and everyone took a moment to calm down. She felt terrible for Chloe—Brooke couldn't imagine dealing with infertility and then discovering a sibling had accidentally had a child despite taking precautions? Brooke couldn't fight the guilt that swamped her.

"I'm fine," Chloe said, and her gaze shifted to Brooke. "So how did my brother stick his foot into it this time?"

The story spilled out of Brooke. She tried to keep to just the facts, but then Chloe would say something like "Those headlines must have *horrified* you," or "He did *what*?" It probably wasn't smart to pour her heart out to this woman she barely knew and only in a professional capacity because Brooke had no idea what might be splashed across the internet tomorrow, but, God, it felt so good to talk to someone besides her mother and Alex. The isolation of the last few months caught up with her all at once, and, before she knew it, she was crying into a tissue and Chloe was rocking the baby and everything was still a huge mess. Amazingly, Brooke felt better.

As Brooke finished the story, Chloe gazed down on

Bean, who was playing with an expensive-looking neck-lace, his eyes drowsy. If Brooke was lucky, Chloe would be able to get the baby back to sleep, and if she was very lucky, no one would shout or slam a door or anything.

Brooke wasn't feeling that lucky.

"So let me see if I've got this right," Chloe said gently. "He told you that you had to marry him? He didn't even *ask*?"

"No!" Brooke said as quietly as she could. Thank God, Chloe got it. "And that's when you walked in."

"Such a jackass. Whoops, sorry, sweetie," she cooed to Bean, who blinked up at her and then launched an-other charming smile at his aunt. "But he didn't lose his temper?"

"I guess not?" Brooke swallowed. "I mean, he's got a right to be upset. But it was nothing like what those head-lines described."

Chloe smirked. "Did he tell you what the fight was about?"

"No?" That didn't sound good.

But Chloe didn't see fit to expand on that comment. In-stead, she looked at Brooke. A shiver went down Brooke's back because there was a calculating gleam in the woman's eyes that hadn't been there a moment ago.

"Here's the thing, though—he's not wrong." Brooke in-haled sharply as Chloe went on, "From a public relations point of view, I mean. If you two are married, we could spin this as a secret long-distance relationship instead of a wayward one-night stand. We could make it sound highly romantic while we release little teases of this supposed re-lationship without revealing too much, while we build up to exclusive interviews and magazine covers. We'd have both your audience and ours *hooked*. The press would be fantastic."

A pit of disquiet began to yawn open in Brooke's stomach. That was probably exactly what the record company would tell her to do, but…

Yes, she wanted to go public with her son. Yes, it made sense to have a plan. And the PR would probably be great.

But was it asking too much for it to be on her terms?

To try to keep some part of her private life private?

"I don't know if I like the sound of that," she told Chloe, trying to be diplomatic about it.

"It's a shame we can't retroactively get last year's date on the wedding certificate," Chloe mused, all of her attention on the baby. Brooke wasn't even sure Chloe had heard her. "But a lie you can prove wrong with a simple records search is a bad lie. Always lie as close to the truth as possible."

Brooke definitely did not like the sound of that. "I don't want to lie anymore."

"Not lie," Chloe went on. "We just want to bend the truth a little. You guys met, had an instant connection, but you couldn't get your schedules lined up…hmm. No, that won't work—Flash was kicked off the rodeo for half the season last year. He could have followed you around easily. No, you were hot and heavy until his arrest, and then you gave him an ultimatum to shape up, which he did."

"Can we slow down for a second here?" Brooke asked, because this was exactly what she was afraid of—Chloe was still going to strong-arm Brooke into doing what Flash wanted, just like Flash had tried to do. The only difference was that Chloe would do it while being all sympathetic and understanding instead of yelling. "There's no way my mother would approve of someone like Flash."

But there was no slowing Chloe. "So he straightened up and you guys have been secretly dating for…five months seems about right. And now that he's passed your tests with flying colors, you guys decided to get married! Yes, I like this. Flash gets his redemption story and you get a huge PR boost for your new album and—"

"I am *not* getting married right now," Brooke burst out.

"I understand your reluctance," Chloe said, not quite as sympathetic as she'd been before. "Flash has that effect on people. But here's the problem—beyond a redemption story or a marketing blitz, what if something happens to you, God forbid?" Before Brooke could panic at this statement—was this a *threat*?—Chloe went on. "Without the legal protection of marriage, would Flash be able to take custody of his own son? Or would your mother keep this perfect little angel away from his own father? Not that we wouldn't fight it in court," Chloe went on, smiling at Bean. "After all, what's the point in being billionaires if you can't buy the best lawyers?"

Billionaires? Brooke inhaled sharply. This *was* a threat.

"But it'd be a long, messy legal battle, one where Flash might not get to see his own son for a long time. I don't know what kind of person your mother is, but if you're concerned about her choices now..." She let the words trail off, her implication clear.

A churning panic took hold of Brooke's stomach because she was not going to get married so Flash could be redeemed and she was not going to marry anyone for the PR, but making sure Flash could care for his own son?

Because Chloe wasn't wrong.

Crissy Bonner might be disappointed that Brooke had gotten knocked up and she would definitely hate Flash, but she loved Bean. She loved being a grandmother and keeping Bean all to herself.

Brooke realized she didn't know how far Crissy would go to keep things that way—all while proclaiming it was *for the best*, no doubt.

"Is that a risk you're willing to take?" Chloe finished softly. "I wouldn't."

"I'm not on death's doorstep," Brooke said, surprised to hear her voice shake. She surged to her feet and plucked

Bean out of Chloe's arms. "I don't have to marry your brother to make sure he gets to see his child, and if you're only here to be the good cop to Flash's bad cop, then you can leave. *Now.*"

She didn't wait for an answer as she stormed from the room and headed downstairs. She was done talking, done with the entire Lawrence family. God, she felt like a fool. Nothing had changed. She and Flash were electric together, but sexual chemistry only got a girl so far. She was not going to let a little lust blind her to the big picture.

She got to the bottom of the stairs and glanced at the front door. Had it only been—what, an hour since Flash had pressed her back against the door and made her feel exactly like the girl she used to be?

Less than an hour. Less than an evening for Flash Lawrence to blow into her life like a twister, leaving a wake of destruction in his path.

And who had to clean up after the storm had passed? She did. Again.

Starting right now, she and Flash were on a no-touching basis. She couldn't afford to be selfish anymore. She had to be a mother, and if that meant it was her against Flash, the Lawrence family, her own family, her record label and, hell, the whole world, then that's the battle Brooke would fight.

She was done hiding and done apologizing. As much as she might miss the girl she'd been before, she was a different woman now. There was no going back.

She strode into the library, her mouth open to tell everyone to get the hell out—but what she saw made her stumble to a stop. Flash had Pete Wellington pinned against the far wall and was punching him in the stomach again and again as Pete grunted in pain, like something out of her nightmares.

"What are you doing?" she cried out in horror.

Nine

Flash spun midpunch, stumbled and almost lost his balance. "Brooke?"

Bean began to cry and Pete said, "Oh, hell."

Damn it.

"It's not what it looks like," he said in what he hoped was a calm voice. He'd just figured out how he'd screwed up. He couldn't afford to make this worse.

"He's not hurting me," Pete called over his shoulder, although the slightly pained tone of his voice made it seem like a lie.

"That's not what it looks like?" Brooke edged toward the door, tucking the baby so Flash couldn't even see the kid.

Oh, God—if she ran now, he had no idea when he'd get to see his son again, and that was a risk he wasn't willing to take. So he said, "It's not. I'm hitting cushions."

"Cushions?" Brooke's eyes bugged out of her head.

"It's okay. No one's in any danger," he said.

It hurt, the look in her eyes. She was furious and scared and exhausted, and Flash wasn't making anything better. God, he never should've ordered her to marry him. Pete had been exactly right. Obviously Brooke felt backed into a corner.

"What's wrong?" Chloe said, running into the room. "Who's hurt?"

"No one," Flash said as calmly as he could—which, all things considered, actually did come out calmly. He owed one to Pete for helping him get to this point because if the man hadn't had the idea to punch a couch, Flash knew he wouldn't be able to think, much less act rationally.

What a mess.

"Brooke? I was hitting cushions."

"Cushions," Pete confirmed. He stepped around Flash, holding the cushions up. "From the couch. See?"

"It's okay," Chloe said softly, reaching out to pat Bean, who was not having a great night, either. None of them were.

"Why would you do that?" Brooke said, looking completely bewildered.

Aw, hell. He'd never wanted a do-over so badly in his entire life. He'd hit the chute at the start of the ride but, unlike in the rodeo, he wasn't going to get a reride. The night had started so well, but then she'd dropped the bomb about the baby, and since then he had not handled things well. He needed to get back to where she was in his arms and he remembered how to be the charming guy she wanted and they weren't on opposite sides.

"Like primal scream therapy, you know? Just blowing off steam so I could think. It was a controlled release. It's okay," he repeated.

"Don't you dare try that—*charm*, Flash Lawrence," Brooke said, her voice cracking as she backed away from Chloe's touch. "Nothing about this is okay!"

"I know," Flash said through gritted teeth, holding his hands out in the sign of surrender. He kept plenty of distance between him and Brooke and shot a look at Chloe that said, *Back off.* Which, to her credit, she did. Crowding Brooke right now would only make the fight-or-flight reaction worse.

"It'll be okay." He lied because he didn't trust her, she clearly didn't trust him, and neither of those facts changed reality—in this case, the baby boy who was making pitifully sad noises.

Brooke looked from worried face to worried face. Chloe helped Pete put the cushions back on the couch, leaving the exit open. Brooke eyed them warily, but she didn't bolt, and for that Flash was thankful.

"You weren't attacking him," she said, dropping her gaze as her cheeks shot scarlet.

Flash had the overwhelming urge to sweep her into his arms, take her upstairs and tuck her in. Then, in the morning, they'd have a good laugh about this. Ha-ha-ha.

"No."

"He really wasn't," Pete added, thankfully no longer sounding winded. Flash glanced back to see Chloe and Pete standing side by side, his arm around her shoulders as she leaned into him, her gaze fastened on Brooke and the baby. Flash got the feeling that Pete was holding Chloe back. He caught Flash's gaze and nodded encouragingly. "Miss Bonner, I know you don't know me from Adam, but I've known Flash for almost eleven years now and I'd swear on a Bible in a court of law that he's not the same immature, hotheaded jerk he used to be."

"Thanks, Pete, but I got it from here," Flash grumbled.

"It was my idea for him to hit the cushions," Pete went on. "I was just holding them."

"Oh, my God, I'm such a fool," Brooke blurted out, shifting Bean so she could swipe the back of her hand over her eyes.

More than her hard *no* to his terrible proposal, more than the surprise of the baby, it was the sight of Brooke trying not to cry that did him in. He was so mad at her—that wasn't going away. But he also wanted to take care of her and those two things weren't playing nicely inside his head.

"No, you're not," Flash said quickly. "Nothing tonight has been normal." There had to be a way to fix this, damn it. But how? Well, an apology was a good place to start. "I'm sorry, babe."

She made a noise that was halfway between a sob and a laugh. "Do you even know what you're apologizing for this time, or are you just guessing again?"

"It's a long list," he agreed, managing to put a good smile into it. "But top of the list is that I shouldn't have told you we had to get married. Even if it's a good idea."

"No," Brooke said, her voice shaky and her eyes huge, "you shouldn't have. No one should've." She cut a glance at Chloe. Flash didn't follow Brooke's gaze, but he heard Chloe sigh. "I don't want to be forced into anything."

That Flash understood completely. He'd always been the kind of guy who'd get a direct order and do the exact opposite just to prove he could. God, why hadn't he seen her reaction coming? He'd just been so convinced of the rightness of him and Brooke being together that he'd stampeded right over her.

Brooke sniffed again, dashing more tears off her cheeks. Flash wanted to fold Brooke into his arms and make everything okay again. But it was clear that doing anything like that would just make Brooke dig in her heels even deeper. Sometimes, a man had to call a tactical retreat if he wanted to live to fight another day.

Figuratively speaking, of course.

"It's been a long night and you've got to be exhausted from the show," he said, trying to give her a nice smile. "I'm truly sorry how this evening has gone down. I think it's time for us to leave so you and James can get some sleep." And he could figure out what Chloe had said that had thrown Brooke into such a panic.

He wanted her. He didn't trust her. He needed to marry her.

God, what a freaking *mess*.

Brooke stared down at the baby. Even Flash could tell the boy was uncomfortable, squirming in his mother's arms. "We can try, anyway."

He came damn close to offering to stay the night so she could sleep and he could rock his son in his arms and get to know the boy. And then he'd be here in the morning when Brooke woke up and they could...

Well, the odds of them having great sex again seemed so small right now as to be nonexistent. But they could talk, hopefully without panic or bitterness.

But discretion was the better part of valor, damn it. And he needed to regroup in a serious way. So, instead, he said, "I'd like to see you again so we can try this whole talking thing. I'm in town through..." He thought quickly. He didn't have to be in Lexington, Kentucky, for ten days, which didn't seem like enough time to get this situation resolved peacefully.

Crud. His lead in the rankings was tenuous. Skipping a rodeo would knock him down several places and might ultimately cost him the Cowboy of the Year championship.

But then he looked at Brooke again and sighed. Missing one rodeo wouldn't be the end of the world. Just so long as it didn't become a habit. Surely, in a week or two they could get some sort of custody plan or visitation schedule set up, and he could come right back to Nashville after the rodeo.

"For as long as you need me to be," he corrected. "We can meet here or in public, wherever you want. Bring Alex."

He didn't want Alex there because Alex would probably beat the ever-loving hell out of him, and Flash would have no choice but to take it.

"You're being charming again," she mumbled, but he caught the way she tucked her lower lip under her teeth and peeked at him.

"Trying to," he agreed with an easy smile. That little flash of normalcy was encouraging. If everything could just calm down, he was sure he could talk sense into Brooke. He truly did want what was best for her and for their son. Brooke in his life was what he wanted. And if that included her being in his bed, well that was just icing on the cake.

"Flash, we need to have a plan—" Chloe started to say.

Flash held up a hand, cutting her off. "Nothing needs to be decided tonight. The only thing that needs to happen right now is Brooke needs to take care of herself and the baby. That's it." And he needed to get a grip on his priorities.

The look Brooke shot him was full of worry and hope and maybe just a little appreciation. At least, he hoped it was appreciation. "I have a meeting at one tomorrow to discuss the Bluebird show. I suppose we could meet after that? Maybe for coffee?" She glanced back at Chloe and Pete again. "Just the two of us. No offense."

It was Pete who answered. "None taken."

Flash worked real hard not to show his disappointment. Because he *wasn't* disappointed that she wasn't asking him to stay. He was happy that she wasn't insisting they bring their seconds to the meeting. Really, it was great news that Brooke was still willing to talk to him at all. "You name the place and I'll be there. Just text me."

She nodded and then looked toward the door. Right. They were leaving—now.

Chloe and Pete got the hint. They stepped forward, Chloe's gaze locked on to the baby. "My deepest apologies for coming on too strong," Chloe said, regret filling her voice. She reached out and, when Brooke didn't shy away, Chloe rubbed James's back. "I hope we can see this special little guy again soon?"

"I'll set it up with Flash." Brooke didn't sound too sure about it, though.

"Thank you," Chloe said, her voice cracking. "He's such a beautiful baby."

Pete held her tight and said, "Miss Bonner, we love your music. Can't wait for the new stuff. And no matter what, welcome to the family." Then he led his wife away.

As the front door opened, Flash heard Chloe almost whimper, "Oh Pete—that baby!"

"I know, hon. I know," Pete replied, his voice choked with emotion.

Then they were gone and Flash was alone with Brooke. "I'm sorry about that. I thought they were going to help," he said quietly.

"Did they?" She didn't move back, didn't shield the baby with her body.

"Pete did. This was—*is* a lot. For both of us." He closed the distance between them and lifted James out of her arms. Thank goodness she didn't resist. He tucked the baby under his chin. This, at least, he was pretty good at. He'd had plenty of practice holding Trixie, after all. He should probably thank Oliver for that—right after Oliver got done tearing him a new one for getting Brooke pregnant in the first place.

Man, this was one of the bigger messes he'd ever been in.

"I don't think I've ever apologized *for* my sister before," he went on. "Usually it's the other way around."

Brooke looked at him, her eyes huge and tired. But despite the toll the night had taken on her—on them all—Flash was pretty damn sure he'd never seen anyone as beautiful as she was. "It's fine, Flash," she said. He couldn't tell if she was being honest or not. "I suspect that you Lawrences are a hardheaded lot."

"Guilty as charged," he said with a good-natured grin. He patted James's back. "Thank you for this—for *him*. I don't know if I said that earlier or not."

"No, you didn't." Her face softened as she looked at the two of them. Wildly, Flash hoped she liked what she saw. Because he wasn't going to give this kid up. Hell, no. Whether she married him or not, whether he forgave her or not, they were in this together.

It'd be so much easier if they were really together, though. There had to be a way.

Flash pressed a tender kiss to the top of James's head. "Sleep for your mom, okay, sweetie?" Then he turned his attention back to Brooke. "Is there anything else I can do for you tonight?"

He knew she wasn't going to ask him to stay, not after he'd made a royal ass of himself tonight. But that didn't change things.

Damn it. He needed to marry her to make things legal for the baby. But did he seriously want to marry her?

He'd dreamed of this woman for a year. He thought he'd been dreaming of the sex, the easy jokes. What if he'd really been dreaming of something more?

Something more had to wait.

He had to man up and make things right. Any potential feelings he had for Brooke would come later, if they came at all.

"I'll… I'll see you tomorrow?" she said softly, taking a sleepy James back from Flash. Then her gaze dropped to his lips.

This wasn't Flash's first rodeo. "Tomorrow," he agreed, his voice barely a whisper. Then he leaned forward and brushed his lips against hers.

He didn't linger, didn't press the issue. "Call me for any reason. I can be right back out here in under twenty minutes." He'd have to see about getting a different hotel room closer to her house.

She nodded, looking breathless. Flash was sorely tempted to lean in for another kiss, something longer and hotter and…

Yeah, no. He backed away before he let his dick do the thinking. That's what had gotten them into this mess in the first place. "Good night, Brooke."

He was almost out of the room when she spoke. "Flash?"

Yes. But he didn't cheer. He turned and asked, "What, babe?"

"This can't get out yet. I can't have my mother finding out about you. Not…" Even across the room in the dark, he saw her swallow nervously. "Not yet."

Hadn't she mentioned her mother earlier? Brooke's record company and mother had all decided that she had to keep her pregnancy and baby a secret because Brooke wouldn't name him as the father? And now Brooke wasn't necessarily afraid of the press finding out about the baby, but she was clearly worried about her mother.

That bothered him. Damn it. He wished his own mother was still here. She'd be able to tell Flash if that was a normal mother-daughter thing or not. But maybe his sister-in-law Renee could shine a little light on how tense mother-daughter relationships worked. He'd have to ask, after Oliver got done chewing him out.

"I won't. No one outside of Chloe and Pete will know until you're ready to tell them. Well," he quickly corrected, "Chloe and Pete and my older brother, Oliver, and his wife, who's Chloe's best friend. It doesn't go farther than that."

They'd all wait to tell Milt Lawrence for a little bit. If Dad found out he had another grandbaby, life would get very complicated very fast.

"Your brother and his wife? Will they keep it quiet?"

"Absolutely. But outside of them, no one will know. You can hold me to that, Brooke."

She sagged in what he hoped was relief. "Okay. Good. Um, good night."

"Night, babe." Then, moving as quickly as he could, he walked his butt right out of that house and started thinking hard about tomorrow.

How did a man propose a marriage of convenience the second time after completely botching the first time?

Ten

"So you'll think about it?" Kari Stockard said, trailing after Brooke as she walked out of the conference room. "The press we'd get from the baby pictures alone could put your album sales over the top, Brooke. You know that."

"Yes, you said as much in the meeting." Repeatedly. Kari was a fine PR manager, but Brooke could take only so much browbeating, and what should've been a quick check-in about the Bluebird performance had instead been Brooke on one side of a conference table and seven—seven!—executives, managers and other people wearing suits on the other side, all trying to tell her what to do with her personal life. And they didn't even know about Flash yet.

Brooke had done a thorough internet check before she'd walked into that meeting this morning, and there was nothing connecting her and Flash. Bless Kyle Morgan's heart, he'd kept his mouth shut.

Brooke wished she'd brought Alex as backup today—but this was supposed to have been a short meeting, not the full-court press, so she'd told her best friend to take the day off because she wasn't up to the conversation Alex would want to have about Flash. Brooke hadn't even brought Mom, who was technically her manager. Instead, Mom was at home with Bean. Not that Mom would've been much help, anyway. She would've agreed to everything the label wanted, as evidenced by her parting shot this morning, which had been, "Sweetheart, don't you think that, with the album release coming up, you're going to want to tell the world about Jimmy?" No one called Bean that except for Crissy Bonner.

"The timing is perfect," Kari went on, still trailing Brooke. "Think of the buzz!"

So, yeah, Brooke was on her own here and it was exhausting. Was it wrong to want someone in her court? She picked up the pace. If she could make it to her car...well, then she could go meet with Flash and fight a completely different battle.

She didn't want it to be a battle, though. She wanted... to feel like she was in control of something. Anything.

Kari wasn't giving up anytime soon. She matched Brooke's pace. "We wouldn't even have to name the father. We could say you'd done in vitro! From a sperm bank?"

"Nope." She was practically jogging at this point. "When I'm ready to take him public, I'll let you know." She made the door.

"Before the album drops?" Kari yelled after her.

"You, too!" Brooke called over her shoulder, intentionally mishearing Kari's question. Her head hurt. Kari didn't know who Flash was so there'd been no discussion of a redemption arc or marriage, but, otherwise, Kari's plan was practically identical to what Chloe had outlined last night.

Brooke got to her car and paused long enough to make sure Kari hadn't trailed her before she slumped back in the seat. The day of public reckoning was coming, that much was certain. But would it involve a wedding or just a baby?

She just wanted to write her songs and perform, and,

yeah, she wanted to make a lot of money—money she controlled, not her mother or her uncle, the rat bastard. Being raised by a single mother meant that Brooke hadn't grown up rich. But everything else that went with being famous? It was all a huge pain in the ass, frankly.

She sat for a moment, trying to get her thoughts in order. Which, of course, took the shape of a melody. Somewhere in the middle of the night, dozing in the chair with Bean, the song in her head had shifted to something darker, something more raw. *Don't say something romantic* was still there, but another song was lurking at the edge of her subconscious.

The stripped-down acoustics of the new melody ran through her mind, full of anguish. A song about being stuck in an impossible situation with no right answers. She opened the notes program on her phone and dictated the lyrics. If nothing else, art imitating her life made for good inspiration.

God, this was a mess.

Because the fact was that everything Chloe Lawrence had said last night hadn't been wrong. Legally, Flash was a persona non grata when it came to Bean. He wasn't on the birth certificate and, until paternity tests happened, he couldn't prove that he was Bean's father, although all anyone had to do was look at the way those two smiled to see the truth.

It didn't matter how Chloe or Kari promised to spin it to her advantage—the simple truth was that for a few weeks, the press would be brutal. All the more so because she'd had the nerve to hide her pregnancy and child this long. Maybe it was selfish or cowardly, but she didn't want to face it alone.

Part of hitting it big last year had been the public perception that Brooke Bonner didn't screw around, do drugs or drink. She might write some saucy songs, but she was a role model to girls—play by the rules and you'll go far. Shattering that mostly true image with an out-of-wedlock baby would cost her fans.

Getting married to Flash—and quickly—meant that she wouldn't have to face the press on her own. It'd also mean she wouldn't have to hide the fact that she was sleeping with him. Assuming she was going to keep sleeping with him.

Was she assuming that?

Just thinking about the orgasm last night kicked her pulse up a notch. But that perfect moment, like the one in Fort Worth over a year ago, was completely overshadowed by what came afterward.

How was marrying Flash the smart thing to do?

The words *but how could I say no?* popped into her mind. Frankly, after that meeting, Brooke could use a drink. *I could use a shot of something stronger*, she dictated, letting the words flow, feeling her way toward what came next.

Can't afford the mistake the whiskey would help me make?

Yeah, it needed work. And she was stalling. She'd told Mom she had a coffee date planned with Kyle Morgan to go over a song. And she was, technically, thinking about lyrics, so it wasn't a total lie. But she had an afternoon to decide the direction of her life for the immediate future before everything spun out of control for her again.

She knew what she had to do. She needed to ask Flash to meet her at a coffee shop. Where are you? she texted.

He answered back in seconds. My hotel. Where do you want to meet? Clearly, he'd been waiting on her. The thought made her relax just a bit.

The responsible thing to do would be to name a bar or restaurant or coffee shop. They needed to stay in public, as part of a crowd, so they could have a mature, rational discussion about parenting and not getting married like adults. That certainly would be the smart course of action.

But all the logic in the world didn't seem to apply when it came to her and Flash. She wanted to feel like she had a choice. And, damn it all, she wanted him. In a bed, this time. Yeah, she was apparently going to keep sleeping with him. What's your room number?

The replay came immediately: 623—you want to meet here?

She wanted a do-over of last night, before it'd all blown up in her face. Just him and her and no big surprises, waiting to ruin everything, lurking in the wings this time. Brooke wanted more than fifteen minutes of satisfaction in Flash's arms. It was selfish, sure. And after last night, it was clearly a mistake of epic proportions.

But, apparently, when it came to Flash, she'd just willfully keep making that mistake.

I'm still not marrying you, she typed, hitting the letters with extra force. Just FYI.

Noted, he replied.

It was so hard to tell if he was looking forward to her showing up or if he was bracing himself for the worst or what. Well, he could just brace. She needed a little more from him. Just for her. Then they could go back to being co-parents or whatever.

I'm coming to you, she texted, and then started the car.

Just as she pulled out of the parking lot, he texted back, Thank God.

Brooke knocked on the door, at least 73 percent sure she was making a mistake. But before she could bail, it swung open and Flash was there.

Damn, he made rugged look *so* good.

He wore a black All-Stars T-shirt, which showed off his muscled forearms. But the funny thing was his feet were bare. No boots, no socks. He gave her that look that she'd always been powerless to resist. "Hey, come in. Thanks for making it."

"No problem."

A memory pushed to the forefront of her mind, of the last time she'd been alone in a hotel room with this man. Of Flash pressing her against the door and whispering in her ear, "Tell me what you want," as he'd ground his erection against her, her entire body humming with need for him. "I'm going to give it to you, Brooke," he'd all but growled in her ear. "But be honest."

She shuddered and shoved the memory away. Now was *so* not the time for erotic flashbacks. God, meeting in his room really was an awful idea, wasn't it? She hadn't even been alone with him for thirty seconds and she was already thinking about sex.

Flash shut the door behind her and, dang it, she startled. He had a knowing smirk on his face. "You sure you want to meet here?"

"No." She didn't like this awkwardness between them and she liked it even less that she was the only one feeling it.

Once upon a time, she had promised him honesty. She'd done a terrible job of that when it came to Bean. Being upfront with Flash now was the very least she could do for him. So she took a deep breath and said, "I don't think I should be alone with you."

He chuckled, not looking the least insulted. God, Brooke just wanted to curl into him but, no, she couldn't. She had to remember why she was here and, more importantly, how she'd gotten to this point. Neither of them would be in this position if she and Flash had been able to keep their hands to themselves.

"If you're not supposed to be alone with me," he asked slowly, "what are you doing here?"

"If we met in public, we'd run the risk of being spotted." It wasn't a great excuse.

And Flash knew it. His gaze sharpened. "Are you saying you've decided to keep *this*," he said, motioning between them, "a secret?"

"No. I'm saying I don't want public perception to force our hand." She turned away from him because it was hard to think with him like that. He looked so damn good in this hotel room.

Wow, she hadn't realized he had a corner suite instead of a regular room. This place was bigger—and nicer—than the apartment she and her mom had shared for most of her adolescence. She certainly hadn't been able to afford rooms this nice when she'd been touring—especially not after her uncle embezzled all her earnings.

This was a *very* nice room. Huge windows behind a dining room table set for eight showed her the view of Music Row and the Cumberland River. She was standing in a living room that not only had a couch and matching accent chairs and tasteful lamps—not industrial light fixtures, but real lamps with stylish shades—but the whole thing was arranged on top of an expensive-looking Persian rug. An office area backed up to a full wet bar. Next to the dining room table, to the left, there was what looked like a full kitchen and a set of doors to the right where, she assumed, there was a bathroom and a bedroom. With a bed. Probably a nice one.

Nope. Not thinking about the bed Flash slept in.

She turned her back on those doorways and walked toward the window overlooking Music Row. Even though this was probably one of the nicer hotel rooms she'd ever been in, she could still tell that Flash had settled in. Behind one of the accent chairs was a duffel bag with a protective vest and ropes spilling out—his bull ropes, no doubt. Chaps were draped over one of the dining room chairs and his black hat was tossed onto the granite countertop. Coffee cups were scattered around the coffeepot on the wet bar, along with a few plastic grocery bags.

Okay, so Flash wasn't the neatest of guys. Somehow, that made him seem more…real. More normal, anyway. He wasn't just this perfect fantasy she'd created or this thug the headlines had painted him to be. He was a flesh-and-blood man.

One who could afford the best room in the hotel, apparently. Rodeo riders weren't known for their tastes for the finer things in life. Half of them lived out of their cars during the summer or crashed on floors because the money from rodeos was only good if one was winning. Hadn't Chloe said something about the Lawrence family being billionaires? It'd been couched in a vaguely threatening statement about affording the best lawyers, but…

Was Flash actually rich?

"I got you some tea," he said, startling her out of her thoughts. "I didn't know which kind, so there's a few sample packs. The concierge found an electric kettle so you wouldn't have coffee-flavored tea to drink."

Oh no—thoughtfulness. This was terrible—if Flash was going to be both charming *and* thoughtful, she was doomed. "Any green tea?"

"Jasmine or peach?" She heard the sound of him rustling through the bags. "Oh—there's a plain green in here, too."

"Jasmine, please." She couldn't let herself be sweet-talked. She had to remember why she was here, and it wasn't because she'd missed Flash or he'd missed her or even that they'd been great in bed together and would probably get even better.

She was here because Bean was almost four months old and had spent a whopping twenty minutes with his father. She was here to ensure that Flash was a man of his word and really had turned his life around. That everyone last night had been telling the truth when they'd said Flash was just hitting pillows and that his whole family and their possible billions of dollars wouldn't be used to cower her into submission. She was here to make sure her son would be safe with Flash.

That *she* was safe with Flash. She wanted to know that he wouldn't make her fall in love with him and then rip her heart right out of her chest. That he wouldn't force her into a marriage and then force her to choose between her child and her career. She needed to believe that he wouldn't abandon her to deal with the hard realities of parenthood alone while he chased the rodeo once the naked lust between them cooled.

Because it would cool, right?

Flash wasn't the kind of guy who settled down. He played the field, kept his options open and never met a woman he didn't love.

Except…was that him? He sure as hell had been that a year ago when she'd taken him up on everything he'd had to offer.

But he'd been waiting for her outside the Bluebird. He'd come to her house. He'd said repeatedly that he hadn't looked at another woman since their night together, and his sister had casually mentioned that she knew Flash had it bad for Brooke. Would he be faithful to her—even if they didn't get hitched? Was she even being fair to ask that of him if she kept telling him no?

The fact was that she wanted it all—great sex with a perfect man who made her feel wonderful *and* her career *and* an equal partner to raise Bean.

But she knew if she asked for that, he'd be hustling her down the aisle before she could do anything else and there'd be no guarantee she'd get anything on her wish list. No matter how much charm Flash wielded right now, he wouldn't be in a big hurry to drop the rodeo and be a stay-at-home dad. The rodeo was in his blood, just like the music was in hers.

She couldn't have it all. There simply weren't enough hours in the day. Which meant she couldn't have Flash. She had to put her son first. Her selfish wants and physical needs came last.

No, not last. Marketing plans and press releases and, *ugh*, magazine covers with exclusive interviews and redemption arcs and record sales—all of those things were dead last on her to-do list. But that didn't mean she could ignore them.

Lord, what a mess. She rubbed her eyes.

"Did you get some sleep?" he asked behind her. She could just make out his reflection in the glass window. He was leaning against the wet bar, watching her. "You look better."

So much for that legendary charm. She knew exactly what she looked like—cutoff shorts, a loose-fitting black tee and a Nashville Predators ball cap pulled over an extremely messy ponytail. She looked exactly like a woman who'd had a terrible night. "That's the best you've got?"

Flash came to stand beside her, grinning wildly. He traced his fingers over her shoulder and down her arm until he laced his fingers with hers. She shivered at the touch and fought the urge to rest her head on his shoulder. "I could say that I've never seen you look more beautiful than you do right now, but we're past flattery, don't you think?" Leaning closer, his voice dropped to a deep whisper. "Here's the thing, babe—I'm not going to lie to you. Never have and I'm not about to start."

She blushed because she realized he was right. He'd told her up front about his arrest record. She was the one who'd kept secrets. "Okay. Yes. I, uh, I apologize again for not telling you about the baby." When he didn't answer right away, she asked, "Are you still mad at me?"

He squeezed her hand—and took his sweet time answering. The longer he was silent, the more her stomach sank. How was this going to work?

Finally, he said, "I'm still working on it. I want to trust you but…" He went on before she could interrupt, "I get that you did the best you could with the information you had." He cleared his throat. "And I'm sorry I didn't handle last night well. I won't attempt to make decisions for you again."

This was the Flash who'd been waiting for her behind the Bluebird Cafe, the one who said all the right things at all the right times. This was the Flash who made her want him.

This was not the Flash who had to walk out of a room before he lost his temper or hit cushions to keep control. This wasn't the Flash who issued life-changing orders and just expected her to go along with them, no questions asked.

Which one was the real Flash Lawrence?

"Seriously, though—did you sleep?" The way he asked made it clear he really wanted to know. He wasn't just making polite small talk.

At least, she hoped he wasn't. "A few hours. No one sleeps well with a fussy four-month-old on their chest. Mom thinks he might be teething. Which is super early, but not unheard-of, apparently."

He winced. "That's going to suck. My niece is teething and it's rough for all of them. I don't want you to have to deal with that on your own."

How was she supposed to interpret that? She'd made it clear she wasn't marrying him—but was he implying that he'd be around to help share the load? Or he'd take Bean back to his place? Which was, presumably… Texas, maybe? Or did he mean he'd hire a nanny or something?

Before she could ask, the kettle beeped and he left her side to get the water. She absolutely wasn't going to miss his warmth, for heaven's sake. He was all of five feet away. It's not like she couldn't go five minutes without touching him. She'd managed a whole year without him!

But then he asked, "How much honey do you take with your tea?" and she knew she was in trouble because, seriously, this level of thoughtfulness was dangerous.

"You remembered I like honey?"

Flash paused midstride and then spun back to her, an almost predatory gleam in his eye. "Do you know," he said, his voice suddenly that much lower and that much deeper, and her traitorous body vibrated like a tuning fork at exactly the right pitch, "that every time I kiss you, I taste honey on your sweet lips?"

"No," she said breathlessly as he backed her against the window, his hard body making her soft with need.

"I do." His breath caressed her lips as his hands came to her hips, pulling her against him. The hot length of his erection pushed against her and she couldn't help the moan that escaped her. "I could get drunk on your kiss and never want for water again."

Oh. Oh, *my*.

"Good line," she whispered, tilting her head up for him.

"You can have it." But he didn't take the kiss she offered. He held himself back, which was probably a sign of maturity or something ridiculous like that. "Not gonna lie, Brooke—I want you so bad." He thrust against her and she moaned. He made a matching sound of need, and she couldn't think, couldn't do anything but feel him against her, want him inside her.

Then he cruelly pulled away. Not far, but enough that he wasn't pressing against her anymore. "Right now, we don't have to do anything except talk." His hand trailed up her side, over her ribs, skimming the edge of her breast before his fingers spread across her throat, and then he cupped her cheek in his palm, his thumb stroking over her skin. Her eyes fluttered closed and she let herself just *feel*.

No one else made her feel like Flash did.

"That's why you're here, isn't it?"

Was it? That's what she'd told herself last night, and then he'd given her an amazing orgasm against the door. She hadn't been able to think until they'd gotten the sex out of the way.

She could've met him in public today, could've insisted on a chaperone. She could've made him come back out to the house and subjected him to her mother, made him change Bean's diapers.

Instead, she'd come straight to his hotel room. He hadn't had to convince her of anything. She was here willingly.

She was *his* willingly.

"No," she whispered, lacing her fingers through his hair and pulling him down to her. "It's not."

Eleven

Hers. That's the word that crossed her mind when she crushed her lips against his.

This man was hers.

He always had been, since the very first moment he'd taken her hand and bowed over it like some lordly duke. If nothing else, they had this.

"Bed?" Flash asked against her mouth, his hands skimming down her back, over her bottom.

"Bed," she agreed.

She loved the hot, heavy sex against the door, but a window wasn't quite as reassuring. Besides, she wanted the luxury of limbs twining together, his bare skin against hers.

The next thing she knew, Flash had bent over and swept her legs out from underneath her. "Whoa!" she squeaked, throwing her arms around his neck for balance.

"I've got you, babe." Oh, she'd needed to hear that. "Do you have any idea what I want to do to you?"

She leaned forward and kissed the side of his neck. His pulse beat wildly against her lips. "Tell me."

"I want to feast on your body and make you scream my name when you come, and then I want to hold you afterwards until you've come back down to earth, and then I want to bury myself in your body until you break again, until I can't take it anymore. I want to lay you out and spend the next two days making love to you," he growled against her ear. Then he wrapped his lips around her lobe and tugged gently as he carried her back through the suite. "Then I want to do it again."

Every muscle in her body clenched at his charged words and, given the wolfish grin he shot her, she knew he'd felt it, too. She'd done that once with him, that glorious night in Fort Worth when he'd swept her off her feet.

Once a year wasn't enough.

Sadly, though, reality wasn't on their side. "We—oh, *Flash*," she moaned as he kissed her neck, "we don't have that kind of time." But Lord, it sounded wonderful, didn't it? A few days to explore how deep this connection went. A few days to selfishly enjoy this man and his tremendous skills.

Because the man had *skills*.

"Then I'll take the time I get with you." He kicked open the door to the bedroom and then kicked it shut, all without missing a single stride.

"Another good line," she murmured as he set her down on the bed and pulled her hat from her head.

"I'm full of them." Her hair tumbled wildly around her shoulders, the ponytail a distant memory. He paused, sucking in air. "God, Brooke—do you have any idea what you do to me?"

She leaned forward, stroking a hand over his obvious erection through his jeans. "I'm getting one."

"You…" He swallowed as she rested her head against his stomach and began to work the buttons on his fly loose.

She shoved his jeans down, then hooked her fingers into the waistband of his blue boxer briefs, which hugged his narrow hips, his ass, his *everything*. Then she pulled and he sprung free.

"If you don't want me to taste you, you let me know."

Flash groaned, his fingers finding her hair as her hands found his hot length. "Please," he got out through gritted teeth as she stroked him. "I want you to do what you want, Brooke," he moaned when she gave him a little squeeze. "I won't tell you what to do."

"You did last night."

There was something powerful about this moment. She had him in the palm of her hand—literally—and she could do what she wanted with him. She looked up at him through her eyelashes and then, slowly, pressed her lips to his tip. He shuddered, but before his hips could flex, she'd pulled away and ran the pad of her thumb over the area she'd kissed.

"A mistake. A huge one," he groaned, his head falling back. "You're killing me, babe."

"Don't mess up again," she said, knowing it sounded like an order. But it wasn't, not really. She was all but begging him.

She'd given him a second chance last night when he'd told her he'd sobered up and straightened himself out, only to have him struggle when she told him about Bean. Yeah, that was partly her fault because she'd broken the news in the absolute worst way possible. But she hadn't forgotten the hard edge to his voice when he'd informed her that they were getting married as soon as possible. And that didn't even take into account the awful moment when she'd thought he'd been attacking his brother-in-law.

She didn't need a domineering, immature jerk in her life. She needed a man, one who did right by her and her son, one who stood up for her, not to her.

She needed Flash to be that man.

"You get one more chance," she told him in all seriousness.

"I won't fail you again." His grip on her hair loosened and then was gone entirely as he tilted her head back. "You can count on me, Brooke—now and forever. No matter what we decide, we're in this together." Even through the haze of lust, she could see how serious he was.

"I know," she whispered, emotion clogging up her throat.

He leaned down and kissed her, the kind of kiss that said as much as his words had. It wasn't a kiss of frenzied passion, but one of heat and something richer, deeper.

Something that might even be love.

No, no—she wasn't going to let love get hopelessly mixed up with lust. Especially not right now. This time with him right now—this was about satisfaction and then about planning. Neither of those two things had a damn thing to do with love.

They'd had so little time together that she hardly knew what this man looked like nude. One night together and a few stolen moments—plus several hard, awkward conversations.

"Take these all the way off," she demanded, releasing her grip on him. "I want you naked."

"God, yes." He stumbled back, kicking out of his pants and yanking his shirt over his head. "I'll always give you what you want. You know that, right?"

She nodded as she did away with what was left of her ponytail and started to pull her shirt off. Flash stopped her. "Just be honest with me, Brooke. Not just about sex—about everything. Be honest with yourself."

Then he grabbed the hem of her shirt and lifted it over her head. She'd gone with the pretty teal bra today, one of the only non-nursing bras she owned that still fit. Her boobs looked *huge* in it.

"Okay to touch?" he asked, stroking a finger down her chest.

She started to nod but then stopped. Last night had been

about reclaiming a part of the girl she'd been before she'd become a mother. But this?

This was the first time Brooke felt like she was having sex as the woman she was now. And he had said he expected complete honesty, so… "Not right now. Let's leave the bra on."

Flash grinned widely as his hands skimmed up her skin and came to a rest on her shoulders, where he kneaded at the tight muscles there. Clearly, the request didn't bother him in the least. "Can do."

She reached for him again, gripping him firmly as she slid her tongue over his tip and took him into her mouth.

He groaned, a noise of pure desire that traveled down her body to where they were connected. She stroked him with her hands, licked him with her tongue. Suddenly, he pulled away.

"Nope," he growled as he pushed her over.

"Nope?" She flung her hands out for balance as she rolled. His hands pressed between her shoulder blades, firm but not hard. "Did I do something wrong?"

He laughed, a noise that sounded almost unhinged as he gently pushed her onto her stomach. "Wrong? Hell, woman. I've never felt anything so right in my life. But you're about to break me and I'm not going down like that. Not until…"

He stripped her shorts and panties off and Brooke let him. She grabbed handfuls of bedding as he nudged her legs apart and then his hands were between her legs, opening her.

"Woman," he growled again, palming her bottom.

She propped herself up on her elbows and looked back at him. "Not until what?"

"Not until you come first." He trailed his hands over the small of her back, but instead of reaching for that space between her legs that was already hot and heavy for him, he knelt on the bed and rested his hands on her shoulders. His strong hands began to massage her shoulders and she let her head drop as her muscles began to relax. "How much time do we have?"

"An hour, maybe." Bean would wake up from his nap and he'd be hungry and she'd need to nurse him. And then there was dealing with Mom...

"Then we'll make that hour count. Don't think, babe," he said, working at a particularly painful knot. "Just let me take care of you."

His hands moved lower, smoothing over her ribs even as he skipped right over her bra strap. The calluses on his hands chafed at her skin, heightening the sensations, making her more and more aware of his every move, his every touch. She stiffened when he ran his hands over her hips. But then he said, "You are *so* beautiful," in a voice that didn't contain a trace of mockery or teasing in it.

"I'm not back to where I was before," she said, cringing as he traced the stretch marks she'd earned with Bean. "So?"

She half rolled and shot him a look. "Seriously? Do you know how many people tell me I need to get back to my prebaby weight? My mother, the record execs—they all say the same thing." Her voice cracked a little on the end.

Flash's eyes—well, they flashed. "Let's get one thing straight," he said, rolling her on to her back and pinning her to the bed. "I loved your body last year. I love your body now. But if you think all you are to me is your body and that any variation in your appearance is going to send me running, then you have sorely misjudged how much I need you. All of you."

God, he really was going to make her cry. She tried to wiggle free, but he held her fast.

"So you're not the same person you were then?" he went on, his erection hot and heavy against her thigh, "Well I'm not, either. We've both grown the hell up, Brooke. And, I think, we've both gotten better." Then he released her wrists and moved lower until she felt his lips pressing against those stretch marks, reverently kissing each and every stripe. "You *are* beautiful," he repeated.

Brooke was glad he wasn't staring into her eyes anymore because it wasn't just the compliments. This wasn't Flash being smooth or charming. This was Flash being fierce and proud—of her. This was the man she wanted in her corner, by her side, when record execs tried to railroad her. This was a man who'd fight for her, for their son, for their family.

How had she failed to realize that romance wasn't just pretty words or a sweet song? Because *this* was romance. It was strong and determined and intense. Just like Flash.

Flash looked up from where he was between her legs. "I wanted you a year ago when we were wild kids looking for a good time," he told her. "I want you now when you've had my son and made me a father. A year from now, five years from now, you won't be the same person you are at this exact moment and *I'll still want you.*"

Oh, Jesus, that was a hell of a good line, one that fit right into *Don't say something romantic*. He rolled her over again, and this time she let herself relax into his touch. Then one hand slid between her legs, stroking over her sensitive flesh, and the lyrics fell away, only the melody drifting through her mind.

"Yeah, just like that," he said, his voice husky as he touched her, rubbed her, kissed her back. "Don't think. Just feel what I do to you." With his other hand, he pushed her hair to the side and then gripped her neck, gently holding her down while he nipped at her shoulder with his teeth, his stubble scraping over her skin.

Then one finger was inside her and she shuddered at the touch. "Yeah, babe," he breathed in her ear as he worked her body with more patience than she'd ever imagined. Until right now, every time with Flash had been hot and heavy, and neither of them had ever been able to hold back.

But now? Now he was holding himself back, overwhelming her senses and demanding her full attention. She gave it willingly. There was no room for PR plans or redemption stories or albums or should haves, could haves, would haves. There was only him and her and the music that wove their lives together.

Because she'd swear Flash could hear the song, too. With two fingers now, he thrust inside of her in rhythm with the melody as he bit into the skin between her shoulder and her neck. The orgasm began to build and she tried to reach back for him, but he didn't let her go. "You want more?" he growled in her ear, and she heard the raw desire in his voice, felt it in the way his body covered hers, the way her body covered his.

Whimpering, she nodded, and then his hand was gone from her neck, his fingers pulled free of her body. "One sec, babe. Do you have any idea what you do to me?" She peered over her shoulder to see him rolling on the condom. Then he lifted her by the hips and she scooted forward on the bed. "This okay?" he asked, kneeling back on the bed and running his hands over her bottom. "Because I've got to tell you, the view is *amazing*."

She laughed and widened her pose, bracing herself on her elbows. "I seem to recall this was better than okay a year ago." Actually, she remembered the shattering orgasm that had hit her so hard it'd knocked her completely off her knees. She'd been unable to do anything but shake while he'd held her for long, glorious minutes.

No one else had ever made her feel the way Flash did. There were reasons she needed to be careful about him—good reasons, no doubt—but right now, as he fit himself against her, his body strong, she couldn't remember what those reasons were. All she knew was that he was going to make her feel wonderful.

"God, woman," he said, giving her backside a light smack before he thrust into her.

"Oh," she moaned in sheer pleasure as he filled her. Even now, she could feel her orgasm straining against him.

"God, I missed you," he murmured, withdrawing and thrusting back in.

"Yes," she got out, dropping her head onto her forearms on the bed, which gave Flash even more access. He squeezed her bottom and teased her delicate flesh with the softest of touches while he drove into her and she lost herself to the rhythm of their bodies. He'd always been so damn good at this, at making her body react at his mere touch. This was why she couldn't keep her hands off him, couldn't kick him to the curb. She simply needed him too much.

He shifted, reaching around and rubbing her in time with his thrusts, and the pressure built and built, and then he wrapped her hair around his fist and pulled her into him until he could bite down on her shoulder.

The climax hit and crescendoed, her body tightening around his as a cry of satisfaction ripped itself from her chest.

"That's it," he murmured against her skin. "Come for me, babe. Just like… Oh, *God.*"

He reared back, grabbing her hips and thrusting with such force that she couldn't keep her knees underneath her as the sensations completely overwhelmed her. The orgasm went on, strengthening until she cried out again.

Seconds later, Flash made a noise of raw lust and collapsed onto her back, driving her into the bed. He managed to roll off to one side, his arm and leg still draped over her. She didn't know how long they lay there, panting, but soon enough the heat from their bodies dissipated and she shivered.

"Oh, babe," Flash sighed, wrapping himself around her and holding on tight. "I…"

She didn't know how he was going to finish that sentence. *Say something romantic.* This time, her brain modulated the key up to A.

No, no—she didn't want him to say something romantic. She didn't want him to make her fall for him all over again, didn't want him to propose when she was weak for him because, after sex like that, she might just say yes.

She just wanted to enjoy him while she could, which she had. Now she needed to focus on reality.

She rolled away from him and out of bed. "I'm still not marrying you," she tossed over her shoulder as she walked—okay, hurried—to the bathroom.

She shut the door before he could answer.

Twelve

She wasn't going to make this easy on him, that much was clear.

While Brooke got cleaned up, Flash flopped across the bed, trying to get his thoughts in order. He wanted nothing more than to pull her right back into bed, curl around her body and nap the rest of the afternoon away, but they didn't have that much time. Not yet, anyway.

Okay, he could do this. He was calm, cool and collected and, thanks to the amazing sex, he could think without getting distracted by her body or his dick. Probably.

First things first—tea.

Just because he wanted her in ways that continually surprised him didn't mean she was his. And it especially didn't mean that he was over her hiding James from him. All it meant was they were…exploring areas of consensus or some such BS.

He launched himself out of bed, disposed of the condom and hurriedly washed his hands in the kitchen. Then he assembled her tea. The water had cooled a little, but it was still hot enough, he hoped. Then he squeezed in a dollop of honey. There.

She still didn't want to get married. She'd made it crystal clear before she'd come over here that she wasn't going to marry him. What he needed to figure out was if she was digging in her heels because he'd pushed too far, too fast or if, when she said she wasn't going to marry him, she was really saying *not right now*. And the sooner he figured that out, the better off they'd all be.

He made it back to the bedroom just as the bathroom door opened. Brooke walked into the bedroom in all her glory, and he was so stunned by her that he damn near dropped the mug. "Babe," he all but groaned, his body straining to muster a response.

She crossed her arms in front of her breasts, still teasingly contained by that pretty bra. "Focus, Flash. We have to talk."

"Right, right." He let his gaze travel down her body, taking in every curve and dip. "Are we talking with or without clothes? I vote without."

"Of course you do." She sighed, but she smiled while she said it. "Is that tea?"

"Jasmine green tea with honey." He held out the tea, making sure not to touch her.

Which was harder than anticipated when she took the mug from him, that satisfied smile on her lips. He'd put that smile there, and he'd do whatever it took to replace it with another one. If she'd let him, he'd make sure she smiled like that every day for the rest of their lives.

Then she frowned and he realized that she wasn't scowling at the tea, but at his hands. His swollen, red hands. "Is that from hitting couch cushions?"

Flash flexed his fingers, wincing. He didn't like that note of doubt in her voice. "Nope. This morning I found a boxing club that let me punch a bag for an hour." He'd had to buy a year's membership, but that hadn't bothered him a bit. Nashville was where Brooke was—her family, her career, her life. He'd be back in town. Often.

Luckily, the boxing club had been three blocks from a jeweler's shop, so he'd been able to kill two birds with one stone, so to speak. The ring itself had seven stones. God, he hoped she liked it.

Brooke looked worried. "And that helps?"

"Absolutely. I have a bag at home, too," he added. "Like I said last night—it's a controlled release. I haven't been in a fight in months."

"Do you remember what it was about?" Clearly, she expected the answer to be *no*.

But he did. "I got into it with Pete right before he and Chloe got hitched—and I was stone-cold sober when I did it. I thought I was protecting my sister, but Chloe let me know in no uncertain terms that she did not need my protection and that I was a jackass for thinking she'd ever want my help." He chuckled, rubbing a hand over his jaw. "Pete'll never let me forget that he broke my jaw. Of course, my face is pretty hard. I broke his hand, so we were even."

She gaped at him. "Seriously?"

"Seriously. I went cold turkey after that—had to. My hands were a mess and my jaw was wired shut for a while. But that was the wake-up call I needed. I almost cost my sister everything she loves, almost ruined my entire career and came damn close to destroying the All-Stars—not to mention risking jail time—all because I couldn't get a handle on my temper."

The thing that still boggled his mind was how damned sure he'd been at the time. When he'd overheard Tex McGraw making horribly crude comments about Brooke, Flash had known he'd needed to defend her honor. That had gotten him arrested and nearly sent to prison. And when he'd gone after Pete, he'd been convinced that the man was taking advantage of Chloe. He'd been positive he'd been right both times.

Now? Now he could see that neither woman had needed his protection. Brooke probably didn't even know Tex existed, much less that he was a sexist jerk. Chloe had been able to handle Pete and the All-Stars just fine on her own. The only thing Flash had ever done was make things worse.

It'd been a hell of a hard lesson to learn but he was learning it. Yeah, last night he'd been 100 percent sure that Brooke needed to marry him immediately, and because of that he'd almost destroyed any chance at a real relationship with her.

"And you're telling me you have a handle on that anger now? That you and Pete are...friends?" Skepticism dripped off every word.

Flash took a deep breath. It was all right if she was skeptical. She'd had months with those headlines eating at her. It would be unreasonable for her to nod and smile and pretend his past didn't bother her at all, especially after last night.

"We get by. And he treats my sister right." He cleared his throat. "Just so you know, I called Oliver, my brother. I told him about James, but not who you were." Although Oliver had figured it out, no doubt. He wasn't the one running the family's energy company by accident.

"I met him, right?"

"I think so, at the Fort Worth rodeo. Oliver's the oldest. He runs Lawrence Energies, which is the family business. He's married to Renee and they have an eight-month-old daughter, Trixie. My dad doesn't run the company anymore."

"Are you really a billionaire?"

"Me, personally? Probably not. Why?"

Brooke's eyes about bugged out of her head. "*Probably* not? You're not sure?"

"I sold my stake in Lawrence Energies when I started riding in the All-Stars to avoid the conflicts of interest. Invested most of it, blew some of it on cars and horses. Bought a nice piece of land a few hours south of Dallas with a big ol' house on it—plenty of room for a boy to have a good time," he added. "I get statements from the brokers, but I don't really read them."

Brooke clutched her tea like it was a life preserver and she was trying not to drown. "You don't even know..." she said quietly.

Flash took advantage of this to climb into bed behind her. He sat in the middle and pulled the sheets up over his waist.

He wasn't going to win the fight to not touch her. As softly as he could, he skimmed his hand over her back. She didn't lean away from him, so that had to count for something. "Is it a problem?"

"No, no. It's just... I didn't grow up rich, and then my uncle stole most of my money or lost it, and..." Her voice trailed off as she focused on him. "And, in the interests of honesty, part of what set me off last night was your sister implying that your family had the money to take me to court and bleed me dry if I didn't cooperate."

Flash groaned. "Yeah, I can see how that'd be upsetting," he said, closing his eyes and pushing back against the frustration. The whole point of calling his sister was so she would *help*, not freak Brooke the hell out! "Sorry about that. The point she should've made was that if you have any outstanding bills for his care or if he needs anything else—diapers or, uh, strollers?" Honestly, he had no idea what a baby would need. "Definitely a pony when he gets old enough."

Brooke grinned at his cluelessness although at least she was trying to hide it behind the mug.

"Or whatever—it's covered," Flash went on. "If there's

anything *you* need, just let me know." He tried to think—what would she want? Then it hit him. "Aside from all the tea you could drink, if you want a recording studio at my place, I'll get one built. If you decide you want a different house, one we share, I'll get it—with your name on the title. I'll start a trust fund for James, too, for college or whatever."

She blinked at him. "You'd build me a studio?"

"Hell, yeah." Actually, the more he thought about it, the better he liked that idea. Brooke could stay for weeks or even months. She could work on her music while Flash taught James how to ride and take care of his pony or took him to a rodeo. Then she wouldn't be tied to Nashville. Although they'd maintain a residence here because obviously Brooke would need to come back here on a regular basis. "I can get contractors started on it next week." He didn't actually know what went into a recording studio, but, hell, money wasn't an object. He'd hire someone who did know and tell them to get top-of-the-line equipment. Problem solved.

"That…" She actually blushed. "That would be lovely."

Yeah, that was exactly how he would show her he was good for her. "But the point is, you've already done the hard part. I want to make things easy for you from here on out, and I don't want the money differences to be a wedge between us."

"I appreciate that." She took a long drink. "Anything else I should know about your family?"

He shrugged. "You've met Chloe, who runs the All-Stars, which used to be part of Lawrence Energies, but now she owns it outright. And me." He launched a self-deprecating grin at her. "I don't run anything."

"But you're one of the best all-around rodeo riders in the world," she said, which had him puffing out his chest a little.

"I try. We haven't told Dad yet because subtlety isn't his strong suit, especially when it comes to grandbabies." Point of fact, the man had gone hog-wild for Trixie, all the more so because Oliver and Renee had named the baby after his beloved wife. It's not like that little girl wanted for anything—Oliver was much better at the whole money thing than Flash would ever be. But every time Milt Lawrence saw his granddaughter, he had another toy, another frilly dress, another keepsake present just for her. The man was over the moon.

"What about your mom? Is she still in the picture?"

Flash swallowed hard as he stroked her back. "She died when I was eleven."

Brooke gasped. "I'm so sorry. I hadn't realized."

"It's okay," he said with the casual shrug he always used when talking about his mom. He was used to her being gone, anyway. That was practically the same thing as it being okay. "I know now that everyone did a lot to shield me from the chaos, but, obviously, everything changed when she lost her fight with cancer."

Mom would've loved Brooke. And there would've been no getting her away from James. She would've known if Flash was doing the right thing. She would've loved her grandson, would've protected Brooke as if she were her own daughter. Trixie Lawrence would've made everything about this better. Flash didn't often miss her—she'd been gone more than half his life—but right now, he missed his mom.

"I'm sorry to hear that," she sniffed, wrapping her arms around his chest and hugging him back.

"It's okay. It was a long time ago. Right after that, Dad won the All-Stars in a poker game and relocated the entire family to Dallas. He couldn't stay in New York where we'd lived with Mom, so we all moved. He started going to rodeos and hanging out with cowboys, and he took me with him. And I learned real quick that there were two kinds of guys at those things—those who were quick with a wink and a joke and those who were quick with their fists."

Dad would disappear to go play cards with his buddies, shooting the breeze and drinking, leaving Flash to run wild. Chloe was usually at the rodeos with them, and she been charged with keeping an eye on him, but Flash had insisted that he hadn't needed a babysitter and had ditched her whenever he could.

"That's where I got my nickname," he told Brooke. "I was small and quick, and I could get into trouble and then disappear—" he snapped his fingers for emphasis "—in a *flash*."

He'd always looked back at his childhood with such fondness. What kid didn't love doing whatever he damn well pleased? But now Flash wondered how things might have been different if Milt Lawrence hadn't been in the grips of a midlife crisis and deep depression following the loss of his beloved wife. Would Flash be a different man today if his father had shown him how to be a different man then?

Brooke sniffed again. "I don't know that I realized you hadn't grown up on a ranch somewhere. You're such a quintessential cowboy."

"I'll take that as a compliment, but I was a city slicker kid from New York."

She curled against his side, and it only made sense for him to drape his arm around her shoulder and hug her close. This was…nice.

"But my point is, for most of my life, I only knew how to be one of two people—a ladies' man who sweet-talked all the pretty girls or a fighter who refused to back down. But when I'm with you, I don't have to stay stuck in those two extremes. I can be someone else."

"Oh, *Flash*," she whispered, looking up at him. He wiped a lingering tear from her cheek.

"I need to be in my son's life on a regular basis," he told her. "And I think it's pretty clear that sex between you and me is gonna be a thing."

"A *good* thing," she murmured, not sounding happy about it. "It'd be easier if it wasn't."

Yeah, if he could keep his hands off her, it'd make what was supposed to be a negotiation more cut-and-dried.

But he couldn't keep his hands off her, as evidenced by the way he stroked her back. "What about your family?"

She shrugged, but he felt the tension ripple through her body. "It's me and Mom. I don't know who my dad was— Mom refuses to talk about him."

"Really?"

"Oh, yeah," she said, slumping back against the bed. "She won't tell me a damn thing about my father, but yet she's been pushing me to sign off on a big baby reveal. Plus, she refuses to see how much of a hypocrite she's being about it. All she can say is it isn't the same—because why? Because I've got a music career? It's BS. Mom is very… focused," she explained. "She pushed me into a singing career from when I was in kindergarten. Which wasn't bad," she added, maybe a little too quickly.

Flash was getting a mental image of her mother that was anything but flattering. The woman sounded domineering, controlling and more than just a little mean. "Are you sure about that?"

She nodded. "I love what I do and I've had some great friends."

"Like Kyle Morgan?" Flash hadn't forgotten the way the older man had given Flash a mean look.

"Yeah, Kyle's been a great mentor. But even the best mentor isn't a replacement for a father. I don't even know if my dad knows I exist and I *hate* it. I've always hated it.

I can't help wondering if he didn't want me." She leaned against him as she said it.

Flash's mind reeled even as he held her tight. True, he'd always butted heads with his father—but he'd always known how much he was loved. His heart hurt for Brooke, for the pain in her voice.

"That's on him," Flash said, furious with this random sperm donor. "Not you, babe. And I would never do that to my child. Even if *this* doesn't work out between you and me, I'm not abandoning my kid. He's a Lawrence no matter what."

She exhaled heavily. "Good. That's good. You know, I'd made peace with it, with her and with him," Brooke went on, her voice small. "Or I thought I had. Then you happened and I got pregnant and it brought it all home—how much Mom kept hidden from me. I love her, but I don't know if I can ever forgive her. Does that make sense?"

Flash felt like she'd punched him. "Yeah," he got out in a strangled voice. "I understand completely."

Because he felt exactly the same way. He cared for Brooke, more than he probably should. And he felt such a powerful, instinctual love for James that he couldn't even put it into words.

But how would he get past the fact that Brooke had kept that baby boy a secret from Flash? Was forgiveness even possible?

"And it was so hard not to call you up and tell you then," she went on, seemingly unaware that she'd just blown Flash's mind. "You've got to believe me, Flash—I always meant to tell you. I never intended to keep you from Bean or him from you. Because I know it's not right. I was just…"

"Waiting for the right time," he said softly after she'd trailed off.

"Yeah." She swallowed. "I wish I'd realized that the right time was actually a few months ago."

That made two of them.

"I'm not going to be like her," she said, her voice stronger as she sat up straighter. "I want Bean to know you and your family. I want us to get to a point where we can make some version of *this* work."

Flash had to swallow a few times. "Yeah, me too."

She tapped a pattern on the tea mug. "The question is, how do we make that happen?"

He scratched a hand through his hair. "The general consensus is that me telling you we *had* to get hitched was the dumbest thing I've done in a long, long time."

"So why did you do it?"

He kept his gaze locked on her face. "*Because*. Which—" he added with a chuckle when her lips twisted off to the side in disapproval "—is a bad answer. I've learned that. But the truth is, you mean something to me, Brooke."

He felt, more than saw, the eye roll. He tried again. "From the moment I laid eyes on you, I haven't looked at another woman—and that's not just a figure of speech. There's something between us, and it's got the potential to be something good. Something great, even. But," he went on before she could tell him where he could shove all his *potential*, "that doesn't mean we make sense married. We both have careers that require near-constant travel, and there's a lot riding on us doing our jobs well."

"That's true," she admitted, sounding almost regretful about it. "I'm not giving up my music."

"Which is absolutely fair. You've been the front line for a year. More than a year," he said. "Have you done it alone?"

She didn't meet his gaze. Instead, her fingers continued to tap out a rhythm on her mug. "I've got Alex. And my mother. She's with Bean now. I may not agree with all of her *choices*, as you put it, but she loves him completely." She winced, her fingers stilling as she shot him an apologetic look. "She'll like you even less than Alex does."

Every single time, Brooke's statements about her mother had been couched in worry and maybe a little bit of fear. If Mrs. Bonner was James's primary babysitter, that probably meant Brooke had needed the time between when she'd left the Bluebird and when Flash had shown up at her house to get her mother out of her house.

Mrs. Bonner was a problem.

Oliver had made it clear why Flash needed to establish paternity immediately, if not sooner. For once, Flash and Oliver had been in agreement about something—marriage would make everything smoother.

Smoother for the Lawrences, yeah. But for Brooke? She needed more than that and, by God, Flash wanted to be the one to give it to her.

"I'm not worried about your mom. I'm worried about *you*." He stroked his thumb over her cheek. Unexpectedly, her eyes began to water. "You impress the hell out of me, you know? You toured while pregnant and had our baby and still wrote a bunch of kick-ass songs. You've done such an amazing job, and I couldn't ask for a better mother for my son."

"Damn it," she sniffed, pulling away from his touch and swiping at her eyes. "Don't be charming, Flash. I'm too tired to cope with you being perfect."

"I'm not being charming," he told her as he put her almost empty mug on the nightstand and then lifted her into his lap. "I'm being honest. I'll always be honest with you. Just be honest with me, too. That's all I ask."

Crying, she settled into his lap, her arms around his neck. This wasn't sexual, although there was no missing the fact that there was little more than a sheet between their nude bodies.

No, this was him taking care of her. He wrapped his arms around her, and relief coursed through him when she rested her head on his shoulder. Leaning back against the headboard, he let his body take her weight while he stroked her back and kissed her forehead and let her get it all out.

Long minutes passed, and he didn't think about her mother or his family or songs or rodeos or anything but this woman.

He wanted her.

It really didn't make sense, except it did. He'd wanted her a year ago and he wanted her now. Would he still want her in another year?

Would she still want him?

It was a huge risk. But, hell, he was Flash Lawrence. Everything he did was a risk.

"Anything between us has to start from trust, and I..." He swallowed hard. "I understand why you did what you did. But I don't trust you as much as I need to right now, and you probably don't trust me as much as you need to, either." She gasped, but he didn't stop. He couldn't. "I'm not going to get it right all the time. I didn't last night. But that doesn't mean I'm going to stop trying."

Another tear trickled down her cheek and he wiped this one away, too. "You're being perfect again," she said in what might have been a scolding voice if it hadn't been so choked with emotion.

"Trying to be, anyway," he said. She laughed, and she was so beautiful, a smile on her face even as tears clung to her eyelashes, that he kissed her. His body surged to attention as he held her tight.

He could get lost in the honeyed sweetness of this woman, and that thought made him realize something—he did want to marry her. It might be a disaster and it'd definitely be messy but...

His father still talked about how he'd taken one look at Trixie Cunningham and that'd been it for him. In the years since her death, he'd never dated, never taken a lover. He was still in love with his wife. She'd been the only woman for him.

How was that different from how Flash had reacted to Brooke? He'd laid eyes on her at the All-Stars Rodeo in Fort Worth and he hadn't stopped thinking about Brooke, hadn't touched another woman, since then.

What if this was the same thing?

What if this was forever?

Thirteen

She pulled away, resting her head on his shoulder again. "We don't have much time."

"Right." Damn it. He tried to get his mind back on track. "Okay. We need a plan."

"Yes. Definitely a plan." But then she gave him a dreamy smile and kissed him again.

She was absolutely *killing* him, but what a way to go. "First things first—what do *you* want to do?"

That dreaminess faded, replaced by a worried furrow between her brows. "You know, I don't think anyone's ever asked."

Flash winced. Yeah, he'd skipped that step last night. "We need to find a workable solution. And that may or may not involve marriage. So be honest."

She was quiet for a long time, but Flash held himself still, and finally she began to talk. "I don't want to use my child as leverage. I want people to see him as a person in his own right instead of a marketing tool. I want to take him to parks and the zoo and introduce him to my friends—who'll all be mad that I've lied to them for the last year. I don't want to lie anymore. I want to feel like I'm in control of at least some part of my own life."

"That all sounds good to me," he said softly. He didn't want to interrupt her.

"I don't want to be forced into anything, like I was when my mother and my record company made the executive decision to hide my pregnancy," she went on. "I don't want to be made to feel ashamed of who I am or who Bean is. I want my new album to do well, and I want to do a smaller, more manageable tour that won't be so exhausting. I want to keep my son with me and I want…" Her gaze cut to him and he hoped like hell he saw desire there.

He leaned forward, hoping to catch that last word, hoping it was *you*.

As her words trailed off, she rolled onto her side and stared at him. "I want to be friends with you, because I like you, too." Her tone was suddenly diplomatic. Was she being honest? "I want to know you better, and you're right—I want to trust you more than I do now. I want Bean to know his whole family. I want everything to be perfect."

She didn't say *not like this*, but Flash heard it anyway.

"That's quite a list."

She swiped at her eyes again. "Yeah. Not going to apologize for any of it."

He could sense the frustration underneath every request—the long nights, the loneliness, the worry that underscored her every moment, and it wrecked him that he hadn't been here for her.

The truth was that he'd nearly ruined his entire life because he'd had some dumb-ass idea that attacking another guy for daring to talk about her was protecting her, but it wasn't. Truly protecting her would've been standing by her side for the last year, backing her up when she'd needed to push against her mother or her record label, holding her hand during labor, being there for the sleepless nights.

He couldn't change the past. The important thing was that she didn't see herself on opposite sides of him or his family. Everything else, he could work with. He wanted her to keep writing, keep singing, and if she wanted to tour, he'd make it work.

Mrs. Bonner was *definitely* going to be a problem, though. Because if there was one thing Flash understood, it was being an adult who everyone still treated like a kid.

He leaned over and pulled the ring box out of the drawer where he'd stashed it when she'd called. "Brooke."

Her eyes went wide as she scrambled into a sitting position—one where she wasn't touching him. "Flash, don't do this."

"I'm not proposing—promise," he corrected quickly. He set the box down in the no-man's land between them. "Let's call it a…business partnership."

She eyed him warily. He hated that look, hated that she still felt she had to guard herself against him. "What kind of partnership?"

"Several things need to happen." Things he'd discussed with Chloe and Pete last night and again with Oliver this morning. At least Oliver had only yelled for a few minutes, although there had been that threat of permanent dismemberment…

"We need a paternity test, for starters. Not because I doubt you," he said, which made her roll her eyes. "Anyone who looks at that boy knows he's mine." Chloe had said as much.

"You do have the same smile," she said quietly, giving him a grin that was almost shy.

"We need the test, because I'm not on the birth certificate and I don't want anyone else to question the fact that he's my son." Anyone like her mother, specifically.

Brooke blew out a long breath. "Yes, of course. There's no question about that."

"Good." The next part, however, was trickier. Chloe had told him what she and Brooke had talked about—including how Chloe had gotten distracted by the baby and started thinking out loud about how they were going to sell this to the public. Flash had called her because he wasn't good at big-picture thinking like that, but he also completely understood why it'd overwhelmed Brooke.

"Have you thought about what Chloe mentioned last night? Before the cushion incident?"

Brooke slumped back onto the bed, her fingers tapping a rhythm only she could hear. Flash was sure she didn't know she was doing it.

"Yes," she said quietly, not looking at him. "It's not a bad plan. It's definitely the kind of thing the record label will sign off on, especially when your name gets out there. But I don't want to get married, you know?"

"Okay. Got that." He'd have to be dead to miss it.

"So what is this?" she asked, nudging the box. "How is a ring—it is a ring, right?" Flash nodded. "How is a ring a business proposal?"

He thought back to that list of things she wanted out of their relationship. The good news was she wanted to be friends with him. Friends spent time together. They hung out, went out, called and texted and sent pictures. Sometimes, friends even stripped each other naked and had extremely satisfying sex.

But she'd also didn't want her choices taken away, and she didn't want to feel ashamed. "Chloe said she could spin our relationship so you're in the driver's seat. We were dating and you got pregnant and then I screwed up and you gave me an ultimatum to shape up or ship out, which I did. Right?"

"Basically…" She crossed her arms and stared at the jeweler's box as if it held the Ring of Sauron or something.

"So we could get engaged." He opened the box, the huge diamond surrounded by sapphires, all catching the light. Brooke gasped in what he hoped was approval.

"Holy crap—look at the size of that rock!" she whispered. Then she looked up at him, her eyes huge. "Engaged? Are you asking me to marry you again?"

Flash took that to be a sign that he'd chosen well. "Nope." She snorted, but her gaze fell back to the ring. "We don't have to set a date, much less book the band and send out invitations. Chloe said we'd tell people we'd be keeping it quiet, like our whole relationship. Then, in a year or whenever, we could break up, ask for privacy during our difficult time, and promise that we would continue to put our child first. And none of that would be a lie, necessarily." Although the thought of her moving on, falling in love with someone else who'd get to spend time raising his son—yeah, that rankled.

"You're serious," she said, sounding breathless. She stretched out a finger toward the ring before she snatched it back, like the ring might burn her.

"Yep." Months of a friendly fake engagement gave Flash room to work. He could take her—and James, of course—out. He could demonstrate he had the chops to be a good father and, most importantly, that he was trustworthy—all without screwing up his big championship year.

Hopefully, during that time, he could get to a point where he could trust her, too. He knew that was a ways off, but he didn't want to spend the rest of his life questioning her every statement or action, either.

And if they were together, it only made sense that they might spend some time in bed, right?

"You can tour for your new album, I can still ride the rodeo on the weekends and, when we can, we make time to work on this parenting thing." He laughed nervously. "I need more work than you do, I reckon."

"And I could call it off whenever I wanted?" she asked softly. This time, she did pick up the ring, studying the huge round-cut diamond.

Yeah, he'd made the right choice. "Of course. You could do that even if it were a real engagement."

"You won't ask me to marry you again?"

He chuckled. "Nope. The offer stands, though." He took the ring from her. "I guessed on the size." He held out his hand for hers.

She made him wait for it, which he probably deserved. "This is the last moment before everything changes. *Again*," she murmured. "After this, it'll be out of our hands."

"No, it won't," he promised, pulling her into a hug. "I won't let anyone run you down. We're in this together."

"What about sex?" she murmured against his bare shoulder.

His pulse stuttered at the thought. "I'm not about to step out on you. The only thing I ask is that you do the same. And…" He had to dig deep to get the words out. "And if we go our separate ways, I want to meet whoever you date before you introduce him to our son."

She nodded against him and said, "Like I have time to date, anyway."

"Yeah," he agreed, letting his hands roam down her back. "I'm going to be busy for the foreseeable future." He had a championship to win, a kid to father and Brooke…

Yeah, he was going to have his hands *full*. "If you want sex to be a part of this *whatever* it is we're going to do, then I'm okay with that." That was the freaking understatement of the century. Just having this conversation was making him hard for her all over again. "If you don't want to be physical, that's okay, too. I still won't sleep with anyone else."

She sighed. "I think…no, I *know* that if we're going to be around each other, we're going to wind up just like this, whether we plan on it or not."

She pulled away and Flash managed not to groan in frustration, so score one for maturity. Damned maturity.

"If we're engaged," she went on, finality in her voice. "I wouldn't want to say it's fake, because I like you, and *this*," she said, motioning between their bodies, "is very, *very* good."

"Happy to hear," he replied, waggling his eyebrows suggestively.

Was she agreeing?

She was.

Taking a deep breath, she squared her shoulders and held out her left hand, palm down. "Okay," she said, sounding for all the world like she was gearing up for battle, not accepting his ring. "Let's do this. For Bean."

"For *us*." Flash didn't realize his own hands were shaking until he slid the diamond onto her finger. "Whatever happens," he told her, his voice low and serious, "we're in this together. Trust me."

The ring fit.

A part of his mind wanted to say it was fate, that she was meant to be his and he would always be hers.

She stared at his ring on her finger. "Trust…" She sighed heavily. A little too heavily. "Because nothing says *trustworthy* like an only sort-of-real engagement, right?"

"It's a challenge," he told her. One that involved working together as a team, developing a physical connection and, *far* down the line, the chance to win it all.

Being almost really engaged to Brooke Bonner was not unlike riding in a rodeo, frankly.

This was Flash's year, and Brooke Bonner was the biggest challenge of his life.

Fourteen

Things happened very quickly after Brooke managed to pull herself out of Flash's arms and out of his bed.

First, she called Alex and updated her friend on the new plan. Not unsurprisingly, Alex wasn't a huge fan of the plan. Or of Flash. "*Engaged? Seriously? I'm not sure this is the best idea.*"

"You got a better one?" Brooke shot back. "I can't keep hiding, Alex. You know I can't. It's not right. And, yes, it's going to suck for a while, but it was always going to suck. We just delayed the suckiness."

"Yeah, yeah, I know." Another longish pause. "You going to marry him?"

"We're *engaged.*" Which wasn't really an answer to that question, but it was the only one she was going to give to Alex, to her mother, to the press. They were engaged. Period. End of discussion.

"I'll break him if he hurts you," she growled into the phone.

Brooke laughed it off because how else was she supposed to respond to what was probably a serious threat?

"I'll fill you in on all the details later." Alex made what

sounded a lot like a retching noise. "But the main thing right now is that we're going to bring Bean to the All-Stars Rodeo Friday night and I hope you'll be able to be there. It'd mean a lot to me." Flash gave her a thumbs-up. "To both of us."

Alex, however, was in no mood to be charmed. "I'm not gonna like him, so quit trying," she snapped, but, in true Alex form, she softened immediately. "Okay, fine. We're all going to the rodeo. Have you told your mom yet?"

"No, that's next. We're going out to the house after this," Brooke said.

"Well, good luck with *that*." She hung up.

Some of Flash's good humor faded. "That didn't sound good."

"It's not." There were no words to describe how little Brooke was looking forward to this introduction.

Flash kissed her forehead before saying, "However you want to handle it is how we'll handle it. I'm here to back you up."

She couldn't help the sigh of relief that escaped her. This was the Flash she wanted. Perfect and charming and thoughtful and beside her. Not out in front, not trying to take over, but supporting her. "Just…maybe focus on demonstrating you're a good father? For all our issues, she does love Bean."

If he tried to charm Mom outright, it'd be a disaster. But if he could convince Crissy Bonner that he'd take good care of her grandson, then maybe it wouldn't be too bad.

"That I can do," he promised, pulling her to her feet and brushing a kiss over her lips, then her cheek. "And then afterwards?"

The next kiss was anything but soft or sweet, and maybe it wasn't the smartest thing to do, but Brooke let herself be swept away by his heat, his taste.

"Will you stay tonight?" she whispered against his

mouth. She could sleep in his arms and maybe he could at least get up with Bean, even if she'd still have to nurse him. And if they were already sharing a bed… "Will you stay with me?"

He touched his forehead to hers, his thumbs stroking over her cheeks. "For as long as you'll let me, babe."

She chose not to think about what he was really saying.

Forty minutes later, Brooke was pretty sure she'd made a tactical error bringing Flash home with her unannounced.

"*Who* is this?" Mom demanded, clutching Bean to her chest as she eyed Flash suspiciously. The look in her eyes promised a storm was about to be unleashed.

But Brooke wasn't going to back down. Not this time. Not ever again.

Mother might know best, but Brooke was a mother now, too. And she knew what was best for her family.

She glanced at Flash. He was family now, especially when he gave her hand an encouraging squeeze and shot her a little wink. Then he turned the full power of his charming smile back to her mother and said, "Mrs. Bonner, I'm Frasier Lawrence. My family owns Lawrence Energies in Dallas." Then, because he was Flash, he threw in a little bow. "I'm Bean's father and," he continued smoothly over Mom's gasp of horror, "I've asked your daughter to marry me." He lifted Brooke's hand and kissed her knuckle, right above the simply huge diamond engagement ring.

She noted that Flash carefully avoided the lie that Brooke had agreed to be his wife. He simply let the jewelry and his real name do the talking for him.

The noise Mom made was barely human. "You *what*? Who the hell *is* this?"

She startled poor Bean, who definitely hadn't recovered from all the excitement the night before. He promptly melted down.

"Now look what you've done!" Mom yelled at Flash over the baby's wails. Bean cried louder.

Brooke tensed because if Flash was going to lose his temper, this would be the moment when it happened.

He didn't. Instead, Flash simply squeezed Brooke's hand and focused on Mom. "Ma'am, I think my son is hungry. Let me check his diaper before I give him to Brooke." He plucked the baby out of Mom's stunned arms. "Hey, honey. I heard you let Mommy sleep a little last night," he cooed to the baby as he headed for the stairs. He shifted so Bean was tucked against his shoulder. "Maybe we'll let her get some more sleep tonight. Won't that be great? Yeah, that's my good boy."

Bean, bless his heart, managed a wobbly grin, even as he gave Brooke a worried look. But he let Flash carry him upstairs.

Brooke's heart clenched with a fierce need because, yeah, he was putting on a show for Mom, but, God, the sight of him cuddling his son, of Bean responding to him—that was what she needed from him. *She* needed to know he'd be a good father.

"You're getting married?" Mom asked, not bothering to wait until Flash and Bean were out of earshot.

"Not today," Brooke replied. "But Flash—that's Frasier's nickname—and I are going to—"

"Wait—that's *Flash* Lawrence?" Mom interrupted, the blood draining from her face. "The criminal?"

"Actually, he's a rodeo rider." Brooke took a cue from Flash and counted her breaths for a moment until she was sure she had her temper under control. "I don't expect you to understand or approve, Mom."

"You're damn right I don't," she fired back. "Do you have any idea what he's capable of? He will destroy your career." With great physical effort, Mom attempted to look caring. She didn't come close. "Honey, let's think about

this. I'm just not sure this *marriage*," she said, like the word
tasted bad in her mouth, "is for the best, you know? We've
kept his…contribution quiet for this long. There's no reason to break that silence right now." She shot Brooke the
look that normally had her dropping her gaze, unwilling to
risk further angering Crissy Bonner. But then her mother
added, "You know I just want what's best for your career,"
in what was probably supposed to be a gentle voice, except
it came out as an order.

Right. If Mom was truly worried about Flash's "criminal" history, she'd be worried about Brooke or about Bean.
But it always came back to the career with Crissy Bonner.

Brooke ignored the sting of rejection layered within her
mother's words. "He can't be any worse for my career than
your brother was when he stole all my money and disappeared to Mexico," Brooke shot back. "But you convinced
me that hiring Uncle Brantley was 'for the best' because it
kept my career in the family, right?"

"He's my brother," Mom snapped. "I trusted him, too.
It's not my fault he made poor choices. Just like it's not my
fault you made poor choices!"

"Do *not* call my child a poor choice," Brooke seethed.

"All I'm trying to do is contain the damage," Mom went
on. "And until we know what that man's motivations are,
it's for the best to keep him out of the picture. That doesn't
make me the bad guy here!"

"Oh? Just like you kept my father out of the picture?"

Mom had already opened her mouth to fire back another excuse, but at Brooke's words, her jaw snapped shut.
"You have no idea what you're talking about," she said in
a dangerous whisper.

"Of course I don't—because you won't tell me!" Brooke
was shouting now, but she didn't care. Years of resentments
bubbled up and poured out. "For God's sake, Mom, I'm
not a little girl anymore! I'm a woman, and I'm more than

capable of deciding what I need to be protected from. Or were you just protecting yourself?" The words came flying out of her mouth before she could stop them. "Maybe you were just afraid that, if I knew my father, I'd choose him over you!"

True hurt flashed over her mother's face, but it was gone in an instant. "After all I've done for you, this is how you repay me?"

That line might've worked on Brooke when she was a teenager, but she wasn't about to fall for that guilt trip now. "Who was he, Mom?"

Everything about Crissy Bonner screamed, *Not telling*, from the tight line of her mouth to the way she'd crossed her arms in front of her.

"Don't you think I deserve to know? At least for Bean's sake. What if there are medical issues we should know about?"

"This discussion is over," Mom snapped. She made a move toward the door.

Brooke blocked her. Somehow, she knew that if Mom walked out that door, she'd never get answers. "I've let you keep your secrets for years, but you owe me this. You made sure I grew up without knowing anything about my father. If you think I'm going to let you do the exact same thing to Bean, then you've underestimated how far I'll go to protect him!"

"You foolish girl—did you ever consider the fact that maybe *he* didn't want you to know who he was?"

"Of course I did." It didn't take a big mental leap to figure that her father simply didn't want her, because if he did, he'd have found a way to be with her. "But does that justify lying to me my entire life?"

Mom tried to push past her, but Brooke wasn't having any of it. She grabbed her mom by her shoulders and demanded, "Who was he?"

"This is a mistake," Mom hissed. She twisted out of Brooke's grasp and made a turn, probably heading for the back door.

Brooke snatched her hand and held tight. "Mom, please. It won't make me love you any less." Who knew, maybe it'd help her understand her mother's *unique* kind of love even more. "Promise."

"You really think I haven't told you just because I'm embarrassed or something? Fine. But you take this up with him. I wash my hands of this whole mess."

"Fine?" Was Crissy Bonner actually going to tell the truth? And Brooke wasn't entirely sure what Mom meant with that *mess* comment. "Who?"

"Kyle Morgan," she snapped. "There. Happy?"

"Kyle? *Kyle?*" Brooke's old friend? The man who'd taught her how to write a song, who'd given her a guitar for her eleventh birthday? Who'd been there the night of her first show at the Bluebird and helped her land her record deal? The man who'd threatened Flash behind the Bluebird?

Kyle Morgan was her father.

And he'd never told her.

"Does he…does he know? Who I am?"

"Of course he does, not that it ever mattered to him. But just because Kyle cut and ran doesn't mean you have to marry *that* man," Mom went on, wrenching her hand away from Brooke and pointing to the second floor. "You've already made one mistake. Two wrongs don't make a right. Trust me on *that*, Brooke."

Numbly, Brooke looked up to see Flash standing at the top of the stairs, Bean in his arms. "Brooke?" he said softly into the eerie silence that settled in the space between Brooke and her mother. "We're ready for you."

She was not going to cry in front of her mother. She was not going to rant and rave and demand to know what the hell Mom and Kyle had been thinking. She was not going to lose it completely. She simply wasn't.

Suddenly she understood why Flash had been punching couch cushions.

"I will cut you out of Bean's life if you ever refer to him as a mistake again," Brooke said, her voice unnaturally calm. "Flash and I are engaged. He's Bean's father and we're together now. And I think it'd be best if I found a manager who understood the difference between managing my career and managing me. I love you, Mom, but I don't know how I'm going to forgive you for this. Or Kyle."

A muscle twitched on Mom's forehead. "Fine. You're on your own."

"Fine." Actually, it was a relief. She was zero-for-two with family members as managers. "Thank you for watching Bean today."

"His name is Jimmy," Mom shot back. "I hate that nickname."

"His name is *James*," Brooke replied, stepping to the side. "James Frasier Lawrence."

Mom stormed past her, slamming the door with all her might.

Brooke stood there for a long moment—okay, several long moments—trying to process everything that had just happened. She'd expected a fight about Flash. She'd considered Mom quitting as her manager a possibility, maybe.

But… Kyle Morgan was her father?

"Babe?" Flash called down softly.

Right.

"Did…" Brooke's voice broke. "Did you hear?"

Flash practically flew down the stairs to stand next to her, close enough to bump her shoulder with his. "Impossible not to."

"Yeah."

"Yeah," he agreed.

The silence stretched but it didn't feel painful. She realized Flash had laced his fingers with hers.

"I…" She cleared her throat and tried again. "I need you to stay. With me. Tonight. I…" Tears began to drip off her chin. "I don't want to be alone right now."

"You won't be."

Fifteen

"Everyone, this is Brooke Bonner, my fiancée, and our son, James Frasier," Flash announced.

Brooke cringed, although she tried not to show it. After so many months of holding her secrets close to her heart, it felt really weird to just announce Bean to four people in this room. She wasn't ready for this. She might never be ready.

But then, she'd be just as bad as her mother and she wasn't having that. So Brooke straightened her spine and lifted her chin. Really, this was no different than walking out onto a stage. Except this wasn't a stage—it was a private luxury suite in the Bridgestone Arena, where the All-Stars Rodeo would happen in a few hours. She was here to put on a show, except instead of singing her heart out, she was putting herself out there as Flash's bride-to-be.

"And this is Alex Andrews, a close friend of Brooke's," Flash went on, launching that charming grin around the room. Thank God, Alex was here. Between her oldest friend's unwavering support and Flash's dogged protectiveness, Brooke was sure she could do this.

Reasonably sure. She still had to give a convincing performance, one that had nothing to do with the last two days of Flash basically living with her, making her dinner and rocking Bean to sleep at naptime so she could lie down, too, and holding her when she cried about her mom and Kyle and the whole mess.

No, this evening had nothing to do with that glimpse into what married life could be like with Flash. It had everything to do with damage control and redemption arcs.

From a far corner, Chloe Lawrence looked up and smiled in welcome. Brooke and Flash had agreed that, for the time being, Kyle's contribution to her life was completely off-limits to anyone outside of the two of them and Alex because Brooke wasn't ready to have that part of her life implode, too.

Unfortunately, Chloe was also on the phone, so the first person Brooke got introduced to was...

"Oliver, this is Brooke," Flash said, leading Brooke over to an imposing-looking man who was clearly Flash's brother, a little taller and broader, with silver shot through his hair. Otherwise, they had practically the same eyes, the same chin. But not the same smile—that much was clear when Oliver grimaced. In an undertone, Flash added, "Be nice or *else*."

If Oliver heard the threat, he didn't react. Instead, in a deeply professional voice, he said, "Ms. Bonner, a pleasure to see you again."

Brooke notched an eyebrow at that. Flash had warned her that his brother could be a bit stiff. She'd barely met the eldest Lawrence sibling at the Fort Worth rodeo before she'd disappeared with Flash. But she remembered someone who'd been very...overwhelming, especially when compared to Flash's easygoing nature. That, at least, hadn't changed.

"Don't worry," the blonde woman next to him said, handing Oliver the baby girl she was struggling to hold on to. "The awkwardness won't last. Welcome to the Lawrence family!"

"This is Renee, Oliver's wife," Flash said, leaning over and giving Renee a kiss on the cheek. Then he mock-whispered to Brooke, "Don't believe a word she says about what we did as kids. It's lies, all lies, I say!"

Renee laughed and stuck out her hand. "I never thought I'd meet the woman who could rein Flash in, but I'm glad I finally have." Renee had a wide smile that seemed vaguely familiar. She patted the little girl. "This is our daughter, Trixie. She's almost nine months old." Trixie barely looked at Brooke before burying her head in her father's neck. "I'm so glad she has a cousin!"

Brooke exhaled in relief. Another mom, another baby—she felt less out to sea already. She only hoped Renee would prove to be as friendly as her smile.

Renee leaned forward, staring at Bean with open adoration. "Look at you," she whispered. "I know tests have to be done, but Oliver, do you see the resemblance?"

Bean chose that moment to launch one of his daddy's smiles into the room, and Renee gasped at the same time Oliver said, "Well, that settles *that*."

"Yeah," Brooke agreed. "We're all in trouble, aren't we?"

Oliver gaped and Brooke was sure she'd screwed up. But then, unexpectedly, Oliver burst out laughing. "You're going to be very good for my brother, aren't you?" he said, slugging Flash on the shoulder.

Apparently, the awkwardness didn't last long. "The better question is, how good will he be for me?"

Oliver beamed, which was sort of unsettling because when he wasn't scowling, he was almost as charming as Flash. "He better be great for you—or else."

"Boys," Renee scolded as she held out her arms. "May I?" Brooke handed over Bean, who immediately gurgled in what sounded like approval. "I practically grew up with

Flash—although he was still Frasier then. Oh, the stories I could tell you!" She fixed him with a piercing gaze. "Remember the elevator incident?"

Next to Brooke, Flash groaned. "You're killing me, Renee."

"It's good for you to be brought down a peg or two," she replied with an easy grin, and it was clear these two had a long history of teasing each other.

"I think discovering fatherhood has run me right out of pegs," Flash countered. "Come on," he said to Oliver, taking Trixie from his big brother's arms, "I could use a drink. A *ginger ale*," he said, meeting Oliver's scowl head-on. "Sheesh, man. Even when I drank, I never drank before a rodeo. Babe, you want green tea? I had them get some just for you."

Brooke's cheeks heated. "That would be wonderful. Thank you."

Flash winked at her, and then the brothers headed off to the side of the suite where a variety of nonalcoholic beverages were displayed on a sideboard.

"I remember when Trixie was this little," Renee said, bouncing Bean in her arms. The baby trilled in delight. She eyed Brooke sympathetically. "How are you holding up?"

"Okay, I guess." Sure, she hadn't seen or spoken to her mother in two days, nor had she decided what to do about Kyle Morgan.

At least Alex was here. Brooke glanced over to see that Flash had somehow gotten Alex over to the drinks and was introducing her to Trixie. It was sweet of Flash to make sure Alex was a part of what was, essentially, a family gathering. And despite all her protestations that she wasn't going to like Flash, Brooke could tell her friend was relieved Flash was including her.

"I understand Chloe has a whole plan in place," Renee said.

Brooke felt awkward standing in the middle of the room,

so she moved to the huge picture windows that overlooked the arena. Renee followed. Below, she saw someone who might be Pete Wellington making the final preparations. In a few minutes, the doors would open and the stands would begin to fill. And once the crowd was in place…

It was just another performance, one where she wouldn't have a guitar in her hands. Just a baby. "Yes. I ran it through the record label's PR department and they signed off on it, as well. I think Chloe's got a job at the label if she ever gets tired of the rodeo."

"Trust me, that'll never happen. The only one who's tired of the rodeo is Oliver."

Redemption arcs for everyone, apparently. Chloe was probably on the phone with Kari right now, coordinating the Big Reveal, as Brooke had started to think of it.

Right before Flash's first event, she and Bean, who had his own set of baby-sized noise-canceling headphones, would go behind the chutes where she would very publicly give Flash a kiss for good luck. The cameras would zoom in to capture the moment. Alex would be right behind her, just in case.

The announcers would draw everyone's attention to her and Flash, at which point Flash would lift Bean out of Brooke's arms and cuddle him. If Bean was cooperative, he would smile, and Brooke would put her head on Flash's shoulder and it would be perfect.

Brooke looked at her son, who was currently attempting to stuff his whole fist in his drooly mouth. Life was so rarely perfect. "It's going to be very messy for a while, though," she said, and sighed.

To Brooke's surprise, Renee wrapped an arm around her shoulders and gave Brooke an awkward hug. "You'll get through this," she said. "No matter what happens, you and this special little guy are family now and family is everything to the Lawrences."

"It is?" Brooke was horrified to hear her voice catch. Family had done nothing but let her down for the last few days. Weeks. Lifetimes, it seemed.

Renee nodded. "It absolutely is. Even when Flash had a rough few years there—which he mostly brought upon himself," she quickly added, "his family stood by him. I don't know your history, aside from your official bio. But my own family was—" she shrugged and turned her attention to Bean "—less than ideal. Having the Lawrences stand with me when everyone else bailed? It's *everything*."

Brooke blinked hard. "I don't really have anyone else but Alex. My mother stopped speaking to me when she found out about Flash." That was a gross simplification of the situation, but it was all she could cop to without crying.

At least with Flash in the house, she'd been able to get some more sleep. She wouldn't have had a prayer of getting through this night otherwise.

Renee handed Bean back to Brooke and then gave her another sideways hug. "I'll be honest—the Lawrences can be overbearing, overwhelming and completely over-the-top. But they'll fight for you and this little guy until the very end, if you let them."

Bean launched his daddy's smile at Brooke. "I just want things to work out," she said softly, hugging her baby tight.

"They will," Renee promised. "Just maybe not the way you thought they would."

Flash stood off to the side, making Trixie giggle as he blew bubbles on her tummy. The whole time, he watched Brooke, who was deep in conversation with Renee.

Chloe came up and topped off her water. "It seems to be going well," she said, nodding toward the two women.

Flash introduced Chloe to Alex. "She's nervous," Alex announced. "Excuse me."

"I'd be worried if she weren't," Chloe agreed. Once Alex had joined Renee and Brooke, Chloe turned her full attention to Flash. "All the pieces are in place. You know what you need to do, right?"

"Yes. I knew the last three times you asked, too."

He was not going to let everyone's nervousness get to him, though. The situation was under control. The babies were happy, the tea was steeping and Brooke's introduction to his family was going well. Really, really well.

He still couldn't get over the fight between Brooke and her mother, though. Meeting Crissy Bonner had made sense of a lot of stuff. He could see how Brooke had been completely overruled by her mother, how Brooke keeping Flash's contribution to their son quiet hadn't necessarily been a selfish act but one of quiet rebellion.

Oh, he was still plenty mad at Crissy Bonner. But between that fight and everything Brooke had told him since then, it was getting a lot harder to hold on to his anger at Brooke herself. He'd always understood on a logical level that she hadn't told him about the baby because she'd seen those headlines and panicked. But when he counted how Brooke's mom had been manipulating her...

Brooke had stood up for Flash. More than that, she'd stood up for herself.

God, she was amazing. And, better than that, she was wearing his ring.

Oliver rumbled, "You *are* going to marry her, aren't you?" while snatching Trixie from Flash's arms.

"That is the literal definition of *engaged*," Flash said, refusing to allow any resentment to take hold at the note of doubt in Oliver's voice. "But I'm not going to drag her down the aisle tomorrow. That was the deal."

"Of course I'm not saying that." This serious declaration was interrupted by Oliver spinning in a circle with his daughter, making the baby shriek with glee. "I'm saying, make it legal."

"Working on it," Flash said through gritted teeth as he squeezed the honey into Brooke's tea.

Chloe slapped Oliver on the arm. "It's been four days, dude. Give the man some room to work. We have a plan." She turned back to Flash. Any gratitude he might have felt toward her for standing up for him evaporated when she added, "You remember your part, right?"

"Would you two back off?" Flash was really proud of the way he kept his voice calm. "I'm not going to blow up and I'm not going to lash out. I know why I'm here and what I'm supposed to do, so stop acting like I'm still nine-teen, got it?"

Chloe and Oliver exchanged a look. It did not inspire a great deal of confidence.

"Got it?" Flash said more forcefully.

His phone buzzed—a message from Dad. Good luck tonight—and bring that girl and that baby home on Mon-day! I want to meet my grandson!

Flash grinned. At least they'd convinced Dad to stay home for this night. Things tended to go haywire when he showed up at rodeos. Besides, Flash hadn't wanted to overwhelm Brooke with relatives and if Milt Lawrence was anything, it was overwhelming.

Will do. Thanks, Dad, he texted back.

"You need to head down," Chloe said after listening to the earpiece. Pete was no doubt on the other end. "Hey—about the Cowboy of the Year championship..."

"Listen," he told his siblings. "I'm still in it to win it, okay? Tomorrow we'll work on setting up visitation sched-ules around the All-Stars and her concert dates. But that's tomorrow. Tonight, I'm counting on you to keep Brooke and James safe and happy. Do *not* upset her. No mentioning lawyers or money or anything that starts with the phrase 'you should.' Can you handle that?"

"Of course," Oliver scoffed, as if he hadn't spent a few decades telling Flash what he should or should not be doing.

"Promise," Chloe added, looking about as chastised as Flash had ever seen her. "The situation is under control."

"The more you say that, the more worried I get," Flash muttered as he cut around them and headed toward Brooke, tea in hand.

Awkward family meetings aside, this was the sort of thing he could get used to. Brooke and James were looking out at the arena. They'd watch him ride and then they'd head back to her place for the night. James would probably exercise his lungs at some point in the wee hours and Flash would get up with him, letting Brooke sleep as long as possible. Then they'd flop back in bed together, taking comfort in each other's bodies.

He hadn't been lying—tomorrow would bring schedules and negotiations and complications. But tonight was his. This was his rodeo and she was...

She might just be his forever.

Because if he married her, there was no going back on that. Lawrence men—and women—were one-and-done people.

"Hey, I've got to head down," he said, slipping his arm around her waist and pulling her back against his chest. Renee shot him a wink and excused herself. Alex did the same, giving him and Brooke as much privacy as possible in the crowded suite. "Your tea. Doing okay?"

"Your sister-in-law is nice," she said, and he was thankful to hear relief in her voice. "I didn't tell her everything, but I got the feeling she'd understand."

"She would. She's one of the nicest people I've ever known, but—and I mean this—don't ever trust her when she's holding water balloons."

Brooke chuckled, which made Bean look up from where he was gumming a rattle.

"You up for this, little man?" Flash asked, stroking his son's soft hair. A week ago, he'd been a single man, pining for the woman of his dreams. Now?

Now he was so much more.

James grinned around his rattle.

"That's my boy." Flash leaned his chin onto Brooke's shoulder. "We're going to get through this, babe. Just a few hours and then we'll be back home. You can do it."

She blew a hard breath. "Trust me, no one knows that the show must go on like I do. Now get going."

"I'm going—but I'm coming back," he said with a grin, kissing her on the neck. "See you soon." When he turned around, he found the attention of every single person in the room on him. Oliver almost smiled, which was the same as a normal person jumping for joy. Chloe gave Flash a thumbs-up, and he could tell that was exactly the sort of display she wanted to see in an hour. Renee beamed a huge smile at him, and even Alex nodded in approval.

So far, so good. Now they just had to get through the rodeo without tanking his place in the standings, and then he could have Brooke all to himself again.

Yup, he was feeling lucky tonight.

Sixteen

"Ready?" Alex muttered.

"Yes."

This was just ten minutes out of Brooke's life. She'd basically handed over the reins of her social media to Chloe and Kari so she wouldn't have to deal with the notifications for a few days. So really, this was no big deal.

Brooke did a final check on Bean's headphones to make sure the baby hadn't knocked them off in the last three minutes. Then she squared her shoulders and put her game face on.

"And Dan Jones makes the time!" an announcer yelled over the roar of the crowd.

Dan was their cue.

"It's time," Chloe said, guiding them out from the tiny alcove created underneath the chutes that had been blocked off from public view by promotional banners. Brooke followed and Alex brought up the rear.

They climbed the rickety metal stairs to the top of the chutes where Flash was waiting. He turned to her just as the announcer said, "Up next is Flash Lawrence, who's having a heck of a comeback year."

"Hey babe," Flash said over the roar of the crowd as he stepped into her. "You okay?"

She knew it was for the show, that they were both playing to the cameras; still, the obvious concern in his eyes was touching. "Holding steady," she said as he lowered her head to hers.

"Good girl," he murmured against her lips.

"That's right," the other announcer said. "After a rough...uh, Jimbo? Who's Flash kissing?"

Brooke kept her eyes closed because she didn't really want to see Flash kissing her blown up on a jumbotron.

"Is that Nashville's own Brooke Bonner, the country superstar?" Jimbo asked. "Larry, is there something going on we didn't know about?"

A hush fell over the arena, and Brooke knew everyone was staring and asking the same questions.

"Almost there," Flash whispered as he lifted Bean out of her arms. "Being good for Mommy?" he asked as he pressed a kiss to the one small section of Bean's head the headphones weren't covering. And, bless his little heart, Bean smiled.

Brooke exhaled in relief and remembered to smile. Hopefully, it looked real and not like she was having a low-grade panic attack, because there was no going back now. Bean was officially public knowledge.

"Jimbo—is that a *baby*? Did you know Flash Lawrence had a baby?"

The crowd gasped in complete unison as Brooke flattened her palm high on Flash's chest so the massive diamond he'd bought her was right next to Bean's back.

"Larry, is that an *engagement* ring?" Jimbo asked.

"Look at the size of that rock!" Larry was clearly impressed.

Seconds later, the crowd erupted into cheers so deafening that even with his protective headphones, Bean flinched.

"Flash, you're up!" Pete said. "Good job, everyone!"

Brooke took Bean back and gave Flash a kiss for luck while the crowd cheered. So far, so good. She'd been in front of enough audiences to know they had the arena eating out of the palms of their hands. This might be a show, but it was a good one.

And Flash knew it.

"Proud of you, Brooke," he said, his satisfied smile almost enough to make her forget they were being watched by thousands.

"Jimbo, I bet there's more to this story—I hope we'll be able to get a word with Flash after the show?" Larry asked.

"Boy, me too," Jimbo agreed. "But first, he's got to make the time on this bronco!" Thankfully, they turned the conversation back to the horse's stats.

"Have a good ride," she told him, digging deep for that smile.

With a nod, he turned and climbed down into the chute onto the bronco's back. Brooke edged away from the chute so Pete could help Flash get his ropes adjusted.

"Damn near perfect," Alex muttered behind Brooke.

She nodded but didn't look away from Flash. The gate opened and his horse spun out, bucking high into the air while Flash held on for dear life.

"That's Daddy, sweetie," she murmured to Bean, shifting the baby so he could watch. "Look at him go!"

Seconds ticked by slowly as Flash clung to the horse's back. The buzzer sounded just as Flash lost his fight with gravity and he went tumbling to the dirt. Brooke gasped and held her breath, but Flash popped right back up again, pumping his fist into the air.

"Looks like it's Flash's lucky night," Jimbo said. "That ride's going to earn him first in the rankings!"

Brooke cheered along with the crowd. She'd almost made it. Now she just had to wait for Flash to get back to the chute, and then he'd escort her backstage, where he'd hand her off to Chloe, who'd take her back to the family's suite for the rest of the rodeo.

"Well, well, well—this explains everything, doesn't it?" a silky voice said, cutting through the crowd noise and the announcers.

Brooke spun just as Alex snarled, "Hey, back off."

The cowboy staring at Brooke wasn't wearing a vest or a rider's number, but he looked vaguely familiar. Had she met him before? Or just seen his picture somewhere?

"Easy, honey," the cowboy said to Alex, which made the big woman growl. "I'm an…old friend of Flash's." He gave Brooke the once-over, and a burst of apprehension shot down her back.

"Explains what?" she asked, looking around for Pete or Chloe or *anyone*. She did not like the look in this guy's eyes.

"He was screwing you the entire time. How about that?" The cowboy laughed but when Alex went to shove him back, he spun gracefully past her, and suddenly only a foot separated Brooke from him.

Oh, hell. She couldn't back up because there was no room and she couldn't get to the stairs without getting past him. "Leave us alone," she ordered.

"Hey!" Flash shouted from the arena floor. How close was he? Where was Pete? Why couldn't Alex catch this guy? "Tex, back off! Pete! Alex! Get him away from her!"

"You know your little boy toy beat the ever-loving shit out of me?" the cowboy apparently named Tex all but purred. Another hush fell over the arena, but Brooke could feel the difference between this one and the way the crowd had quieted at the reveal of the baby and the ring. "Broke my jaw and my leg, all because I hoped you'd be a good fuck. He ended my career, all for a little piece like you!"

Behind Tex, Alex lunged but the man had catlike reflexes, apparently, because he easily danced out of her way—which only brought him closer to Brooke.

"I had nothing to do with that," she told him, curling around Bean. That's why she recognized him—his picture had been in the articles about Flash's arrest and trial. Had the fight been about her? Because this creep made some creepy comments?

Someone in the crowd shrieked. "Larry, what's Tex McGraw doing here?" Jimbo asked.

"He quit the All-Stars, didn't he?" Larry responded, sounding worried. "After that fight with Flash?"

"The bastard took away everything I love," Tex said, charging forward, his hand clamping around her arm with so much force that it took her breath away. "It's time I returned the favor."

Brooke tried to yell, but her throat wasn't working as Tex twisted her arm hard enough that she saw stars. The baby! She spun, trying to keep hold of Bean, who began to scream bloody murder.

"Brooke!" A body slammed into Tex—oh, thank God, it was Flash.

Brooke stumbled before Tex's grip on her arm gave, and then Flash and Tex crashed off the top of the chute, landing in the dirt with a thud. Flash came up swinging.

"Jesus," Alex said, grabbing Brooke and hustling her down the stairs. "Is Bean okay?"

Brooke stumbled to a stop, staring in horror as Flash threw a punch and then another one. His fists were a blur. "You touch her again and I'll *end* you," he roared as blood flew off his knuckles.

"Move, Bonner," Alex bellowed, shoving Brooke past the fight and into the tunnel under the stands. *"Move!"*

Brooke looked back over her shoulder as Alex pushed her away from the arena. Complete pandemonium had broken out—Pete and a bunch of cowboys were trying to get Flash off Tex, who was throwing a few punches of his own.

The last thing Brooke saw before Alex dragged her through a pair of doors was Flash's head snap back as Tex's fist connected with his jaw and Flash turning a bloody grin on Tex, letting his fist fly.

Brooke's stomach turned and she began to run.

God help her, that man was enjoying the fight.

Seventeen

"The *good* news," Chloe said in the tone of voice that made it clear there wasn't a whole lot to go around, "is that, despite your record and your history with Tex, the prosecutors are declining to press charges on assault for you. The whole fight was caught on camera. You were clearly defending your family. Oliver's talking to them now."

That was the good news? Flash moved the ice off his face and squinted at Chloe. "The bad news?"

Wincing at his black eyes, Chloe held her phone out for Flash to read. Which was a challenge. The words drifted before him like they were floating down a lazy river, but he managed to get one eye to focus.

What he saw chilled him colder than any ice pack ever could. Brooke had sent a group text to Chloe, Oliver and Flash: Thank you for welcoming me and James into the Lawrence family. We will be in touch to set up a visitation schedule. No mention of Flash coming back to her house tonight, no mention of engagements—nothing.

His vision narrowed to those few lines of text. He forgot how to count, how to breathe.

We will be in touch.

If it were possible for five words to break him, those five might just do the trick.

She'd promised. *Promised!* They were in this together now! They were a team! She'd sworn she wouldn't keep him from his son—not again!

No. He refused to accept this.

He had to make this right. He struggled up, which made the room spin. "I need to go," he said, except his jaw wasn't moving right—again. If people could stop breaking the damn thing, that'd be great. He couldn't talk to Brooke with a broken jaw and he definitely couldn't ride.

"No," Pete said, putting a firm hand on Flash's shoulder, "you don't. You show up looking like someone flattened your face with a steamroller and it'll only scare her more."

"Worse than the cushion incident in the library," Chloe agreed, picking up the ice and putting it back on Flash's face.

He tried to bat it away because, yeah, he probably looked horrifying, but he couldn't let Brooke hide behind that cold text. "Tomorrow, then," he managed to get out.

"Shit, man—is your jaw busted again?" Pete said, crouching before Flash and studying his face.

"You should see the other guy," Flash tried to say but that was way too much talking. Crap.

"Buddy, you're done for the season," Pete said. "Chloe, we've got to get him to a hospital."

"On it," she said, and sighed.

His championship season…gone. Just like that.

But the moment self-pity tried to crowd into his head, it was pushed aside by the look of terror on Brooke's face when Tex had grabbed her. In that moment, she'd been more important than anything else—his jaw, the rodeo… none of it mattered. What had mattered was making sure she was okay and Bean was safe.

He couldn't wait until tomorrow.

He needed to see with his own eyes that she was fine, that the baby was okay, that Brooke understood he'd do anything to protect her.

We will be in touch.

He needed her to have some faith in him. Instead, she was pulling back, locking him out.

He wasn't going to stand for it.

"I will knock your ass out if you try to stand up again," Pete warned, shoving him back into the chair. "I've done it before and I'll do it again."

The room spun. Flash might have blacked out, he wasn't sure. Maybe Pete really had tagged him. The next thing he knew, he was being loaded into the back of an ambulance and Oliver was next to him, looking as worried as hell.

"It's going to be okay," Oliver said, his voice sounding strained.

"Brooke," Flash moaned. The ambulance began to move and the world got spinny again.

"It'll be okay," Oliver repeated, holding on to Flash's arm.

As Flash slipped back into the darkness, he was pretty sure it wouldn't be okay. Not until he could get to Brooke.

Thankfully, Bean was fine. Once Brooke settled in the rocker with the baby on her lap, he was out like a light.

Brooke, however, was not fine.

She had forgotten what *fine* felt like. Every one of her nightmares had played out in real time—Flash Lawrence, out of control.

"You're still shaking," Alex said, sounding as close to crying as Brooke had ever heard her.

"Am I?" Brooke laughed, a high-pitched noise that startled Bean. Brooke adjusted him to the other side. "Sorry."

"I sent that text you wanted," Alex said, sitting down on the footstool.

"What text?"

The worry lines deepened on Alex's face. She pulled out a phone—Brooke's phone, she recognized it—and read the text. "You told me to send it when we got home, so I did."

"Then I must have wanted you to." She didn't remember telling Alex that, but who knew. She was pretty sure she was in a state of shock.

She'd been nearly assaulted and then her fiancé had snapped, and none of that took into account the situation with her mother and Kyle or the press...

It was safe to say she was *not* coping well. Nope.

"Brooke? If he shows up, do you want to see him?"

"I don't..." She cleared her throat. A part of her wished that Flash would stroll into the nursery, a mug of hot tea with honey in his hand and a charming smile on his face. That he'd bring the music back with him and they'd write the ending to their song together.

But how could she trust him? How could she trust that she'd make the right decision this time?

Thank God she hadn't married him.

She held up her left hand, where his enormous ring was heavy on her finger. It hadn't been real. That was a comfort, right? No one would blame her for breaking it off with him, not after what had happened tonight.

"I don't think so," she said softly.

"Are you sure that's the right thing to do?" Alex asked, her voice gruff.

"I thought you didn't like him."

"I don't. But Brooke, he was defending you. Because I missed." Tears overflowed Alex's eyes. Brooke stared in shock. Had Alex ever cried? "I wasn't quick enough to catch that guy, but Flash was faster. If I'd done my job..." A sob racked her big body. "I'm so sorry I let you down. But don't hold it against Flash. He was *protecting* you."

Was Alex right? After all, hadn't Brooke been up there

on that chute, praying he'd get to her in time? And he had. He had!

Someone rang the damned doorbell and Bean startled, mewling in displeasure.

"I'll get it," Alex growled, rubbing at her watery eyes.

Sighing, Brooke began to pat the baby's back. "If it's Flash, I'm not home." Maybe Alex was right, maybe she wasn't. But Brooke wasn't going to deal with any of that tonight. No way, no how.

Being around Flash was too intoxicating. He made her forget things, like how Bean was her first priority and how she didn't need someone who was good in bed—she could go whole years without sex. She had after she'd met him, hadn't she? But the moment he got within ten feet of her, she craved him like a junkie craved a hit.

That wasn't healthy.

Two sets of footsteps echoed on the stairs. Oh, no—Alex had decided to let Flash in after all, hadn't she? "I told you, I didn't want to see…"

But it wasn't Flash who followed Alex into the room—it was Kyle Morgan. Of course. Because Brooke didn't have enough going on today.

"What do you want?"

Kyle had the decency to look embarrassed. "Caught the rodeo on TV tonight."

"So? What do you care?"

Kyle blushed. "Didn't know you'd had a baby. Sorry I missed that."

"Are you?" She knew she was being a total witch, but she couldn't help it. Anyone who was expecting her to go along to get along was in for a hell of a surprise. "Are you my father?"

Kyle dropped his gaze, scrubbing his hand through his short silver hair. "She finally told you, huh?"

"I will never let you see your grandson ever again if

you don't cut the crap, Morgan. I've had a shitty evening and you're not helping. You've been my friend for years and never once even hinted that you were my damned father, so *spill it*."

"Look, I got your mother pregnant. We had a couple of wild nights and…"

Alex growled menacingly behind him.

"And I didn't want to be a father. I was too young and I'll be honest—I was doing a lot of drugs. I wasn't fit to be around a baby. Told your mother as much. Told her I wasn't going to be a father to any child she had. She made the choice to keep you."

"Oh. Okay. So you really didn't want me. Sure."

If this night got any worse, Brooke was going to lose her mind. She couldn't take another shock.

"Morgan, that's the crappiest excuse I've ever heard," Alex rumbled.

"Yeah, I know," he shot back, but he kept his attention on Brooke. "By the time you were a kid, I'd gotten clean and my songs started selling and you had so much talent…" He cleared his throat. "I'm not father material. Never was. But a mentor? I could do that. Your mother saw the same thing I did—you had what it took to be a star. And I could help make it happen."

Brooke let her head fall back against the chair. This man was her father. And in his screwed-up way, he'd done his part to look after her. It hadn't been enough, but it'd been something.

"Look, I may have messed up," Kyle began.

"You think?" Brooke shot back.

"But I did the best I could. I didn't have anything else to give, especially before I stopped using. It's been the joy of my life, being a part of your music." He stared at Bean. "Wish your mother had told me you were going to have a baby, though. Sorry I missed that," he repeated.

Brooke couldn't look at him. She closed her eyes and her mind immediately turned to Flash. What would he do, if he were here? Would he throw Kyle out on his rear? Get into another fight? Or would he stand next to Brooke, holding her hand and ready to back her up, no matter what she decided?

Kyle had had a fling with Crissy Bonner and left her high and dry. When he'd found out about Brooke, he'd cut and run.

Flash hadn't done that, though.

Instead, he'd offered her and Bean the protection of his name and his family's power and wealth. He'd done it in a crappy way at first, but one thing had been clear from the very moment he'd found out about Bean—he'd move heaven and earth to be a father to his son.

Was that still true?

"Why is my name Bonner?"

"Morgan is a stage name." She cracked open one eye to glare at him. "What? I had a lot of kids calling me Bonnie when I was growing up. I married your mother to give you a name and then we got a quiet, quick divorce."

Of all the damn things…insisting that he give her his real name but not anything else took the cake. "I am going to hate you for a while." Which was a lie. She was going to hate him for as long as she damn well wanted. And she wasn't going to think too kindly about Mom, either. The level of deception they'd sunk to was mind-boggling. And for what?

She was so tired of lies wrapped in lies and buried under more lies.

Kyle looked hurt but he nodded grimly. "That's fine." He stood to leave. "I've always cared about you, honey. That doesn't mean I haven't been the world's worst father," he said over the combined sounds of Brooke and Alex scoffing in unison, "but I still care. If you let me, I'll care about that boy of yours, too."

"Don't push your luck, *Kyle*." Because she wasn't calling him Dad. He definitely hadn't earned that right.

He nodded in resignation again and turned to go. "One last thing—that fiancé of yours?"

"I don't think we're engaged anymore," Brooke mumbled.

"Yeah, I looked him up after the Bluebird. Those headlines must have pissed your mother off in a major way—too close to what happened to her and me, I think."

Brooke scowled at him again. "You got a point? I've had a long night and I want James to get some sleep." She might not get any, but someone in this house should.

"James. Good name. Fits him." He leaned forward and Brooke let him brush a kiss against her forehead. "I walked away from you and your mother. It's always been my biggest regret, that I threw away the love of my life and my family just because it got hard. Don't make the same mistakes I did."

"That supposed to be fatherly advice?" she snipped, because it was either be snippy or start bawling.

Kyle gave her a sad smile as he turned to go. "Just... think about it. Let me know when you want to talk." He straightened. "I'm not going to throw away a second chance to be a part of your life. You have always been my greatest hit, honey."

Alex showed him out, leaving Brooke alone with her tumbled thoughts and her sleeping son. Now that some of the shock of the attack and fight was wearing off, she was more confused than ever.

Kyle Morgan was her father, but he'd completely abdicated any responsibility for her, choosing to be a friend instead of a parent. He'd abandoned Mom, but had helped Brooke as she'd worked her way up in country music. But he hadn't wanted her unless she was easy and talented. He was a selfish, egotistical asshole, and forgiveness would be a long time coming, if ever.

Flash, on the other hand, wanted to marry her and make it legal—not just in name only, like Kyle and Crissy had, but as a real family. He wanted to be a part of Bean's life. He'd talked about building her a studio on his ranch in Texas and buying Bean a pony. He'd introduced her to his family and staked his claim in front of what felt like the whole world.

Was what happened tonight a deal breaker? Or was she overreacting? If she walked away from Flash, was she doing the same thing Kyle had done? Pushing Flash out of her life because it was easier?

She simply didn't know what the right answer was.

Probably because there wasn't one.

Eighteen

Flash woke up in the hospital to find Milt Lawrence sitting next to the bed, watching baseball. That seemed off. Dad was supposed to be in Texas. Texas was a long way from Nashville. Or was Flash in Texas?

"What time is it?" Flash asked groggily. Or tried to. Damn it, his jaw had been wired shut again.

"High time you woke up," Dad replied, clicking off the television. "That was a hell of a concussion that ass gave you. But don't worry," he went on, and Flash thought the old man winked, but it was hard to tell because one of Flash's eyes was swollen. "You did a hell of a lot more damage."

That sounded bad. "Didn't kill him?"

"Naw, he's alive and pissed. You've bested him twice. His pride is never going to recover and Oliver's working to have him brought up on charges. Plus, your sister has banned him from ever entering an All-Stars event again and I believe she's gotten him kicked off the Total Bull Challenge, too. She can be very persuasive when she wants to be." Dad chuckled. "Mighty proud of that girl, going to the mat for her family like that."

Flash grunted.

Dad stood on bow legs and peered down at Flash's face. It took Flash's eyes a second to focus. "Never known anyone who had such a glass jaw but could keep fighting."

"Thanks, Dad," he slurred. He didn't care about his jaw at the moment. He only cared about two things. "Brooke? Baby?"

Dad's smile cracked a little and he sat back down. "They're fine. Not really in the mood to deal with your brother and sister. That friend of hers has been sending updates, though."

Flash tried to think, but he could tell he was on painkillers. His brain was muddy and he couldn't see through the silt. Dad couldn't be saying what Flash was afraid he was saying. "Need her."

"Not sure that's the best idea at the moment," Dad said, sounding sad about it. "You gave her quite a fright. But, hell, I saw the tape. I'd have done the exact same thing. When someone threatens the woman you love, you step up and throw down to protect her. You did the right thing."

"Don't *love* her." Funny, those words really hurt to say.

Thankfully, Dad was having no trouble understanding Flash's slurring. "That's not what it looked like to me, boy."

"Like her. Lots." Protecting her had been the most important thing he'd ever done and, if he had to, he'd beat the hell out of Tex again. Anything to take care of her and James. "Need her."

"Son," Dad began in that tone that signaled Flash was in for a hell of a lecture, "I don't know who you think you're trying to fool, but I've got eyes and I've loved my Trixie far longer than you've been walking on this planet."

"She doesn't trust me," Flash said, or tried to say. "She hid the baby from me."

"So?"

Flash managed to roll his eyes at that, although it hurt like hell.

"I'm serious," Dad said, leaning forward to meet Flash's gaze. "No, I don't think she should've kept that kid from you—but I can count, son. I did the math. I'm betting she saw those headlines, just like everyone else did. And your sister says that Brooke's mother is a problem."

"Huge problem," Flash agreed. His father was making sense. Never a good sign.

"So she had her reasons. And you have yours. But if you're waiting for the stars to line up and everything to be perfect in a relationship, then you're gonna spend the rest of your life alone, pining for the girl that got away from you. You're in love with her, and don't even try to deny it—I *know* you, boy. She's pretty crazy for you, too, from what I can tell. But everything that comes after that, including faith and trust and love, is a choice. Every day you have to choose to do what it takes to be in love, to stay in love and then? Then you've got to do the work."

Flash blinked at his old man in confusion. "But...you and Mom?"

Milt Lawrence snorted. "There were times your mother, bless her soul, didn't like me very much. More than once she almost strung me up by my toes and I'm not too proud to admit I deserved it. And, as much as it pains me to say, there were days when she drove me up a wall. We had our fights, although we made sure you kids didn't know. But the next day, we'd choose to love each other all over again and *do the work*. Every single day, I made it my job to show her not just that I loved her and needed her and trusted her, but that I was the man she could love, trust and need, come hell or high water." He snorted again. "I never cheated. I made time for her. I put her needs first and I was there for you kids. And let me tell you, flowers never hurt a thing."

Was Flash hearing this right? His parents' marriage had always seemed so perfect—a love story for the ages. At no point had it looked like *work*.

"A year ago..." Dad rubbed his chin thoughtfully. "A year ago, I don't think you would've been capable of it. I sure as hell wouldn't have told you to go get your girl. Wouldn't have been fair to the girl," he added with a chuckle.

"Thanks, Dad," Flash slurred. His head was spinning and he had no idea if it was the drugs or the concussion or the jaw or...

The truth.

He and Brooke hadn't chosen each other after their one-night stand. But doing the work...that sounded a lot like proving Brooke could trust him.

Would she choose to prove he could trust her? Or would she bail?

Dad kept going. "But you got your act together. You did the work on yourself and, Lord knows, I've never been prouder of you. So now? Now I know you can do the right thing. I know you've got it in you, Flash."

A warm feeling spread through Flash's chest. He had, hadn't he? That year of sobriety and anger management and, yes, celibacy had been the longest, hardest year of his life. Every single day he'd had to get up and choose to stay on the straight and narrow, even when it sucked.

There wasn't just one thing he could do or say that would prove to Brooke he was worthy of her. He had to show her, day in and day out. It'd take a lifetime to prove it, but it'd be a lifetime with her.

Because he loved her.

Damn it, he hated when his dad was right. Made the man insufferable.

"So give her a few days to cool off. You don't have a choice—you're being held for observation for that concussion." He sighed heavily. "Flash, you're not gonna want to hear this, but..."

For a panicked second, Flash thought Brooke had called

in lawyers. But then Dad wouldn't be giving him that pep talk if Brooke was done with him, right?

"Your jaw can't take another break," Dad said, his voice...sad, almost. "This one is going to take a few more surgeries before it's all said and done." He cleared his throat, a sound like a tractor engine turning over. "Might not be best for you to compete anymore."

That sounded like... *the end*. The end of a career.

Like his body couldn't take the jarring from bucking broncos and bulls, like steer wrestling was completely off the table. Maybe he could still do calf roping?

Oh, hell—was he done? *Done* done?

No.

No! This was his year! Cowboy of the Year was his for the taking! He'd finally earned his place at the table and he was the best in the world! Hell, he'd been chasing the rodeo for over half his life. If he wasn't chasing the buckle, what was he doing?

But the moment the question crossed his fuzzy mind, the answer followed it. He'd known it since he'd seen Brooke up there, trying to protect their son from Tex.

Nothing mattered more than she did.

Brooke and Bean were everything to him. The rodeo was...just a job.

He'd be a husband and a father. He'd be there to read bedtime stories to his son and travel with Brooke when she toured. Maybe there'd be more children, babies he'd be able to hold the moment they came into the world. Brooke would test her songs out for him, and he'd be by her side when she did things like walk the red carpet at the Grammys or the Country Music Awards.

A family of love and laughter, for the rest of his life. That was his future. Not another buckle or another brawl.

Or another broken jaw.

He'd show up and do the work because Brooke was worth it.

One problem with that plan.

He needed to get to Brooke right *now*.

Dad grabbed his hand away from the IV before Flash could pull it out. "Knock that off, son. You're no good to anyone all busted up."

"How long?" He had hazy memories of time passing, but clearly he'd been sedated so the doctors could work on his jaw. Stupid head injuries.

"Day and a half. Oliver sent the company jet to get me." His phone chimed. "Hey, listen to this—your sister forwarded this to me. Know what the press is saying? Here. 'Flash Lawrence Defends Fiancée Brooke Bonner in All-Stars Brawl.' You're a hero, son."

Yeah, a hero to everyone. Did that include Brooke?

"Need her," he mumbled to his father.

"I know you do. Lawrence men fall hard and fast and forever. It was the same with your mother, God rest her soul."

A hush settled in the hospital room, except for all the beeping. Hey, he'd noticed the beeping! Maybe his head was starting to clear.

Then it came to him. Flowers were great, but he needed to show Brooke that he knew her and cared for her.

"Tea," Flash managed to say. Yeah, his head was definitely clearing because his jaw was starting to throb. But the pain was good. It centered him and gave him something to fight against.

"What was that?" Dad leaned in closer.

"Send her tea. And honey. Good honey. From me."

Dad leaned into Flash's line of sight, a crafty grin on his face. "That," he said, "I can do."

Nineteen

"Just so we're all operating on the same page, let's look at the footage," Kari Stockard, the PR exec, said as the footage of the All-Stars Rodeo from two weeks ago began to run. "As you can see, we arranged for Brooke and the baby to be behind the chutes for a touching moment with Flash Lawrence."

Two weeks since Brooke had last seen Flash. It felt like a lifetime. She kept telling herself she was still making up her mind about him, but that was a lie.

She was doing the exact same thing she'd done after she'd discovered she was pregnant. She was hiding.

And she hated it.

Brooke stared in horrified fascination as her life played out on the screen in a conference room at her record label's executive offices, surrounded by men in suits and her new manager, Janet Worthington. Bean trilled in delight when the camera zoomed in on Brooke's face. Because Bean went everywhere with her now. She didn't have to hide him anymore. And also, because Mom was no longer his primary babysitter.

She didn't want to watch the exact moment she'd lost

control of her life again. She was still having nightmares about living it.

But she was seeing it now while Kari talked over the video. Brooke watched as Flash kissed her and then cuddled Bean, and it took Brooke's breath away because it'd all been for show, right?

But that's not what she saw. What she saw was *real*. Real adoration in Flash's eyes when he'd looked at her, real tenderness as he'd held his son.

She saw real love in her eyes when she'd kissed him for good luck.

It was as plain as day that Flash Lawrence loved her.

It was all over his face, in every single movement he made, in every touch between them. He was head over heels in love with her. And she…

The camera caught her touching her lips as Flash walked away from her, a happy smile lighting up her face. She didn't even remember doing that, but apparently she had.

Oh, God—it hadn't been for show.

It'd been real. All of it.

The camera cut back to Brooke and Bean, still on top of the chute. This time, that terrible Tex McGraw started advancing on her.

Brooke gasped in shock to see the horror that'd been on her face. She watched helplessly as Alex lunged but missed and suddenly Tex had hold of Brooke, his hand digging into her arm and then…

Then Flash had been there, moving so fast he was little more than a blur. He'd gotten Tex off her and she had to swallow back tears as she watched herself stumble, struggling to hold on to her son. Then Alex rushed her down from the chutes, and that was when the video clicked off and a graph came up on the screen.

Kari was talking again but Brooke couldn't listen. She had to keep her gaze on the top of Bean's head while she struggled for control. The incident was every bit as bad as she remembered and yet...not as bad, either.

Because Flash loved her. It was *so* obvious.

Why hadn't she seen it at the time?

What would Tex McGraw have done if Flash hadn't been there?

Alex had been right. Brooke hadn't been able to separate her terror at the attack from her feelings for Flash. All those emotions had sloshed around, mixing together.

She looked down at Flash's ring glinting brightly on her finger.

It'd been real to Flash. She remembered him saying he wouldn't ask her to marry him again, but the offer was on the table. She'd thought he'd been asking her out of duty or a concern about custody.

But had he really been asking her to marry him?

"As you can see from this chart, the number of social media hits from the last two weeks has been tremendous and the reception has been overwhelmingly positive," Kari explained to the bored-looking suits. "People are not only excited for Brooke's new album, but they can't get enough of Brooke and Flash!"

He had. He'd been asking Brooke to marry him because he wanted her. Not just her body or a quickie against the door but her, Brooke Bonner. Hadn't he said as much?

And what had she done?

The one thing Kyle Morgan had told her not to do because it'd be the regret of her life. She was perilously close to walking away.

What was she *doing*?

"Brooke?"

Brooke startled. Everyone in the room was staring at her, expecting an answer, maybe? "Yes?"

Kari's smile tightened. "When can we schedule an interview and photo shoot with you, Flash and that beautiful baby boy?" Clearly, she'd already asked once.

How could Brooke schedule interviews and photo shoots? She hadn't spoken to Flash since that awful night! She'd ignored his gifts, his notes.

Brooke looked helplessly at Janet Worthington, her new manager. Janet had heard the whole messy story, mostly so she could successfully run interference in situations like this.

"Who did you have in mind?" Janet asked, keeping her tone cool.

"*People* is our first choice, but we've had offers..." Kari launched into the pros and cons of the print publications.

Brooke tuned it all out because it was nothing but noise.

Because Flash had sent the most thoughtful, charming, *perfect* gifts, starting with a box of jasmine green tea and local clover honey with a note that read, "I will never stop fighting for you and Bean."

The next day, a sampler of black teas and a different honey—wildflower—had been delivered. "I have faith in you," the note had said.

Every day since, different flavors of tea and honey and occasionally delicate teacups or thermal mugs and, once, even a plastic toy tea set for Bean had shown up, each with a short note written in Flash's scrawl. He missed her. He hoped Bean was letting her sleep and having fun getting out and about. He asked about how the plans for her album were going. Was she doing okay with Kyle and her mother? Did she need anything from him? He'd be there for her.

The last note—the one from yesterday—had said, "I choose you. I want to do the work. You're worth it."

Flash loved her.

He hadn't said the words—it was true—but his love was in every cup of tea she drank, in every bit of honey sweetness.

He wasn't backing her into a corner and he wasn't forcing her to make a choice. Instead, he'd spent the last two weeks showing her how much he cared, and she hadn't responded. Not even to check on him.

Bean fussed. Brooke took the chance to escape. "Is there anything else you need me for?"

Janet got the hint immediately. "We'll get back to you on dates."

Brooke slipped out while Janet settled the details. For two danged weeks, Brooke had been hemming and hawing, asking herself how she could trust him when, really, she'd been trying to figure out how she could trust herself.

She couldn't do it. She couldn't walk away.

All she needed to do was make a leap of faith.

She texted Flash, Where are you?

My hotel room, was the immediate reply. In Nashville.

Relief coursed through her. Still here?

Never left, babe. I might walk away from you and you might walk away from me when we need to calm down, but I will always come back for you. Been hoping you'll come back to me, too.

Dear God, he really did love her. I need to talk to you.

Where?

She was more than half tempted to ask for his room number, but she had a drowsy infant in the back seat. Meet me at my house in half an hour.

Just as she pulled out of the parking lot, Flash texted back, Thank God.

Flash hadn't waited half an hour. He was on Brooke's doorstep less than fifteen minutes later, waiting. Dad hadn't been happy about Flash driving himself, but a man had to do what a man had to do.

Finally.

It'd taken two weeks of every kind of tea and tea accessory known to mankind, but she'd reached out to him.

Please let this be good, he prayed.

Of course, she needed to talk to him, which was kind of a problem because right now, Flash wasn't doing a whole lot of talking. And kissing—good, deep kissing, the kind that led to clothing-optional activities—was also off the table. Nibbling was strictly forbidden.

Stupid busted jaw.

It felt like an eternity before Brooke drove up, and Flash was thrilled to see she was alone except for the baby.

He hurried to open Brooke's door but the next thing he knew, she was in his arms and he was struggling to hold back the tears because for two long, awful weeks he'd been afraid he'd lost her, and Brooke Bonner wasn't the kind of woman a man just got over.

"Missed you," he mumbled into her hair as best he could.

"Missed you, too. Let me put the baby down and then we'll talk?"

Reluctantly he let her go. He held the door for her as she pulled a napping James Frasier out of the back seat and then got the front door for her as she carried the baby inside.

They got Bean into the crib without waking him. Flash wrapped his arm around Brooke's shoulders and held her as they stared at their son.

Yep. This was right. This was where he belonged.

Now he just had to convince Brooke of that.

Silently she led him back down to the library where he'd nearly ruined everything. "God, I'm so sorry," she said, basically launching herself at him. "Your face!"

Flash grunted at the impact but, hell, he could play with the pain. The bruises had mostly faded to sickly greens and yellows, except where he'd had more work done on his jaw. But he knew he still looked terrible.

He picked her up and carried her to the couch—with its now-lumpy cushions. Then he pulled out his tablet and began typing.

"Are you okay?"

She read the message and then stared at him. "What's wrong with your mouth?"

"Broken jaw. Wired shut. Won't be able to do much talking or anything for a few more weeks. I'm officially retired from the rodeo. Doctors say I'm done—can't risk any more damage."

She went pale. "Oh, my God! Flash! I'm so sorry!"

"It's okay, babe," he typed. "Everything's okay as long as I'm with you."

Her eyes got all watery again. "It was all real, wasn't it? The proposals and this huge ring and all that tea and honey and…it's all real, isn't it?"

He nodded and touched his forehead to hers. "Love you," he tried to say.

"Don't talk, babe. You…" She sniffed and he wiped the tears off her cheeks. "You said so much in all your notes. I was just too confused to see it."

He kissed her then, *gently*, before he tucked her against his chest so he could type. "I love you. I think I always have, ever since that first night. But I didn't fight for you then. I let you go and I've regretted it ever since. I don't want to let you go again. I'm going to fight for you and for our family every day of my life."

"Oh, Flash," she whispered through her tears. "I'm so, so sorry because I was doing the same thing I did last time. I shut you out because I was scared. I was doing the exact same thing my mom and Kyle did, and I was wrong. I know you were protecting me, but everything got so screwed up in my mind that…"

"You had to walk away for a little bit," he typed quickly, his heart pounding. "Just to calm down. I understand. I had faith you'd fight for me, too." He swallowed, a raspy sound, and then added, "You are, right?"

Because it'd about kill him if she said no. He could let the rodeo go and the world would keep right on spinning.

But life without Brooke...no, he wasn't about to let her go.

Lawrence men fell hard and fast and forever.

That's what this was. *Forever.*

"I understand now," she told him. "I didn't before. But I talked with my...with Kyle, and he told me he didn't fight for me, didn't try to get right with my mom. He only wanted me when I was easy and talented. But that's not life, is it? It's hard work. That's what I want—someone who's willing to fight for me, who'll stick it out when it gets hard and help make things better. And that's you."

"That's you, too," he typed back, his hands shaking.

She shook her head, tears dripping down her face. "Not enough. I need to fight harder. Not just for you, but for myself. For us."

"We'll work on it," he typed back. He couldn't wait until he could talk to her again. It was damn near impossible to whisper sweet nothings into a girl's ear on a tablet. "Together. We're a team. Today, tomorrow, every day." When she gasped, he gritted his teeth and made the one concession he was willing to make. "We don't have to get married, but the offer stands. It'll always stand. I'm not giving up on you or on us. I want this to work. Every day, I'll prove it to you. That's a promise."

She took the tablet from his hands and tossed it aside. "But...what if I want to get married? Is that something you still want?"

Flash groaned. "Yes," he said out loud, although it sounded like a tire deflating. "God, yes."

"How will it work?" she asked, stroking her fingertips over his busted jaw.

He picked up the tablet again. "I'm done with chasing the rodeo. It's time I did the stay-at-home-dad thing. Go with you on tour. Be there for you. For our family."

"Oh, Flash," she whispered, carefully throwing her arms around his neck. "That's what I want. You and me and our family. With less broken bones, though."

"Working on it," he got out, holding her tight.

Then he set her aside and got to one knee next to the couch, taking her hands in his. She still had on his ring, thank God. She'd worn it this whole time.

"Brooke, would you marry me?" Although it didn't come out exactly right.

"For real?" she asked, her eyes shimmering with tears.

"For real," he replied, kissing her hands.

"Yes, Flash. Because I am always coming back for you, too," she sobbed.

Flash surged to his feet and pulled her into a hug. This was home. Brooke was home. "Thank God," he mumbled.

Thank God, he'd never have to get over Brooke Bonner.

* * * * *

COMING SOON!

We really hope you enjoyed reading this book. If you're looking for more romance, be sure to head to the shops when new books are available on

Thursday 4th April

To see which titles are coming soon, please visit

millsandboon.co.uk/nextmonth

LET'S TALK
Romance

For exclusive extracts, competitions
and special offers, find us online:

 facebook.com/millsandboon

🐦 @MillsandBoon

📷 @MillsandBoonUK

Get in touch on 01413 063232

For all the latest titles coming soon, visit
millsandboon.co.uk/nextmonth